Wool and Iron

WOOL AND IRON

Brian J. Croasdell

iUniverse, Inc.
New York Lincoln Shanghai

Wool and Iron

iUniverse, Inc.

For information address:
iUniverse, Inc.
2021 Pine Lake Road, Suite 100
Lincoln, NE 68512
www.iuniverse.com

This book is a work of fiction. Names, characters and places are products of the author's imagination. Any resemblance to actual persons is entirely coincidental.

ISBN: 0-595-31059-1

Printed in the United States of America

FOR DOT

List of Characters

EGYPT

PYTHEAS   :   Seaman and businessman.

PHILIP   :   Son. Intelligence specialist.

ALEXANDER   :   Merchant banker.

IRELAND

BRIGIT   :   Military advisor to the High King of All Ireland.

NIALL   :   Counsellor.

BRITAIN

CUNEBELINOS   :   High King of Britain.

TOGODUMNOS   :   Son and heir.

CARATACOS   :   Son. Governor of the Atrebates tribe.

ADMINIOS   :   Son. Governor of the Cantii until his defection.

CERI   :   Grandson. Governor of the Cantii.

FOX   :   Counsellor.

ENA	:	A Chief of the Cantii.
SEGONAX	:	Son of another Chief of the Cantii.
BIVAN	:	Pilot.
BUDUOC	:	King of the Northern Dobunni.
CARTIMANDUA	:	Queen of the Brigantes.
PRASUTAGOS	:	King of the Iceni.
PHYLUS	:	Medicine salesman and Roman agent.
AMBON	:	Roman agent.

CITY OF ROME

CLAUDIUS	:	Water Commissioner. Uncle of the Emperor.
NARCISSUS	:	His secretary-general.
Aurelius VICTORINUS	:	Policeman.
TITUS	:	His friend.
DOMITILLA	:	Titus's girlfriend.
Valerius ASIATICUS	:	Senator, businessman and thief.
Rufrius POLLIO	:	Officer of the Praetorian Guard.
Titus SELEUCUS	:	Naval Captain.
BERICOS	:	King and former ruler of the British Atrebates.
SCOTA	:	His daughter.
COGIDUMNOS	:	A Chief of the British Atrebates.

ROMAN EUROPE

Servius GALBA	:	Governor of Upper Germany.
Aulus PLAUTIUS	:	Commander of the Invasion Task Force.
Hosideus GETA	:	His second in command.
Sentius SATURNINUS	:	His rear areas commander.
Flavius VESPASIAN	:	Legate of Legion II Augusta.
Anicius MAXIMUS	:	Camp Commandant of Legion II Augusta.
Fangs MACER	:	Legionary of Legion II Augusta.
Rufus SITA	:	Cavalryman.
VIRIDOMAR	:	British agent.

WOOL AND IRON

The wind drove from the east and dragged sand particles in hissing rivulets between the straining stems of the dune's grass. They stung and stuck to the fugitive's bare wet ankles and filled in the shallow depressions of his footprints where he had scrambled over the crest of the dune. The cold wet trouser legs slapped his muscular calves, the chequered wool of his clothing flattening to the left side of his body and snapping like a flag to his right, tugging at brooch and belt.

Grains of sand clung to the stubble of his jaw and to the damp of his fluttering moustache. His hair, stiffened with lime, hardly stirred. Behind him heaved the grey and glittery seas. On the horizon, the pale smear of his former land showed below the streaming sky. He stared south with salt-reddened eyes. With the back of one sore hand, he rubbed the recent sword cut that ran from left eyebrow into the hairline. With something like a groan, he shouldered his equipment and started to walk.

CHAPTER 1

▼

ROME

I do not go to the Games these days. This is not due to inadequate religious observance on my part, nor to a lack of interest in martial skills, although neither would, perhaps, be surprising, given my specialist duties during the greatest military enterprise of this reign. Very few young men have survived my single experience as the centre of attraction in the arena and willingly go near the place again. My proportion of Celtic blood inclines me towards impulsiveness, and that nearly resulted in a premature mess on the sand.

My opponent was an awkward looking fellow, long in the body and short of leg, like your typical citizen, but of a thinness and hairiness of leg just short of disgusting. His professional nickname was Spider. I can never look on one of those usually harmless creatures without a pang.

Strutting out into the crowd noise, I was brimming with confidence and good health. Any concerns I had at that moment were related to the very remote possibility that my father would find out what I was up to—and by then, one way or another, it would be too late—and the more immediate concern that my helmet was not a good fit.

In the interest of proper appearances, the helmet I had been allocated as a novice was a towering ornate device with a bristling crest. It gave me even more height over the scuttling Spider but, as an item of protective equipment, it was heavy, unbalanced and, potentially at least, a liability. In the event, the helmet did not remain a problem for long. A small round shield was tightly strapped to my left arm and I was armed with a long double-edged blade in the Celtic style.

Full of bravery, I walked around the Spider, taunting him and making jokes at his expense to the part of the crowd nearest to me. There were some commoners in the higher tiers who laughed openly. A number of their elders and perhaps betters lower down eyed me more cynically. However, I had no serious misgivings, even when I noted that my opponent did not react to my threatening feints except by turning so as to remain facing me. The glowing black eyes in the swarthy, oiled face watched expressionlessly over the oblong legionary-style shield. His short stabbing sword pointed unequivocally at my midriff. I felt the rising tide of excitement and confidence threatening to choke me and made such a fuss of saluting the patron's box that I nearly missed the starting signal.

I went at him like a wild man, swinging and hacking like the novice I was, my blade ringing and thudding on metal and leather. Like a rising wind, the crowd drove me forward, the desire thick in my throat to chop my way through the Spider's guard and through the little man behind it.

The next instant, I was flat on my back, my helmet off and my head ringing like the bells of Isis. My left arm was tangled in the straps of my shield on which the Spider was standing and the gritty sole of his other foot was pushing the side of my face into the cold sand of the arena. My sword had gone. From the waves of crowd sound, it seemed that my erstwhile supporters found my present position entirely satisfactory.

Squinting sideways through my tears, I had an unedifying view of the Spider's foreshortened skinny shanks with, above, his two bony fists closed around his reversed sword, the bright point of which menaced my heaving unprotected chest. He had evidently discarded his damaged shield but did not seem even out of breath. After all, I suppose that I had been doing all the work. The noise died away as some noble nincompoop pondered as to whether I lived or died.

Fortunately, panic took over. My right hand, fumbling for sand to throw into the victor's face, gripped the rim of my beautiful, dented helmet and drove it upwards, like a monstrous iron boxing glove, between the Spider's thighs. The angle was not right and I did not have a proper grip on the helmet or the contest would have been over then and there. The thin, hairy legs drove the victim skywards with a force that would have excited admiration from his namesake and only the bristled helmet crest threatened the future of the arachnid race. When he landed, however, a sharp blow with the edge of my shield on his unprotected toes reduced the rest of the unseemly scuffle to near formality.

The patron would not allow me to finish him off, preferring to treat my victory as a comic interlude which had placed the crowd in a rare good humour for the rest of the ceremonies. He would not even allow me the ivory tablet certifying my survival of my first gladiatorial contest.

I have since heard the contest described in various parts of the world and I am now used to the intervention of helpless laughter in the description of the event. If the match was meant to show the crowd the inevitable victory of Roman professionalism over Celtic impulsiveness and cowardice, I have the last laugh. Although of Celtic stock, I am as much a citizen as anyone born free in Rome and, whatever the antics, in the end I won.

CHAPTER 2

▼

ROME

There was no time for rejoicing over either victory or survival. The next pair of combatants was waiting, clean, oiled and pink-faced at the entrance of the dressing rooms. They were also novices but even they knew enough not to lay a hand on me while I plodded past them. I was, I admit, in a very confused state of mind. Despite the fact that they were in every way prepared to fight, while I was the object of popular derision and armed only with a battered helmet dangling from a broken chinstrap, they easily restrained any impulse to comment or laugh. One of them, the one who subsequently died, gravely informed me that there was a messenger from my father.

This was alarming news, made worse by the fact that the messenger was none other than the truly superior being who occupied the position of steward in my father's household. Eno did not call himself steward out of deference to the fact that my grandfather had himself been the steward to a family with estates below the Alps. My grandfather had been granted freedom before my father was born. My father has therefore been born free and so, in turn, had I. More than that, due to a State decree widening the scope of citizenship when recruiting into the legions was low, my father had become a citizen before my birth and I was born to be a citizen. As a freedman, my father had been eligible for service in the auxiliaries or the Fleet. As a citizen he would have been eligible for military service in the legions had he not been married. There, he would have been surrounded by the lowest class of countrymen and townspeople distinguished only by their status as citizens of Rome. Instead, he swiftly removed my mother and elder brother Marcus to a coastal town where he had prospered in the marketing of ships' supplies. He and Eno were of an age and, although I never got to the bottom of it, I have always suspected that they have shared memories of mischief. A descendant of a freedman and a new citizen would have had many obstacles to overcome when struggling to set up a business, and seaports were no more law-abiding and friendly then than they are now.

The public relationship displayed between my father and Eno was that of master and trusted estate manager. For estate-owner my father now was. He had purchased a modest property to add to his dignity and to distance his family from its main source of wealth, trade in ships' supplies. We were no longer considered solely as merchants and, if we were nowhere near being noble, at least we were approaching being gentry.

Eno had always been the object of some respect on the part of Marcus, my sister Letitia and myself. My mother, a good Roman matron, took no part in public life but contented herself in running the growing household. She held the official view that, other than a few State religious appointments such as the Vestals, the running of all arms of the State and Government was the duty of citizens. In other words, free Roman males over the age of fourteen and, at the last census, there had been just under five million of them across the world. More than enough, she said, to do a proper job. Since my mother's death during Letitia's birth, my father had thrown himself with even greater energy into the business of making the family financially secure and, in many ways, Eno had run the household. His close-set icy eyes missed very little and, what they did, the long bent nose sniffed out. We, as children, were considerably in awe of the man and, as a young adult, I found this sentiment had not changed appreciably.

The fact that, in the cramped, bustling changing rooms off the arena, Eno had both gained admittance and been granted the use of a small alcove for this interview, indicated that others had also found him to be difficult to deny—unless, of course, my peers and superiors had simply accommodated him for the purpose of eavesdropping to my later embarrassment.

He was dressed in a new tunic for his attendance at the Games and was holding himself even more erectly than usual.

"Master Tiberias," he intoned by way of greeting. "I have seen you looking better."

Since I had just completed a fairly desperate single combat, this was hardly surprising. My childhood training very nearly had me hanging my head and shuffling my feet on the stone flags.

"Your father," he boomed, "has heard of this escapade with much displeasure."

That unsettled me, make no mistake. My father's displeasure was something to be avoided as many a lazy timber merchant or swindling tar manufacturer had found out to his sorrow.

"With your brother the recognised heir to your father's interests, your position as a student water-engineer would have provided you—in time—with a suitably dignified and appropriate place in society."

There was the faintest glimmer of emotion in those level eyes.

"It may surprise you to learn that one of the daughters of the port's Chief Engineer has been found to be pregnant."

That did, in fact, surprise me. I had thought that they both were.

"That aspect has been resolved, but your father does not require you to return home. He has a close business relationship with the girl's father and your presence would adversely affect this. There is, however, no possibility for you to continue risking your life to pander to that."

He jerked his heard towards the sound of distant cheering.

I was mentally forced to concede that my prospects of a career in the arena might be bright but would almost certainly be short and limited.

"Quite aside from the gratuitous exposure to physical danger in the name of religion, one which is not necessarily your own, your maiden appearance was one which might be best forgotton. No, do not assume that look, sir. I assure you that I observed the performance and was not impressed."

My legs were now, in fact, trembling with fatigue and I had little difficulty in restraining my urge to bend his nose the other way.

"I have bought the remainder of your contract from the Games' organiser and your father has secured for you a suitable position with one of the Urban Cohorts in Rome. You are going to be a policeman."

CHAPTER 3

▼

ROME

I found life in Urban Cohort XII in Rome to be at about midlevel in the hierarchy of those Services permanently based in the City.

It was nowhere near the status of the gilded Praetorian Guard whose lordly members still affect great martial superiority even over the rough, tough legions out on the frontiers. The Guard, six thousand of them, only actually deign to go to war when the Emperor himself takes the field. It seemed very unlikely at the time of my enlistment that Emperor Gaius Caligula was personally going to do that again in the near future. It seemed to me, as a military expert of a few weeks' standing, that the Praetorian Guard was a colossal waste of first-rate soldiers. I received a friendly warning from my training optio that to repeat this assessment in the presence of guardsmen—in whose Camp the Urban Cohorts are quartered—might result in a sudden change in my personal circumstances.

The fact that they had been present on the beaches opposite Britain when the Emperor had quailed from ordering his surly invasion force to embark, had made the Guard, as a unit, very touchy. The fact that they had had to participate in the farce that followed, using infantry weapons and artillery to attack the Ocean, if you can believe it, had left its mark on each guardsman. The legions had gone back to the borders where the barbarians did not know any better, but the Guard had to return to Rome to face its knowing public. Praetorians still provide a glistening backdrop to Imperial functions but, especially in those days, they were often a target for the commoner humourists.

Lower in status than the three Urban Cohorts were the seven thousand men of the night watch and fire service called Vigiles. These brave men, distinguished by huge eyes and pale complexions, are rarely seen in daylight. I have worked after dark in the City myself but only on specific cases with sufficient support close at hand. The thought of patrolling the streets every night, sniffing for smoke and waiting for something dangerous and potentially lethal to happen, does not appeal to me. Many of them seem actively to enjoy the solitude and, of course, directing the wheeled traffic that is allowed into the City only after dark does offer certain opportunities for graft. On balance, however, I am a daylight man.

Each of the three Urban Cohort numbers a thousand men in theory but, as a rough guide, a Cohort commander can only reckon on having seven hundred men on duty on any day. The daily parade strength of the three Cohorts is spread unevenly over the fourteen districts of Rome. The Cohort commanders report directly to the City Prefect, discuss crime trends and overnight reports from the Vigiles with him, receive schedules of State, municipal and guild functions and plan daily deployments accordingly.

All this is far above the level of the ordinary foot soldier, especially one such as myself who has just completed training. Wearing my tall new helmet of antique design, and the rest of my policeman's disguise, I emerged for the first time to bring peace to the streets of the City. Since my first and only appearance in the arena, my name had become, and remains, Aurelius Victorinus. That day in Rome I had the ridiculous feeling, spiced with some trepidation, that this was in every way the first day in a new life.

The more experienced men in the Cohort had been dispatched to attend to burglaries, to thefts and to domestic disputes. Others had been sent to make their appearances in various courts and others to work in support of various municipal departments. A small group had been retained to respond to emergencies. I had been instructed to walk a beat. I had walked this particular beat close to the river while under the tutelage of a trained patrolman, so I knew the various points at which my superiors could check my progress. Even more importantly for my first duty alone, I could direct any visitor to the sights.

I walked downhill towards the river, looking into the shops at the foot of the blocks of flats. The weather was fine but it had been raining and the roadway was clean. The public toilets did not smell, there were no new graffiti and there were no loiterers outside. The water of the public fountains contained no litter. Throngs of people were on the move and the general mood seemed happy. The patter of sandals and bare feet on stone was a counterpoint to the talk and laughter. Yellow and white seemed to be the predominant colours.

Even the Tiber looked fairly clean when I made my first point on the river embankment. It was less busy here. While waiting to see if a supervisor put in an appearance, I watched a few individuals with parcels of what smelt like food make their way to the bridge to the Temple of Aesculapius. Breakfast for the sick that had spent the night under the roof of the god of healing, waiting for a cure. The fact that they were being brought food suggested that relatives were not convinced this act of piety was going to be rewarded. I idly wondered about a charge of sacrilege.

Along the embankment, a young boy reported an accident, someone injured. Remembering the first rule of police work— 'Walk to a fight, run to an accident'—I hurried to the construction site, mentally rehearsing my first aid training. A crane had very evidently collapsed. Thankfully, an official from the municipal building department was already on the scene together with a doctor who had been on his way to the Temple. Even so, it took me by surprise when the little crowd opened respectfully at the appearance of my uniform and the doctor reported to me. At that moment, I would gladly have joined the spectators. With professional callousness he told me that one of the workmen had lost most of his teeth and another had a badly crushed foot—no serious injuries, he said. The other workmen had made themselves scarce—probably illegals.

The crane had apparently been lifting a section of pillar for the portico of a municipal building fronting the river. Now it was a mass of broken wood and tangled rope. Hoping that my voice did not come out as a frightened squeak, I stood erect.

"Who is in charge here?" I demanded.

The doctor and the municipal official looked at each other.

"Who is in charge of the builders, I mean?" I amended.

The official looked at a nuggety, shifty fellow in a dusty tunic. Splashes of cement adorned his wiry brown arms.

"Er, I'm the foreman," he volunteered under intense silent pressure from the bystanders.

"What happened here, then?" I was getting good at this.

"I've already asked him that," snarled the official.

"And I've already told him," the foreman whined to me. "The equipment was faulty—it just fell apart."

"Rubbish," said the official, who was starting to get on my nerves.

"Unlikely," said the doctor.

"Horseshit," said someone in the crowd.

They all looked at me.

Inspiration deserted me although cunning did not.

I resisted the temptation to proclaim an instant assessment that might be instantly disproved by some wiseacre. I approached the wreckage. Everyone gave me room. Traces of blood on the pillar segment indicated what had crushed the one workman's foot. The lifting rope was still secure around it. The crane's jib was lying flat on the ground with the rope through the pulley at the end. The treadmill was still standing but surrounded by a ravel of rope which should have been neatly wound round it. Traces of blood showed on the treads and I did not need to look for broken teeth to identify how the second workman had come by his injuries. But, why had the equipment failed? I resisted the temptation to scratch my head.

In the crowd stood a sailor. I have lived in a port and know the stance. His profession was confirmed by his sleeveless tunic and the tattoos on his folded arms. There is a large detachment of the Misene Fleet based in Rome. They are equally responsible for Imperial communications throughout the world and the more mundane task of handling of the shade awnings at the Theatre in the City. We in the Urban Cohorts usually get on well with the Fleet. His right index finger was tapping the tattoo of an anchor on his left bicep. Anchor. Anchorage!

When a crane treadmill starts to turn and the weight of the load starts to bear on the tip of the jib, the only thing preventing the jib falling towards the load is the efficiency of the guy ropes holding the tip of the jib in the correct position. The guys need to be so anchored that the weight of the load cannot drag down the jib.

"The guys were not anchored properly," I pronounced, grasping the foreman by the arm.

"Good," said the doctor.

"About time," said the official.

"Bloody obvious," said the same voice in the crowd.

The sailor had gone.

When the supervisor had heard my report to the end, he actually smiled.

"Got the names and addresses of the injured parties, have you?"

"Well, no. Their superiors were at the site when I got there."

"I see. Well, during your meal break just go and find the injured, record their particulars, personally check that their next of kin have been notified and then, when you have done that, you can eat. Get on with it."

By the time I had completed the documentation in the City centre, my ever-considerate colleagues had eaten all the food sent up from the Camp kitchens.

Back on my beat, I checked the prices in the shops. Cheese, olives, even bread and wine were expensive in this area. Shopkeepers have to cover their shop rental and municipal taxes. What I needed was a street vendor and the supervisor would not be looking for me yet. Close to the Cock Inn, I located a sausage seller who still had some stock in his portable oven. He offered to present me with a free sausage but there was no way I was going down that route. I paid and got out of the way of traffic, mainly now flowing towards the Baths.

It was almost inevitable. No sooner was I standing in a doorway, chewing a mouthful of hot sausage and with grease running down my forearm, than there was a change in crowd movement, craning of necks, a change in the rhythm of conversation and a few distant shouts. It could be a fight. I certainly was not running to that.

There was a backward surge in the crowd in front of me and, before I could dispose of the sausage and stride majestically into the street to take charge, an eddy in the crowd's ebbing tide pressed me into the doorway. It was faintly ridiculous, but the long—if greasy—arm of the law was immobilised in a bookseller's doorway by the broad backs of a crowd of heavily breathing members of the public.

The backs hemming me in were broad, but the figures concerned were not tall. The crowd stilled as a State escort of lictors, shouldering their bundles of sticks, paced past. The litter that followed carried a small veiled figure in white, a Vestal on her way to watch over the sacred fire, no doubt. The six Vestal Virgins maintain this watch in turn at their Temple, the hearth of the nation. They are the only female State officials of rank, but, when they are on the move, even the Consuls get out of their way. No one wants to be implicated in the catastrophe that would follow the fire being allowed to die out.

The crowd relaxed after she was safely on her way and the doorway emptied as suddenly as it had been occupied. I doubt whether any of the citizens had even noticed their protector, helpless at the back. As I stirred, my foot struck a letter lying on the floor. It was unopened, the two halves of wax tablet still secured by twine, the seal intact. I looked out of the bookseller's doorway but could not identify any of my recent companions. They had completely merged with the traffic.

The bookseller's business is hectic in literate Rome and City-dwellers are used to important people passing by. The clerks had not left their desks inside where they were industriously copying books in their well-known Tironean abbreviations. A boy was making more ink, mixing the soot and gum. The bookseller himself was labeling the finished scrolls with the titles of the books and stowing them in purple cases for sale. No one, he told me, had lost a letter there and, although he did sell wax tablets and steel styluses for inscribing them, even the materials for the letter did not come from his shop. I asked him to hold the letter against the owner's coming to look for it but he shook his head.

"There is no need," he said. "See here, the address is on the outside. The Senator is often away seeing to his estates beyond the Alps but he has a townhouse here. He must be in town now."

"Odd that a Gallic Senator should be called Asiaticus. Why would that be?"

"Wait until you see him, or maybe the original family interests were in that part of the world. I don't know, I'm sure. Now, would you like the boy to show you the house?"

As it happened, I knew the house, long and low with shops around the outside at street level. I had never been inside and it had had the look of being closed up, the owner away. I declined the offer of a diminutive guide and stepped out into the afternoon shade. I was already off my beat and could imagine the supervisor standing at one of my points, slapping his leg with his cane. Better, perhaps, to be seen returning from the good Senator's house having delivered the property which I might have found in my area of duty rather than arriving from off my beat with something found elsewhere.

The food shops were now doing good business with take-away evening meals. Because of the ever-present fire risk, very few flat-dwellers dare cook in their homes. Start a fire in a second floor flat and not even the Vigiles can save everyone above. Many of the customers buying cooked food were hurrying homewards with clean, flushed faces from the Baths. My time to parade off-duty was approaching and I stepped out briskly through the clean and hungry crowd.

At my second knock, the magnificent front door between two shops swung silently inwards on its pintles and a very haughty person with the beard of a slave was revealed. A maid hovered behind.

"Senator Asiaticus?" I enquired, pleasantly.

"And who might you be?"

"Ti—, er, patrolman Aurelius Victorinus of Urban Cohort XII."

"I shall enquire," and the man tried to close the door only to find it obstructed by the foot of patrolman Aurelius Victorinus.

This did not please his beardship who made a comment to the maid which set her giggling. I had not forgotten the language of my boyhood in the plains below the Alps and, in rusty Celtic, I commented upon his social status, his physical appearance, his probable ancestry and his very unlikely gender. I stopped when heavy-handed applause broke out from within and a very tall figure loomed behind the servants. Wide hipped and narrow of shoulder, the man's complexion showed almost yellow in the dusk and his slanting eyes were nearly lost in shadow under a long forehead. He had discarded his toga and changed his outdoor shoes for slippers, but the quality of his tunic and the old iron signet ring on his right hand merely confirmed that I had found the enigmatic Senator.

He tensed when he saw my uniform and what I held in my hand, but recovered immediately and invited me in. The maid scurried on ahead to open his study while I swept past a fuming but silent doorman and was ushered through the darkening atrium. I narrowly avoided measuring my length in the shallow rainwater pool in its centre, but fetched up safely in a large but stuffy office at the rear of the house. The maid was lighting the oil lamps on a large candelabrum. She trimmed the wicks with a small set of tweezers and withdrew a bolt from the stem of the candelabrum and raised the top to the required height before replacing the bolt.

In the light now falling fairly evenly over the room, I could see that she was no ordinary maid. Her dark tinted hair was tied in a shining knot and she wore a simple stola of good quality to her ankles. It did nothing to conceal the lithe and shapely figure beneath. The giveaways were the keys and the make up. Her arms and face had been whitened with powdered chalk, antimony eyeliner enhanced the gleaming dark eyes and the cheeks and lips had been reddened, probably with wine sediment. A tiny key formed part of one of the rings on her slim fingers and a large latchkey was attached to her girdle. Whatever the Senator's marital status, this was the lady of this house.

I was conscious of the intensity of the Senator's inspection of the sealing of the letter and found it slightly offensive. In the end, he did not comment on its condition nor on its possible sender. He did not open it then but left it at his elbow while we shared a silver jug of very good wine and made a little small talk, mostly about life in the Celtic Provinces from Spain to the Black Sea, and in the few aboriginal Celtic areas still outside the Empire.

His estates were beyond the Alps in southern Gaul. When the first Emperor, the divine Augustus, emerged the victor in the civil wars, he had settled retiring veterans of his Legion VIII on land grants where they could keep an eye on the Greek colony of Massilia on the coast and could provide support and farm produce to his new Fleet base nearby. As is the way of such things, not all retired soldiers are good farmers, and, in any case, many of their sons preferred to join the Army rather than to follow the plough. As the land grants came up for sale, Asiaticus, and his forefathers, bought them up and imported slaves to work the soil. I told him about the farming in the area in which I grew up and we compared the respective merits of the Celtic against the Roman plough.

The Senator was mildly amused that I, a descendent of the barbarian army that had captured and held Rome to ransom in ancient times, now patrolled its streets and enforced its laws. This was a little flattering but I had not thought it necessary to tell him that this was my first day on duty alone.

He seemed tired from his journey to the City and glanced with increasing frequency at the sealed letter. I had not expected to be received with such informal civility by a Senator. Gratitude, interest in our respective backgrounds and the absence, as yet, of most of his household staff had contributed to the relaxation of formality. Although I found it very pleasant sitting in the mellow lamplight, the distant sound of the porter firing the furnace for the central heating and the smell of cooking gave me an additional hint that it was time to take my leave. I would have been missed at the end-of-duty parade and had better make my appearance before a search was ordered. Also, it seemed that I was not going to be offered any more wine.

He thanked me fairly graciously beside the illuminated shrine to the household gods and offered me the services of his porter to see me back to Camp. This I thought wisest to decline. That, I thought, other than my official report, was the end of it. I was wrong.

Faintly, the grind of rims and the screech of badly oiled axles heralded the nightly entry of wheeled transport into the City. Vigiles and municipal sanitary workers were out on the streets.

Walking through the gloom from a Senator's house, tired, hungry again and just slightly drunk, I ended my first day as a real policeman.

CHAPTER 4

▼

ROME

The atmosphere in the Praetorian Camp was not easy to define. The Praetorians practice at being soldiers all day and sometimes part of the night as well. There are ceremonial functions and guard duties for them to undertake and plenty of parties for them after-hours. They enjoy accompanying the Emperor on excursions to various parts of his domains but, mostly, when he is not personally at war, they are very obviously present in and near Rome, a glaring and expensive extravagance in the eyes of many. Individually, and as a unit, they react to this with a sometimes stunning arrogance. As an irreverent colleague of mine described it, "Overpaid, over-sexed and overbearing!"

We in the Urban Cohorts were quartered in their Camp under the authority of the Praetorian Prefect for discipline and administration, but the Cohort commanders, as I have said, reporting to the City Prefect. We spent very little time retraining but went daily into action against the City crime lords. In many ways we were much more attuned to the popular feelings in the City than the Praetorians despite their powerful political connections. The simple act of walking the streets, usually alone, looking out for trouble, generates a certain grudging respect for patrolmen. It means that individual members become known to the public and anyone who has dangerous information to impart would naturally prefer to place his safety in the hands of someone he knows, however distantly, than in those of someone he does not. However much individual citizens might sometimes dislike our interest in their activities, most of the population concedes that we are always needed and, probably, are underpaid for what we do.

Had I been more experienced at the time, I might have noticed an alteration in the tempo of barrack activities or possibly an air of suppressed excitement among the more immature Praetorian officers, but I did not. I did notice an increased sensitivity towards any of our men straying into Praetorian territory in our Camp but thought this simply a symptom of Guards' urge to exclusivity.

At one morning parade, an elderly Centurion of the Cohort detailed several of us to stand aside for a briefing on a particular investigation. I was still very junior and was intrigued by my selection. He produced an inspector of the City's water department who tucked his thumbs into his girdle and surveyed his small audience.

"Not a very inspiring body," he observed in a loud voice to the Centurion. "From the cripple on the right to the bent weed on the left." He turned to the Centurion. "I did not know we were still recruiting children."

The Centurion, who was no less than forty, growled at him to get on with it and to stop messing about.

"Right, children. You guard the greatest City in the world. What is its lifeblood?"

As he was from the water department, it was clear what he thought was Rome's lifeblood, so we answered variously in suitably squeaky child-like voices.

"Alien labour, sir."

"The municipal sewerage system."

"Farm produce, inspector."

"Wine from Etruria, sir."

"Idiots!" he roared. "Does any one of you know the difference between an aqueduct and a reservoir? I thought not. Listen and learn."

The Centurion looked at me but I said nothing and neither did he.

"Water is brought many miles into the City from springs in the countryside under the control of the department. When it reaches the City, it is distributed from reservoirs—storage tanks to you—mainly to public fountains. Water for public use is free to the consumer; only water connected to private homes and businesses is taxed. As even you may know, the Emperor two years ago commissioned two additional water sources to be developed, one in the Sabine mountains and the other from the Anio River. The one is fifty-six kilometers from the City and the other no less than one hundred kilometers. Construction work is underway at several points along each of the surveyed lines of the aqueducts."

He paused and gave us the benefit of his sarcastic smile.

"Aqueducts, children, are channels or pipes to convey the water to the City. Now, we cannot guard every single construction site. Tools, equipment, and, particularly, lead piping is being stolen wholesale. The piping belongs to the municipality and we want you to stop the thefts, preferably yesterday."

He strutted about a bit and then fixed us with what he thought to be a steely stare.

"The Emperor's uncle, Claudius, is now overseeing the work and he wants action."

The implied menace of the Emperor's uncle failed to impress. Poor Claudius was known to have been disabled by a childhood illness and was believed to be several dice short of a full cup. He was treated with barely concealed contempt even by the Imperial family.

"There are two areas for investigation," declared the waterman. "The port of Ostia and the construction sites themselves…"

"Thank you, inspector," interjected the Centurion heavily. "I'll take it from here."

"Oh. Very well." The inspector looked at us, shook his head sadly and strode away.

The Centurion divided the team into two parties.

"Right, first party, go directly to the Fleet landing stage where there is a boat waiting for you. Have the sailors head downstream to Ostia and check every boatyard, shipyard and scrap metal merchant on the way. Don't waste time looking for tools. Any tools with a mark that cannot be removed will be at the bottom of the river and not in a toolbox. Don't waste time looking at what the yard foremen want to show you. They'll soon know that you are coming and will want to delay you. Go straight to any sign of fire on the premises and search carefully around melting pots and furnaces. Examine any lead you can find, including any already nailed to the hulls of boats. If you find any part of the municipal stamp on lead pipe or sheet, detain the management, close the yard and guard the evidence. Send the sailors back here with any aggressive prisoners under escort. No questions? Good. On your way." He paused to take a breath.

"Second party. The two new aqueducts are planned to meet about nine kilometers outside the City on the Sublacensis Road. Deploy now as if you are going to patrol beats in the City on that side. Lead pipes are too heavy to carry and too long, generally, to hide while being moved. This evening, instead of making your ways back to parade off-duty, assemble at the Gate and instruct the Vigiles not to allow any transport in. Search, starting from the back of the queue. I can see, Titus, that you think that your Centurion has forgotten that Vigiles search the incoming transport. Well, what load-carrying carts are quite long and are almost never searched by our colleagues? No, restrain your enthusiasm. You are quite right. They are the carts that collect the corpses for proper burial outside the

City. Stop that groaning. No one told you that work in the Urban Cohort was light, clean and paid well. Get out there and find the lead!"

The Centurion looked at me and jerked his head.

"My office," he said.

I found myself facing him over a cluttered desk. The silence lengthened. Eventually, it was he who broke it.

"I do not delve too deeply into the past of my men, provided that they come to the Cohorts recommended by reputable sponsors and work well. But I have reason to believe that you know something about water reticulation. Without admitting or denying it, what else needs to be done?"

"Illegal connections."

"Right. For what purpose?"

"Avoidance of municipal taxes on businesses and private homes. From what I've seen, the few private houses in the City are owned by the very wealthy who, maybe, would not steal to avoid a tax."

"Maybe is right. So—probably businesses then. What sort of business?"

"I would like to give that more thought. There is, of course, the departmental inspectorate." I paused as a thought struck me. "Which appears, right now, to be directing our attention outside the City."

The Centurion grinned suddenly. He rummaged behind his desk, cleared the surface with a sweep of a large hand and flattened a worn document across it.

"This is a plan of the City—about two years old. Here is the Tiber, there is the Forum, and we are here. These fine lines represent the water distribution network from the main reservoirs to the smaller water tanks and then to public fountains and private consumers. Unfortunately, there may have been many new connections in the last two years but I cannot call for an up-to-date version without signaling a special interest."

"Sir, I understand that. We need to find any illegal connections, but from this plan, it looks like an impossible job. We would have to check all the legitimate connections recorded here, locate all the ones which do not appear on this plan, then eliminate the new ones which were made legitimately. That will be a major exercise. Months of work, perhaps, even using half the Cohort; no way could that be kept secret."

My superior pondered. I saw his frown suddenly disappear and a grin spread across his unlovely features.

"You," he said, pointing a blunt forefinger at my chest, "are an investigator." His grin widened. I waited. " So. Go and investigate."

CHAPTER 5

▼

ROME

It did not take me long to work out which businesses needed large quantities of clean water, preferably free. Tanneries, for example, use a great deal of water but it does not have to be clean. Tiber River water is quite good enough. On the other hand, one of the biggest service industries in Rome is the cleaning of clothing. The City is not like a village where the women simply take the washing down to the nearest stream. The citizens, with their passion for Baths, change clothes often. City fashion dictates the wearing of clothing made with long runs of material and housewives simply do not have the time, access to water, or space to launder togas, for example, at home. They go to the public fullers' and the fullers need lots of clean water.

Unfortunately, identification of the type of business needing my investigatorial attention was only the first step. I had no idea how many fullers there are in Rome but I was sure there were scores if not hundreds. Assuming that I lived long enough to visit all of them, the City officials would be alerted long before I finished the task. Still, it was early, before the heat of the day, and I knew very little about the operation of the cleaning business. In the Cohort, we wash our own clothes, unless we can persuade a girlfriend to take care of them, and with a sponge and brush I had managed to keep my cloak presentable. Now, it was time to see how the experts do it.

The nearest business was not large but did cater to the wealthier Praetorians. Despite watching very carefully for it, I could not detect any disdain on the face of the proprietor as he examined my work-a-day garment, kneaded the material and picked off a thread or two. He handed it to a staff member who enthusiastically doused it in a tub of lupine solution and then, with an excessive amount of energy, beat the sodden lump on a stone table. When it was suitably subdued, it was dropped into a water tub where it was trampled underfoot by an off-duty wine maker. The suds having been, mostly, expelled, it was hauled out and stubborn stains attacked with what smelled suspiciously like urine. Generously, I chose to assume it was nitre. Thankfully, it was then again washed in clean water before being hung up to dry. A press with two screws was being used to finish dried garments but I did not wait for this process.

As I had known, a lot of clean water was used even for one item of clothing and the fullers had been busy. A lot of used water was drained out onto the street where it eventually found its way, no doubt, into the City sewerage system. Walking casually round to the rear of the premises, I located the incoming water pipe and traced it back to the neighbourhood municipal water tank. The municipal stamp was clearly visible in the lead piping.

I could not make a direct approach to the municipality for access to tax records and the only water-distribution map I had was from the Centurion and it was out of date. Nevertheless, like a good investigator, I had a plan.

The following morning, fully rested and in uniform, on my way to collect my clean cloak, I met the haggard members of the overnight search party. Red-eyed and irritable, they confirmed that they had searched every incoming hearse without finding anything other than two frightened illegal work-seekers. I suspected that the appearance of two white-faced apparitions from within a corpse-cart, seen by flickering torchlight, might have created more fright among the searchers than it did for those found. I told them that, as far as I knew, the investigating team on the river was still racing the news of its approach downstream. Certainly, no prisoners had been sent back as yet.

At the fullers' I collected my clean, pressed cloak with expressions of satisfaction. The proprietor relaxed a little, accepted my money and gave me the address of the head of his guild for me to express my approval of his work.

I always enjoy walking through the morning crowds in the City. There seems to be an atmosphere of anticipation and optimism in the air, especially when the weather is fine. The honest citizens had eaten and slept and the rubbish had been cleared away overnight. They had packed their shining children off to school and were out to work, shop or gossip, often all three. Even the sight of the Cohort on the street was treated with some cheerfulness. It would be different by mid-morning when the late-night revelers, prostitutes and criminals would be creeping into the sunlight looking for something for their hangovers and to replenish their purses.

The Master of the Guild, as might be expected, had large premises near the Forum and was busy with the morning trade. He quickly found time for me when he somehow developed the impression that I was not there on official business. He acknowledged my appreciation of his colleague's work in a voice loud enough to carry to all customers within distant earshot but he did not invite me into his minute office in the back.

"Now," he said, darting glances past me to check on his business, "is there anything I can do for the community's guardians?"

"Not really." I leaned against a wall, made small talk until a faint frown of irritation appeared on his face and his eyes began to focus on me.

"But," I pronounced airily, "be that as it may. There have been a rising number of crowd control problems during guild processions…"

"Nothing to do with this Guild…"

"Perhaps, but the Bakers…"

"Yes, well, what do you expect? Rough lot, the Bakers. Their Master has a terrible time getting in membership subscriptions and there are always arguments about pay-outs to the widows and orphans."

"The Bakers' procession ended in a near-riot. Four people hurt and a lot of property damage. My superiors had to deploy stand-by staff…"

"I heard that there was some sort of disturbance…"

"…and," I continued, "it ended up with guild members smashing up bakers' shops on the procession route."

"I see. I'll bet you half my day's takings that they were not proper bakers in those shops." The light of battle appeared in the Master's narrowed eyes. "I'll bet you that that they were a bunch of slaves and freedmen operating without membership of the Bakers' Guild. Am I right? In competition with legitimate guild members without the expense of subscriptions and, probably, avoiding municipal taxes, as well. You should close them all down. It's a disgrace."

"Well, I don't know anything about the businesses being illegal, but it could be so."

"Of course it's so. The place is overrun with foreigners and crooks. We have exactly the same problem. They pretend to be proper fullers, undercut our prices and give us a bad name. None of them are trained, none of them do the job properly and I have to deal with the complaints."

"I cannot comment on their businesses being illegal. If they are, I am sure you have brought it to the attention of the City Prefect's office."

"Hah."

"My superiors merely want to know where potential trouble spots are for your next procession."

"I see."

"In order to eliminate any danger to public order, it may well be necessary for the Cohort to question them. Some might have to be detained."

"Wait there. I'll get the list."

I should, of course, have hurried back to the Praetorian Camp and reported to my Centurion, presented the list of illegal fullers and modestly accepted his congratulations. Two things caused me to modify this commendable course of action. The first was that I had a shrewd suspicion that any congratulations available would be those bestowed on the Centurion himself when he described to the Cohort commander how he had solved the mystery of the missing lead piping. The second was that the list only bore five addresses—hardly enough, I would have thought, to have caused the Master any sleepless nights. Few enough for me to check out before making an official report. It was not yet even noon.

I did have to go back to the Camp and change out of uniform, however. I shared a dormitory with seven other patrolmen but only one would be there at midday. It was possible to reach my quarters without being seen by Cohort administration staff, but only if I circled around through Praetorian Guard domains. This was not without its dangers, but the possibility of an outraged report to my Centurion, or a summary beating up by guardsmen, might be worth it—and they had to catch me first. I did not believe that many of those muscle-bound clothes hangers could develop my turn of speed if danger threatened.

The sentries at the Camp gates seemed preoccupied and almost nervous. They looked at me more closely than usual as I strode confidently in but did not make any move to stop me. The Praetorians' accommodation was eerily deserted, not even a hurrying orderly to be seen. As I flitted from cover to cover, I could hear the rumble of a large crowd apparently gathered in the centre of their administration area. A high voice was declaiming some passionate belief and the crowd responses carried an impression of shock and anger. This was no place for me to linger.

I was poised to dart across the open space to where the Cohort quarters began when the speaker's voice rose even higher.

"…our Commander in Chief proposes to make his horse a god. His *horse!*"

There was a momentary silence, then a roar of disbelief merging into fury.

I ran.

Safe in my quarters, I sat on my bunk and caught my breath. Like all such buildings, my eight-man mess slept in the outer room and stored equipment and personal possessions in the inner room. Usually there would be at least one member on hand keeping an eye on our property and cooking our evening meal in the Camp kitchens. He must be away drawing rations or checking the guard list for night duty.

In the meantime, what were the Praetorians so incensed about? The Commander in Chief could only mean the Emperor, Gaius Caligula. All Rome had been scandalised when he had tried to get himself declared a god while he was still alive and had tried to get his horse elected as Consul. Could it really be true that he had made the outrageous suggestion that his horse, Incitatus, be declared a god? In the Celtic tradition, there is a horse-goddess and the mythical half-men-halfhorses known as the centaurs are well-known, but the Emperor's personal horse? The religious conservatives would be horrified. The common gossip-mongers would not let the subject rest for months, if not years.

I resisted the impulse to laugh aloud. The Cohorts serve the Emperor only indirectly but, for the Praetorian Guard, the Emperor is indeed their Commander in Chief. Any aberrant actions on his part reflect directly on them and, recently, he had given them very little to boast about. True, the Army had had success in Mauretania, but it had been gained by ordinary soldiers under Hosideus Geta, not Praetorians, and even that was success in putting down a bitter revolt which had been sparked by the Emperor's own illogical actions. The Praetorians were going to have difficulty explaining away the proposed deification of their boss's transport.

✶   ✶   ✶   ✶

Titus burst into the barrack room, giving me such a fright I nearly brained myself on the upper bunk. He was bedraggled, breathless and almost beside himself. It took some time before I could understand him.

It appeared that the Praetorians had caught him trying to eavesdrop on their unit meeting at the tribunal, and, with their present temper, they were not after him to offer promotion. He claimed to have lost his pursuers but I knew better. They would not give up until they vented their anger on someone, and who better than a junior member, or two, of the Cohorts—the Cohorts which were closer than the Guard to the commoners of Rome, those same commoners whose derision was making life a misery for the gilded Guard? And if those junior members of a Cohort came to grief before the righteous anger of the Praetorians, under whose disciplinary code would the subsequent enquiry be convened? It was clearly time to adopt that military activity known as headlong flight.

Unfortunately, Titus was from peasant stock in his native Etruria and once an idea had sunk into his skull, it was very difficult to dislodge it. He had been on a day's quiet Camp duty for our mess when his inquisitive nature had led him into a whirlpool of trouble. He had headed for our quarters like a mouse for a hole and, now he thought himself safe, he had no intention of leaving it again.

"We must barricade ourselves in here until their officers come," bawled this innocent. "They will sort them out."

"Have you seen any officers?" I snarled at him.

"Only Rufrius Pollio," he wailed. "But he is as big as any two Guardsmen. He'll get them under control."

"Well, that's fine," I said, doing some quick mental arithmetic. "With two of them taken care of, there are only five thousand, nine hundred and ninety eight we have to worry about."

It took precious time to convince him of the danger of staying where we were and then even more precious time to prevent him from drawing weapons and armour from our inner room. What he thought he could achieve with a short sword against about six thousand angry Praetorians I do not know. What finally broke through his stubbornness was the sound of hobnails on stone flags—a lot of them—and of doors being kicked open. Dressed in tunics and sandals, as we were, Titus and I could possibly pass as civilians, but that would only help if we could reach the City's streets. It would not much matter to the Praetorians if they caught nosey members of the Cohort or civilians—possibly spies at worst, at best humourists from the Roman mob—within the Camp.

I peered through a crack in our door. A large group of Praetorians was sweeping along the lines. They had clearly attended the unit meeting in full uniform but now one was without his helmet. Several had drawn swords in hand. They looked flushed and ugly, not at all the haughty protectors of the Emperor. Definitely time to go.

We burst from that doorway like balls from a ballista, curved left and picked up even more speed. I did not hear any shouts of alarm but there was no mistaking the metallic pounding of the military in pursuit. We headed for the Main Gate Left, hoping to skim out of there while the sentries were still gazing at the City.

We are all trained to run in armour with weapons. Titus and I were unencumbered and should have been able to outdistance the armoured heavyweights behind us. So much for the theory. It was a long straight stretch to the Camp wall where we would have to turn right to reach the Gate. We were drawing away from our pursuers and, encouraged, we even relaxed a little as we rounded the centurion's quarters at the end of the line—and stopped.

A huge crowd of Praetorians had gathered in the space between the wall and the ends of the lines of accommodation blocks. They were all facing us, except for an immensely tall soldier who had his back to us. At about fifty paces I could see their faces clearly and frowns were giving way to anticipation as they stared at Titus and I. The same sort of expression as a fox may have in a chicken run.

Titus took one look at them, turned on his heel and fled down the length of the Camp wall just as the first of our pursuers ran out, sword in hand, from behind the centurion's house. He was the one without the helmet. He tried to turn after Titus but, with a screech of hobnails on stone, he fell with a crash flat on his back and slid for several paces, his tunic riding up his thighs. The rest of the pursuers, like a pack of hounds, hurdled their prone leader and tore off after my comrade.

I think it was the laughter that got to me. It was totally illogical. Their colleague had slipped and fallen and the mass of the Praetorians was laughing, mainly at him. But they were also laughing at an unarmed man running away for his life. They were laughing at me, weaponless, at bay in front of hundreds of allegedly the best soldiers in the Empire. They were prepared to kill us because they were embarrassed, their dignity had been harmed and now they were laughing at us. A true Roman might have been able to turn this to his advantage. With a few well-chosen words, with a little judicious groveling, he might be able to change that laughter into something friendly. I am a citizen but not a true Roman. The Celtic element in my blood started to fizz and sing in my ears, rage rose in my throat and, with some sort of scream, I launched myself at the scores of armed men in the front rank of the crowd. I have no idea what I was trying to do except to wipe the smiles off some faces.

Fifty paces is not far and is covered quickly. The tall soldier had turned to face me in astonishment. The smiles disappeared from the crowd and those in front even gave a little ground. Weapons appeared foreshortened as they were aimed at me. The tall man had time to draw a weapon but he did not, nor did he step back. A faint glimmer of reason directed me at him. I hurled myself at him, my red-rimmed vision fixed on his sword arm.

At the last moment he twisted aside. The collision knocked the breath out of me but I had not knocked him down. I had lost impetus and two huge hands fastened on the front of my tunic. I lashed out, butted and kicked but could not land a decisive blow. I am tall and not a lightweight, but this man was a giant. He ducked his helmet to protect his face, braced his elbows against the front of his cuirass, flexed his legs and lifted me right off the ground. Armed men appeared all around with weapons poised to drive in under my rib cage.

"Leave him," the giant roared to them into my face.

The weapons withdrew a few centimeters.

"Leave the manikin to me."

Through the dissipating mists of anger, I was conscious that garlic formed a significant element of his diet. I tried a round-arm punch to his head and only skinned my knuckles on his cheek-piece. I jabbed for his eyes but he jerked his head away with a flash of very large teeth. I was in a frankly ludicrous position. His grip on the front of my clothing, and my own exertions, were pulling the tunic through the girdle round my waist, exposing my nether regions. I subsided, waiting for an opportunity to plant an incapacitating kick. He was too shrewd for that and flung me suddenly away from him. I did not get my legs under me in time and landed on my backside, surrounded by sharp steel.

"Now little man, what do you think you are doing, haring around my Camp and attacking half the Praetorian Guard?"

This got something of a laugh from the wall of armed men. It was subtly different from the earlier crowd-noise.

"A member of Urban Cohort XII, are you? Well, pull your tunic down before you have to arrest yourself for indecent exposure."

More grins.

"Do you have any complaint about the Praetorian Guard? No? I should think not. Just remember, the Urban Cohorts are guests here. You are not allowed to go around attacking peace-loving guardsmen in their own Camp. Now get yourself about your duties before I remember you throwing yourself at me like a toddler at her mother."

Laughter and the sheathing of swords as I got to my feet.

"And get something for that bruise on your buttocks."

I got as far as saying that I did not have a bruise when I received a mighty kick to the backside and Rufrius Pollio led away his men.

We found Titus later behind the latrines. He had been beaten half to death. In the subsequent enquiry, the Praetorian officers' board found that no suspect could be adequately identified.

CHAPTER 6

▼

EGYPT

On the other side of the world, Philip walked in the sun beside the canal Pharoah Necos had abandoned in his attempt to link the Delta with the Red Sea. One hundred and twenty thousand Egyptian labourers had died in that attempt. It was left to the Great King Darius of Persia to complete the work some five hundred years ago, connecting the Mediterranean to the southern ports of his empire.

The Greeks had, of course, eventually beaten the Persians. A Greek dynasty had ruled in Egypt until Cleopatra VI had been driven to suicide. In the seventy years since her death, the western demand for Chinese silk had declined. Little traffic was moving along this route now. Philip's father, Pytheas, known during his service with the Fleet as Antoninus Maximus, intended to change that.

Pytheas had not sailed out of the Mediterranean during his military service, nor had any real wish to follow his namesake, the ancient colonial Greek explorer, to the Cassiterides Islands of the far north. His independent attitude and strong views had retarded his career. Politically he was suspect in being unable to conceal from his superiors his simmering rage at the conversion of the sovereign and ancient kingdom of Egypt into a mere food producing Province for the voracious and ignorant electorate of the Empire. The corn produced in the fertile flood plains of the Nile was confiscated annually for the spongers and idlers of Rome.

Most of his naval officers had been of Greek descent but some were not, and, one year before the completion of his enlistment, Antoninus Maximus was discharged from service with the Fleet without any terminal benefits.

This was a devastating, but not uncommon, sanction. He had given twenty-five years of his life to military service, to be denied, by one year, of the grant of Roman citizenship to himself and to his descendents. More bitter still, men in military service were still not officially permitted to marry although, of course, many did so. The honourable discharge granted after completing the term of service automatically legitimised both an unofficial marriage and the children from it. The other benefits of the grant were as nothing compared to the official deprivation of official recognition from his family.

One of those deprived, his son Philip, was now on his way home from Syria with sufficient intelligence sewn into his clothing and filed in his memory to launch the non-recognised family's fortunes eastwards to India. Philip trudged on towards Fayum.

To the north-west, the waters of Alexandria Harbour were crowded with shipping. A forest of masts spiked the clear sky and fringed the windowsill of the office of the international banker named as the founder of the second largest city in the Empire. Alexander was a middle aged Jew, a financier with colleagues throughout the Empire, co-religionists for the most part and friends and advisors to the powerful. He was an Alexandrine and never tired of the mercantile vibrancy of his city, which he rarely left and never stayed away from longer than was imperative. Busy always, his office was never busier than during the month of May and it was now mid May. Every morning, the cleaners had to sponge walls and furniture to remove the soot from batteries of oil lamps that had burned late into the previous night. The corn fleet must sail in June.

The clerks he had barred from his last meeting swarmed almost silently into his office. He had handpicked them from among the many Jewish and Greek applicants who came to his door. The Romans who, while they were by no means stupid, had an exaggerated concern for their personal dignity, and the Egyptians from the rural hinterland, accustomed to undue subservience, were not represented on his staff.

Alexander took a few minutes to reflect on his discussion with his last visitor. The risk profile of investment in any region depended absolutely on its environment. Any information on that environment was invaluable. The intensity of the exposition of the swirling complexities of religion and politics in Palestine had been worth every disturbing minute. His visitor had received some rudimentary legal training and was a naturally good observer. Mark's account of the religious and political upheavals caused by the preaching of his teacher, Jesus, had been masterful. Unfortunately, Jesus had been executed ten years ago. Alexander would have liked to have met the man. The financier had made a cash contribution to Mark's cause. It had been no more than just reward for business intelligence received.

The waiting client was shown in and stood, head up, feet apart and apparently at ease.

"Pytheas. How are you? Please take a seat. How is business? And the family? All well, I trust?"

Alexander examined the burly figure in front of him. No sign of illness in the clear eyes and ruddy cheeks. More silver in the hair and beard than when they had last met. No citizen's toga, of course, but very muscular forearms below a well-cut tunic, the legacy of years at the oar. The ridged brown calluses across the palms at the base of the fingers had probably gone by now but the tattoo of a steering oar, glimpsed below his sleeve, never would.

Pytheas' gaze did not waver.

"I sold the business to a friend in Fayum."

"And, no doubt, invested the proceeds wisely as you have already cleared your debt with me," said Alexander, nodding.

"No. I have put the money aside to await the outcome of certain research I have commissioned. I am looking at a business opportunity that, I believe, has great promise."

"And the research is now complete?"

"Yes."

"And it is now time to talk about the financing of the enterprise?"

"That's right."

"You do not feel that the time is right to retire to your smallholding and watch the wheat grow?"

Both men laughed a little.

"So. What can you tell me of your researches? How is your son Philip?"

Pytheas' eyes widened but he retained his composure.

"I can tell you this. We export glass, copper, tin, lead, textiles and pottery to the East from Alexandria. Most of that the Indians can make or mine themselves. We get back incense, some precious stones, muslin and spices, especially pepper. The skipper of every Arab coaster and the headman of every flea-bitten village from the Red Sea to the Indus takes his cut. The problem is that what we export is not of much use to the noblemen out there and they are not prepared to spend much to supplement their subjects' requirements. For what we send out, we get comparatively little back. Bad business."

"You have not mentioned silk," put in Alexander delicately.

"Yes. The most valuable import of all. Popularised here by Cleopatra Ptolomy until her death and now discouraged by our masters throughout the Empire as being contrary to proper Roman austerity." There was no sneer in his bald statement.

"And yet still it arrives."

"Yes. Mostly overland through Syria and ruinously expensive, too. The Greeks in Palmyra control that trade. I sent Philip to Palmyra."

"Ah", said Alexander.

"He reports that the river, the Orontes, has been made navigable from the Mediterranean to Antioch and from there it is overland to Palmyra where the caravan traffic is organised down the line of the Euphrates to the Persian Gulf. There they meet our friends the Arab coasters, operating to the Indus River. The silk arrives there from beyond India somewhere. The Arab skippers say that silk is commonplace in India although apparently it is not made there."

"This confirms what we have already heard." Alexander mused for a moment while Pytheas noted the "we".

"So," said the banker, "we have a market and we have a supplier, but we are not offering the required goods for trade. Also, we are losing too much potential profit in commissions on the way."

"Right again."

The retired sailor and Alexander looked at one another.

"Ships and money."

"Right."

Alexander fingered his beard. "There is a monster of a ship being built at Myos Hormus on the Red Sea."

"Five hundred tons displacement, it will be the biggest man-made object on the sea. And since Hippalus—a Greek, by the way, dead these hundred years— discovered and recorded the wind patterns of the annual monsoons, there is no reason why we cannot sail directly to the west coast of India, outside the reach of the coasters and the Palmyra crowd."

"And you need a loan to complete it."

"No."

"No?"

"The ship is paid for. I bought my share with the sale of my business. We need the money to buy silk."

"To buy silk? But we have sent barrels of money east in the past."

"You have sent barrels of bronze and copper coins minted locally. Indian nobles can't use them except to melt them down for armour. You can be sure they give very little armour to their people. What they want is gold coin which is only made at the Imperial mints. They want the Emperor's head on it as a qual-ity-guarantee, and they want as much as we can send. Palmyra is outside the Empire and cannot siphon off enough gold coin to trade properly. But you can."

Alexander sat back breathless. "There's a shipload on its way here now," he said.

*   *   *   *

The post of Prefect of the Fleet at Alexandria was a political and an adminis-trative appointment at least as much as it was a military one. The new incumbent felt a faint stirring of unease. He had served his political and administrative internship and had done well in the City, in Spain and in Syria, but his military service had been as a junior tribune in a peaceful area. He had absorbed a modest amount of instruction from his superior officers in the legion. The Senior Tri-bune, the formidable Camp Commandant and the Legate himself, had all three tried to impart to him what a young officer needed to know but, in truth, his learning capacity was clouded by his inability to get on good terms with his men. The hard centurions and profane legionaries secretly scared him and some of them, at least, suspected it. Still, that was a long time ago. Fortunately he came from a notable family which had largely survived the purges in the reign of the Emperor Tiberius. When Gaius Caligula came to the throne, the family had con-stituted a significant part of his support base and the Prefect's appointment was the reward.

The shipping crammed into Alexandria harbour, and beached and anchored all along the foreshore, constituted only an administrative problem, not a military one. He was confident that this was well within his powers although the scale of the political crisis which would result from any failure on his part gave rise to reg-ular qualms. If the Egyptian corn did not reach the population of Rome on time, there would be riots which the military would have to put down and a lot of vot-ers would be hurt. The consequences of that would be dire, both nationally and personally. With a suppressed sigh, he turned from his contemplation of Alexan-dria's huge lighthouse and bustling port from his office window and faced the two military men politely waiting for his attention.

He was immediately aware of an atmosphere of tension between the admiral, or Navarch, of the warships based in Alexandria and the commander of the Nile River Guard who stood before him. The Navarch looked unhappy and almost defiant while his junior colleague seethed with some emotion behind an almost blank mask. Trouble. The Navarch, as a naval officer, should have been called upon to report first. However, the Prefect, who knew professional jealousy when he saw it, told the River Guard commander to report.

"Sir. I have closed down one reception point and transferred the staff to the other three. The staff has been threatened. Probing the sacks before being weighed has turned up several tons of corn with logs of wood, stones and other rubbish included. The farmers have been arrested but death threats have been made against my personnel by the families and I do not have sufficient men to guard all four points."

"Very well. Proceed." This was routine. The bad news hovered invisibly, so far unsaid.

"Yesterday, we escorted forty seven loaded barges from the reception points, supervised the transshipment of the corn into the merchant ship and sealed the holds. Navy personnel were present when the sealing was done and the loaded and sealed ships were handed over to the Fleet, with the documentation, in the Delta."

"How much of the harvest is still to come?"

"I hear that the granaries are nearly empty. Another six days should do it."

"Good. Any other problems other than the would-be swindlers?"

"Not on my side," said the River Guard commander, with a sidelong glance.

"Thank you, commander. I have no additional instructions for you. You may go."

"Ah…"

"Good day, commander."

The Prefect turned to look again at the Navarch.

"Sir. Firstly, thank you for that," the naval officer nodded towards the office door. "Because of the needs of Hosideus Geta in Mauretania, most of our warships are in the far west and will be there, most probably, until the revolt is put down. Here, 'Libertas' is careened for essential repairs. The other two, 'Concordia' and 'Athenonike', were taking it in turns to escort the loaded merchantmen from the Delta to anchor here."

"Were?"

"Yes," the Navarch took an audible breath. "Yesterday, while turning in the Delta, 'Concordia' rammed 'Athenonike'…"

"What!" the Prefect surged from his chair.

"Yes," the Navarch hurried on. "Both ships are damaged. 'Athenonike' is beached below Heliopolis and will need dockyard help. 'Concordia's' ram is broken off and she is leaking like a sieve, but is limping back here. Crew are taking shifts rowing and pumping. She should arrive tomorrow if the weather holds."

Leaning on his desk with clenched fists, the Prefect collected himself.

"Did anyone else witness this…this event?"

"There were several merchant vessels at the hand-over point and some River Guard boats."

"Any casualties?"

"One believed fatality. A helmsman went over the side. A crocodile probably got him."

"Good." The Prefect slowly subsided onto his chair. "Now, how long before 'Libertas' is ready for sea?'

"Three days."

"So," shock was being replaced, and the rising tide of anger was clearly visible on the Prefect's face. "So, Navarch of the Alexandrine Fleet, at this moment you do not have a single viable warship to command. Tell me why I need a Navarch with no ships."

The naval officer decided not to respond directly to this reasonable but distinctly disturbing question.

"One of our warships should be arriving any day now from Mauretania to collect pay for the troops there, but we cannot retain it here without the danger of unrest in Hosideus Geta's expeditionary force. Another warship is also on its way here with the money, but it will be from either the Misenum or the Ravenna Fleet. If we try to delay it after unloading I can also foresee administrative problems."

"No need to be coy, Navarch. The Prefects of the two Fleets based in Italy outrank me by far, and are a lot closer to the Imperial ear. That ship will have to return as soon as it has completed its task here."

"Yes sir, which leaves requisitioning a ship or ships. Or the River Guard. Which," he added hastily, "I do not recommend."

The Prefect grunted agreement. The Nile guard boats were too small and frail for the open sea and the merchant skippers would take great delight in ignoring and leaving behind any River Guard vessel which tried to marshal their ships in their own element. He surveyed the Navarch.

"Requisitioning shipping while the corn fleet is assembling?"

"Very difficult. There is, sir, a financier. A Jew…"

"There is, almost always, a Jewish financier."

"…who may be in a position to assist. He is waiting outside. His name is Alexander."

Alexander entered with an air of diffidence which the Navarch noted with a wry smile. The seated Roman Prefect, who had adjusted his toga and smoothed his hair before having the financier shown in, adopted a dignified and relaxed posture as he indicated a seat in front of his desk.

"I understand from the Navarch that you are aware of the present needs."

"I have heard of the unfortunate incident in the Delta but, then, so has a very large proportion of the population."

The Prefect's dignity underwent a subtle change.

"And you feel that you may be able to assist Egypt in its Imperial task?"

"I am in a position to lease a seaworthy ship to the Alexandrine Fleet should it be required and the terms be agreeable."

The Navarch fought down an urge to smile. It was well known that Alexander had friends and debtors in high places and not only in Alexandria. He felt it unnecessary to intervene. The Prefect continued.

"Merchant shipping is at a premium. I had not thought that a sea-going vessel would be available, much less one which you consider might be of service to the Fleet."

"It is not a military liburnian but it is not an ordinary cargo ship either. It was an experiment by a consortium running silk, woven in Antioch, to the market in Rome. The members are now each pursuing other business interests and the ship has been used to settle the consortium's account with me. The business ran into difficulties because the flow of woven silk was dependent on the overland caravans through Palmyra. No one can accurately predict this, and it is uneconomic to have a purpose-built ship lying idle for lengthy periods."

"What makes you think that the ship will be suitable for military purposes?"

"That is for the Navarch, perhaps, to say. I can tell you though that it is fast. It is fitted both with rowers' benches and with sails. It is on passage here from the Orontes and should arrive tomorrow. It left five days ago."

The Prefect looked at the naval officer who nodded. Six days was good time for the time of year. He turned back to the financier.

"Very well. Your ship's suitability will be reported upon and it certainly sounds promising. Now, as to terms…"

It was Alexander's turn to look at the Navarch, which he did with a smile. The Prefect took the hint and dismissed his subordinate with unnecessary injunctions about keeping him advised on progress in restoring his stricken ships. He turned again to face the financier.

$$* \qquad * \qquad * \qquad *$$

"Pytheas," said Alexander later, "I believe we may have a deal."

The old sailor rested his forearms on the desk between them and peered into the bright eyes of the bearded banker.

"Tell me," he said simply.

"You need gold coin and the Prefect of the Fleet, as the ranking military officer left in the Province, needs some form of warship under his control right now. No, don't worry, 'Cleopatra' could not be used for his task even if she could be transferred from the Red Sea to the Mediterranean. I have a ship I can lend him if it is found to be suitable, and it will be."

"And you will lend me the gold he pays you?"

"Not exactly. He does not have sufficient gold on hand to make your enterprise worthwhile. But a warship loaded with gold coin, 'Minerva' from the Misenum Fleet, is about to dock in Alexandria. The money is the quarterly pay for the army and almost all the soldiers are away in Mauretania. A warship is doubtless on its way from there to collect the pay brought by 'Minerva'. But, you know, there is nothing much to spend it on there and many of the senior soldiers have families here in Alexandria. The ordinary legionary may want his pay in hand to waste in that desert but the family men know better." He added, almost as an aside, "Centurions get paid thirty two times what a common legionary receives." Alexander watched the expression on Pytheas' face.

"So,' he continued, "the Prefect will ratify the many private arrangements I made with officers and legionary standard bearers before the Army left for Mauretania. Their pay will be deposited with me and my office will pay the monthly allotments to the families. This can be done in bronze and copper coin and the gold will be available for—ah—investment."

Pytheas thumped the desk in satisfaction and gave Alexander the benefit of a huge smile.

"There is one thing further," said the banker. "I have a friend in a very influential position in Rome who will do everything in his power to stimulate the market for the silk you bring back."

"That is very good indeed. We obviously need to discuss the terms of your loan to me and what can be done for your friend. Also, the Prefect was very fortunate in having the use of a valuable ship for merely ratifying an existing and sensible arrangement for the military."

"Well, the Prefect has undertaken to provide something else as well. But, as to my terms, interest on the loan will suffice; I do not wish to buy a share in the first voyage. Subsequent ones might be different. I will accept half my usual rate of interest."

"Half? What makes me think that the rest of my end of the deal might cause me some heartache?"

Alexander smiled. "My friend has a need for someone he can trust in the centre of Imperial communications, the detachment of the Misenum Fleet in Rome."

There was a pause.

"You are thinking of Philip," stated the ex-sailor. "He has courage and a level head and enjoys intelligence work, but…"

"I have an undertaking that he would never be asked to do anything contrary to Imperial interests…"

"To hell with Imperial interests. You know as well as I do that the bloody Navy did me and my family out of my rights by discharging me a year early."

"Yes. I do know that, and that," said Alexander, "is the other contribution that the Prefect is going to make."

A short while later, Alexander walked with Pytheas, all smiles, to the door of his office, his hand on his shoulder. Before opening the door, Pytheas turned to him.

"You know, when this new route is established, I can foresee a continuous drain of gold flowing out of the Empire through Alexandria and a continuous stream of silk flowing in. Silk is perishable. At most it lasts for a few years. The demand for it will be continuous and growing. The demand for Roman gold will also be continuous and growing. What would happen if gold supplies in the Empire were to dry up?"

"That, my Greek friend," said the smiling Jew, "would be a truly Imperial problem."

CHAPTER 7

▼

BRITAIN

West of Britain, in the Irish Sea, the delegation of the High King of Ireland steered into the wide estuary of the Severn. So wide is the estuary that the original Greek navigator, Pytheas, had thought that it was a channel dividing the huge western promontory of Britain from the rest of the land. The Irish knew better. Since the Celts from Spain first landed in Ireland under Queen Scota and her son Ir, the Irish had probed and explored, traded and raided the entire west coast of Britain and beyond. They spoke a language similar but not the same as the Celts of west Britain and they shared an admiration of heroic single combat with a brave enemy, keeping the heads of honoured vanquished enemies as reminders of their bravery. However well educated, they committed nothing to writing, at least not in Celtic, and relied on the support of the international Celtic association of the Druids in matters of record, diplomacy and negotiation.

This delegation was small. One substantial war boat, at dawn in the Severn estuary, contained twelve high-born Irish warriors, a Druid called Niall and its leader, Brigit Mong Ruadh, military co-ordinator of the Irish and sister of the High King. As it was a peace mission, a green branch was displayed at the mast-head and weapons were not drawn. The well-born shuffled their feet, fiddled with their torcs and arm rings and bailed a little. No matter how fine an appearance the delegation presented, wet feet in the bottom of a boat made of smelly oxhide and creaking struts were incentives to hurry on shore and fight or talk. So far, however, there was no signal to confirm the landing place.

"No sign of any river traffic, not even a ferry or a fishing boat, Niall".

"No, lady, they know we are here but they do not yet know if we have a substantial armed force on the water behind us."

"I remember that the people on the west bank are rare fighters on the water or off it."

"The Silures? Yes, many a hard knock for very little profit there. My colleagues there know why we are here and I doubt that anyone will interfere with us. There was a time when almost all trade from Continental Europe came by Ocean-going ship to south-west Britain where the Durotriges controlled land and river transport. This estuary was on a major north-south trade route then, and the Silures important people."

"And then came Caesar."

"Destroyed the Celtic fleets and burned their ports on the Continent, and their capital Vannes, scattered the Veneti seamen from their homes, many of them ending up in Britain. They interested the locals in the use of the slingshot and helped them improve their military engineering on the hillforts."

"Making life more difficult for your honest Irish raider."

"True, lady, but your average Irish skull is more than a match for a British pebble."

There was the merest ripple of amusement among the soldiers.

"And, I suppose, Niall, Irish legs will carry the owner up any British wall."

"True again, lady, although Druids among the Durotriges tell me that one of their fortifications, Mai Dun, is something to marvel at."

"But Caesar had major political problems at home, even when he allegedly conquered the Continental Celtish kingdoms..."

"And," interrupted Niall, his measured academic tone becoming uneven, "doing his best to wipe out the Order of Druids."

"Which," said Brigit soothingly, "he rightly saw as the major force binding all the Celts in Europe and parts of Asia against the expansion of Rome. Every Celt from the High Kings down knows the importance of the legal, social, teaching and archival service provided by the Druids to the confederation of Celtic nations. It is, of course, your religious duties that the Romans draw attention to and profess horror at our sacrifice of criminals and our lack of organised slave markets for prisoners of war. They prefer to condemn people to the death of slavery for the rest of their lives. Roman society cannot function without incessant warfare and they have not sufficient freeborn to both fight and farm. You can see where this is going to lead. Ordinary Romans, fighting for the expansion of their Empire, lose their own land in their absence to fat local landowners because..."

She looked hard at the grave faces of her escort.

"*Because,*" she emphasised the word, "their womenfolk are deprived of proper recourse to the courts. The landowners seize the farmland and work their expanding estates with slaves. The Roman soldiers, if they survive, are compensated with captured land on the frontiers when they retire. Will the slaves fight if the Roman Army falters? Only for themselves. Rome is hollow at the centre. Soon may it collapse."

Gulls, investigating the drifting vessel for any sign of fishing, screamed in disappointment. The crew stirred and arms pointed at the three pillars of smoke rising into the dark sky from the eastern shore of the estuary.

"Heroes, bend your backs. Niall, steer for the reception committee. What is the name of their King again?"

"Buduoc, lady. He is an appointee of High King Cunebelinos to rule the northern part of the Dobunni tribe when they acknowledged his authority recently. Neither the Silures nor the Durotriges have formally conceded, but King Buduoc's new realm gives High King Cunobelinos direct rule from Camelodunon. From the east coast to the river Severn in the west."

"A key figure then. As we are to be received by a British king and to be escorted to his High King, I had better make myself presentable. Hail his new subjects, Niall, and announce the mission of the High King of Ireland, Connaire Mor, led by his royal sister, Brigit Mong Ruadh, to Cunibelinos the High King of Britain."

Three days later, the Irish party was getting the tour of Kaleoua, the former capital of the Atrebates' King. The territory was now governed by Caratacos, son of the British High King. He was younger than Brigit had expected, compact, energetic and ruddy complexioned. There were other sons, she knew, the eldest governed in the High King's capital, Camulodunon on the British east coast, and another governed the tribe of the British south-east, the Cantii. All three were grown men and would be among the candidates for election when their father eventually entered the Otherworld. And that, her brother had told her, would probably be soon.

Brigit had luxuriated in the soap and warm water provided on her arrival. Chariots were fun but hard on the legs and arms. It had been a real relief to throw off her mud-spattered tunic and trousers, almost bliss to loosen the tight bindings of her breasts and to discard her loincloth. With comb and enameled mirror she had untangled her red hair and then, washed, had dressed in clean underwear and put on a fresh tunic over a bell-shaped skirt. A decorated belt and clean sandals had been dug out of the baggage and, from her jewelry box, several gold chains now augmented the royal torc around her throat. A jet bracelet and a gold ring completed the transformation.

The townsmen and women of Kaleoua seemed a relatively contented community although this, Caratacos told her, had not always been the case. They had initially been resentful of the pressure of the Cassi family under the High King and had wanted to retain the independence of the Atrebates tribe. Militarily, they were not really capable of standing up to the forces of the High King, descendents of those warriors who had twice repelled the Romans under one of their most famous generals some ninety years before.

The Atrebates had claimed land from the Thames south to the coast, but they were hemmed in by potential enemies and were prevented from cross-Channel trading. That was claimed as the High King's prerogative. The good quality iron they produced from the Weald eventually determined that they would become his subjects. In the end, their own king, Bericos, fled to the Romans, followed by some of his kinsmen. A few other troublemakers had met with accidents and now peace and development was taking hold, or so it was said.

Caratacos pointed out land which had been allocated to the support of the social services, the granaries, water mills and covered threshing-floors. Weaving, brewing and metalworking was mainly done at home in the round, thatched buildings of the homesteads. This was all familiar to the Irish.

The Irish warriors solemnly listened to an explanation of the brewing technique in the odd British tongue. The conversion of the barley grain into braich malt was, they were told, followed by its being dried in a kiln until it was hard. The ground malt was apparently then made into a mash with water and this was fermented, boiled and strained. Although this method in no way differed from that used back home, the soldiers expressed deep surprise and intense interest in the presentation. Brigit and Caratacos watched the Irishmen solicit samples from the gullible British countrymen, solemnly taste substantial quantities, compare samples and render informed judgement.

They saw their British host watching them and offered wide Irish grins.

"Carry on lads," said Caratacos. "It is always a pleasure to watch professionals at work."

A harvesting machine was demonstrated. Two oxen pushed a wheeled box into a cornfield. It was open in front and lined at the bottom of the opening with narrow teeth. As the box rumbled forward, the teeth combed the cornstalks and stripped off the heads which fell into the box.

"A certain amount of leaf and stalk also finds its way into the box, but this is separated out at threshing time and, in any case, is no more than you get when harvesting is done by lines of people with sickles."

In the city, half-timbered tenements up to three stories high housed the townspeople, mainly comprising the unfree class or those who owned no land of their own.

The public courts attracted Niall immediately and the others politely kept him company while he listened intently to a dispute referred from a community on the coast over the annual lottery for deep sea fishing grounds. When the arbitration, guided by the Magistrate, had concluded and the compensation had been agreed, it was Brigit who then detained the party.

A woman, divorced by her husband, had lawfully retained her dowry and other personal property she had brought into the partnership. Now that she was again free, her action was to confirm her ownership of the offspring of the cattle her father had given her as a bride. Without hesitation, the court found in her favour. The Magistrate reminded the ex-husband of the equality of rights enjoyed by Celtic women and, for good measure, of the heavy penalties provided for any offences against the honour of women. The man did not appear at all chastened. The case had been a foregone conclusion. Nevertheless, Caratacos was pleased to see that it had put his Irish guest in high good humour. As they swept, smiling, from the court, the Magistrate caught Niall's eye and Niall subsided.

A tall figure stood before the court. Though dressed in colourful tunic and trousers in the Celtic fashion, he was undeniably foreign. The brooch securing his woollen cloak was of Celtic, but not British, design, and his short hair and shaved upper lip suggested his origin as being from occupied Gaul. His name, he announced, was Phylus.

The Magistrate held up a small square of slate. "What is this?" he demanded.

"That," said the stranger with some composure, "gives my name, my profession and the sort of treatment I am able to provide. I give them out to potential clients."

"I can read Latin," said the Magistrate sharply, "as well as Greek, and your name sounds Greek to me. Give an account of yourself, sir. Who are you, and what are you doing in the combined kingdoms of High King Cunobelinos?"

"For professional reasons I have adopted a Greek name. I am of the sovereign tribe of the Sequani. I arrived by fishing boat two days ago and I am here to practice my profession of healer, if the local authorities permit."

There was a murmur among the spectators. The foreigner's composure bordered on insolence and the stir of hostility was not lost on the Magistrate. He looked at Niall who shook his head slightly. He turned back to the stranger.

"The Sequani of east Gaul may have been sovereign once, but they are now under the Roman heel. That is not the situation here. We will come to the legality of your arrival here under an assumed name in a moment. Be aware that you are standing before what you are pleased to term 'the local authorities' and it is more than simply permission for you to conduct business which is being decided here. There are heavy penalties provided for unlawful entry into these lands and even heavier penalties for quacks pretending to be properly qualified medical men. I can see you are not a Druid and this has been confirmed by an eminent member of the Order here present." The Magistrate bowed slightly in Niall's direction. "Druids, and only Druids, are physicians and surgeons here and any imposter will find himself deprived of every right of citizenship except life. As a foreigner, your family or tribe could be required to pay very substantial compensation to any unsuspecting patient injured by your ministrations. Until such time as the payment was forthcoming you would be required to perform community service in the quarries or on the roads. Do you understand your position?"

Phylus had not physically quailed, but was distinctly paler as he nodded.

"It may be that I have accidentally given the wrong impression to the court. I am aware that Druidical training is long and intensive..."

"Up to twenty years," put in the Magistrate, sharply.

"...I am not in any way a doctor. I have taken a Greek name because most medical men in the Roman world seem to be Greeks and it is good for business. I am here to sell medicine made by others. Assuming, of course, that this is permitted. I have sold nothing so far and I reported my arrival immediately."

"So," said the Magistrate. "That is as it should be. Now, what guarantee do you offer to this community? How does the potential patient know that what you sell is safe?"

"Guarantee?" said Phylus, looking slightly more comfortable. "Well, I have written recommendations from several noble clients..."

"Inadequate." The Magistrate, having cut off the salesman's prepared presentation, stirred the array of small glass bottles in front of him.

"What are these preparations supposed to do?"

"They contain a remedy for eye infections, sir. Many reputable Romans suffer, more so, I think, than do the Celts..."

"Hardly surprising. If they insist on bathing communally in hot water, what would they expect? They need to change their lifestyle. Do you personally guarantee the safety of this product? And its efficacy?"

The Magistrate looked around the court and beckoned a little girl from right at the back. He smiled and talked gently to her, looking into her weeping red eyes. Detaching a shred of wool from the edge of his robe, he gently wiped her eyes and sent her scampering back with a pat on the bottom.

Obeying the crooked finger of the Magistrate, Phylus stepped forward and stood still as the magistrate carefully wiped his eyes with the damp wool.

"Now, sir," said the magistrate, "the court will retain custody of your product and your slates. You may stay at the community guesthouse. Return here in three days for examination and to collect one bottle of your remedy. In seven days the court will examine you again and make a finding. The court is adjourned."

Caratacos' hall outside Kaleoua was new and smelled pleasantly of recently cut wood and fresh thatch. The meal of oysters, salmon baked in honey and cummin, and roast boar had been a success. The presence of Brigit and Caratacos' wife at the top of the table had slowed the drinking and inhibited the more unseemly of the scuffling among the younger male element. There were, of course, the inevitable Irish jokes and British jokes but nothing got to the weapons stage. At times, the poet's hoarse voice and the harpist's instrument could be quite clearly heard. The most interesting debate was over the respective merits of the Irish wolfhound as against the British mastiff. Politics were held over until later.

The evening was warm. No fire had been necessary in the hall and the ground was dry underfoot as Brigit and Caratacos walked at leisure beside the farmland. A British and an Irish guard walked some distance behind, carrying their superiors' swords. The Atrebatans were not all resigned to the High King's protection.

"In Ireland," said Brigit, "we have a tribe called the Brigantes. We hear that there is a tribe of the same name in Britain."

"In Britain, it is not so much a tribe as a federation of tribes north of the River Trent. It is outside the High King's domains and those of our immediate neighbours. It stretches across the waist of the island, from the Irish Sea, over the Pennies to the North Sea."

"Does its ruler acknowledge the authority of the High King?"

"Rulers. Queen Cartimandua, although very young, is very—political. Her husband, King Venutios, is not. They each have a substantial following among their tribes and lean different ways. They acknowledge the influence of the High King."

"But not, as yet, his authority?" Brigit gently insisted.

"Only because he does not choose to make an issue of it." Caratacos breathed deeply and stretched. "We have business south of that territory and it suits the

Cassi family very well to have a loose federation of small tribes as a buffer against the wild men from further north."

They walked around a weedy pond where a frog croaked. They both looked at the sky.

"The Cassi family always provides the High King? Are you going to be the next one?"

"No, but over the last hundred years it has usually been a family member who has held the post." Caratacos laughed. "And no again. My elder brother, Togo-dumnos, governs the traditional Cassi heartland for my father. He is the likely successor. There is another grown brother, Adminios, who has recently been appointed our father's administrator with the Cantii in the south east. I am likely to remain the administrator of the Atrebates, for the foreseeable future anyway."

"And your father?"

Caratacos chose to misunderstand Brigit's enquiry after High King Cunobeli-nos' health.

"My father moved his capital to the east coast, north of the Thames estuary. It was formerly the principal city and port of the Trinovantes tribe but they are now, of course, part of the High King's jurisdiction."

Brigit decided to be more direct.

"And the business of the Cassi family is the expansion of the High King's domains?"

Caratacos did not answer directly.

"There are forces in the world, which survive by continuously eating up their neighbours. Nothing, for them, is enough. They take what they want and divide the best between themselves. The rest they batter into the shape they require and feed it into their organs of state, into their military and into their religion. There is never anything left. They are all teeth and stomach."

Brigit did not say anything. Caratacos had not finished.

"We do not wish to become such a force, we do not wish to swallow nations whole and digest them and change them into us. But such a force is coming and, strong as we are, we are too small to fight it alone. Without changing ourselves, we must gather, we must prepare."

They stopped and looked intently into one another's faces.

"So," said Caratacos. "Tell me about Ireland."

Smiling, they turned towards the lamplight of the hall. The armed men saun-tered behind.

Like all big rivers, the Thames in winter can be dangerous. Tales had been told in Kaleoua of huge volumes of icy water coursing through defiles and sprawling in floods over low-lying country, of scoured farmland, buckled bridges and the remains of homes riding the rushing current. Now, in summer, it was different. Reminders of the violence of winter could only be seen in the debris lodged in the high branches of the island trees and in the tall trees felled into the stream by the river's winter bites out of its own banks. Warm, moist air filled the Thames Valley with the fragrance of heated greenery and the smell of the brown, clear water as it slid sleekly towards the sea. The sun smiled hotly down.

It should have been like a holiday, a pleasant restful cruise to eastern Britain and the High King's court for the mission from Ireland. It did not start that way. Before dawn, the British and the Irish soldiers inspected and launched the two warboats. They packed and loaded the baggage, tools and weapons, hurrying to make an early start. They chose and tested oars for strength and flexibility and loaded additional ones as well. They added bailers to try to keep their feet dry and pots of tar for waterproofing the seams of the leather sides. They allocated, argued over, gambled for and, eventually, agreed each man's place in each of the boats. They cooked and ate their breakfast and made the appropriate offering. Then they waited.

They waited a long time. The sun was high when Brigit Mong Ruadh arrived, laughing. With her were Caratacos, his wife, Niall and a party of relaxed and happy well-wishers. She had apparently been detained on matters of State and affected not to notice the atmosphere simmering around her escort. She airily told them that they would have to make room for one more passenger as she had given permission for Phylus, the Gallic medicine man, to travel with them. He could, in fact, have been fairly easily accommodated as the boats were big and two of the Irish soldiers had to be left behind anyway. One of them had been hurt taking part in a boar hunt with the locals and the other had lost his temper after he had been told one too many Irish jokes. Both were expected to make a full recovery. However, the escort were not in the mood to accept delays and changes of plan graciously.

Brigit lightly boarded her boat. Niall's expressionless stare at her crew quelled any murmuring but Phylus, momentarily distracted, found himself having to splash frenziedly through the shallows after the departing stern of his allocated boat. Caratacos, in the second boat, noted the lightening of the atmosphere among his men at the sight of the frantic Phylus. He waved goodbye to his wife and supporters as his boat slid into the stream.

As might have been imagined, in the absence of their superiors, the crewmembers had made sure that all the Irish soldiers were in one boat and all the British soldiers in the other. Caratacos quickly noticed that his oarsmens' rate of strike was excessively high and his boat was rapidly overhauling that of Brigit. The Irishmen rose to the challenge, clenched their teeth and leaned back into their strokes. Within a hundred paces, both boats had developed respectable bow waves and their crews were rowing as if the river demons were after them.

The Irish envoy and the son of the British High King looked at each through droplets of spray and decided to let competition work off any petty frustrations. The Irish had been chosen for the mission to Britain because of their skill at sea and, when a course was set, could drive a boat through heavy waves. The British were mainly rivermen, lacking the sheer power of the sea voyagers, but able instantly to compensate for sudden changes of course without losing balance or timing.

The gleaming Thames flowed heavily under the trailing branches of the thickets on its banks. Breaking through the shadowed undergrowth, green summer fields stretched to the water's edge. Reeds shivered as the current fingered their stems. Where farmland breached the barriers of undergrowth on the banks, slight but perceptible breezes ruffled the water's surface. Deep, slow eddies marked underwater obstructions as the great river wound its curving course. The sharp prows of wooded islands divided the stream and sandbanks glowed beneath the surface.

For a while, the Irish and British leaders resisted the temptation to become involved in the developing boat race, but only for a while. Frustration within the crews dissolved dramatically as their leaders allowed themselves to be drawn into optimising the effort being expended.

Brigit, as on a sea-raid, took over the steering and Niall settled into the rowing position nearest to her. Brigit's displaced helmsman took up a vacant place in the benches. Phylus, the Gallic purveyor of eye-lotion, was simply in the way. He was told to take his sore eyes to the bow and to shout a warning of any river obstruction. Sulking, he went, impelled on the way by the butts of several oars in motion.

Caratacos, with a full crew of British rivermen, reorganised his people differently. He did take the steering oar himself, but sent the helmsman, an experienced river pilot called Bivan, to the bow with a boat hook.

Helmsman Bivan watched the river surface with disciplined concentration while Caratacos steered to take maximum advantage from the following current in the centre of each deep-water channel.

Phylus' usefulness as a lookout for Brigit was limited, but his post in the bows kept him from impeding the huge force generated by the Irish oarsmen. Brigit laid off sections of her course as if in long reaches of the open sea to allow them the best opportunity to turn that force into speed. At sea, as the Irish well knew, there was always the danger of hitting a wave with an oar on the backswing. This tended to tilt the horizontal axis of the boat in the opposite direction just as all the oars were about to bite into the water. The sudden lowering of the freeboard on that side often induced oar-blades to enter the water before being square to its surface. It was not unknown that, as the blade of the oar dived towards the sea-bottom, the handle would lift the rower out of a fast moving boat. He would have 'caught a crab.'

On the river, there were no significant waves to think about. The factor which might now unbalance the crew with disastrous results, would be unexpected changes of course and these Brigit was determined to avoid. The powerful Irish crew quickly hauled their hide and wicker boat into a lead of four boat's lengths. Behind lay a straight wake, bracketed with circles of oar-disturbed water.

The smooth alterations in course, made continuously by the British boat, did not leave such an admirable wake. Caratacos could rely on the rivermen's ability to maintain their own balance and the timing of the oars' strokes. His adjustments in course took advantage of the slightest changes in river conditions and he gradually began to eat into the Irish lead whose straight-line course brought them close to the north bank.

Warm air flowed over the straining shoulders of the oarsmen, calloused hands had become mechanical claws, forearm tendons bar-taut. Reedbank, thicket and open field seemed to stream close past the left of the Irish boat. Dragonflies bobbed and weaved over the disturbed wake. Sleepy cattle, cooling their legs, took fright from the water's edge with much snorting and sucking. The boat swept through a still layer of sweet cattle-smell. The British, in centre stream, with a slightly slower strike rate, edged up. Three lengths.

Brigit, with a reedy shout, warned her people of a change of course. The river was bending to the right and she intended to go straight across the river to the south bank to shave the bend as closely as possible. Warned, the Irish crew on the right of the boat continued their strokes with full force. Those on the left simply maintained the rhythm with reduced power. All concentrated on maintaining their balance until Brigit settled on her intended course.

Caratacos did not increase the strike rate of his boat nor did he change course. Let the Irish do all the work. The Irish boat crossed his bows, its lead decreasing dramatically. The British crew had to concentrate as the boat ploughed through their opponents' disturbed water.

Caratacos glanced inboard at his crew's faces. They were alert, full of fight with no sign that the deep reserves of endurance were at all depleted. Glancing forward, Brigit's red head sprinkled with jewels of water and, beyond, strained Irish faces looked back at him. Several were definitely beginning to blow. Rowing with the much slower following-current at the river's edge, and compensating for occasional but major course changes, was drawing down on their fitness. Go on like this, thought Caratacos, and there will be no Irish soldiers awake on guard duty tonight and probably precious few British soldiers either. He warned his crew first and then shouted past their faces.

"Brigit! Brigit Mong Ruadh!"

Wisely, she did not look back, concentrating on the point in the curve round which she would steer her boat. Caratacos heard her shrill acknowledgement and inflated his lungs.

"Round this bend there is a long straight and then a bend to the left. Just after that, a bridge. We'll finish there. Agree?"

It was not Brigit but Niall who replied with a gasping roar, "Agreed!"

Even at two boats' lengths behind, Caratacos could see the Irish faces brighten and tauten with determination. His own crew was pulling steadily and several of them grinned. The stern of the Irish boat was now to Caratacos' right front. Bivan signaled from the bows that the Irish were cutting it fine, but should negotiate the bend.

"All right, rivermen," Caratacos pitched his voice high. "I want you abreast of the Irish after this bend. Then it's a nice straight, a bend to our advantage and then home. Build up the stroke, watch your timing and start putting some real muscle into it. Don't worry about the sea pirates. They think that fresh water is only for washing in, and that not too often! Pull!"

Despite the shorter route the Irish boat was taking into the bend, Niall was horrified to see that the British boat was edging up on them. He shook water out of his eyes and croaked a warning to Brigit. He was not an athletic man and was starting to feel the strain. She glanced to her left. The British strike rate had increased and, without doubt, their boat was gaining. She almost looked too long.

Her bows had drifted shorewards and the racing blades were tearing at the edges of the reeds. She did not panic. Gently, she nudged the steering oar and, slowly, the bow swung away. It would miss the edge of the reed bed. Slowly, the bows swung clear and then, even more slowly, clear water appeared for the oars.

Exultant, Brigit screamed, "Now! Pull! Pull your hearts out!"

Phylus, in the bow, did not understand the Irish but twisted around, shock at the woman's scream etched on his face. He turned back.

As he did so, a family of swans sailed majestically out of the reeds in front of the rushing bows of the Irish boat. Another huge bird, committed to landing with the family, tried, by frantic flapping of wings and paddling of webbed feet, to get airborne again. Too late. The intersection of the boat's course and the swan's intended flight path was squarely on Phylus' chest. He had a moment to comprehend the whistling rush of the great bird's wings, and the change in the quality of the light in front of him, before an immensely heavy, airborne body drove the breath from his chest and lifted him into the rowing benches.

Unexpectedly attacked by a maddened whirlwind of huge thrashing wings and a hissing, stabbing beak on a muscular darting neck, several quick-thinking Irish veterans simply flung themselves over the side. Two, tangled with the felled Gallic medicine man, cowered in confusion. Brigit tried to smother the bird's frantic struggles with a spare cloak. The boat, dragging several abandoned oars, slowed to a disorganised stop in the centre of the wakes of the disturbed—and angry—waterborne swans.

Niall, who had been trying to subdue the on-board bird with a bailer, assisted Brigit to confine its wild struggles and then, together, they heaved the convulsing bundle of cloak and bird over the side. The frantic swan immediately fought its way out of the cloak. The heavy splash stimulated the oarsmen in the water to make for the reeds at their best speed.

The Irish boat, bereft of most of its crew and their oars, and half-full of water, turned slowly in the current. Phylus, clutching his chest, sat up and looked dazedly around.

"I've never liked birds," he muttered darkly.

For some reason, everyone heard this comment. Starting with a giggle from Brigit, a curse and a guffaw from Niall, a waterlogged cough and a chortle from one of the swimmers, a wave of laughter developed and swept back and forth between the two boats. Even Bivan was reliably reported to have smiled.

The swans, wagging their tails in offended dignity, swam rapidly away with many outraged glares behind them.

The Irishmen loudly protested their willingness to camp on an island as had been the original intention, despite their wet clothes and bedding, and, in reality, with a good fire on a summer evening, it would not have been a great hardship. Brigit, however, would have none of it and Caratacos agreed that they would stop at the next large homestead.

No sooner had the decision been made than it was sealed by the appearance of a small boat, paddled by two tired fishermen who had spent the day hauling and mending their nets. They had had a good catch, including a huge predator pike and a large number of perch and chub. They also had news.

A party of important people was in the region, travelling up-river from the port of Lud Dun by road. The fishermen had reported the presence of some out-laws in the thickets and the party had turned aside to investigate. Its leader, Ceri, asked that Caratacos wait for him at a place the fishermen would show him.

Brigit looked enquiringly at Caratacos.

"Ceri is my dead brother's son," he explained. "He is normally based in Lud Dun but will be paying a visit to Kaleoua while I am away."

"I see. Learning the arts of administration and politics?"

"Energetic, inquisitive and with already a good military grounding. The out-laws won't detain him long, unless…"

"Unless?"

"He loves a bit of drama. Well, we'll see."

The fishermen proudly led the two warboats to the landing place of a substan-tial homestead set back from the river. The middle-aged farmer, his wife and brother, met the boats at the water's edge. A large, cheerful crowd of neighbours, servants, farm labourers and children gathered behind them. Dogs and geese were also represented.

The farmer made a short, lucid address of welcome and indicated his house. Brigit walked with the farmer's wife as she issued rapid instructions which sent servants and farm-hands scattering. The Irish warriors made much of the chil-dren. Caratacos listened quietly to the farmer's report while the farmer's brother gravely accepted the shining pike from the fishermen as their contribution to the evening meal.

At the main house, the crowd had politely thinned down to the family and the senior guests. The farmer settled everyone and produced a tall sealed container, pointed at the bottom and with two handles at the top. Everyone looked at it with interest.

"Your nephew left this in my care as his gift to you. He asks that you ensure it is empty by the time he returns."

They had all seen or heard of an amphora, the standard container in which Roman merchants exported better-quality wine or olive oil around the world. They were not yet, however, very common in Ireland. The farmer indicated some incised lettering on a tablet on the clay body of the container.

"See here. I can read some Greek but I suppose this is Latin. I cannot make it out at all."

"Not surprising, my friend," said Caratacos. "I think it is Latin, but in abbreviations I can't translate. We need Phylus in here. With your permission?"

Phylus appeared and his expression brightened as he saw the amphora.

"No, my Gallic pedlar, you are not invited for a drink. Just translate that label, please."

Phylus peered at the lettering, RVBR.VET.V.P.CII.

"It is the abbreviation for the Latin 'rubrum vetus vinum picatum CII.'"

"Right. Old, pitched red wine. Contents, one hundred and two, ah, one hundred and two what, Phylus?"

"I have no idea."

"So much for your accuracy in the mixing of potions. You are excused, go and find a strainer and something to remove a clay and cement stopper without harming the wine."

Caratacos stopped and apologised to the farmer's wife for issuing orders in her house. She smiled and shook her head.

"This is your house too." She raised her voice. "Phylus, while you are about it, bring cups."

The wine was not an unqualified success. Niall refused to try it. Caratacos and Brigit had both tasted wine from the Continent before and were not impressed. The brothers were not inclined to comment adversely on a gift to their guest. The lady of the house, however, had no such inhibitions and she firmly set aside her grey, glazed cup.

"It is probably made for far hotter climates than this, although, goodness knows, it has been warm enough here recently. It is more bitter than I had expected and I don't like the aftertaste."

"I think the merchants shipped it too soon," said Caratacos. "That taste is the burnt myrrh which is rubbed on the amphora after cleaning. After it is filled and closed it should stand in a smoky atmosphere for a period to mellow the flavour."

"Greedy merchants are everywhere," said Brigit, "but generous nephews are a rarity. Let's savour what we have until my comrades have seriously depleted your stocks of beer. Then they can have the rest of the wine and, whatever it tastes like, I can guarantee it will disappear like ice in summer."

There was the long sonorous bray of a carnyx downriver.

"Speaking of nephews," said Caratacos. "Ceri's signaler has lungs like a metal-worker's bellows."

For a second time that afternoon, a crowd of men, women, children, dogs and geese walked, bounded and waddled down to the river's edge. Just coming into sight was a small flotilla of boats filled with men and some women. A further, and quite unnecessary, blast on the carnyx boomed up-river from the leading boat. It did not immediately turn in to the river side but continued upstream for a while to allow the spectators a view of the flotilla's prizes. Most of the river craft were quite obviously locally requisitioned boats; but two, under tow, were dug-out canoes, camouflaged with low superstructures of fresh branches and reeds.

The lead boat at last turned into the landing place and a tall, thin youth with a grave face, suddenly flashed an immense grin, vaulted over the side and splashed ashore. Caratacos had to smile at the sight of Ceri's curly head, with its prominent ears and small, intelligent eyes, approaching him rapidly above the heads of the crowd.

"Welcome!" Ceri shouted, and, without waiting for a response, pointed at the disorderly disembarkation taking place below. "Have you ever seen the like? They were hidden in a reed bed with a dry camp on a tiny mound. Six outlaws—well, three now—and two canoes captured. We destroyed their camp as well. Only one of mine injured."

"Let me introduce you," said Caratacos evenly. "Brigit Mong Ruadh, war leader to the High King of All Ireland. My nephew Ceri, administrator designate of Kaleoua."

Ceri was not at all abashed but bowed slightly and murmured "Lady" before his grin widened and he added, "I am, in addition, today the conqueror of the smallest territory in the domains of the High King of Britain." He turned back to Caratacos: "What about the prisoners?"

"After dinner."

Later, the three prisoners were paraded, two men and a woman, dirty, unkempt and obviously hungry but not without a certain dignity. The woman replied in a clear voice with a local accent when they were called upon to give an account of themselves. They were, she said, not criminals but refugees. They had stolen, it was true, but only to feed and clothe themselves and they had not killed anyone.

"Where did you flee from?" demanded Caratacos. "And why?"

The woman was defiantly silent. One of the men volunteered a transparent lie which was demolished instantly in a conference among the audience. They all turned back to the woman.

"Well?" said Caratacos.

"Well," she said. "We fled from the oppressive rule of Buduoc who calls himself King of the northern Dobunni."

"He is the King of the northern Dobunni," said Caratacos.

"Others fled in different directions, even to the southern Dobunni, but were, all of them, without fail, handed back to King Buduoc. The tribes are anxious not to offend the High King. We tried to hide in the High King's own jurisdiction and, perhaps, make our way out of Britain altogether. It was too far and too difficult."

Brigit, as a visitor, had distanced herself slightly from the examination and had asked no questions. Niall, on the other hand, as the only Druid present, sat close to Caratacos. He now glanced at Caratacos for permission and asked:

"Who were you expecting to shelter you outside Britain? The Romans?"

"No," she said with some scorn. "The Romans have only one use for refugees—as puppets. We have contacts in the Celtic communities in occupied Gaul. They will shelter us until it is time to return."

"And that will be?" enquired Caratacos.

"When Buduoc is no longer in power."

Caratacos glanced casually around, absorbing the feeling of the assembly. The sympathy for the woman's spirit had been degraded by her defiance. She would be dangerous to Buduoc and, therefore, to the High King's interests. The men appeared to be nonentities. He turned back to the prisoners and they tensed.

"You claim to be refugees and not criminals. Yet you are outlaws, rejecting allegiance to your King. It may be that you have committed crimes against him. We will hear about that soon enough. You have certainly admitted that you have committed crimes in this jurisdiction. Normally, you would be required to pay a fine for your thefts or your families would be invited to ransom you. However, you do not have any property and it is unlikely that your families under King Buduoc would wish to support you. My options are to sentence you to community service to those you have wronged or to execute you."

"Execute us then!" demanded the woman.

Niall stirred but did not interrupt.

"As you know," said Caratacos to the woman, "we do not execute women. I was speaking to your companions. Which is it to be, men?"

"Community service," mumbled the one. The other nodded.

"Very well. Community service for one year under the supervision of the local authority here, which means that you have been accepted provisionally into the lowest rank of citizenship. Complete it satisfactorily and you will be citizens again. Run away and you will be executed."

He turned to the woman.

"Three years community service under the same conditions except execution. If you run away and are again caught, it will be assumed that you reject my offer of citizenship and reject Britain as a homeland. You will then be taken to the middle of the North Sea and left in a boat alone to go where you please. You will not be provided with sails, oars, food or water."

Caratacos steadily returned the woman's defiant glare. There was no sign of fear. A dangerous subject for a weak monarch.

After business, the company relaxed in music and stories. Ceri had not brought a professional bard with him, and Niall's specialist training had been in the law, but there were plenty of amateur entertainers.

Ceri told the story of the Battle of the Smallest Domain. With small eyes flashing in the firelight, gauging the effect of his words on his audience, he told it well. Even though it had only occurred that afternoon, he had already managed to develop a rudimentary rhyme. The assembly laughed and cheered the gallant soldiers and hissed the wicked outlaws.

Brigit told the story of the Repulse of the Swan, her clear white skin shining, her eyes shadowed by her glinting hair. Her high voice with its intriguing Irish accent carried well. The women looked at her thoughtfully while the men initially watched the reaction of their other Irish guests to her story. The first soldier laughed as he recognized his own hurried departure over the side of the boat and any restraint was broken completely by her description of the Druid's counter-attack on the Swan with the boat's bailer. Slapping knees and nudging one another, British and Irish enjoyed the tale.

Under courteous pressure, Niall told a story of a mighty Irish giant called Finn. It was, perhaps, overlong and the old Irish phraseology difficult, but the Druid's strong baritone voice was easy to listen to and he brought it to an end before the children started to fidget.

By popular acclaim, the farmer's wife sang a song, accompanied by her husband and her brother-in-law on stringed instruments. It was a love story, developing in parallel with the agricultural year. Sparked during Brigantia, the first day of spring when the ewes come into milk, and heated by Beltane, the first day of summer when the rays of Bel, the sun, warm the world, the love of two young people progressed to their marriage just after the harvest festival of Ludnasa. The singer's flushed and pretty face saddened. At the end of the pastoral year though, when the Otherworld becomes visible to humans at the festival of Samhain, the young man dies, bravely defending his home, but his pregnant wife survives and, coming full circle, his son is born at Brigantia next year.

Brigit watched their middle-aged hosts. The firelight smoothed away the sign of the years from the singer's skin and outlined the similar strong bone structures of the brothers' faces. Work-worn hands, one with a blackened nail, plucked music gently from the strings of the lyres.

Caratacos was not allowed to escape. He told an old, old story, eagerly received, a story of politics and intrigue and of heroic combat. Long ago, the story went, Caratacos' great, great, great, great grandfather had been High King just as his father was now. Irish listeners in the audience turned to the British who nodded in confirmation. That High King sought to extend his benevolent protection over the Trinovantes on the east coast where the capital of the Cassi now stands, Camulodunon. The Trinovantes then were proud, and mistakenly thought that they could do without the offered protection. Some Irish faces looked just a little skeptical. Most of the Trinovantes realised their mistake but some fled, seeking military support elsewhere without even fighting. Noises of disapproval from the audience. Worse still, some traitors, British traitors, went overseas to enlist help from the Romans against their own High King. There was a growl of disbelief and anger even though the story was well known. The Romans came twice with ships and alien professional soldiers under their most famous general and with their puppet candidate as King of the Trinovantes. Twice the High King called Britain to arms and twice British forces pushed the Romans back to the seashore where the Ocean smashed their ships. Faces around the fire were alight with triumph. Their general, Julius Caesar, told his people that he had defeated the British, that the High King had agreed to pay tribute to Rome and that Caesar had placed his candidate on the throne of the Trinovantes. There were cries of scorn for such lies. The British had twice defeated Julius Caesar and his little armoured men and they had never paid one coin in so-called tribute. But, said Caratacos and the circle grew closer, but the High King did allow Rome's candidate to sit for a time on the throne of the Trinovantes. The Romans called their candidate Mandubratius because, not being learned, they did not know the meaning of the name the Celts used for him. The assembly drew a collective breath. The Romans did not know what the name Mandubrad meant in Celtic. Some of the children gasped but their parents still held their breath. So, said Caratacos, for the rest of his short life, the puppet on the throne of the Trinovantes was solemnly called by the Romans by his Celtic title, King Black Traitor, and the Romans never knew! The pent-up breath was released in a roar of derision and quietened into companionable laughter.

It was towards midnight when the gathering broke up. Men and women, some carrying sleeping children, drifted away to bed.

And it was still dark the following morning when Caratacos was awakened. It was reported that Ceri's woman-prisoner had been killed by a guard while trying to steal a boat. The geese had given her away.

River traffic increased on the Thames as the party approached the port town of Lud Dun in the late afternoon. A wide smudge of smoke against the overcast sky indicated an urban population preparing for an evening meal on a cool afternoon. Ferries, barges and fishing boats were still in evidence but mostly heading downstream for the night. Children played on the banks and herded cattle at the water's edge. The Irish looked with interest at the large numbers of horses.

Caratacos looked back and called, "Last bridge coming up." He immediately regretted this as his guests' boat slowed to a stop. From the Irish muttering carrying across the water and the unorganised activity in their boat, he gathered that Brigit was insisting that her people make themselves presentable. The lady herself, standing in the stern of her boat with a comb in one hand, was trying to tug the creases out of her tunic. She wobbled dangerously when one of her oarsmen leaned over the side to wash his face. Her comments on his carelessness raised tired grins in the British boat.

At last she was ready. The Irish gathered their oars and picked up the stroke.

They passed under a substantial bridge without having to duck their heads and veered towards the north bank where wooden piers jutted out into the stream. Several coasters were tied up alongside and two ocean-going merchant ships were anchored in midstream, waiting for a berth. The party studiously ignored the interest shown by the crews of the Roman merchant ships and steered for a colourful crowd on the quay below the wooden walls of the town.

The official welcoming party stood on the floating landing stage below the quay. Several well-dressed men of various ages represented the town's management but the centre of the group was a plain faced middle-aged women in a simple blue dress, her grey hair hanging down her back. With a serene smile on her face, she held out chubby arms in greeting, her gaze fixed on Caratacos. He brought his boat neatly alongside and leaped out, leaving the tidying up to Bivan.

Brigit successfully brought her boat to the landing stage. Phylus nearly committed a blunder by trying to disembark first. His attempt to do so was abruptly halted by a large Irish fist gripping the back of his tunic, leaving him standing unsteadily with one leg in the boat and the other poised in mid-air. Ignoring the medicine seller's predicament, Brigit stepped demurely onto the landing stage.

The port officials had obviously given up any idea of a formal speech of welcome as Caratacos swept the older woman off her feet and hugged her. They smiled and murmured approval. The boats' crews grinned as they held on to the gently heaving landing stage.

"This," said Caratacos to Brigit, "is Grainne, my nurse, my mentor and my friend."

The two women appraised one another. Brigit saw an alert protector behind that bland and pleasant exterior and Grainne saw that she knew it. Grainne also saw, in Brigit, behind the red mane and white skin, a thirty-year-old woman with forty years of experience, probably once a wife, certainly at some time a mother and now a diplomat and a warrior.

"Welcome, dear," said Grainne. "I have a very nice house for you, back from the harbour and close to the law court."

"Thank you," said Brigit. "Caratacos' lady wife asked me to give you her love."

Grainne smiled. "This way, dear," she said.

After the evening meal and entertainment in the absent Ceri's hall, the gathering broke up early. Tired oarsmen knew that the next two or three days, down to the sea and then north-east up the coast, would be taxing. The morning's ebb-tide was early. Bivan appeared silently beside Caratacos.

"Phylus," he said.

"Yes?"

"Left immediately after eating."

"And?"

"Met with a seaman off one of the Roman ships."

"Anything else?"

"No."

"Watch him."

"Like a hawk."

In the quiet dawn mist, the crews bailed and loaded the boats as the river gurgled under the landing stage. A few dogs barked and a pet cockerel crowed. The smell of woodsmoke and of the river swirled gently. More well-wrapped figures appeared out of the gloom and stepped onto the landing stage. Quiet farewells were said. Grainne hugged Caratacos and patted Brigit's hand. The boats were pushed off and turned downstream towards the sea. With a final wave towards the landing stage and a glance at the darkened shapes of the anchored merchant ships, Caratacos settled beside Bivan at the steering oar.

Despite the early start, and the prospect of getting into the Irishmen's preferred element, progress was not as good as Caratacos had hoped. He never liked this stretch of the journey. The broad, powerful river expended its strength in sprawling meanders. The banks receded and the deep-water channels wound through wide stinking mud flats with smaller channels draining between tiny islands of tussock grass and reeds towards the sea. The bird cries all seemed distant and mournful, the sky vast and featureless.

In the early afternoon, with the tide turned against them, they were intercepted by a guard boat manned by Cantii from their homeland south of the estuary. After exchanging greetings and news, the Cantii invited them to camp with them. Their camp was well established on good ground at the mouth of the Medu River which flowed into the estuary from the south, cutting through the mud to join the waters of the Thames. The river guards were simple people, supplementing their official duties with fishing and the collecting of shellfish. They knew of their tribal capital in the east and they told proudly of the four tribal divisions of the Cantii, two on either side of the Medu river. They also knew of the High King and his court north east of the estuary.

When Caratacos asked them about the High King's representative in the area, they said they had heard that there was one, but they did not know him. The name Adminios did not mean anything to them. Their duties, they reported, were to prevent armed intruders travelling up-river, either on the Thames or the Medu. As Cantii, there was no doubt as to which of those aspects was the more important.

They shyly demonstrated their ability to remember lists of shipping, by day and tide, over considerable periods of time. Niall, the Druid, listened with some respect. Their superiors were apparently based upstream at a crossing place on the Medu where there was a small town. Despite the relatively short distance, the crews were not enthusiastic about more rowing that day so the party did not explore the Medu. Instead, they slept in the thatched camp overlooking the wide estuary.

The following day was much better. The rested crews gained the open sea by mid-morning. The Irish, in particular, were reinvigorated by the keen salt breeze and by their opportunity to show off their oarsmanship in the long waves. The British rivermen were hard pressed to keep up as the party coasted north-eastwards towards the High King's court.

When Brigit looked into the High King's eyes she knew the man was dying. They were fairly private. Niall was with her, of course. The High King's own Druid and counsellor, Louernios, known to everyone as Fox, was, naturally, also present. In the background, Caratacos stood with his elder brother, Togodumnus. Otherwise they were alone.

There was silence in the round, thatched room other than for the rain outside and the crackle and pop of a small bright fire.

Cunobelinos had been High King of Britain since his early manhood. Through persuasion, guile and a carefully regulated application of naked force, he had sustained and extended his grip on the office. Assassinations and inexplicable sudden deaths had occurred from time to time amongst his opponents but no blood had every been seen on his hands. Any opponent of the High King, military or political, had walked the threshold of the Otherworld.

Now, his gaunt old figure sat in Camulodunon, the capital and port he had wrested from the Trinovantes. His eldest son maintained his family's presence in his old capital to the west. Further west still, Caratacos governed the Atrebates from Kaleoua and, on the banks of the river Severn, King Buduoc was the High King's puppet. To the south east, the senior men of the Cantii grudgingly accepted his other son, Adminios, as the High King's representative. In peace, his diplomacy and, in general, his leadership, was accepted throughout southern Britain. In war, his right to exercise it was undisputed.

Throughout his long years of expansion and consolidation, High King Cunobelinos had maintained two strategic policies intact. He had never interfered seriously in the affairs of the tribal confederation of Brigantes which shielded his domain from the north. He had also been careful never to provoke the Romans in occupied Gaul. It is true that he had never paid them the tribute they claimed on the basis of Julius Caesar's lies; his power base would never have permitted that. He had, however, allowed access to Roman traders and, when Roman sailors had been shipwrecked on British shores, he had ensured that they had been well-treated, nursed back to health and returned home with appropriate gifts.

The policies had each paid off. During his decades in office, no incursion came through the Brigates' barrier in the north and, in the south, the only Roman invasion to come any where near embarking was the disgraceful performance by the Roman forces under their pitiful Emperor, Gaius Caligula. Under a leader like that, no wonder the Roman soldiers refused to face the dangers of the Ocean backed up by the weapons of the waiting British armies. No, the only attacks impacting on southern Britain consisted of the Irish compulsion to small-scale coastal raiding, which, like breathing, went on all the time.

High King Cunobelinos' breathing was laboured. The strong bones of his face were covered by fragile yellowish skin and his large white moustache was thin. His warrior's hands, shorn of one little finger and laced with blue veins, trembled on his knees. Under his shaggy brows, dull, hooded eyes looked out.

"I am dying," said the High King in a soft, hoarse voice. No one protested. "So, I have little time to demonstrate my vaunted diplomacy." The white moustache moved in a small smile. "I am grateful to my brother, High King Conaire Mor, for allowing you to be here. Kindly take him my appreciation and this small gift."

The Fox, well-named for his stiff, ginger hair alone, came from behind the High King and presented, to Niall, a flat box filled with mistletoe leaves on top of which rested a thick torc made of twisted gold wires. The gold, with its silver and enameled terminals, gleamed richly in the firelight. Niall, his eyes widened with fright, showed the gift slowly to Brigit. She hid her dismay and thanked Cunobelinos on behalf of her brother, the High King of Ireland.

She was tempted, for a moment only, to represent the gift she had as being her personal present to Cunobelinos. She immediately realised that this would be completely transparent and even more inappropriate than the exchange of two nearly identical gifts between High Kings. She signaled to Niall who stepped forward and presented the gift of the High King of Ireland, a torc fashioned of twisted gold and silver wires with large gold terminals set with coral. Fox gravely accepted the gift from an ashen-faced Niall and showed it to the High King.

Cunobelinos inspected the gift carefully in a moment of silence. Only Brigit could see his moustache twitch. He then reached up and began to struggle with the torc he was wearing. His sons helped him remove it and to replace it with the splendid gift from Ireland. The torc was closed around the old man's neck and settled on his collarbone. The silver actually showed better against his yellow skin than did the gold. He asked Brigit to convey his thanks.

"Many representatives of the peoples of Britain grace my capital at this moment," said the High King in his soft, hoarse voice. "Many of them are royalty, such as Queen Cartimandua, and her husband, of the federation of the Brigantes. None of them, though, is more welcome than Brigit Mong Ruadh of Ireland."

Brigit, a touch of colour at her cheeks, thanked the old politician and made a suitable reply.

"They are here," he went on, "and you are here, to think about the next High King—of Britain, of course. I shall soon enter the Otherworld to await my return to this world. In these stable times, some may think it premature to talk about a successor. I do not. I am part of that stability and my imminent departure will change many things. Succession by the election of my eldest son is by no means a foregone conclusion."

Togodumnos stirred and Brigit, at last, felt she could look at him properly. She saw a broad-shouldered, youngish man, taller than Caratacos, running to a little fat, with fair, ruddy skin. His moustache was so fair as to be almost white, in contrast to thin, reddish hair. Deep in his eyes, there was an uncomfortable red glow. Beside him, Caratacos looked fairly ordinary.

The High King watched her inspection and reaction carefully.

"Yes," he said hoarsely. "He does have that effect on women. King Prasutagos of the Iceni, for example, is an ally, but his new wife, Boudicca, is most definitely not. What did you do to Boudicca, anyway?"

Togodumnos did not respond and the High King, visibly tiring, did not pursue it.

The rain still pattered on the thatch and the fire burned lower. Fox did not put any firewood onto it. Brigit, taking the hint, prepared to excuse herself.

"I must give myself the pleasure of greeting all my valued guests," said Cunobelinos, "and there will be an entertainment when it becomes light, so we might not have this opportunity again. Please convey to my brother, the High King of Ireland, my appreciation of his efforts to curb the raiding of my coasts by certain disobedient subjects of his." He almost paused. "Particularly of those lands under my direct control."

Brigit heard the words and understood the meaning. Irish raiding should be limited to the coasts of British monarchs who did not acknowledge the British High King's authority. That, in turn, would emphasise the need to accept the High King's appointee in that area, King Buduoc. Provided Conaire Mor's raiding took place only in the far west of Britain, and he did not land a proper Irish army, the raiding worked to Cunebelinos' political advantage.

The High King smiled again. "Caratacos is in charge of my small gift to you. He will look after it until you decide you have to leave us."

Brigit and Niall took their leave and breathed deeply of the cold, damp air outside. Fox accompanied them for a few steps and paused at the sound of raised voices behind them. He shook his head.

"No," said Fox. "It is not about you. A family matter, only." He bowed slightly and, silently, went back inside.

"Well," said Brigit lightly as they walked towards the warmth of their quarters. "We know what the High King of Britain wants of Ireland. Did we tell him what the High King of Ireland wants of Britain?"

"Not in so many words," said Niall the Druid.

Celtic days start and end at sunset, and so the sun was high above the smoky horizon of Camulodunon, on the same day, when Brigit found her seat overlooking the vast parade ground outside the capital.

Royalty was present in the chubby, dimpled form of the young Cartimandua, Queen of the Brigantes, and in the tall, somehow melancholy appearance of King Prasutagos of the Iceni, quite outshone by his much younger and statuesque wife, Boudicca. Although not officially royalty herself, Brigit had been placed close by because of whom she represented and she watched, with interest, Cartimandua's animated talk accompanied by many gestures with her small white hands. Prasutagos listened with a lop-sided smile. Boudicca sat still and upright with the faintest of curls to her lip.

The High King had had to be almost smuggled to his seat of honour by his family and household. Most of the huge, colourful crowd, assembled round three sides of the ground, was not aware that the most powerful man in Britain was now unable to dismount unaided from his horse. By the time the crowd became aware that the High King was present, he was already seated between Queen Cartimandua and King Prasutagos. His son, Togodumnos, stepped up and placed himself directly behind the High King's chair. A sigh, almost of contentment, swept quietly through the throng. The High King's nomination of his successor was noted. Perhaps in order to emphasise the unspoken choice, neither Caratacos nor Adminios were in view. There was to be a military display, but the main business of the gathering had already been done.

Fox stepped forward with raised hands to quiet an almost silent crowd. Only a baby's wail and a dog barking on the fringes of the crowd broke the silence. There was a yelp and even the dog was quiet. The Druid turned and faced the High King. Cunobelinos did not intend to try to pitch his old man's voice against the vastness of the ground and sky. Without rising, he made a gesture for the entertainment to commence.

There was a distant, harsh shout and, with the accelerating sound of galloping hooves, a chariot, with its two-horse team at full stretch, burst onto the earthen parade ground from the open side. Trailing puffs of condensation from the horses' flaring nostrils, the little vehicle, with its two human occupants, crossed the ground diagonally at top speed towards the corner on the High King's right. In that corner, attention on the rapidly approaching chariot was fixed. There were shouts of alarm. Some members of the crowd stood up, others surged backwards while still seated. It was apparent to everyone that the chariot, out of control, was going to smash into the crowd at that corner.

The chariot-driver, teeth gritted and neck tendons standing out, suddenly hauled on his right hand reins, bracing himself as best he could on the small, rocking platform. The warrior with him leaned out of the vehicle as far as he could over the spinning left wheel. The horses, eyes staring and ears back, swerved to the right without breaking pace. Only the weight of the passenger hanging over the side prevented the chariot from overturning. As it was, it took the turn on one wheel with the entire vehicle just at the point of balance.

It settled with a crash onto both wheels and, showering the spectators with dust and stones, swept down in front of the High King's chair, the warrior saluting with raised javelins as it galloped past. At the next corner, the unit, without slowing, executed another right-hand turn and set off diagonally across the ground. Another galloping team and bouncing chariot were already on the ground, heading in the opposite direction, followed by another, and another. Soon the entire ground seemed filled with hurtling vehicles and galloping teams, criss-crossing the surface with their crews grimly hanging on and the crowd, all now standing, surging backwards and forwards at each new menace and laughing shakily at each reprieve. They had become as unsettled as the enemy's ranks would be at the start of battle.

Out of the crowd streaked a dog. Frenziedly barking, it threw itself in front of galloping hooves and behind spinning wheels. Excitedly fixated on the twinkling spokes of one wheel, it threw itself bodily at the spinning disc. The chariot was going too fast for the dog and it missed. It landed right in front of another galloping team and the horses shied in different directions. Both went down.

The drawbar snapped like a stick and the chariot, wheels turning, somersaulted over the fallen horses, emptying out the crew as it went. The driver, injured and dazed in the dirt, made a loop of the reins tied to his wrist and sliced through them with his knife. Free, he staggered to his feet and another chariot collided with him, killing him instantly. The warrior lay inert beside the shattered chariot. No one saw what became of the dog.

There were a several partial collisions and many near-misses, involving both the wreckage and the casualties, but the drivers and crew-members were experienced men, the High King's best. Once they had the position of the wreck established in their minds, they avoided further collisions and continued the fast-moving demonstration without pause.

The charioteers swung their vehicles into line facing away from the High King and the warriors leapt from the open rears of the vehicles, hurled javelins, drew their long swords and launched a realistic attack on foot. Their duty complete, they ran back to their waiting vehicles, picking up the javelins on the way, and jumped onto the platforms. The chariots, still in line abreast, rolled gently off the ground to sustained rounds of applause.

Brigit was on her feet, cheering with the rest. She paid little attention to the efficient removal of bodies and wreckage but chattered excitedly to her neighbours about the display. She had just caught her breath, and was shading her eyes to look at the cavalry on their big, glossy horses that she could see assembling at the open end of the ground, when Fox was suddenly beside her. There was, it seemed, a minor problem. The young soldier injured in the chariot wreck needed urgent medical attention. The Camulodunon medical team was competent but would be grateful if Niall could be allowed to attend.

Brigit thought swiftly. All Druids acquired some medical expertise during their twenty long years of training but Niall had specialised in the law, as Fox well knew.

"This soldier," she said, "he is of high rank?"

"Segonax has only just reached manhood. Sixteen years of age. His father sent him to the High King to train in chariot warfare."

"Ah. And his father is…?"

Fox half-smiled. "One of the four chiefs of the Cantii."

Brigit considered the political implications. The High King's son Adminios was not popular among the Cantii. This must impact on the High King's prestige, huge though it was. The accidental death of a young soldier in military training would not reflect adversely on Cunobelinos. But, if the injured man were to die of medical neglect or medical incompetence, that would be a different matter. Fox was asking for a trained, impartial witness to be present.

She nodded to the Irish Druid who quickly followed Fox away from the crowd-noise and north to a stand of ancient, gnarled oak trees. No one guarded the way into the grove. No one needed to. This was Druid territory.

Inside the grove, there was a clearing. There they said a prayer before entering the roofless enclosure where the surgeon waited with the patient. Niall was introduced and the surgeon was invited to present the case. He rubbed his clean hands.

"Segonax is a healthy, well-developed young man for his age, sixteen years. He has reportedly been in a chariot accident and his injuries are consistent with that."

He turned to the pale, semi-naked figure lying in the sunlight.

"There are contusions here and here, and this laceration was, in all probability, caused by an iron tyre. However, the only life-threatening injury is to the patient's head, the seat of the spirit."

The Druids moved closer. Dark brown hair had been shaved away from the right side of the head. There was not much blood.

"Segonax is sinking into unconsciousness. His reactions have been getting progressively slower and weaker, even over the short time he has been here." The surgeon placed his hands gently over the patient's open eyes.

"You will have to look closely. Pupil reaction is not easy to see in brown eyes. Some foreign ancestry here I shouldn't wonder."

He quickly removed his hands.

"No reaction in the right eye," observed Niall.

"You can see the point of impact." The surgeon, nevertheless, pointed to a shallow depression in the blue/white skin above the right ear. "I don't know what struck him or what he fell onto but that is not material. What is apparent is that the skull is fractured and is pressing on his spirit, progressively affecting all his functions. I believe I must operate."

Fox looked at Niall. Without looking at him, Niall nodded.

"I concur," said Fox.

They moved to a small table where the medical assistants stood, waiting. The bronze instruments were clean. Without touching them, Niall examined the needle and gut thread, the scalpel, forceps, burring drill and bone elevator. Again, he nodded.

"Proceed," said Fox.

One of the medical assistants turned the patient's head to the left, ensured that the airway was clear, and took the head in a gentle but firm grip. The surgeon took up a scalpel and cut a flap in the skin next to the depressed area of the skull. He discarded the scalpel and pinned the flap open and out of the way with a quick stitch. He nodded with satisfaction at the sight of the whole bone below. His assistants made sure the patient's head and limbs were immobilised. There was only the feeblest resistance.

The surgeon placed the wide, flat head of the drill against the exposed bone of the patient's skull. Holding it in place with his left hand, he began to turn with his right, progressively applying more pressure as the edges of the drill bit began to chew into the bone and there was less chance of slippage. He stopped frequently to clear away the fragments created by the drill's burring action and to wash out the miniature well he was creating in the bone. He carefully inspected the depth at these intervals and reduced the pressure as he proceeded. Finally with a little jerk, he pulled back the drill as it broke through. Blood, trapped within the skull, escaped through the hole.

"Allow it to bleed," said the surgeon sharply as one of the assistants picked up a cloth. He washed and carefully dried his hands so that they would not slip.

The bleeding soon stopped and the Druids examined the healthy organ below. The hole was clean with no loose fragments. They checked on their patient's condition and the assistants adjusted their grips. The surgeon selected the bone elevator, a narrow, flat spatula with a handle set at an angle.

Delicately, he inserted the tip of the elevator into the hole and edged it under the bone towards the depression. The slight rasping sound set Fox's teeth on edge. The surgeon put his left hand over the depressed area of the skull and, with his right on the handle, applied upward pressure against the broken bone with the end of the elevator. Nothing happened. He relaxed and adjusted the angle of the elevator. Again he applied pressure and there was a hint of movement under his left hand. With tiny adjustments of angle and pressure, the surgeon worked on. Eventually, without removing the elevator, he silently invited inspection. Both the other Druids nodded.

The elevator was carefully extracted. The hole received a final inspection and the flap of skin sewn back into place.

"Don't make the stitches too tight," admonished the surgeon, washing his hands again. "I want any blood outside, not trapped."

The medical assistants were good. The wound was covered with a light dressing. A thick ring bandage was laid on top so that no pressure was applied directly to the protected area and the whole was fastened into place. The patient's head and limbs were restrained with bandages and blankets covered him.

"Well," said the surgeon, cheerily. "He's alive. His pulse and colour are not bad and his breathing has improved. Above all, he is young and healthy. I think he has a good chance. What do you think?"

"Well done," said Niall, sincerely.

"Excellent procedure," said Fox.

The two walked out of the grove together. The military display was obviously over and had been a great success. Great crowds of men, women and children streamed away from the parade ground, laughing and teasing one another over the frights they had had from friendly military activity. Lines of cavalrymen walked their steaming horses towards the farms surrounding the city. The chariots had already gone.

Part of the crowd had paused and gathered in a knot around a prone horse and a woman's voice was raised in extreme anger. The Druids pushed their way through. The horse was obviously in deep trouble. So was the young cavalryman.

A burly woman, with her hair hanging around her exasperated face, was giving the white-faced trooper the tongue-lashing of his life. Fox, ginger hair bristling, ignored them to attend to the important thing, the stricken horse.

The mare had raised her head and now made a feeble attempt to get her legs under her. White patches of old sweat marked the short coat where the saddle and girth had been and a swathe of it on either side of the neck had developed from the rubbing of the reins. Pink-stained drools hung from the horse's mouth under fluttering nostrils. Her flanks heaved. She struggled to reach the water in a wide, earthernware pot in front of her. Fox laid a hand on her neck and spoke soothingly. The skin was sweaty and cold.

"You deliver the High King's foals, you raise them and you train them," the woman shouted at the appreciative audience. "And what happens?" she appealed to the sky. "By the great goddess Epona, you have to hand the darlings over to ham-fisted cretins who don't know a horse from a hamlet! Call yourself a horse-man!" She turned on the trooper and gave him a violent shove. He fell over his own military saddle into the unsympathetic crowd. Niall also ignored the side-show and stooped beside Fox.

"It's exhaustion," murmured Fox, "and we may be able to mend that, but I don't like the look of this bloody froth."

They stripped off the bridle, gently disengaging the steel bit from the large, quivering lips. Niall tossed the tack towards the saddle and was mildly surprised to see that the cavalryman had regained his feet and had not retreated. The woman hovered over the Druid's shoulder, tears running down her fat cheeks.

It needed two pairs of hands to hold the great head steady and to examine the mouth equipped with big yellow teeth. The mare's eyes rolled and her ears tended to lay back but Fox's steady, soothing voice seemed to reassure her.

"There. Lacerations to the inside of the cheeks, near the first grinders."

"Bit injuries," said Niall with relief. "Ridden into the ground."

Then, as anger flooded him, he rose and faced the trooper who recoiled from his expression as if from a raised fist.

"Niall," said Fox gently. "First, the horse."

Niall blew out a long breath. "Yes."

Fox looked at the woman.

"Have you got any beer?" he said.

The smallest of smiles crossed the tearful face before him.

"You ask me, a horse farmer, if I have any beer?" she joked weakly.

"A large pot of beer, warm if you can arrange it, for the mare. Also, something to keep her warm until she can stand. You!" The cavalryman jumped as if Fox's finger was a dagger pointed at him. "You are going to stay here, with your horse, until she is better. However long that takes. The beer will provide for her thirst, settle her stomach and give her a little sustenance. Keep her warm and she may sleep. You may not."

"When she has recovered a little," Niall added, "feed her small meals often. And this is the important part." The Druid smiled grimly. "Since you have damaged her mouth it will be you who washes the lacerations inside her cheeks after every meal until they have healed. I notice that she is looking at you very carefully. Count your fingers after each washing. We will be checking on you and on her progress."

The small crowd rumbled in satisfaction and started to disperse.

As the Druids walked away, Niall broke the short silence.

"She said she is a horse-farmer."

"Yes. Most of our horses, probably like yours, are the small, pony type. Suitable for pulling loads, but they can't carry much weight. We need bigger horses for cavalry mounts. The High King, and his predecessors, imported foreign stock decades ago, before the Romans embargoed their export. We rear and train them separately on farms around here. They are never used for farm work, of course. Too valuable. We still use oxen for that."

They were approaching the High King's hall. Caratacos was standing alone, apparently waiting for them.

"Tell me, Niall," said Fox, looking intently at the solitary figure. "Do you believe that troubles generally come in threes?"

"As surely as there are three leaves on a shamrock."

Fox did not know what a shamrock was but he had no doubt from Caratacos's flushed appearance and blazing eyes that they were about to learn something to everyone's disadvantage.

"Our brother Adminios," said Caratacos, without a greeting, "has gone." He stared bleakly into their startled faces. "We believe he has defected."

✳   ✳   ✳   ✳

Caratacos met with Togodumnos alone. Not even Fox was present. Bel, the sun, would be well above the horizon but was hidden behind thick, dark clouds. The brothers, wrapped in cloaks, walked slowly through the dripping oak trees, old acorns, missed by foraging pigs, crunching under their feet.

"How did he get away?" Togodumnos' intense anger had burned itself out.

"A collection of half-wits, led by me." Caratacos was still seething. "I told someone to watch that Phylus, which he duly did. He was closely watching while he made a fortune with his medicine sales to the gullible. In the meantime, the regular guards at the south gate persuaded more of the gullible to stand guard for them while they watched the chariots."

"He's gone to Rome, you know."

"Not out of Lud Dun. Grainne had the port authority order the Roman ships out of the port as a precaution. Ceri will make sure he does not get away to the west. In any case, I agree with you. It is Rome, so he is heading for the south coast. There are parties after him on fast horses but, if he keeps moving, he will be there before them, and before we can warn the fishermen to guard their boats."

"Agreed."

Togodumnos stopped and pulled his cloak tighter around his slightly overweight figure.

"Well, good riddance. May the Ocean swallow him for the traitor he is."

"He was always able to convince himself that he was hard done by. In the hands of the Romans, he can be dangerous."

"Hah! I'd like to see him trying to lead a Roman army ashore. Every Celt in Europe would be after his blood and, in any case, the Roman army is frightened of the sea. With all that armour, they'd go to the bottom like stones."

"Roman ships travel all over the world and their troops don't have to wear armour. Ours don't. Don't forget that Caesar made it over the Ocean twice. With armoured soldiers."

"What do they call those little armoured men, again? Snails?"

They laughed and started walking again.

"Caesar was their greatest commander ever," said Togodumnos. "Even he could not stay here long. Not enough food and the good Ocean wrecked his ships. Look who they've got to lead them now. An Emperor who thinks he and his horse are gods. His horse is probably saner than he is. No, his army refused to embark once, he won't try again."

"Our brother and he will make a fine pair. Long may the Emperor reign."

As they came out from under the trees it began to rain in earnest.

"End of the year," said Caratacos, walking steadily. "Soon be the first day of winter."

"Yes, Samhain. I think our father's spirit will leave us then."

"Probably. And you will be High King."

Togodumnos, thin hair plastered to his scalp, looked closely at his brother. "I'm not elected yet. How do you feel about it?"

"Rather you than me. You control our heartland from here and deal with political relations with the Romans and the Brigantes. After—Samhain, I'll rejoin my family in Kaleoua, keep an eye on King Buduoc and try and subvert the Durotriges. Extend our influence westwards."

"Good. Send Ceri back when you get to Kaleoua. We can trust Grainne in Lud Dun but she is getting on and needs to train a successor."

"You'll keep Fox?"

"Of course. Find your own Druid. Speaking of westwards influence, how are diplomatic relations with Brigit Mong Ruadh?"

"Purely diplomatic. You know my wife. Brigit's saying goodbye to father now."

*   *   *   *

Crowded under the dripping eaves of the buildings around the High King's hall, the Irish troopers chattered excitedly but quietly, out of deference for the sick old man inside. They were pleased to be going home and to be making the journey by road as far as the Severn estuary. Rowing upstream along the Thames route did not have much appeal, they had already seen the country from that perspective. Saddled horses with bulging saddlebags huddled ready under the eaves. The Irish would pick up their two recovered comrades at Kaleoua.

As the rain eased, Brigit walked briskly into the yard with Niall at her heels. The Irish immediately began to bustle, swinging themselves into the saddle. She kissed Togodumnos while Niall and Fox bowed slightly to one another. A youth with an enormous bandage bulging to the right side of his head, shyly led out Caratacos' saddled horse. Segonax was not allowed to ride yet, but it would not be long.

Mounted, Caratacos saw, with approval, Brigit ignore helping hands and swing nimbly into the saddle. He turned his horse and the cavalcade, with an occasional splash and skitter, walked slowly through the misty streets to the open country. Out of the city, they allowed the fresh horses a short canter and then halted briefly to tighten girths.

"This is not the direct route to Kaleoua", said Niall.

"No," said Caratacos. "I have instructions from the High King."

They turned into the farmland, the troopers looking in wonder and some avarice at the slowly-moving herds of big horses grazing under guard. Niall recognised the horse-farmer as she stood waiting for them outside a large, thatched barn. He had last seen her publicly berating the reckless cavalryman over his abused horse. Brigit, her eyes sparkling, slid off her horse and followed the farmer into the barn.

Her shout from inside brought two of the Irish off their horses, but it was delight, not alarm. They led out three big mares, all in foal and meticulously groomed.

"A present," said Caratacos, "to the envoy of the High King of Ireland from the High King of Britain." There were murmurs of approval and admiration. After a while, the mares were led from the yard and started on the road to Kale-oua. He gave his guests a moment, then dug in his saddle bag.

"And a present to the brave escort of the envoy, from my father." He handed a small purse of gold coins to each of the grinning troopers.

He turned to Niall and opened the palm of his hand in front of him. A small sickle made of gold lay in his hand.

"Fox tells me that this is suitable," said Caratacos and Niall took it reverently from his hand.

"My prayers at the gathering of the mistletoe will start with those for the High King of Britain and his family," said the Druid.

Brigit, her eyes brimming, put her hands on Caratacos' shoulders and kissed him. She smelled of mown grass and her lips were salty. He put his arm round her waist and looked up, surrounded by wide Irish smiles.

"Lastly, my personal gift to you all. Leave these horses and saddles with King Buduoc. He will keep them to carry you back here on your next visit. Make it soon."

She did not resist as Caratacos lifted her into the saddle and, for a moment, Brigit rested her hand on his. Then she gathered up the reins, looked around her people and led them clattering out of the yard. There was a distant shout of "god save Ireland" as they broke into a gallop, and then they were gone.

That Samhain, the first day of winter, Cunobelinos, 'the hound of Bel', High King of Britain, died in his sleep. His eldest son, Togodumnos, was elected without opposition as his successor. The day of his inauguration dawned well. The ceremony took place in the open so that the participants could feel at one with the damp earth, the breeze from the sea, the few spots of rain and the rays of the sun lancing through the clouds. They were dressed in the bright, thick wool of winter. Gold and silver shone at their throats and wrists.

Royalty was represented by King Buduoc. The four chieftains of the Cantii were there, one of them a woman. Chieftains of the Trinovantes, the Atrebates and the Catuvellauni were also present, several of them women. Caratacos and Ceri stood side by side in the small crowd of rulers. Togodumnos, with his thin hair and light moustache ruffling in the breeze, stood impassively facing them, only Fox and Segonax standing behind him. In their hands lay the old ceremonial horned helmet of wisdom and the High King's sword.

With their heads back and their eyes half-closed, hair colour varied from light ginger to chestnut, the leaders intoned the oath of allegiance. The deep voices of the men, leavened by the clearer tones of the women, committed their persons to the bargain while involving the natural elements in the oath.

"We will keep faith unless the sky falls and crushes us, or the earth opens and swallows us, or the sea rises and overwhelms us."

The old words were concluded and Togodumnos, corpulent and imposing, touched first the helmet and then the sword. He was the High King of Britain.

The fearful two-day festival of Samhain was long past and the old High King long buried. The cold hand of mid-winter lay on Britain.

High King Togodumnos rode to visit the halls of his many chieftains in the lands of the Cantii, the Atrebates, the northern Dobunni, the Catuvelauni and the Trinovantes. He was always welcomed, sometimes cautiously, sometimes enthusiastically. He was escorted only by Fox and a few soldiers for Britain was at peace. Even the raiders in the far west did not relish crossing the Irish Sea in winter.

The Silurians on the west bank of the Severn estuary, and their neighbours, mined their iron, lead, silver and gold and looked to their weapons because in the spring, after the coming into milk of the ewes, the Irish would be back.

To the north, the Brigantes huddled in their smoky huts and gossiped about the doings of their young Queen, Cartimandua, and her interest in young charioteers. The Gallic medicine-man with the Greek name, Phylus, visited her court and treated many of her subjects.

The Iceni rejoiced. Their King's strong young wife, Boudicca, had an easy delivery of their first child and heir, a girl.

Caratacos and Cerri fished the slow, cold waters of the Thames from its ice-fringed banks. White drifts of snow decorated the frozen black earth and the translucent fangs of icicles hung from the trees' stiff branches. A small, bright fire crackled on top of the bank where one of Caratacos' children roasted chestnuts for her elders and heated rocks for them to put their feet on. Their voices echoed in the frozen woods.

"I don't believe there are any fish at all in this river."

"If there are," said Cerri, small eyes shining in the gloom of the river bank, "and I say *if* there are, they are frozen solid and sunk to the bottom."

"I think you've let the poachers get out of hand while I've been away. They've taken every fish in the river."

"After I arrested all your poachers, who were already totally out of hand, I instructed your magistrates to sentence offenders to beat the river. They've chased all your fish downstream. I'll have good fishing in Lud Dun when I get back."

There was silence, broken only by the hiss and plink of the lines in water.

There was a young girl's cry from the top of the bank and the muffled thump of horse's hooves. Both fishermen abruptly turned. Then a familiar voice reverberated through the trees.

"It's all right! It's only me!" Then in a quieter voice: "Hello, darling. Come and give your uncle a kiss. Here, I'll take those for you."

Togodumnos appeared at the top of the bank and, leaning backwards, started to stride downhill, clutching something in both hands. Halfway down, his heel did not dig in, he stumbled and broke into an uncontrolled trot. Cerri and Caratacos scattered out of the way as the High King of Britain slid to a stop, putting one foot in the frigid water with a gasp and a curse.

"I'll thank you not to use that sort of language in front of my daughter," said Caratacos primly.

A little girl of about six ran easily down to her father and Caratacos swung her up and wrapped his cloak around her. She turned an accusing gaze on Togodumnus.

"Did you drop my chestnuts, uncle?"

"No. No, dear. See, they are safe. I put my foot in the river, though."

"That's all right then."

Togodumnos looked around.

"Have you eaten all the fish, you gannets, or have you got them in a keep-net somewhere?"

"The governor-designate of Lud Dun has stolen away all the fish of the governor of Kaleoua. We've caught nothing."

"It's a good job I came then. I can see that you have been treating this task in a frivolous and non-professional manner. Time I took charge. Cerri come with me, your uncle is too old to be taught how to fish properly, he can guard the chestnuts. Don't eat them all before we get back."

Caratacos sat on a log and wrapped his cloak and his arms around his child.

The two other men, one tall and corpulent, the other younger, tall and thin, moved away along the river bank.

"I need you back in Lud Dun, as soon as possible. Grainne is not well—no, nothing too serious—just a heavy winter cold, I think, but she can't get around the way she did. You need more urban administration experience but there is something more pressing. I hear, and Grainne confirms, that there is movement in occupied Gaul. Mainly around the Romans' old troop-embarkation port just across the Channel from Dobra. They call it Gesoriacum or some such. It may be nothing, it may be routine maintenance or it may be some development we need to know about."

"I'll leave first thing tomorrow."

"Leave Grainne to keep an eye on your officials. Go and visit the Cantii but don't let them tie you down with meaningless functions. Tap into their intelligence networks with the Continent if you can. Whether they let you do that or not, start to develop your own."

"I haven't done much of that."

"No. Tackle it on two levels. Have the skippers of ships from the Continent report to you personally when they want to dock in Lud Dun. Have them told that you have to issue them with a visa or you want to check their manifest, something like that. Cross-check their gossip until you get a clear idea of what's happening. On the other level, identify people you can trust who would have a good reason to be in Gaul. Grainne will help. Keep them separate. Send them over and have them report back only to you."

"Right."

"Remember, the Romans are doing exactly the same thing. Cross-check and cross-check again. Don't trust anyone simply because he's a Celt. The Gauls are Celts but have been under Roman domination for nearly a hundred years. Your people must move among the Gauls unseen, like…"

"Like fish in this river?"

"Yes, you've got it…dammit, where are these fish?"

If anything, the day had got even colder. Icy fingers seemed to probe back muscles even under the warmest cloaks. They scrambled up the bank and put out the fire. Cerri led the horse with the little girl perched happily on the big saddle. The brothers walked behind, brittle winter leaves crackling underfoot.

"How is King Buduoc doing, Togo?"

"Better. He still reminds me of a weasel, furtive and dangerous, but he seems to have gathered some support. The southern Dobunni still want nothing to do with him. I'm not going to replace him—yet."

"What about the Irish party?"

"Brigit? She had left. They don't want to be shipping livestock this late in the season, but they decided to chance it before the mares gave birth. Buduoc helped them organise a barge. Not very fast but stable enough. They should have reached Tara long ago, all being well."

"And the Durotriges? How did they react to your visit?"

"Polite. Not very welcoming. Interested to get a look at the new High King but careful not to compromise their independence. Are you making any inroads there?"

"After all these years, they are still very sensitive about losing their monopoly of trade with the Continent and across the neck of Britain's south-west peninsula. I keep pointing out that it was the Romans who destroyed Gaul's deep-sea fleets and closed all the Continental ports except Gesoriacum. As beneficiaries, they still hold us responsible for their decline. Did you see the Mai Dun fortifications?"

"Oh, yes. They made very sure of that. Quite impressive. Whoever designed the approach to the gate, knew something about missile warfare. No internal water supply though. I didn't get to see the other fortresses on the old trade route this time."

"I've been thinking," said Caratacos slowly. "If there was the right person on King Buduoc's throne, the Durotriges might find it easier to offer him allegiance than they would to one of our family, High King or not. And we would still control the monarch on Buduoc's throne."

"Do you want to be King of the West?" Togodumnos asked with a small smile.

"No."

"No. You have enough to do here. With Adminios gone, we are running short of candidates. The idea is good. Look for a suitable person."

"Right."

They walked a while before Caratacos spoke again.

"Adminios stole a fishing boat as we expected. There was quite a fight on the beach. He was wounded but got away with one of his companions. Two others were killed. The pursuit did their very best. They lost several horses and took several casualties themselves."

"I know. Stop blaming yourself. It's over. As far as I am concerned, I don't have a brother called Adminios. Whoever it is that they've got locked up in Rome, I hope they feed him to those lion things."

CHAPTER 8

▼

ROME

Titus had a girlfriend, lucky man. Domitilla was a slave in a big household in the City and I had often seen her around, well spoken, beautifully groomed and intelligent. I have never fathomed what she saw in my numbskull messmate when she could have had her pick of citizen, freedman or slave. He was a citizen, but from Etruria. He was no Greek god to look at and he believed that his head was for use in a fight as a battering ram.

I was supposed to be hunting down the receivers of stolen piping but could not leave Titus unsupervised in the Camp. The military doctor had dealt briskly with his broken collarbone and ribs and pronounced the head injuries as trivial, in the way of medicos, but had shaken his head dubiously at the blood-stained urine that Titus continued to produce. Not only was I concerned that the Praetorians might come back to finish the job but, equally, there was every chance that Titus would rise from his sick bed and stagger off to assault his attackers. I had a duty to protect the Praetorian Guard.

Domitilla rushed into our quarters when all of us were at our ease, cracking jokes at Titus' expense and explaining to him how damage to the kidneys usually resulted in impotence. This peaceful scene was quite disrupted by her arrival and several of my more timid colleagues fled the scene in their underwear. After railing at male callousness, she cooed at the patient while cradling his frowsty, bandaged head in her white arms. He whimpered shamelessly. She then turned on me, demanding explanations and action.

Titus, she said, must be moved at once before he died of neglect and maltreatment at the hands of selfish incompetents. I nodded gravely at this description of my colleagues and was somewhat hurt when I realized she was including me. He must be taken, this very night, to the house where she worked and she would ensure that he got proper treatment, safe from his so-called friends. Titus let out a long wavering groan. She would allow him to return only when he was fully recovered. A sigh and a horrible cough from the patient.

I told her that we would be happy for Titus to go. He was urinating blood and this, as she knew, was an infallible sign of sexually transmitted disease in an advanced stage. With a strangled roar, the invalid tried to get out of bed. With some dignity, I departed to attend to my duties.

We had no money for a sedan but we did manage, for a small bribe, to borrow the handcart used to bring firewood from the woodyard to the guardroom. Titus was not a model passenger. From the fuss he made, you would think he was being stretched on the rack and not being laid on an improvised ambulance. Clattering cheerfully through the dark streets with Domitilla and a couple of my comrades, we made our way to the edge of the City where we were stopped by the Vigiles.

"Ho, there," said the one with the sense of humour. "You are too early. That corpse is still alive." We managed to restrain Titus.

"And where might you be going?"

Domitilla stepped forward. "To the British Palace," she said.

I intervened with a brief edited version of our mission and proof of our identity. With interested glances at Domitilla, the Vigiles let us pass.

"The British Palace?" I queried.

"Yes. It's not really a palace, just a big house on the edge of the City. It's getting to be quite crowded with refugees."

"I'm not sure that we should leave the casualty with a household of barbarians. They might mistake him for a brave soldier, chop off his head and keep it in a wooden chest."

"Titus will be quite safe in the servants' quarters there. He has been there before."

The patient's face took on a smug look, which Domitilla noticed.

"Of course," she continued. "A head in that condition would be no good as a trophy anyway."

The main door of the British Palace was guarded by a muscular and alert looking porter whose professional scowl disappeared when he saw Domitilla. It was a very large house. More like a country villa than a townhouse and the servants' quarters were at the back. We off-loaded the handcart into a spare room and my comrades trundled it happily away in the direction of the Camp. After Domitilla had got Titus settled, the porter invited us for a drink in his lodge at the main door.

I had not, so far, seen any of the residents and asked him about them. After two cups of suspiciously good quality wine, the porter became almost expansive.

"Well, they are barbarians, of course, although well-born, some of them. They have no idea of indoor plumbing when they get here. And they won't eat poultry. The men shave their chins like civilized people but usually insist on keeping their moustaches. They are forever laughing, shouting and kicking up a row, and the women are almost as bad. Playing music all day long when I am trying to sleep."

"There are women here?" I prompted.

"Oh yes, big, strong redheads mostly, but with nice white—er—skin. They usually arrive in trousers and Domitilla has to really work at making them presentable."

"They bring a lot of jewelry with them," Domitilla put in. " Big solid torcs of gold and silver alloy, but the men wear them as well. Some of the pieces though are really fine, inlaid with enamel or coral. They make the enamel in all sorts of colours, not just red. Sometimes pearl pendants, as well."

"You know," said the porter pouring more wine. "I always thought their homeland was a wet desert. There must be some wealth there though, despite what Julius Caesar said."

"He had his own agenda," I said. "Twice he went there and twice withdrew with his armies disorganised and half his fleets wrecked. We know," I emphasised, " that they were two victorious expeditions. The only reason he could not bring back much booty was because the land was so poor. Maybe."

The wine was loosening my tongue and a policeman with a loose tongue does not last long in the Cohorts.

"What unnerves me about them," said the porter, who had become noticeably drunk, "is all the blue and grey eyes about the place, everywhere you look."

"What unnerves me about them," said Domitilla quietly, "is the way the men treat the women. Just as if they are not women at all. As if they are just people."

The porter laughed loudly.

"Well, you won't get that from me, girl," he said. "We are not people. We are slaves."

CHAPTER 9

▼

ROME

'Minerva' made a good nine-day passage from the Alexandria homeport to the main Fleet Base at Misenum, south-east of Rome. The officers and crew had been given a fairly warm sendoff from the merchant seamen of the corn fleet, who had enjoyed their free demonstration put on by the warship. Formal but heartfelt thanks had been offered in a public speech by the Prefect of the Alexandrine Fleet. What was much more appreciated was the deposit with the Captain of a large amount of copper and bronze coinage for distribution to the crew on their arrival in Italy. Shore leave in Alexandria, still thronged with merchant marine crews, had not been permitted before 'Minerva's' departure.

Philip's status in the eyes of the crew had never been very clear but his quick reactions on deck had been noted and were much talked about. He did nothing to clarify his status, which, if anything, enhanced it. His first mentor, he of the difficult Balkan accent, had begun treating the supernumerary with something approaching respect. They stood together at the front of the ship above the large eyes painted on either side. The air was distinctly cooler. The Captain, in his shore-going uniform, loomed behind them.

"Misenum," he said, pointing ahead with his freshly-shaven chin. "Biggest Fleet Base in the world. Eighty ships, ten thousand sailors. Not all of them at home at once, of course. Detachments all over the western Mediterranean and warships on courier duties everywhere where there's water."

"What about Ravenna, sir?"

"A Fleet about half our size but on the wrong side of Italy for Rome's daily business. They do a good job," he said, eyeing Philip's mentor, "in keeping the

Balkans under control. Our biggest detachment is, strange to say, on land, in Rome. Imperial communications, you see."

Philip nodded with real interest, which the Captain noted with some pleasure.

"After the sea-battle of Actium, only seventy years ago, even though he was the winner, the Emperor the divine Augustus, had more problems than a human could cope with. His most immediate problem was that he had hundreds of war-ships and scores of legions filled with men who, for years, had been desperately trying to kill one another. It would not have taken much to spark the fire again."

"So he rationalised the military."

"Yes. Discharged the time-expired men wholesale. Split some legions into two, abolished others completely, halved the total number of legions in the end. Incidentally, that's why you cannot rely just on the official number to identify a legion. Several have the same number because they were on different sides. So you have to use their title as well."

The Captain was starting to look around, gauging the activities on his ship. Philip saw the Captain had not much time left for socialising.

"What about the Navy, Captain," he asked quickly.

"Yes, well. That was, I think, a stroke of genius. He sent all the warships to Forum Julii, then a Fleet Base on a river lagoon on the south coast of Gaul. There is an old colony of veteran soldiers established near there. The warships and crews were reorganised there and crews then sent to here for retraining. There is a naval retraining facility on the crater-lake of Avernus. The crewmen who did not make the grade were discharged piecemeal and surplus ships dismantled. Forum Julii is still there but only a shadow of what it was, I believe. Now I must go. Don't let this one off the hook. Make sure he gives you hard facts about the Navy not fairy tales from the Danube."

Philip was determined not to be impressed by Rome. From a very early age, he had continuously heard about the wonders, the orderliness and the cleanliness of the capital. Romans emphatically confirmed this, even if they had never been to the City. Provincials, drawn into the Roman web, and often profiting by it, were even more convincing.

Greeks, who had once ruled the ancient monarchies of Egypt and Asia Minor, as well as a myriad of Mediterranean islands and colonies, did not concede Roman cultural superiority. Roman military might had subverted and then con-quered those ancient kingdoms and vibrant colonies. Roman civil servants had converted them into dull provinces of Empire. Egypt had become a farm. Its wondrous monuments were merely quarries for building materials and the descendents of their builders merely farm labourers. Alexandria, however, yielded to no city in mercantile enterprise and in learning.

Roman temple architecture was no surprise to Philip, being based closely on Greek designs. What was a surprise was that monumental architecture in Rome was so crowded around by public buildings and housing that the beauty of its dimensions could not even be fully seen, let alone appreciated. The Greeks built temples alone on hills. The Romans appeared to clear a space in the urban congestion and drop them in.

He got directions to the Praetorian Camp east of the City easily enough but decided not to make an immediate report there as his travel instructions dictated. He had already seen enough of the military mind to know that, once he did that, every moment of his time would have to be accounted for and he had another instruction to follow.

The offices of the City's Water Department were seething with surveyors, contractors, clerks and inspectors. Rolled plans were everywhere and meetings assembled and dispersed without any apparent pattern. Terms such as fountain houses, cisterns and aqueducts littered the talk. Philip interrupted a discussion between an inspector and an individual with a folded ruler stuck in his girdle. The inspector did not look up from a plan held down by cement-spotted hands but simply pointed to a door with his thumb.

Inside, in a posture that seemed almost universal in these offices, a man leaned on both hands over an unrolled plan.

"Know anything about venters?" he asked without looking up.

"Simple sailors from Alexandria do not know much about fresh-water reticulation."

The young man slowly looked up. His balding head, painted to represent natural hair, made him look older than he was. There was gleam of gold bridgework when he smiled.

"Who are you then, simple sailor?"

Philip told him.

"I have been expecting you. I am Narcissus."

They sat on wooden benches and took stock of each other. Narcissus was dressed simply but not cheaply. There was a faint smear of ink on the front of his new tunic. He listened intently to Philip's description of the voyage and asked seemingly innocuous questions about domestic conditions in Egypt, about 'Minerva's' demonstration in front of seamen of the corn fleet, of the warship's crew's gossip and of his impressions of Misenum. When Philip described his swearing in to military service, Narcissus nodded without shifting his gaze. He asked in Greek.

"How did you feel about that?"

"Surprised. I thought at first that the Emperor had died."

"And afterwards?"

"Uncomfortable. I had made an even greater commitment than I had expected. The penalties for breaking an oath to a god will extend after death if—as—the Emperor is now divine. The East has a history of monarchs who were gods in their lifetimes and I have no doubt I shall come to accept it here."

"Perhaps more readily than many Romans."

Narcissus shifted slightly and clasped his hands, forearms on his knees.

"I am a freedman," he said unnecessarily. "I was a literate household slave belonging to Claudius, the Emperor's uncle. His close relations tend to die unexpectedly, you know, but he has survived—so far. He had a childhood illness that has left him with some physical impairment and people think there is something wrong with his mind. They are wrong. I was able to help him with his divorces and other things, and he set me free."

"How did you feel about that?"

Unconsciously, Philip returned the question Narcissus had earlier put to him. The question was considered.

"At first emotionless, then frightened. Now, at times, it disgusts me."

"Disgusts?"

"I still work for Claudius. He's in charge of the City's water supply. Every day I deal with citizens. Some are poor, ignorant louts who are pleased to treat me with contempt. I find that funny. Some are from old, famous families who treat me with greasy servility, and then snigger behind my back. I find that disgusting."

A short silence followed. Then Narcissus unclasped his hands. He did not seem able to sit still for long and there was a slight tremor in his hands. His voice remained calm and pleasant.

"The Prefect of the Alexandrine Fleet has reported well on you, as has the Captain of 'Minerva'.

Philip automatically thanked Narcissus while absorbing the fact that a freedman, working in a noisy municipal office concerned with City water supply, had access to official Fleet reports. Narcissus would not have deliberately provided that insight simply as a pleasantry. Despite his odd appearance, Philip did not believe that Narcissus made unconsidered comments. Philip returned his stare before replying.

"Official reports do not provide the full story."

"Good. I have other, even more significant reports of your background and abilities."

Before Philip could formulate a response, Narcissus continued.

"My responsibilities extend beyond this office. I need what official reports do not provide. I need to know and understand the environments, military, religious and political, in which those reports are generated."

"Religious?" Philip felt on the verge of being left behind.

"Oh, yes. We Greeks are inclined to think that we own the pantheon of gods. Many other nations, however, as you know, have their own. The Romans simply take them over, all of them, and make them part of the structure of the Empire. The theory is that no newly conquered people can feel too humiliated when they realise that the gods they relied on in a conflict with Rome were Roman all the time."

They both laughed.

"And," continued Narcissus, "custodianship of the gods of our Empire is a high State appointment. Claudius is the Pontiff."

"So," said Philip slowly. "Claudius has access to military records and formal religious matters. As a member of one of the Imperial families and a member of the Senate he must surely have a broad view of Imperial concerns and of City politics?"

"You would think so, wouldn't you? In recent times, City politics have become more and more a simple reflection of the Emperor's will. As far as members of the Imperial families becoming well versed in the mechanisms of Empire, well, it is a grim fact that to take such an interest is dangerous. Such members are likely to become excluded from them completely—one way or another."

"Your patron, then, is in danger through lack of informal information. The gathering of such information is itself dangerous."

Narcissus stood and stretched. He had a steel stylus tucked through his girdle. He did not respond immediately. The writing instrument gleamed like the weapon it was.

"An error has been detected in the public records office," he said. "It has now been established that Antoninus Maximus completed his full enlistment period in the Navy, after all."

Philip was momentarily confused by his father's official military name.

"The diploma granting him an honourable discharge is being prepared for presentation by the Prefect of the Fleet. Your distinguished father, and his family, will shortly be citizens. You will be a citizen. Congratulations."

Philip was able to mumble an acknowledgement as he also stood.

Narcissus nodded his painted head. "I wish you every success in your career in the Misene Fleet detachment in Rome. I hope to see you often."

"I am at your service."

"Good." Narcissus walked to the door. "How was that old Jewish moneybags when you left home?"

"Alexander?" said Philip, thinking quickly. "You know him?"

"Oh, yes," said Narcissus. "He's Claudius' banker."

It was in a very preoccupied state of mind that Philip pushed though the outer offices and out onto the wet streets. It had started to rain.

CHAPTER 10

▼

ROME

I felt much more comfortable with Titus in Domitilla's safe hands, especially as he was among barbarians. She would make sure that they would not interfere with him and the Celts would discourage any casual intrusions into the British Palace by bored Praetorians.

My own pressing problem was to run down the excellent information provided by the Master of the Guild of Fullers before my Centurion demanded a report. The work I had put in was on the verge of paying off, but, if I was asked for an accounting at this moment, all I could produce to my superior was the list. It was not unknown at such a point in an investigation that a superior would take over the case on the grounds of insufficient progress and would reap the rewards for himself.

There were only five names of illegal fullers on the Master's list for me to check. A report after those premises had been located and visited would carry more weight than the list alone, and also make it more difficult for my Centurion to claim all the credit. The deciding factor was, however, that I had an excuse. During the near-riot in the Praetorian Camp, no officers, other than Rufrius Pollio of the big boot, had been in evidence. I certainly could not make an official report to a Centurion who had made himself scarce when the Praetorians were on the rampage. The investigation team sent down-river to Ostia must be about due back. That would bring our respected superior out of hiding and so I must hurry.

Leaving my uniform at the British Palace, I borrowed clothing from Domitilla's laundry and set off in a gusting rain. The hooded woollen cloak was of excellent quality and I thanked the unknown British sheep for their contribution to Roman comfort.

On the basis that the illegal fullers did indeed enjoy official protection, I chose the most central of the premises to visit first and, not far from the old Forum of Augustus, located the first of the illegals on the list. Usually, it seems, when an investigator sets himself to check a lengthy list of items, it is the last one which yields the result he seeks. In this case, Fortune smiled in the rain.

If an illegal business can be described as brazen, that might describe the imposing shop fronting onto a busy central street that I found from the Master's list. Even on a damp day, with water squelching in shoes and icy drops gusting about bare ankles, a number of pedestrians hurried through the street. Occasionally one crossed the threshold of the shop I was watching from fairly limited shelter across the street.

There was a public fountain at a nearby intersection but, for the fuller to draw water from there for the business would simply advertise its illegal status. All legal fullers rely on mains water supply. I prowled the streets uphill from the fuller's until I located the local reservoir for the neighbourhood. I identified the inlet pipe by its larger bore. There were several outlet pipes, as I expected in that well-to-do area, all correctly imprinted with the municipal stamp. There was no sign of an illegal connection at the reservoir. I then had an idea.

I went back to the public fountain I had seen earlier and traced its inlet pipe uphill towards the reservoir. Except where it was crossed by a roadway, it ran above ground and was easy to follow. At the point where it was crossed by the street beside the illegal fuller's, the pipe came up through the pavement, the hole filled in with gravel. I glanced about. The rain was heavier, pedestrians fewer.

There are severe restrictions about civilians going about armed in the settled Provinces of the Empire, more so in Rome itself. Even magistrates, however, accept that many tradesmen require a knife for business and I did not fear being challenged when I took out my blade. Being challenged for interfering with the City's water supply was an entirely different matter. Keeping my hooded head down and disguising my intentions under my British cloak, I dug out the wet gravel as quickly as I could, using my hands to scoop it out after I had loosened the surface. About a hand's length beneath pavement level, I felt what I had been expecting. Another pipe had been connected into the public water supply. It ran off along the street beside the fuller's premises.

I pushed most of the gravel back into the hole, put away my knife and stood up. Under my sodden hood I surveyed the almost deserted street while I trod down the gravel. Walking along the side street, I quickly came to the side wall of the fuller's shop and looked around again. There was no sign of the illicit pipe but a paving stone was missing from the sidewalk next to the wall of the building.

Again, I dug into the gravel fill with knife and hands and delved into the hole. I located the lead pipe making a right angle turn through the wall of the fuller's premises. I refilled the hole and straightened my back.

There was now no one moving on the street. The rain was coming down in gusting sheets, thumping into the wet fabric of my cloak and bouncing from the pavement. There was no warning at all.

A paving stone smashed, with appalling force, into the wall beside my head. Before I could turn completely, something like a runaway hay-wagon drove me against the wall. Bruised, breathless and tangled in a sodden cloak, my attacker should have strangled me like a baby in swaddling clothes. Instead, he opted to scoop up the broken paving stone which, standing over me, he raised above his head to finish the job.

I managed to draw a tortured breath and, finding a gap in my cloak, drove my knife halfway to its hilt into his hairy leg. I twisted away to avoid the paving stone as it again crashed down on the pavement. Hopping backwards, the knife still pinning his leg, my assailant stepped in one of the channels in the roadway which serve for drainage and carts' wheels, tripped over the pedestrian stepping-stone in the centre and fell hard.

He was game. With my knife in his hand, he was struggling to regain his feet when I reached him in a sort of scrambling rush and enveloped him in my wet cloak. Knowing how sharp my knife was, I stood back, panting and looking around feverishly until I saw a sizeable piece of the broken paving stone. With it, I hit likely lumps in the cloak until my assailant finally subsided.

I unwrapped him, recovered my knife and looked around. The street was deserted but that did not mean that the brief fight had not been seen. A witness might even now be looking for a member of the Cohort and complaining that there was never a policeman around when he was needed. My attacker was unconscious, rain hitting his face and streaking blood into his slave's beard. Even though he was not at his best, there was no doubt of his identity. I had last seen him when being entertained to drinks in his town house by a member of the Senate. He belonged to Senator Asiaticus and the Senator was probably not going to be pleased. With his hands tied, a sore head and a wounded leg, he probably would not get far before the Cohort arrived.

Washing things in the public fountains is illegal, and washing bloody knives and hands is not only illegal but totally outrageous. I accomplished the clean-up without discovery and walked in the front door of the illegal fuller's like any other wet and bruised customer. The typical warmth and chemical smells struck me as I entered and scanned the premises for potential opponents. The main business of the day appeared to be over although a number of garments were stretched over racks to dry. One slave was brushing a dress without too much enthusiasm while two others chatted.

Before they had a chance to bar my way, I turned right towards the side of the premises which was of interest. I kept walking, as they rapidly became more alert and asked me my business. I did not stop but asked them where their clothes-press was. By this time there was a note of alarm in the questioning voices. A restraining hand reached towards me. There, protruding through the wall, was a lead waterpipe with the municipal stamp clearly visible. Hanging from the valve was a drop of the City's water.

I turned, and spun the tense slaves a yarn about having them dry my cloak in their clothes-press which, indeed, stood in the background. Their questioning looks faded and they started to relax. At that moment, the dull light from the street dimmed further and, throwing her damp scarf off her shining hair, Senator Asiaticus' beautiful housekeeper stood in the doorway. She had fuzzy spots of blood close to the hem of her dress. Her eyes widened when she saw me and then became hard, narrow chips. The slaves looked at her and then looked at me.

The first voice to break the silence, however, was from outside. Rough, hectoring demands and confident footfalls announced the arrival of two large representatives of Urban Cohort X. The housekeeper disappeared into the rain. The patrolmen did not know me and I had to spend some time convincing them of my credentials. Senator Asiaticus' wounded slave had gone.

My superior's office, when he at last granted me permission to enter, was no tidier than it had been last time. The Centurion, as I had thought, had put in an appearance after the disturbances in the Praetorian Camp, acting as if he had never been absent. After a cursory enquiry about Titus' chances of recovery, he did not refer to the events of that day again. Now, after waiting for what seemed like half the evening, he had acknowledged my presence and invited me in. He pushed aside the remains of his evening meal—I hadn't eaten—and, with a casual wave of his hand, he invited me to speak.

At the start of my report he sat slumped at his ease, his blunt features flushed and relaxed. By the time I had reached the part where I had been attacked while tracing the illegal water connection, he was sitting bolt upright and swearing vengeance on all undisciplined and murderous slaves. When I reached the point of the identification of the slave and the housekeeper and who was their master, his eyes had glazed and, even in the lamplight, he looked pale. His mouth hung open slightly with a toothpick still clinging to his lower lip. My boss was seriously thinking. His eyes gradually focused on me and his mouth slowly closed.

"Right. Now see here Aurelius Victorinus! I sent you out to investigate a theft of lead piping…"

I was more or less prepared for this approach and interrupted quickly.

"Which is what I did. And located some too."

"…and, instead, you come back with a long story about slaves and stepping stones…"

"Paving stones."

"…pretty housewives…"

"Housekeepers."

"…belonging to a most respected member of the Senate. Good god man, Asiaticus is a candidate for one of the Consulships next year."

"People belonging to the Senator are stealing municipal water," I said evenly. "Probably for quite a long time. They are using stolen lead piping to do so. City officials are in collusion with them. The Senator could be involved…"

My Centurion made a noise like a cough. I took the opportunity to press on.

"…and I have not checked all the other suspect premises yet. He could own them all."

My superior reared back in his chair.

"Wait," he said holding up a large hand. "Just wait. Just what evidence do we have? Go through it again."

I did so, watching him carefully. For the most part, he seemed to be listening, only occasionally did the spectre of a demolished career cloud his eyes.

"Very well," he said finally. "Obviously, there are political implications here and I shall have to consult with the Commander tomorrow morning. He may decide to drop the matter in the public interest."

I tried to restrain myself.

"Difficult," was all I said.

"What do you mean, difficult?"

"Theft, corruption and attempted murder uncovered in an investigation. An investigation ordered by the Emperor's uncle I believe."

The Centurion's interestingly pale complexion became suddenly enhanced by a light sheen of perspiration.

He did not quite dare to ask me who else knew of my findings although I had a lie prepared. He held out his hand and smiled most horribly.

"Give me the list."

"Here is your copy." I did not emphasise the last word.

"Sir!" he said.

"Sir," I obediently repeated.

I spent that night in safety at the British Palace but was outside the Centurion's office the following morning on his return from his meeting with the Commander of the Cohort. He was looking less oppressed by his burdens of office. I greeted him respectfully, having gone quite close to the edge the previous night.

"Go and see this freedman fellow in the Water Commissioner's office", he instructed me, quite pleasantly. "Tell him your story. He may want to discuss our investigation with me. If so, get a few dates from him and I'll confirm an appointment in due course."

I looked at the name on the slip he handed to me.

"Do you know who this is, sir?"

"No. Why?"

"It doesn't matter. I'll report back after the meeting. Sir."

I was looking forward to meeting Narcissus. It is not every day you meet the man who runs the uncle of the Emperor.

When I closed the door of his office behind me, however, there were two unknown men looking at me.

"I have an appointment with Narcissus." I said, speaking to the air between the two. The burly old man sitting behind the drawing board grunted. The one standing flashed me a golden smile.

"I'm Narcissus, and you are the investigator?"

I introduced myself.

Narcissus turned to his companion and then faced me again.

"I don't believe that you have met," he then rolled the names, "Tiberius Drusus Nero Germanicus Claudius. Have you?"

Uncle Claudius!

"Sit down, investigator," said the Emperor's uncle in a deep, pleasant voice with only a hint of a lisp. "You look a little shaky on your legs, if you don't mind my saying so. Not as shaky as me, though, hey Narcissus?"

They laughed, old friends.

Claudius calmly surveyed me through tired, clever eyes.

"I understand that you have a result in the investigation. I am surprised your immediate superior is not here with you."

"Er—I don't think he realised that the report was to be made to…"

"To the Water Commissioner?"

"Yes."

"No," said Narcissus, smiling, though his jaw was taut. "He thought it was to be made to a simple freedman in the Water Commissioner's office, didn't he?"

"Er—yes."

"Very well," said Uncle Claudius, resting his muscular forearms on the drawing board and hunching his big shoulders. "Proceed with your report."

He sat still while I spoke, trying to moderate my voice that tends to get into a loud, boring rhythm when reporting. Narcissus moved about his office, picking things up and putting them down. When I had finished Claudius spoke almost as if he had not heard a word I had said.

"I am told that the officers of the Praetorian Guard successfully put down a near mutiny. Some rumour about the deification of a horse. It is surprising that military men consider themselves qualified to judge religious matters. Were you there?"

"Yes, but…"

"Which officers spoke to you?"

"I was not a mutineer. I am not a member of the Guards. The only Guards officer I saw was Rufrius Pollio."

Claudius looked over my head and nodded to Narcissus. I heard the door close behind him.

"Narcissus will deal with the internal corruption side of the investigation. No, I realise that you are not a guardsman. You appear to have far more sense. They do have their uses though, especially if you have to deal with a person of the status of Valerius Asiaticus."

"I know the Senator, sir. In fact, I have been to his house."

"Have you indeed?" Claudius spoke quite softly. "How did that come about?"

So I told him of finding the letter and my reception by Asiaticus and our informal discussion about his Gallic business interests.

"I see. Asiaticus and his family have done good work for Rome in the East—as you might imagine from the name—but now it's Gaul. I was born there myself, you know."

I did not. Claudius might have been born on the moon for all I knew. One thing I did know, was that his words bore no relationship to whatever was being considered in the Water Commissioner's mind. I had long known that Asiaticus was a candidate for one of the two Consulships next year and it was apparent that even the Emperor's uncle, responsible for several important State functions, was going to tread warily. His prudence should not have been surprising. There were very few close relatives of the Emperor left alive.

He shouldered his toga and heaved himself to his feet. As he properly draped the robe about him, he told me to stay until my evidence was written down. He nodded and headed towards the door with a slight lurch to his gait, thin ankles visible below the broad purple stripe on the hem of his Senator's toga.

At the door, he turned and spoke loudly, the lisp much more pronounced.

"Tell your Centurion," he said, "he is to report here at the start of business tomorrow morning. I believe that Narcissus has something he wishes to discuss with him."

He looked at me closely, then gave a little grin and lurched away.

CHAPTER 11

▼

ROME

Except in mid-winter, the Fleet landing stage on the River Tiber was always a busy place. The day Philip tracked down his designated superior there was no exception. Ranks of Fleet boats were clustered about, discharging bags of Imperial mail or waiting for dispatches. A stream of signalers hurried between the landing stage and the Fleet offices within the Praetorian Camp. Several marines kept the approaches clear. On production of his travel warrant, Philip was allowed onto the platform but decided not to intrude on the discussion taking place between a Fleet Centurion and an officer of the same rank from the Urban Cohorts. Fleet boats were being waved off to make space.

Two heavily overloaded river craft edged in towards the landing stage. The first was a Fleet boat with navy crew and several policemen. The barge being towed behind was very low in the water. On top of its load of lead, sat a very uncomfortable group of prisoners, each prisoner shackled to a lead ingot. There was obviously no danger of an escape by swimming. The faces of the policemen were stiff with pride, the sailors more relaxed as they made fast.

The police Centurion did not, at first, acknowledge his subordinates' success. He marched over the landing stage to peer short-sightedly at the stamp on the ingots and crooked a finger at one of the policemen. Philip eased closer to hear.

"See here," said the Centurion. "I sent you downriver to investigate the disposal of stolen lead piping. What are these ingots? That is not a municipal stamp on them."

"No," said one sailor, shooting a glance at his own Centurion who did not tell him to keep quiet. "That is a British stamp. I've seen it before. Those ingots are supposed to have been imported from Britain."

The Centurion was wary of being made to look a fool and decided on caution.

"What has British export lead got to do with the investigation?"

"We also found this."

With a flourish, the policeman produced a metal stamp and placed one end against an ingot. The sailor obligingly picked up another ingot and, using it as a hammer, struck the other end of the stamp. A second imprint of the 'British' stamp appeared on the ingot.

"These crooks," said the policeman, somewhat unnecessarily, "were disguising stolen piping as imported lead ingots."

"Have you confiscated samples of the piping?"

"Better than that. See here."

The Centurion looked at him sharply but made no comment. The other policemen manhandled an obviously heavy object out of the boat. Everyone crowded round. It was a fire-blackened pot half filled with solid lead. Embedded in the lead were several short lengths of lead piping.

"They must have heard we were coming and tried to melt the last of the stolen piping in a potful of already molten lead."

The policemen had been watching their Centurion's face expectantly. The Fleet Centurion leaned forward suddenly and pointed at a mark on one of the lead pipes.

"Look. The municipal stamp."

"Right," said the Cohort Centurion, smugly. "I thought you would find the evidence I needed in a ship yard."

"Not in a ship yard. In an import/export warehouse at Ostia. Owned by a family called Asiaticus."

Philip thought that the Centurion was suddenly not looking as smug as he had been. A tall Cohort patrolman pushed his way through the onlookers and delivered a verbal message to the Centurion that made him look distinctly unhappy. This did not distract from the delight of his subordinates. They marshalled their prisoners and loaded them with the evidence that would convict them.

The Fleet Centurion turned from ordering the barge of lead ingots to be moved from the landing stage, and Philip formally reported himself to his new superior. It seemed that Philip was posted to the Fleets' mail sorting room. The huge building received dispatches and correspondence destined for the Emperor and the Senate from the Imperial and Senatorial Provinces. As so many more Provinces were under the direct control of the Emperor rather than the Senate, as well as virtually the whole of the military establishment, Philip was expecting that the Emperor's office would receive and generate the greater volume of mail. This was not the case. The numerous members of the Senate, with fewer Provincial responsibilities, were inveterate letter-writers.

Philip, with his background of commercial intelligence, could guess at the volume and value of the information flowing through the sorting room daily. It would not be only enemies of Rome who would wish to have well placed agents in the Fleet sorting room. At its simplest, from a purely business perspective, knowledge of where the Emperor next intended to concentrate part of his attention would be worth a fortune in potential State contracts. Philip was certain that he was not the only agent on the staff.

His job, however, did not involve tampering with the mail, for which the severest penalties were decreed, but was based on the other, unofficial function of the Fleet sorting room; that of being the clearing-house of gossip from all over the Empire. Most of the gossip travelled at least as fast as the mail and was probably almost as accurate. Furthermore, over the miles, while the contents of the mail-bags remained unchanging, the gossip did not. It was dissected, correlated and distilled in endless discussions on decks and benches until it often gave the recipient a more digested perspective of the facts than the official version. At the least, it provided an insight into Imperial beliefs and thinking at the broad lower levels.

As a Provincial himself, Philip was not yet finely attuned to the environment in Rome. It was immediately apparent, however, that there was a marked gulf between beliefs and attitudes in the City and those in the Provinces. The seldom-spoken opinion in the City was that the Emperor was a wasteful, unjust, adult brat and probably deranged as well. His extension of existing public holidays and establishing of new ones drove the industrious to distraction and ruined their businesses. This, and the relentless bloodletting in the arena, had emptied a full treasury so that forcible bequests and other forms of Imperial extortion were needed to avoid bankruptcy. The Provincials, on the other hand, complained of Imperial taxes but were more rarely directly affected by the Emperor's personal flaws. When he turned his attention to systematically confiscating their wealth, that would change.

Ordinary soldiers on the distant frontiers complained incessantly of low pay, little chance of booty and, above all, the never-ending toil of road-making. Perhaps their officers worried about the stability of their Commander-in-Chief. They did not make their opinions known. Mutinies on the Rhine had been recently subdued by Imperial bribes and the staunchness of a few senior front-line officers. The Praetorian Guard in Rome, however, was not reticent, viewing with increasing anger the Emperor's insulting behaviour towards their own senior officers and his pandering to the unproductive Roman mob.

Philip was certain that Narcissus and Claudius were well aware of these general ground-swells of opinion. Through his own appointment, they were aware of the dissatisfaction in the Fleet over the common practice of discharging servicemen without terminal benefits one year before the end of their normal service.

After some thought, he decided to produce, as his first project, a report on Navy concerns about the dilapidated condition of the port of Ostia, the Fleet's gateway to Rome.

CHAPTER 12

▼

ROME

It is not every day that a patrolman of the Urban Cohorts may be required to testify publicly against a member of the Senate and I had to admit to myself that the thought might be making me just a little tense. It was not just that Asiaticus was a Senator, and a candidate for Consul at that, but that he had an aura of being a very bad man to cross. I had had a drink with the man in his private study and did not relish the prospect of looking up into those shadowed eyes and telling him he was a crook.

There are plenty of distinguished Senators whose after-hours activities are freely discussed in the Cohorts and among the Vigiles. Public pillars of rectitude are frequently to be seen sliding unshaven out of drinking dens and brothels for both sexes in the early hours, and the news is on the law-enforcement gossip circuit before dawn. Often the crowds listening to renowned Senatorial orators speaking on the Roman virtue of austerity are puzzled by the knowing grins on the faces of patrolmen nearby. There are also plenty of Senators who happen to suddenly invest in companies which are then fortunate enough to be awarded big State contracts. The electorate is not unaware and is generally fairly tolerant.

The Asiaticus case was something different. His warehouse in Ostia had been receiving stolen public property and systematically disguising its origin so that it could be sold as legitimately imported lead ingots. At the same time, public property stolen from the same source had been used to siphon off public water to supply illegal businesses run by his staff. This was clear criminality no matter how much blame he might try and shed onto his people.

Uncle Claudius had acted swiftly. While my Centurion was receiving a brief survey of his career prospects from Narcissus, the giant Guards' officer, Rufrius

Pollio, went into a private meeting with Claudius. We small fry from the Urban Cohort sat in an outer office, miraculously cleared of the usual throng of officials and contractors, and dictated our depositions to clerks. We were still at it when our superior officer emerged from his attitude-readjustment session, white faced and tottering. I felt quite sorry for our old Centurion, but it does not do—even for a citizen—to snub a freedman of an Imperial family.

Rufrius Pollio opened the door and pointed at me. Keeping my backside clear of his boots, I edged sideways into the Water Commissioner's office. Claudius was sitting behind his desk in what was becoming a familiar pose, big forearms on the surface with his hands clasped on the single document visible.

"Aurelius Victorinus," he lisped, nodding pleasantly. "Welcome. You know Pollio, here I believe?"

"Oh yes, sir," I said airily. "I know old Pollio." I ignored the murderous glare from the Guards' officer.

"Ah, yes," said Claudius. "Well, I have here a subpoena to be served on Senator Valerius Asiaticus to attend a hearing convened by myself as Water Commissioner for the City of Rome. In view of his status, it is to be served privately on the Senator by a very senior officer of the Praetorian Guard. That senior officer has suggested that you be present."

I looked at the simmering giant but his face gave no clue. The Water Commissioner did not explain either but handed the document to Rufrius Pollio before turning back to me. He rested his watery, friendly eyes on me for quite a long time without speaking. Then he gave that small grin.

"Investigations into charges of corruption within this Department are being concluded." He did not miss the question in my mind. "The list you gave me? All owned or leased by Asiaticus. Go get him."

Outside the Water Commissioner's office, I found my foot pinned to the pavement by the hobnails of a Guards' boot. Garlic-laden breath fanned around my upturned face.

"'Old Pollio' hey?" said the articulate giant. "Do that one more time, little man, and I'll drive you through a crack in this pavement like a rusty razor!"

I deemed it wise to make no reply.

He clumped off down the street with me hobbling behind. We made a fairly lengthy detour around streets closed off for the Emperor's convenience and stopped just short of the Senator's town house, still with that deserted look I remembered. A patrolman from Cohort XI confirmed that the Senator was at home.

The front door swung open to the guardsman's thunderous knock and a distinguished-looking steward admitted us to the atrium. He left us standing next to the sunken rainwater tank while he tapped on the door of the study. There was a fine mosaic underfoot and the red walls of the atrium had been newly painted with full-length portraits. White clouds hung motionless in the open sky above.

Just before we began to fidget, we were admitted to the study and the door closed behind us. The window-shutters were open onto the small, sunlit, enclosed garden at the rear of the house. They provided air and light to the small room. The Senator, imposing in toga and complete with iron signet ring, sat with his back to the light. The room smelt mainly of garden herbs. The walls had been sponged and the candelabrum moved to one side but there was still a faint smell of burnt lamp-oil and ink.

Rufrius Pollio, moderating his parade ground bellow, stated who we were and our mission. I could see the Senator's face a little better now. Asiaticus was watching me. When he had finished, Pollio placed the subpoena on the desk. The Senator ignored it. The Guardsman turned it around so that it could be read from the Senator's position. He still ignored it. His right hand on the desk slowly closed and he rapped once. The door behind us immediately opened.

"You may go," he said conversationally.

Rufrius Pollio turned and stalked out, but the door closed in my face as I made to follow. I turned. I half-expected the Senator to offer me money and I had rehearsed an elegant and witty rejection. He had no such intention.

"Victorinus," said Senator Valerius Asiaticus. "You are a dead man."

My scalp crawled.

"Go fuck yourself," I responded briefly.

The steward opened the study door once more. After that definitive exchange, there did not seem to be anything else to say. I left.

"What happened?" demanded Rufrius Pollio in the street. I told him. After a moment, he gave vent to a loud snort followed shortly afterwards by several others. He was not having a seizure. He was laughing.

"Don't apply for a job in the diplomatic service."

"You set this up," I accused.

"Of course. A Senator's testimony far out-weighs any patrolman's in any Court in the Empire. With all the other official testimony, plus the physical evidence, there may be a conviction. It will be touch and go. He has to get rid of the star witness or plead guilty."

"Thanks very much."

"That means he either bribes you or threatens you or both. He is wealthy in property but not in cash. The Water Commission could match any money bribe he could offer, so that is out. Threat it had to be. You told him that threats won't work. He's going to have to humiliate himself before the Water Commissioner."

I thought about that.

"Claudius agreed to my going along for this purpose?"

"Contrary to what he said, it was he, not I, who suggested this. We had a bet on the outcome."

"Who won?" I asked, with real interest.

"Claudius is a damaged person," said the giant guardsman. "He is by no means a fool."

In the event, there was no Court case. Asiaticus had a private interview with the Water Commissioner after which he publicly withdrew his candidature for the next Consuls' election. Another Senator, Sentius Saturninus, put his name forward for one of the two posts and, three months later, he got the job. Shortly after that, the world changed.

Asiaticus appeared to have lost heart. He put up his City businesses for sale and asked the Emperor's permission to retire to his estates. While he waited for a reply, he seldom left his town house. My friends in the Cohorts kept me informed.

The conclusion of the case brought me a gift and a new posting. Narcissus gave me a lightweight vest of chain links which I wore under my tunic, when I remembered. At much the same time, the Cohort posted me to the British Palace, ostensibly as a protector but actually to eavesdrop on the Celtic refugees.

CHAPTER 13

▼

ROME

Off-duty, Philip made his way to the Water Commission's office for his evening meeting with Narcissus. He carried no notes and rehearsed the points of his report in his mind as he walked the wet streets fragrant with the smells of evening meals being prepared. He turned a corner and paused in a doorway until he was fairly certain he was not being followed.

Narcissus welcomed him to the almost deserted offices. He was bathed, shaved and dressed for some evening function. A good wig made him look younger and he was in good spirits. A fine silk robe was carefully laid over his drawing board.

They sat, as before, on wooden benches, Philip with a cup of warmed wine in his hands.

"You like the robe?" Narcissus saw his interest and immediately sprang up and touched the material. "It's silk, from Palmyra. You were there. Do you recognise the weave?"

"Not in this light," said Philip, "but they do good work. As the sole suppliers they certainly inflate the price don't they?"

Narcissus smiled. "How is your father? And that monster ship of his?"

"Nearly ready but it is too late in this season. 'Cleopatra' will sail from the Red Sea in July when the prevailing winds are from the south-west. All being well, she will return from India next year at about this time when the prevailing winds will be from the north-east."

"There is a vast potential market for silk in Rome. All the young things—and the matrons—want to get their hands on it. The one barrier is the much-vaunted Roman male tradition of austerity. Show that you are wealthy by public donation, not by personal extravagance."

"Will this change?"

"It has to. You cannot exclude the female half of the population from public life and expect it to wear sackcloth and eat radishes."

Narcissus sat. "What about business in the City?"

"Bad," said Philip. "It seems that the Roman Games are no sooner over than Rome is ready for the Plebeian Games. In no time it will mid-December and time for Saturnalia. No one has time for work and no one is going to invest in a business where the workers are never available. A Senator called Asiaticus cannot even sell his businesses and they are in the City centre."

"Really?" said Narcissus, his mind seemingly on another track. "Ah, yes. Saturnalia. When I was a slave, I really enjoyed that holiday. Wearing the master's clothes and he wearing a slave's. Taking the master's place at table and being served by him and his family. It was great fun clapping our hands for more wine and telling him to get a move on. Of course with Claudius, he would enter into the spirit of the thing and protest that he was going as fast as he could with his gammy leg. He actually enjoyed it as much as we did." The freedman's brow darkened. "There are other masters, though."

"What was it like to be a slave?" said Philip, somewhat daring.

"Secure employment in a wealthy, stable, household. Very insecure in a poorer one. If times are hard, the first expense to be retrenched is a slave, with no guarantee as to the buyer. The new master might be a rich idler who just wants someone to do a little light gardening. Or, it might be the mines." The freedman shuddered slightly. "The worst thing for an intelligent slave, though, is suppressing the invention of any labour-saving devices which might result in his retrenchment."

Philip had to laugh. "Such as?"

"You laugh?" said Narcissus. "All over the greatest Empire the world has seen, administrators, officials and ordinary citizens struggle to read after dark by the poor light provided by the smelliest, soot-producing contraptions known to man. Do you imagine that no one ever invented a better oil lamp? They have. Often. Do you imagine that such an invention would be welcomed by the slave population? Never. Slaves would either have to work all night as well as all day, or they would be retrenched because they were no longer required to clean the walls and furniture in the mornings. I can assure you, my friend, that any bright, economical, sweet-smelling lamps invented will always be quickly disabled by the slaves responsible for lighting them."

"Speaking of the mines," said Philip, sobering. "The mint is complaining of inadequate supplies of new silver."

"Tax receipts are down all over and the Treasury is low, so there is not much old gold or silver for recycling. What is wrong at the mines?"

"Flooding, I hear. At least as far as the Spanish silver mines are concerned. They are now so deep that more slaves are employed on the water treadmills than there are digging the ore. They are wearing out almost before they become skilled. The slave markets cannot keep up with replacements."

"Yes," said Narcissus, sadly. "Still, Galba has the solution in his own hands."

He noted the incomprehension on Philip's face.

"Servius Sulpicius Galba is the Governor of Upper Germany, strict disciplinarian, successful soldier, well-connected and rich. He is only just over forty. We are going to hear more of him. He owns most of the Spanish mines. The legions on his part of the Rhine have just crushed that attempted German invasion of Gaul and a lot of prisoners of war will have become available for the slave market. Germans are used to cold and wet and we all know how tough they are."

Narcissus jumped up and paced around the small office. He obviously did not feel the same sympathy for German slaves as he did for others. Greek slaves for example.

"What about the Navy?" asked Narcissus.

"Two points," said Philip. "I want to thank you again for what you did for my father and our family. But junior ranks are still very bitter about the continuing practice of discharging men early to avoid granting them their full terminal benefits. At least, that is how they see it."

"That is in hand," Narcissus replied, still pacing, head down. "The changes will take a while to work through the system. The other point?"

"Senior ranks complain about the state of the Port of Ostia. It is too small, too congested and is in the process of silting up, apparently. As a gateway up the Tiber to Rome, it is said to be totally inadequate. I am preparing a written report for you."

Narcissus looked up sharply.

"Destroy it."

"Sorry?"

"Put nothing in writing. Particularly about the military. Destroy it all, notes as well."

Philip's confusion was obvious. Narcissus decided to explain.

"As far as anyone else is concerned, you and I meet because of a common interest in the silk trade. Our working lives only intersect on the level of that business. Nothing more. A certain amount of discussion on general topics would not be unexpected but you must understand that the military affairs of the

Empire—all its military affairs, down to the number of horsehair bristles in a centurion's helmet-crest—is the province of the Emperor and the Emperor alone. Our Emperor, the divine Gaius Caligula, is particularly sensitive in this regard." The freedman nodded several times in emphasis.

"Particularly sensitive," he repeated. "He has twenty six legions, hundreds of thousands of fighting men and hundreds of ships across the world. There is no separate head of the Army, no separate head of the Navy. He alone is their commander and the owner of their bases and the administrator of the provinces in which they operate. He does not like other people reporting on them."

"But…" Philip began.

"Yes. In theory he, himself, reports to the elected Senate, headed by the two Consuls. In fact, as long as the military supports him, the Emperor conducts Imperial business as he chooses."

"I see."

Narcissus looked at Philip closely and then nodded again.

"One more thing. You are valuable to me in your present position simply by reporting trends. If you start investigating to try and authenticate them, you become obvious and you will soon—ah—be lost. I have other resources which can confirm or explain the trends you pick up."

Narcissus gave his golden smile.

"So," he said. "Report to me on them. But not in writing."

CHAPTER 14

▼

ROME

Living in a house full of barbarians was not all bad. The constant noise, music, loud laughter and harsh voices, took some time to get used to. The smell of strange cooking was also odd but not unpleasant. Domitilla prevented the residents from forcing the kitchen staff to cook anything truly outrageous but she had more difficulty in preventing the British women—high born or not—from taking over the kitchen and cooking the food themselves. They all, men and women, like to drink. Fortunately so do I, and I owe my lifelong taste for beer to my duty at the British Palace in Rome. There was wine in the house but I suspect most of it went down the throats of the staff.

What was most difficult to come to terms with was their incredibly high opinion of themselves. To hear these ludicrous barbarians compare the Temple of Mars and the Forum—unfavourably, mark you—with their muddy sacred groves and the hovels of their market towns was enough to beggar description. They were dismissive of the City's water-borne sewage system and public toilets, saying that they preferred rural scenery and privacy to the straining faces of the citizens. Of Rome's mains water supply, they complained that the water tasted of the lead piping and tainted their beer. The women looked with interest at the finer fabrics but rejected silk as being too flimsy to serve even as scarves. The men passed remarks on the smaller physique of the Roman men, in all portions of their anatomy, and endlessly recalled the undeniable fact that hundreds of years ago a victorious Celtic army dictated its terms inside the City of Rome.

Once you got used to this fixation of racial superiority, and the haughtiness they frequently adopted when meeting strangers, you had to feel a bit sorry for them. Refugees they call themselves, but to their countrymen in wild Britain they were traitors. To the lowliest Roman citizen, they were nothing but barbarians and therefore, by definition, inferior.

When I reported for duty at the British Palace, there were about twenty refugees in residence, mostly men. The most senior was a white-haired old cove called Bericos, the former King of the Atrebates tribe in southern Britain. The most influential refugee, though, was undoubtedly Cogidumnos, one of his followers who went on later to great things. Alone among the male refugees, Cogidumnos shaved his upper lip and wore his hair short in the Roman style. Although the others teased him about this, they looked to him to solve their quarrels and listened to what he said.

The staff in the big house were all Roman slaves from various parts of the Empire, quite happy with the light housekeeping work they were required to do and used to receiving complicated instructions in a language they barely understood. There were no guards as such, just the usual porter at the front door and now myself and the convalescent Titus from Urban Cohort XII. An officer from the Praetorian Guard visited every week to pay out allowances, check the household accounts and bully the staff. Otherwise we were left pretty much on our own. The refugees were free to come and go as they wished but they did not go out as often as you would think. Perhaps the weight of their Roman exile and their distance from home and countrymen depressed them.

Cogidumnos wasted no time in interviewing me in the study of the house which he had taken over as his own office. He already spoke Latin reasonably well.

"You are Aurelius Victorinus, an officer in the Urban Cohorts."

"Not an officer."

"An official then. I understand you are of Celtic descent and understand our language."

Oh, well done, Titus, I thought.

"Yes. We spoke it at home near Trento when I was a child."

"Do you know that, in Britain, one of the major rivers is the Trent?"

"No."

"True. Celts or Gaels have settled across the world from Ireland to Galatia in Asia Minor. There are Celtic place names everywhere."

It was time to reassert my position in this household.

"I am a Roman, as are all the Celts between the British Isles and Galatia. I am a patrolman in Urban Cohort XII and I am here to maintain liaison between the British refugees and the Urban Cohorts."

"Because you speak the language?" Cogidumnos had not even blinked.

"That, yes." I had to smile. "And because I have just completed a major case in which my life has been threatened."

"I see. Well, I shall tell my colleagues that you speak the language to avoid any mutual embarrassment. I shall also tell them that that fact should not go any further. Your comrade, Titus, has made friends here. You will both be safe with us."

I did not believe that for a minute. Asiaticus would not forget and there are plenty of gangsters for hire in Rome.

Titus, in fact, was almost completely recovered from the beating he had received from semi-mutinous members of the Praetorian Guard. I suspected that he was not struggling as hard as he might to get back to duty and that the reason for that was the slave Domitilla. The British did not seem to make any sort of distinction between slave and free. Several of the refugees were showing a close interest in her but she showed an interest for no one other than my thick-headed friend from Etruria.

I walked Titus to the Baths most afternoons and the refugees often went too although they insisted on using their own soap rather than the oil and scrapers used by civilized men. We used popular streets and went as a group where possible.

About a week before the Plebeian Games were due to commence, our Centurion came to the British Palace with two items of bad news for me. The first was that the Cohort was short-handed due to crowd-control requirements and Titus was needed back on duty. He was ordered to be back in the Praetorian Camp by the following morning. The second was that the Senator's housekeeper had been seen visiting a gangster called Septimus, a well-known enforcer and protection specialist. I could draw my own conclusions from that.

Cogidumnos asked me what was worrying me as I had been like a ghost walking. I did not like the man overmuch but he there was no denying he was both perceptive and competent.

"This Septimus," he said. "He's a criminal? A murderer? Why is he not dead or in one of your prisons?"

I explained about his history of withdrawn complaints, disappearing evidence and forgetful witnesses.

"I see. Your colleagues in the Cohort would be able to tell you where the man is at about dusk tomorrow. Have them tell you, and you tell me, will you?"

He strolled away to talk to the other refugees.

Two days later, Septimus and his bodyguard were found dead in an alleyway. The Cohort investigated but did not detect any suspect.

That same day, Asiaticus's housekeeper was at a gambling den run by another gangster. That evening there was a brawl among the patrons and, when the gangster intervened, he was killed. Both his bouncers were seriously injured and decided to retire. The Cohort investigated the murder without success. The housekeeper did not go out much after that.

I found that I was developing a certain respect for Cogidumnos. Although I no longer felt I was under such immediate threat, I still wore Narcissus' chain-mail vest when I remembered.

CHAPTER 15

▼

ROME

Saturnalia was approaching and a bitter wind streamed through the darkening City streets as Philip hurried to his evening meeting with Narcissus. Despatches were still arriving in good time from within Italy and Senators and their staffs could therefore still maintain a steady flow of correspondence. The volume of incoming Imperial mail, however, had fallen dramatically over the past month. Military activity had been curtailed for the year and the legions had gone into winter quarters. Intelligence reports and those on supply matters were still being sent, but the flow of military operational reports and instructions had been noticeably reduced. Road links to the Imperial Provinces in the north and west had been affected. Heavy falls of snow had been reported in the passes of the Alps and the Pyrannees. The Fleets had laid up most of their vessels for refitting and those ships maintained in service for Imperial communications were now often delayed by bad weather, one had already been lost at sea.

Philip was grateful for the warm fug in Narcissus' office. Charcoal glowed in a brazier on a tripod well away from the drawing board. Narcissus laid aside yet another rolled plan and welcomed his chilled visitor. They looked at several samples of silk draped over the drawing board. Philip noticed that the freedman's balding head had been painted again, the new wig obviously too unreliable in the winter winds.

"This is not the way to inspect silk," said Narcissus. "Artificial light does not do justice to the dye."

"You haven't invented a better oil lamp, then?"

"Yes, but I immediately scrapped it," joked Narcissus. "In case lazy slaves took to reading in bed."

They sat on benches and Philip unhurriedly presented his verbal report. He had come to value these sessions. Narcissus was invariably alert and interested, sometimes seizing on items which had seemed to Philip to have been of minor importance. Obviously, Narcissus was correlating what he was being told with other fragments filed in a remarkable memory. Often, Philip gained more of an insight from what Narcissus found interesting than from what Narcissus told him.

"I had thought," said Philip, "that the Misene Fleet Detachment in Rome would have become almost dormant in winter but we seem to have become busy in a different way."

Narcissus noted the word 'we' as he nodded encouragingly.

"Sailors are still being needed to handle the weather-awnings at all sorts of public gatherings, and there are plenty of those. Additionally, the Fleet is deploying small boat crews to supplement dispatch riders as the roads grow more treacherous. On top of that, because of the first-hand information we get from ships and horsemen, we seem to be running a weather-information service for half the official population of Rome."

"Yes. I would imagine that a few officials are genuinely disappointed that the weather is preventing their travelling. Most, however, are grateful for any official excuse not to leave their warm offices." Narcissus looked around him. "Like me," he added.

"I hear a rumour from the Fleet Base at Misenum," said Philip, seriously.

"Yes?" Narcissus' attention perceptibly sharpened.

"Orders from the Fleet Prefect. Shipyard teams to concentrate on preparing several selected ships for a mid-winter voyage."

"A mid-winter voyage," Narcissus repeated. "They are going to travel together?"

"At much the same time anyway."

"Where to?"

"I don't know. One of the ships, though, is to be fitted for a very high-ranking person. I don't know who."

Narcissus gaze was intent. "But you can guess?"

"The Fleet Base Supply Division has issued an order for several bolts of purple fabric from Rome."

"The Emperor," said Narcissus, quietly.

He jumped to his feet, handed Philip his cloak and, thanking him most courteously, rapidly ushered him out of the office. Stuffing the samples into his girdle, Narcissus caught up his own hooded cloak and swept out of the building.

Claudius was having a dinner party. It had been going on since mid-afternoon and the guests were almost sated with food and wine. The musicians were tired and were trooping out of the dining room as Narcissus was admitted to the apartment by a freedman of the household. They had known one another for years.

"How is the old man?"

"He's snoring," said Pallas with a knowing look. "The party is political, Sentius Saturninus is the guest of honour. He might get the Consulship. He certainly thinks so."

Slaves came out of the wide doorway carrying the table complete with the remains of the main courses.

"Before they bring the second table in," said Narcissus urgently. "Has Claudius vomited yet? All right, get him out here. I'll be in his study."

Claudius lurched, dribbling, into his study and Pallas closed the door behind him. He looked around and straightened up, wiping his mouth with a napkin. The foodstains on the front of his clothing he left alone. His eyes appeared to focus and he gave Narcissus a little grin.

"This, I'm sure, is important. Even if it isn't, I owe you my thanks. I've never heard such pretentious drivel."

"An unconfirmed report has it that the Emperor is preparing to make a mid-winter voyage."

There was a fairly long pause. Claudius gave his chin a final swipe and threw aside the napkin.

"He's going after money, then. The Treasury's empty, public entertainments are increasing, not decreasing, and the winter won't kill off enough of the aged-wealthy to bring in much bequest money."

"But, where?"

"That's easy. He cannot touch military pay without setting off a round of mutinies which will bring him down. Even this grovelling Senate will not allow him to strip its Provinces. So, which of the Emperor's own Provinces is wealthy, and has only a relatively small military complement?"

"Yes, there is no real alternative, is there? It must be Egypt."

They changed positions. Claudius, the Emperor's despised uncle, settled heavily into his chair and clasped his hands on the desk. Narcissus strode jerkily around the study.

"What does 'mid-winter' mean?" said Claudius.

"I gather that the ships must be ready to sail by the middle of January."

"After the election of the Consuls." Claudius unclasped his hands and closed them into fists. "Sentius Saturninus must be elected."

"Right."

"Get word to our Jewish friend in Alexandria. Tell Alexander to hide his money and to spread the rumour that the corn crop next year is going to be confiscated and the Roman electorate is actually going to have to work for its porridge."

"The Egyptian peasants will love it." Perspiration was beading Narcissus' brow. "The rumour from Egypt will hit the City before my messenger gets back. There'll be riots." He paused for a long moment. "The Emperor might fall."

"Not until the he announces his journey to Egypt. Then it will seem like confirmation. And perhaps we are wrong. Perhaps that is not his intention at all. Perhaps."

Claudius lurched to his feet. At the door, he turned to the immobile freedman.

"You know, Narcissus, you're looking a little queasy. Must be something you ate."

CHAPTER 16

▼

ROME

I have always known that the Urban Cohorts of Rome are fundamentally different from the Praetorian Guards and the Fleet Detachments, even though we share the same Camp. We are responsible for—and to—the population of Rome through the City Prefect. The other military organisations are responsible directly to the Emperor.

Most policemen are conservatives by temperament, almost by definition. We approve of the established institutions of state and, generally, support the actions of its officers—even against the population—until it cannot be denied that the powers of office are being abused. Then the defence of the population against the corrupt in office is our responsibility.

The one member of the Imperial families who survived the blood-letting of recent years—only because he had no chance of election—was Uncle Claudius. I had seen him in private but, the first time I saw him trying to make a speech in public, I could not believe it was the same person. His deep voice, with its not unpleasant lisp, had gone. His head nodded and his voice stammered like a cart on cobblestones, leaving no doubt that he was totally unable to hold office and was no threat to anyone other than himself. He was not worth killing. Gaius Caligula, with very few possible successors surviving, was our Emperor.

One thing we policemen usually do not have to worry about is the protection of the person of the Emperor. The Praetorian Guard provides the formal, state protection in the shape of towering figures in silvered metal and horsehair plumes. There is also always an inner circle of personal bodyguards recruited from among the barbaric German nations. They can usually speak only German and so are difficult to subvert. Anyone trying to do so stands a very good chance of being impaled on the long narrow blades of their short-handled spears. We enforce crowd-control before—and sometimes after—the Emperor turns his Germans loose on the unarmed citizens.

One day in winter, I was chatting with the porter in his lodge at the British Palace. My Centurion was due to pay a routine visit and I was in uniform with my sword and helmet to hand. He was late, probably due to traffic problems. The morning Imperial procession to the arena frequently caused hold-ups. The street outside the porter's lodge was almost deserted and the businesses were closed for the holiday but there was the usual distant rumble of crowd-noise.

The porter paused in his story of an incredibly complicated love-life and cocked his head. I had already heard the change in crowd-sound and slipped the baldric of my sword over my head and picked up my helmet. The distant noise surged and ebbed like the waves. We stepped out into the street, leaving the main door open behind us. For a moment, nothing happened. Then a youth appeared, running easily from the direction of the arena. He had a mad grin on his face and his eyes were wide and glazed. I held up my hand but he brushed past me like a bead curtain without even a break in his stride. Over his shoulder he shouted that the Germans were killing everyone. Without comment the porter vanished into the house.

I stood irresolute in the centre of the street, my helmet in hand. The main door of the British Palace opened partially and a hand appeared, beckoning frantically to me. The porter's voice repeatedly called my name in an agitated stage-whisper. More runners appeared from down the street. Two teenage boys going like the wind, followed by a middle-aged citizen making good time on wobbly legs. He shouted to me in a breathless voice but did not stop. A young mother, clutching a baby-sized bundle, ran past crying. The sound of harsh shouts, getting closer. To hell with this.

I put on my helmet, gritting my teeth as I fastened the chinstrap. The porter ran, crouching, across the pavement and pulled on my arm as if he was trying to empty a pillowcase. I shook him off and he scuttled into cover again like a crab heading for an overhang.

Several running figures appeared, some of them turning into doorways and side streets. Only three kept coming, a young refugee girl in trousers, making for the safety of the British Palace, and two big athletic men with yellow hair and murderous intent.

She saw me in the middle of the street and her eyes fixed on mine, a small smile tightened the loose mouth and her hands started to rise from her sides towards me. Then she shuddered, her running legs becoming disorganised and clumsy, her head starting to tilt backwards. Her grey eyes held mine for a moment and then she went down on her knees, head tilting further back and her long hair dragging on the pavement, until she slid to a stop twenty paces in front of me. She slowly rolled onto her side, the spear shaft showing like an obscene panhandle in her back.

Trying not to look at the corpse, and to keep my hands still at my sides, I looked at the two pursuers as they came to a stop beside the murdered girl. They might have been brothers. Big framed and lean, their chests heaved and cheeks fluttered with exertion. From the state of their tunics and trousers they might have been workers in a family butcher's shop. Their eyes were staring and they positively had froth in the corners of their mouths. One of them had his spear poised at my chest and the other wrenched his out of the girl's back and held it like a sword. Both the blades ran red.

I drew myself to my full height. Despite the helmet, it was still considerably less than theirs. Run to an accident, walk to a fight. I took two steps forward. They tensed. I took a deep breath. Fortunately, it came out as a strangled roar and not as a squeak.

"Stop!"

They did not flinch. They did not move. If there was any reason behind those red eyes, I did not appear to be connecting with it. Keeping my hands still, and away from my sword, I tried again.

"Enough!'

They were fit, those two. Their panting was already subsiding, and was there maybe a suspicion of calm creeping back into those bearded faces? I tried again. Lowering my voice slightly, I kept it simple.

"Enough. Go back."

Greatly daring, I raised my right arm and pointed behind them. Watchful faces had appeared in doorways and around street corners.

The porter now decided to take a hand. Safe in his lodge, his indignant voice echoed into the street.

"Kill them, Aurelius!"

I froze, eyes watering, waiting for the shock of the blades in my chest.

The Germans tensed, identified the source of the new voice and peered at the tightly-closed door and open shutter. One made a feint at it with his spear and the shutter slammed shut. He coughed and wiped his beard with back of a red hand. The other looked at him and guffawed. They both chuckled briefly.

I took two careful steps towards them, allowing my shoulders to slump slightly, and spoke in a lower tone.

"Back. Go on back, now."

One of them feinted at me with his red spear. I managed not to flinch and he displayed large white teeth. The other looked at the tightly-closed shutter and said something which sounded like 'swine hound', then they both abruptly turned on their heels and began marching back down the street.

The other watchers had more brains than the porter and pulled in their heads as the Germans went past and did not provoke them.

I was glad of the chattering crowd which converged on me, people frenziedly telling one another of the part they had played in the little drama. I took the opportunity to fill my lungs again and brace my quivering knees.

"Why didn't you arrest them? You had a sword. Why didn't you arrest them?" Needless to say, perhaps, but it was the valiant porter, recently emerged from his lair.

"For very good reason you twittering little twerp," a rough and familiar voice preceded the blunt features of my Centurion as he ploughed his way through the unarmed and unsettled crowd. "The Germans obey only the Emperor and the Emperor told them to disperse the crowd. Now, I don't question the Emperor's orders, do you? I can arrange for you to meet the top German if you wish. No? Oh, very well. Get that poor girl's body off the street."

He did not have to order the crowd to disperse. It was already moving. Incredibly, some were even shakily laughing at the porter. He did not seem to have a ready reply.

The Centurion laid a heavy hand on my shoulder.

"Touch-and-go there. Again. It is going to become your nickname, son."

"What happened?"

"Emperor decided to change his route without warning and the crowd got in his way. One thing led to another. Someone shouted something he didn't like and he turned his Germans loose. Horrible mess in the City centre."

We walked into the welcome warmth of the house while the porter looked for help with the body. I was still shivering. I led the way to Cogidumnos' office and the Centurion took his chair. Other than the kitchen, the study is normally the warmest room in the house.

"Well," said my superior, settling down. "Got any wine?"

I got up again and found some in the kitchen. The staff were helping the porter. All the residents were out.

"That's better," said the Centurion as I ran the wine through the strainer into his cup. "The German barbarians kill a Celtic barbarian right front of you and your hand has almost stopped shaking. It's worked out quite well, really."

"What do you mean?"

"You have a sudden vacancy in the house and I've got a replacement on the way."

There were voices in the atrium and a sudden wail. The door burst open and Cogidumnos glared into the study.

"Which godless savage murdered King Bericos' daughter? By the great Bel, I'll crush his genitals and nail his head to the front door!"

"Good morning," said my boss, holding his wine cup with his little finger extended.

"Get out of my chair!" said Cogidumnos.

"No."

This seemed to surprise Cogidumnos. I could actually see him calming himself and reorganising his thoughts.

"You are here to investigate the murder?" He managed a fairly civil tone.

"There are a lot of murders about," said the Centurion looking him right in the eye. "This, however, was an execution. There is no court will convict a member of the Emperor's bodyguard acting on his instructions." Wordlessly, he held out his empty wine cup to me. Wordlessly, I filled it.

Cogidumnos smiled through clenched teeth.

"We will find who did it. He will die."

"So be it. The Germans, I'm told, are well able to take care of themselves. Of course, should you succeed and the Emperor finds out, he may feel that you may have abused his hospitality. I think it's possible he might get cross with you. Yes," he added with a sigh, "very possible."

The tendons in Cogidumnos' neck were suddenly quite prominent. His voice had developed a grating quality.

"What are you doing here?"

"And," said my superior, as if Cogidumnos had not spoken, "I doubt that you'll find many gangsters, even in Rome, who will want to antagonise the Germans. A rough lot, the Germans."

"What," repeated Cogidumnos, "are you doing here?"

"Ah, yes. What am I doing here?" the Centurion's frown of puzzlement disappeared and he beamed. "I'm bringing you another bar—Briton. Name of Adminius or Adminios, something like that."

"Adminios," Cogidumnos in a voice just above a whisper. "It cannot be. Yes, yes Adminios."

We were both looking at him very closely. He shook his head slightly.

"Yes. Adminios. Son of the High King, The same High King who dispossessed King Bericos and chased the rest of us out of Britain. He is a Catuvellauni is he?"

"I'm sure I don't know. He's a refugee like you, is what I know, and the Emperor's guest, like you. Any more wine in that jug? Pity. Well I must be going."

The Centurion heaved himself to his feet and stood eye-to-eye with Cogidumnos.

"I'm going to bring Adminios here now and he's going to stay here in peace. There is to be no trouble between the Emperor's guests. If there is—even a sniff of it—then Victorinus here will notify me. I will notify the Emperor and then you'll see more Germans than you might want to."

With the back of his hand, my superior gently, but apparently effortlessly, shifted the simmering Briton out of the doorway and we listened to the sound of his departing hobnails on the mosaic floor.

CHAPTER 17

▼

ROME

Claudius gathered up his research documents and notes and piled them together on a side table. His latest manuscript, full of revisions, he tossed towards the waiting household clerk, together with a list of requirements from the public records office and the public libraries. The man scurried almost silently out of his study. History was an absorbing subject but current politics was more pressing.

He draped his toga around him and shuffled in his socks onto the balcony. The cold air probed his nostrils and made his eyes water. Senator Sentius Saturninus, shown into an empty study, followed him out onto the balcony.

"We missed you at the arena," he said by way of greeting.

"Yes. I sent my apologies. A slight cold which doctor Xenaphon felt might be aggravated by long exposure to the weather." To illustrate, Claudius coughed delicately.

"Of course. I noticed Xenaphon working in the City centre. There had been a disturbance. A number of citizens needed attention and he assisted."

"A good man. I have suggested to the Senate that a proportion of the doctors practicing in the City have their tax liability reduced if they treat the poor free of charge. What do think about that?"

"It will pass. It will make someone very popular. Look, can't we go inside before I need a doctor myself?"

Seated in the study, with the doors closed, Saturninus stretched chubby, blue hands towards the brazier. Claudius pulled up another chair.

"You seem confident that the proposal for free medical services to the poor will pass the Senate. What about the Emperor?"

"I don't think he is likely to be interested. The loss in tax receipts will be small and will not be lost to the Emperor but to the Senate. As I said, it will make someone popular among the poor of the electorate. I would think that that would be the only reason it might be of interest to the Emperor. If so, he might even decide to sponsor it himself."

"The Emperor certainly does not discuss matters of state with me but I am his uncle. I can see that he is not unduly concerned with personal popularity. Except with the military, of course."

"Of course, that is his office."

"An office originally created to deal with military emergencies. A temporary office."

Senator Sentius Saturninus withdrew his warmed hands from the charcoal's glow and pulled his toga closer about him. The gesture seemed more defensive than related to warmth.

"You are a Republican, Claudius."

"Always have been. Always will be."

"You are also a historian. You know it took Rome five hundred years to fight her way to dominance of the Italian peninsular, but only another hundred to dominate the entire Mediterranean basin. The Republican form of government evolved over the five hundred years to run a city-state. It is not adequate to run the world."

Claudius cleared his throat, but the Senator pressed on.

"We need professional armies, not part-time soldiers available only when their farms don't need them. We need a single military authority, not a Consul like me taking time off from running the Senate—or even worse, both Consuls playing at soldiers at the same time with supreme authority rotating between them on a daily basis."

"You are right. I am a historian. Rome grew slowly over the centuries, with setbacks but without stopping, because of its unique ability to bring order out of any form of chaos, to absorb any kind of culture and fit it into the Roman pattern. Roman Republican institutions are founded in hundreds of years of gradual evolution and testing. The only way to eat an elephant is one mouthful at a time."

"So, you think that, with the frontiers stabilised and piracy swept from the sea, there is no real need for the office of Emperor?"

"No," said Claudius. "I'm a traditionalist. There will always be a need for the office. But there are times when it should revert to being dormant. The Senate should then take back control of the military and take over the administration of the new Provinces."

"Too late, Claudius. The Empire is suddenly so big. We have swallowed the elephant whole, and the motions of the Senate are too slow to digest it. All the consultation and debate—we can hardly solve administrative problems across such a variety of nationalities, never mind taking on the military ones. Remember, we are elected politicians with only a smattering of military expertise. I have hardly even held a sword. Have you?"

There was a resounding silence.

"Sorry," said the Senator, red-faced.

"Not at all," said Claudius genuinely. "It is refreshing when someone forgets that I am militarily challenged."

Saturninus loosened his toga. "Become warm in here all of a sudden," he said.

Claudius smiled. "How does next year's program of legislation look to a new Consul?"

CHAPTER 18

▼

ROME

There are a lot of rattling tongues and lethargic brains in the City. Rumours always seem to develop a quick currency in Rome, particularly on public holidays when everyone has a lot of time on his hands. The one surging through the lower orders in the City was that the Emperor's proposed visit to Egypt had to do with the confiscation and sale of the corn crop to replenish his empty Treasury. Everyone, not only the poor, was suddenly talking about it. No discussion as to who would pay for it. No debate as to who would buy it. I personally thought it was a lot of nonsense. If the Emperor was going to refill his Treasury and was going to Egypt to do it, rich Alexandrines had more to fear than the poor of either Egypt or Rome. I was in the minority.

I had found one of Claudius' books and was reading it in my quarters in the British Palace one morning before the official start of the day. I was fully dressed, even to my mail vest, which, as it turned out, was just as well.

Domitilla brought Titus in. He had apparently detoured on his way to his beat to try and persuade her to leave the British Palace. She was puzzled and annoyed that he was so adamant and yet so evasive as to the reason. I was not surprised. His life was always in tension between his duty to his employers and to his friends and, like all the stolid peasants in his ancestry, he could be very stubborn. Making soothing noises, I ushered Domitilla out of my bedroom and firmly closed the door. There had been many a time when I had wished that the movement had been in the reverse direction.

Titus told me that the Praetorian Camp was again in ferment, worse than before. The officers had performed their customary vanishing trick. This time, though, the guardsmen had been too quick for some of them and had cordoned the Praetorian Prefect's house. By dawn, a huge crowd of soldiers were chanting demands for him to address them.

Now, you would think that, having recently recovered from painful injuries inflicted by the Praetorian Guard for eavesdropping on one of their meetings, Titus would have clapped on his helmet and marched smartly away from the sounds of disturbance. Not a chance. My friend of the short life expectancy had crept as close as he dared to listen to what was being said.

I refrained from commenting upon his idiocy.

"Well, what were they saying, then?" I snapped.

"At first," said Titus, "it was just crowd-noise. A lot of shouts for the Prefect but he didn't appear. Not while I was there, anyway. There were a lot of coarse jokes about gods and horses and corn. Some of them quite funny."

He saw my expression and hurried on.

"And then they got into a sort of chant and that went on and on."

"What, Titus. What were they chanting?"

"Just one word over and over. 'Britain! Britain!' Like that."

We sat in the British Palace and looked at one another. If the Praetorian Guard was angry with Britain they could either march across Europe, swim the Ocean and attack the island—or they could come here. No prizes for the correct answer.

I jerked open the door and a white-faced Domitilla almost toppled into the room.

"We must get everyone away," she said with some dignity, arranging her hair.

"Where to?" I snarled. "There are thousands of Praetorians. Get Cogidumnos in here and then run, run to the Water Commissioner's office. Find a freedman called Narcissus and tell him what's happened."

"I know Narcissus." She smiled sweetly.

"Good. Then go!" I roared. She vanished like an officer of the Urban Cohorts.

"Weapons," said Titus. Given time, he does tend to secure a grip on the obvious.

"Weapons and barricades," I agreed. "Cogidumnos! Get in here."

"What," he said, "is the meaning of this uproar?"

So I told him.

I had seen him do it before. He hardly missed a beat.

"There are fifteen Britons in the house this morning. We'll see to the barricades and improvise weapons. You go and slow down that armoured mob."

"Listen. I'm in charge of your safety. If they are already on their way, the only way the two of us could slow them down is for us to be trampled underfoot.

Barricades and improvised weapons, certainly. Do that. Put the slaves and your women in the kitchen out of the way."

"British women will fight. Some of the slaves too, perhaps. The porter?"

"Tie him to the front door knob and he might. Now, Titus and I are going to leave you for a while."

"You are?"

"We are?" said Titus.

"Yes. These are Praetorians we are talking about, not elderly housebreakers. You need some proper weapons and we are going to get them."

"I see. Leave me your swords then."

"No. Without them we would be out of uniform and would never be allowed near any weapons-store."

He looked at me. I looked at him.

"Right," said Cogidumnos. "See you soon then." He strode out of the door and his shouts started echoing around the house.

The streets looked remarkably normal as we marched rapidly towards the Camp but they did get quieter as we approached the Gate. Sentries were on duty, properly turned out and alert. There was no sign of bustle or of anger.

"Are you sure, Titus?" I asked.

"Yes," he said, shortly. I believed him.

"If the Gates are guarded, sentries at other vital points will be in place. We won't be able to get into the armoury. Keep moving. If we stop, someone is going to ask us what we are doing here."

"Let's try the barracks."

There were shields in the equipment-room of our quarters but no swords. Our messmates had them on duty and there was no sign of the barrack detail. We took two shields as our excuse for returning to barracks during duty time. Then Titus remembered something. One of the sections in our block had been on a lengthy investigation together and had been granted leave at the same time. A quick scan around, followed by some swift breaking and entering, and we had eight perfectly serviceable swords. We took only three each, tied them tightly together with their baldrics and fastened them to the handgrips inside our shields. The shields were now especially heavy and unwieldy but we were used to practice shields during weekly sword drill and thought we could manage.

We would have left Camp without question had not the guard commander seen a senior officer approaching from the City as we were about to leave. He decided to publish his efficiency by loudly demanding why we were equipped with shields. I was explaining about fictitous crowd-control duties when an even louder voice shocked him into rigidity.

"Where is the Prefect," boomed Rufrius Pollio as he strode into the gateway.

"He has not left by this Gate, sir, but I do not believe he is in the Camp."

"Find out." Pollio turned on Titus and I. "What are you doing idling about my Gate? Get about your duties!"

He must have recognised me, but not by a twitch did he acknowledge it. We rapidly got about our duties.

Cogidumnos was actually out on the street keeping watch for us, his hand clamped on the porter's shoulder. Once inside, with the main door barred, Cogidumnos led the way to the study. The rooms were darker than I had seen them in the daylight before, as all the shutters were closed. Plenty of light still came into the centre of the house where the atrium opens to the sky.

King Bericos was sitting in the study, the axe from the woodpile lying on the desk in front of him. He was looking pleased at the prospect of a brawl. Several of his senior people were there, armed with a variety of kitchen knives and gardening tools. Adminios had been unable to squeeze his way in. Space was made for us, however, and Titus and I thankfully shed the heavy shields and swords. Faces brightened all round. Cogidumnos directed a rapid re-organisation of weapons, pointedly leaving out Adminios. I had to insist that Adminios received one of the swords.

Most of the slaves had refused to be armed. Considering the penalties under Roman law for slaves found with weapons, this was not too surprising. There are also heavy penalties for anyone offering to provide slaves with arms, but we were beyond the point of worrying about that.

There was a shout from almost overhead. Bericos' elder daughter had been made to perch on the rafters under the roof. I was given a leg up through a hole broken in the ceiling and squatted next to her, the woodwork creaking alarmingly. She displayed very white teeth in the hot, musty, gloom. Another one looking for a fight, and, judging from the fearsome pruning hook hanging next to her perch, she was prepared. She shifted a tile from in front of us and a bloom of daylight illuminated clear, pale skin, bright green eyes and dark auburn hair. I was conscious of the clean, sweaty, woman-smell very close.

Concentrating, I looked out through the sloping roof. Because of the angle, not much of the small rear herb-garden could be seen but there were definitely helmeted heads bobbing outside the rear wall. I shouted a warning to Cogidumnos and there was a scramble from below.

The helmets grouped together behind the wall. No plumes or crests and the shape of them was wrong for Praetorian Guards. Suddenly Domitilla rose from amongst the helmets as if she were levitating and, with a flutter of long skirts and longer legs, she landed in the garden. Titus must have been watching from the rear of the house for she was plucked inside almost as she landed.

Titus shouted that Domitilla had brought reinforcements arranged by Narcissus. Men from the Urban Cohort meanwhile started to drop heavily into the garden. Several of them helped the bulky figure of our Centurion to alight with some dignity.

My companion seemed almost disappointed that armed help had arrived. She told me her name was Scota. It was with some reluctance that I descended into the office and brushed dust from my clothes. The arrival of the Centurion and our colleagues settled the outcome of the defence of the British Palace. However, it was only mid-morning.

"Yes," said the Centurion, tiredly. "Yes. I should have known. Victorinus at it again. Why can't you skulk in the back of a bakery and eat fresh bread like all the other patrolmen. No, I don't want your report on the situation, I'll get it from Cogi—whatsis. You listen to what this young lady has to say." He indicated with a thumb.

I managed to pry Domitilla away from Titus. They weren't touching but their eyes seemed invisibly connected. It was not a verbal message she had, but a written one and it was from Narcissus. He was a model of brevity but short on specifics. I was to go immediately to the Theatre, assess the situation there, and report in person at the Water Commissioner's office. The Centurion released Titus as well and we departed like small boys over the back wall.

There was no one in the service lane at the rear of the houses and no sign of any bloodthirsty Praetorians when we turned into the street. We noticed passers-by looking at us, members of the Urban Cohorts in a hurry, so we reduced our pace to a routine saunter, blending into the street scene.

Whatever our outward appearances, though, I, at least, felt pressure building as we paced towards the Theatre. The performances should have already started and the Emperor would be present. He usually was. That meant a substantial body of Praetorians in attendance as well as a team of the Emperor's personal bodyguards with their short, sharp spears. In addition, not very far away, a crowd-control unit of the Urban Cohorts would be waiting.

Praetorians were in evidence on the approaches and we were stopped by a nervous junior officer just short of the Theatre. I did not like the way his eyes kept sliding away from my face. With as much confidence as I could muster, I told him that we were from the City Prefect's office, sent urgently to investigate a report of the scene-changing machinery backstage being in a dangerous condition. He told us to come back tomorrow. No, I told him, the collapse of the machinery was reportedly imminent. But, the performances had already started, he said. Then we would wait for the lunch break, I told him. No, no, he protested, that was impossible. He was now looking actually frightened. If the machinery breaks down during the performance, I intoned, the Emperor might storm out looking for a culprit.

I remember wondering where they recruited Praetorian officers. Some noble lady's little darling, no doubt. I remember also the impression that he was more concerned that the Emperor might leave early than that he might be identified as the culprit. I should have thought more about that. Wide-eyed, he glared about, looking for advice. There was none.

"Very well," he said, taking a deep breath. "The Emperor must not be disturbed. Follow me and keep it quiet." He led us down a guarded, covered way into the backstage area. I had to snarl quietly at Titus to make him take a silly grin off his face.

The dressing rooms were crowded with actors in make-up and exaggerated costumes, many of them smelled as if they had not bathed for weeks. Nearer the stage, harassed stage-hands twisted through the throng. There were even some sailors, handling the ropes, pulleys and winches controlling scene-changes. An actor boomed on-stage. We made a considerable show of checking the stability of scenery and of the condition of the machinery to handle it. I let Titus take the lead, striding about, issuing instructions in a hoarse whisper and pushing people out of the way, the Praetorian officer fluttering about behind. I got behind the backdrop and tried to find a hole to look into the auditorium. I could not find one. Time was pressing and I fumbled for my knife.

"No need for that," said a voice next to me, making me jump. "There."

It was a fair-haired sailor who looked familiar. I found the hole he indicated and looked out beyond the actor into the banks of seats facing the stage. There was a peculiar quality to the light out there and I judged that the canvas awnings had been stretched out over the seats in case of rain. All the seats were occupied. In the centre of the lowest tier, a young man sat at his ease amongst cushions on the stone seat. His neighbours on either side leaned slightly in towards him. The purple splashed on his clothes and the circlet around his forehead confirmed to me that I was looking at our Emperor. High up behind him, figures moved in the gloom of the awnings, more sailors, perhaps, or restless German bodyguards.

"Come away," the junior officer was tugging on my sleeve. "Enough. You are going to leave now. Now. It is nearly lunchtime."

Titus had got hold of a wax tablet and a stylus from somewhere and had inscribed an impressive list which he was studying with pursed lips. The man was a natural. The Praetorian grabbed hold of his sleeve with his free hand and we allowed him to begin to tow us back towards the dressing rooms. It was too late. The declamation on stage ended abruptly in a spattering of applause and the actor, passion still in his eyes, swept off-stage. The winches started to clatter and the ropes groan, the light from front of house faded as the curtain rose. More Praetorians appeared and began pushing stage-hands out of the way and evicting actors from the dressing room area, clearing a route to the covered way we had used to enter the Theatre. Our escort was in a quandary. He had a policeman in each hand and nowhere to go.

"This was not supposed to happen," said the sailor in my ear. "The Emperor was supposed to leave from the front."

I glared about but could not see where the danger was coming from. Several Senators climbed up to the stage and headed for the covered passage at the rear. One of them lurched along with his head nodding. Uncle Claudius in his public role. He was with the new Consul, Sentius Saturninus. Our Praetorian seemed to have gone into some form of shock. In the middle of that surging back-stage crowd, he stood stock-still, mouth hanging open, with his bony fists locked on the material of our sleeves. Moments later, the young Emperor appeared back-stage, almost dwarfed by the Guards' officers escorting him. They bustled into the covered way. More Praetorian officers slammed the door behind them and put their backs against it. They drew their swords.

"Assassination," I said, and tore my sleeve from Praetorian grasp. The junior officer tried to hang onto Titus and got his features imprinted on a wax tablet. A terrible scream echoed from within the covered way. The Praetorian guards flinched but their swords did not waver. Several actors screamed in sympathy. The sailor grabbed my arm and I nearly struck him.

"No," he said. "There's no way through here. Out the front. Over the stage."

I used my sword on the curtain but the fabric was tough and my sword was double-edged. I could not get sufficient purchase to rip a big enough hole. There was fighting now in the wings. Titus and I gripped either side of the hole I had jabbed in the curtain and tore it apart. The auditorium was virtually empty. Several bodyguards were dropping down the tiers of benches towards the stage. A Senator coughed and kicked among the discarded cushions and half-eaten fruit.

I got clear of the curtain with Titus right behind me. The sailor also got free but the press of frantic people behind impeded individual escape. The curtain bulged with arms, legs and heads writhing in the torn opening like some netted sea creature.

A German officer gave an echoing shout in a language I could not understand, he had decided that there was no quick way to the Emperor through the Praetorians at the stage. His men would have to go around the outside of the Theatre. A spear, thrown in frustration, struck sparks off a stone seat and spun over my head. There was a yelp of pain behind me but no time to look. I followed the half dozen German bodyguards in their rush for the exit.

Running out into broad daylight, we entered an extraordinary scene. A fruit-seller, who had obviously got in the way of the Germans, lay dying, but the unarmed Roman crowd of Theatre-goers, food-sellers and shop-keepers had not fled from the German onrush. Had the bodyguards charged straight into the crowd, they might have carved their way through but, confused, they hesitated. Our appearance behind them created a sensation in the crowd; apparently two members of their Urban Cohorts, supported by a representative of the Fleet, had chased the dreaded Germans out of the Theatre.

That was the spark. With a scream and a roar the crowd surged forward, knives glinting, stones and fruit and roof tiles appeared to take flight and rain down on the bodyguards. Their officer tried to gather his men, inflated his chest to shout an order but a thrown brazier of glowing charcoal emptied over his head and shoulders. One of the Germans, arms red to the elbows, tried to run back into the Theatre where Titus and I took him down.

We worked our way round the hacking, stamping crowd, the sailor and I having to actually pull the over-excited Titus away Free of the crowd, we ran for a short distance and turned into a smelly alleyway where we paused for breath. I noticed for the first time that the sailor appeared to be wearing a red scarf.

"I'm all right, I'm all right", he said between gasps.

Titus propped him against a dirty wall and examined his throat. I peered out of the mouth of the alley. The street was totally deserted but there was the distant tramp of an organised unit on the move.

Time for some housekeeping. I sheathed my sword. My shoes were still properly done up. I retied my loin-cloth which was about to part company with me, tugged down my tunic and tightened the girdle. My nipples were sore from the rubbing of the mail-vest but there was nothing I could do about that except to throw it away, and this did not seem to be the time. I wiped most of the sweat from my brow and from the leather lining of my helmet, put it back on and re-fastened the chin-strap. I drew my sword again and was almost as good as new.

"He is all right," said Titus. "Lost part of his ear and a few cupfuls of blood. He'll be fine."

"I'm Philip," said the sailor, who did not look as confident of his condition as Titus' cheerful diagnosis suggested. I must have looked blank because he went on with some emphasis, "I work for Narcissus. I've seen you there."

I looked at Titus who was wiping his forehead with a torn sleeve. I opened my mouth but Titus raised a finger. The sound of marching feet echoed in the street and a rasping voice penetrated the noise. We involuntarily straightened up.

Files of the Urban Cohorts' crowd-control unit bobbed past the end of the alleyway, eyes wide and jaws compressed by tightly-fastened helmet straps, they marched towards the sound of rioting. Their centurion marched beside them, half the age and half the bulk of our old boy. I did not recognise him. He looked straight at us but he had more on his mind than a few stray patrolmen. His rasping tones faded with the sound of marching feet.

"They'll be too late for the Germans," said Titus musingly. "Fancy dying at the hands of a rabble of townsmen, far from your homeland, knowing that you have just failed your boss."

"Woden will not be pleased with them," said the sailor, Philip, with some satisfaction. He wound a scarf around his head.

"We'll postpone philosophical discussions on death and German gods. I agree that the Emperor is probably dead."

"Got to be," said Titus, in no way put down. "It wasn't the Praetorian officers screaming in that tunnel."

"So, Narcissus must be told," I finished.

"Never mind about Narcissus," said Titus forcefully. "What about Uncle Claudius?"

We looked at each other, in that alley, for what seemed like a long time. Claudius had been on his way to lunch, probably at the Palace although possibly at Consul Sentius Saturninus' house. There were other German Imperial bodyguards at the Palace as well as a considerable contingent of the Praetorian Guard. If Claudius was not at the Palace, it would not take long for them to work out where he was, and then they could either kill him as the assassinated Emperor's uncle or…or what? Or perhaps they could make him Emperor. It was not as if there were many obvious candidates around.

I gave my knife to Philip; he had lost his somewhere, and I persuaded him to go and find Narcissus. He sidled out of the alley as if glad to get moving and departed without a word. Titus and I set off for the Palace.

Why did we do it? Claudius was old, at least fifty. He was crippled and defenceless. There were plenty of reasons for us to simply lie low until it was all over. But, we were policemen. Also, there might be fame and promotion in it. It was early afternoon.

At first we were cautious but the streets were deserted and crowd noise had died away completely. All the doors and shutters I noticed were tightly closed. There was no smell of food cooking and no smoke from the baths. A few withered cabbage leaves stirred in the cold breeze. We stepped out more confidently in the wider streets but we kept our hands on our weapons.

"What are we going to do when we get to the Palace?" asked Titus sensibly.

"I've been thinking about that. My considered conclusion is that I have absolutely no idea."

The Palace appeared to be as deserted as the streets outside. A few bundles stacked at the foot of the steps could be identified, even at a distance, as the remains of more bodyguards. We mounted the steps with an appearance of confidence, expecting at any moment to be challenged. There was no challenge, no sentries, not even a porter. The main doors, under the overhanging roof, stood open on their pintles. We stood just inside the doors and listened. The Palace is vast and we could hear a number of voices, as if in debate, at a great distance. Titus, the chronic eavesdropper, wanted to move closer. I wondered how to locate Claudius' apartment in the complex. We compromised on a decision to try to locate the kitchens in order to collar a servant who would know his way about.

We walked quietly through that huge building trying unsuccessfully to look either as if we were its owners or as if we were two of the full-length portraits on the walls. Whichever way we went, it seemed that we were getting closer to the source of many voices, and some laughter, rising and falling in argument.

Suddenly, a figure flitted across an open doorway and Titus was after him, dashing through the opening before he had even got his sword properly out of his scabbard. The fugitive was too clever for Titus. Truth be told, he was too clever for both of us. As I hurled myself at the entrance, dragging at my sword hilt, the little man, who had taken cover just inside the doorway, launched himself out and we met head on. I had an instant to register a sharp weapon coming at me before a tremendous shock in the centre of my chest rattled my teeth and blurred my vision. I clutched a handful of his clothing as I went over and he swayed and staggered as he tried to maintain his momentum, dragging my weight across the marble. Titus caught up and felled him with a heavy punch to the back of the head. Thankfully, I released his clothing and examined the damage.

The mail vest had done its job. Several links were flattened and fused and I was going to have a huge bruise in the centre of my chest but, otherwise, no harm done. I coughed a couple of times.

"Titus," I croaked. "If you don't release his throat, he can't tell you who he is."

"I'm Pallas," snuffled the fugitive. His nose was bleeding from contact with the floor. "I'm a freedman in Claudius' household."

"Just the man we're looking for. What do you mean attacking my friend without provocation?"

"What do you mean chasing after me with swords?" Pallas responded indignantly. I could see that this was not going anywhere.

"Where's Claudius?" I managed to interrupt.

"Praetorians have got him," said Pallas. "Scores of them. In the Emperor's reception room. They are deciding what to do with him."

I was astonished to see tears in his eyes. I put it down to the pain in his nose.

"Can we get him away?"

"I don't think so. I couldn't get close. They've put sentries out. Why do you want to get him away?"

"We are friends. We've sent for Narcissus."

"Oh, good. We must move. Narcissus will go straight to the apartment."

I left Pallas and Titus at the apartment and crept towards the sound of the on-going debate. I had my sword out this time and massaged my chest with my free hand. I supposed that, during a normal day, the Palace would be all laughter, light and bustle. That particular afternoon, it seemed a place of dread and menace. The occasional echoing laughter, growing louder as I approached, did nothing to alleviate the sense of foreboding that seemed to hang about the statues and wall-portraits. The laughter itself was harsh and derisory.

The scrape of a hobnail in the shadow of a pillar warned me of the presence of one of the sentries seen by Pallas. I shrank against the wall. It seemed excessively dark even for a winter's afternoon. The interaction of many voices had ceased and a single voice droned for a while. Suddenly there were several loud shouts which made me jump and my blade pinged on a statue next to me. Laughter and a rising chorus of cheers drowned the noise and double doors burst open and a disorderly column of Praetorian Guards poured out. One of its members seemed twice as tall as the others and nearly struck its head on the door lintel. In a moment I realised that, carried on the shoulders of two ordinary-sized guardsmen, was none other than a very pale, but composed, Uncle Claudius. As the procession turned towards his apartment, I fled through the shadows ahead of them.

I burst into the apartment just ahead of the noisy soldiers. White faces turned towards me. Narcissus was there, Titus with his hand on his sword, Pallas poised for flight again and a man in a bandage whom I recognised as Philip. I reassured them as quickly as I could while making for hiding, Titus and Philip close behind. Narcissus stopped us before we got out of sight.

"Wait," he said, "wait."

The apartment door burst open again and the room seemed filled with armour and horsehair. We were all told to identify ourselves by a burly, red-faced officer. When it got to our turn, Narcissus smoothly intervened and told him that Titus and I were personal guards allocated to Claudius by the City Prefect, if you please. Claudius was lowered to his unsteady feet. He braced himself and made a neat speech of thanks. Narcissus distributed money and Pallas, all smiles, held open the door and bowed out the noisy visitors one by one. We all then barred the door except for Narcissus who walked his master straight through to the main bedroom.

Titus, again showing his firm grasp of essentials, pointed a finger at the other freedman.

"Pallas, right?"

"Yes."

"Wine."

"All right."

We drank two or three cups of wine, which seemed to have no effect whatsoever, and sat slackly on the heavy furniture. It was early evening and, in the absence of any other staff, Pallas bestirred himself and started lighting lamps.

Narcissus reappeared, swallowed once or twice, and announced, quite quietly.

"Tiberius Drusus Nero Germanicus Claudius, Emperor-designate of Rome."

Claudius had washed his face and combed his hair. He had put on a plain white toga and had composed himself. It did not matter that he needed a shave. We all did.

I said, "Congratulations, sire," and, of course, he immediately took me up on it.

"No-one is Emperor until appointed by the Senate. I am nominated but not appointed."

I said, "No, sire," with a bit more emphasis. I began to wonder if he could manage it. He looked hard at me without replying, then he settled heavily in a chair facing the door and placed his large hands on his knees. They were not trembling. He nodded to Narcissus who licked his lips and began.

"There will be a Senate debate tomorrow morning in which nominations for the office of Emperor will be considered and an appointment made. It is conceivable that the Senate might decide that it will govern without an Emperor. But it is not likely. The City is in a ferment, the Praetorians will make their wishes known, and the rest of the military has become used to having a single supreme commander. Our patron's name will be the first but not necessarily the only nomination. He has the support of the Praetorians and his family…"

"Narcissus," said Claudius. "There is not much time."

"Yes. We have a lot to do tonight before the debate. Nothing is settled yet. We need to consolidate and there is no way back. If anyone else receives the Senate appointment, someone like our friend Senator Asiaticus for example, we will all be too dangerous as competition to survive."

That was a sobering thought if we needed one. I looked around at the others. The middle-aged candidate, born in Gaul, two Greek ex-slaves, Philip from Egypt and two policeman, one of whom, at least, was part Celtic; we had to make history.

"Now," said Narcissus, "several powerful men will take the risk of pledging their support before the Senate makes its decision. It suits us and it suits them as it may lead to Imperial patronage, but first they have to know the position and, at this moment, they do not. Philip!"

The injured sailor sat upright.

"Get cleaned up and take these letters to the Consul Sentius Saturninus and to Governor Galba. The Governor is in the City for the Consuls' inauguration and is still here. Saturninus will know where he is. Then go to the Fleet Communications offices, we need to know what messages are going out on the military network. When you get there, use whatever method you see fit to get word of the present situation to Rufrius Pollio of the Praetorian Guard. He may not be up-to-date. Pallas!"

The freedman did not flinch. He had been in politically dangerous positions before.

"The Emperor-designate's wife must be informed. Take this to the lady Messalina; she can mobilise support." Narcissus did not look at Claudius but I saw Pallas look quickly at him. His face was impassive.

Narcissus pressed on.

"The City is dangerous and these messages must reach our supporters. Titus and Aurelius, you escort Pallas and Philip to their destinations and bring Pallas safe back here."

"No," I said.

"No?" said Claudius, sharply.

"No, sire," I repeated. "Titus and I stay here. The Praetorians have just killed one Emperor and only a hundred or so have declared for you. They could still change their minds, kill you, and no one would be the wiser. There are many other Praetorians we haven't heard from yet and the bas—soldiers could do anything."

"On top of that," added Titus. "What about the Germans? There are bound to be some survivors skulking in the Palace, looking for a target."

"But what about Pallas and Philip? They need escorts." The Imperial candidate sounded almost plaintive.

Without making too much of a fuss about it, I unbarred the door and swung it open, startling the two Praetorians who were preening themselves outside.

"You!" I barked at them.

"Me?" asked the intelligent one.

"Yes, you. Go get your officer."

The burly red-faced officer strutted, bareheaded, into sight. He opened his mouth to speak. I did not give him a chance. I pointed at the two immaculate guardsmen.

"These two. Slovenly, dirty, half-asleep. Replace them. While you are at it, detail appropriate escorts for two Imperial messengers. Now. Knock when you are ready."

I slammed the door on his stunned face. I listened at the panel. There was a prolonged silence, then a muffled word of command, marching feet and distant shouting.

I heard strange sounds behind me. The Imperial candidate was making a wheezing noise, tears squeezing out of the corners of his eyes. Narcissus gave me the benefit of his entire golden bridgework and the others laughed uncontrollably. I felt my own stomach muscles relax. It was hysteria perhaps.

"Slovenly, dirty..." repeated Titus, and then went off into a gale of laughter.

There was a quiet knock on the door. The officer stood there, helmet on. A file of guards stood rigid in the background. Narcissus gently intervened.

"Very well," he said. "The messengers will be ready shortly. Now be so good as to find the servants and send them in."

The officer looked over Narcissus shoulder towards Claudius sitting regally at the end of the room. He drew himself up and saluted. Claudius nodded distantly.

"The servants?" hissed the officer at Narcissus. "Where will I find your servants?"

"I don't know," said the freedman, airily. "You chased them away. You find them." And he closed the door again.

"Before you go," I said to Pallas and Philip. "We need reinforcements, not to mention a change of clothing."

"Especially underwear," said Titus, with a grin.

"After you have been to the lady Messalina, would you go to the British Palace, do you know it?" Pallas nodded. "There is an Urban Cohort detachment there. Tell the centurion what is happening. You can trust him."

"He can organise reliable armed men I'm sure," agreed Pallas, "but can he get them into this building? The Praetorians are very touchy about things like that."

"They won't allow Urban Cohort members into the Palace, but they will not refuse entry to lictors escorting one of Rome's Consuls." I turned to Philip but did not need to say anything further.

"I'll arrange it," he said. "I'm sure that it won't be the first time that swords have been hidden in their rods of office."

And so, during that night, they came to offer their respect and support. Household staff reappeared, including, thankfully, a barber. Pallas returned, mission accomplished. Rufrius Pollio diplomatically pleaded that the assassins be spared and that the restoration of the Praetorian Guards' prestige should be an Imperial priority. The politician, Sentius Saturninus, arrived with some pomp and told Claudius emphatically, in private, that the Senate would indeed appoint an Emperor and he better hope that it was Claudius. When the Consul left, he was escorted by four lictors fewer than he had arrived with. The arrival of reinforcements from Urban Cohort XII in disguise was as welcome as the clean uniforms they brought.

It was about midnight, while I was snatching a bath, that Titus managed to prevent the Praetorians from hacking to pieces a haggard, unarmed German who presented himself at the door. He, with his surviving comrades, was pardoned by a visibly drooping Claudius. We were not done yet, however.

A few hours before dawn, a fierce, little man arrived. He had bulging eyes, a flattened nose and bandy legs and was, by no means a figure of fun. Servius Sulpicius Galba was then about forty three, the Governor of Upper Germany, the suppressor of more than one army mutiny and the crusher of a German invasion of Gaul. In his own right he was a millionaire and, fortunately for us, related to Claudius through their common grandmother, Livia, wife of the first Roman Emperor. As a soldier, he was renowned as both a trainer and a leader of troops. He, if anyone, could speak for the legions, the real backbone of any Emperor's authority. Titus saluted him elaborately, and so did I. He looked at me so closely, I was glad I had had time for a shave.

Claudius and Galba left the room, followed by Narcissus. In a moment, the freedman was back and beckoned to me. They were in the study, Claudius sitting behind the desk, Galba leaning against the wall. We stood erect.

"I am not a candidate," Galba was saying. "You are older, better connected and even uglier than me. You must be Emperor." Claudius was nodding dolefully.

"And the legions?" he asked.

"The legions in Upper Germany will declare for you," said the Governor, decisively. "My colleagues' legions in Lower Germany also, without question. Your brother is still remembered there. I believe that you can probably count on those on the Danube as well. Governor Aulus Plautius is a kinsman of your first wife. No hard feelings over the divorce, I understand?"

"No," said Claudius, still looking mournful. "It was political."

Narcissus looked at me with controlled delight. The legions on the Rhine and the Danube comprised the bulk of the army in the west.

"As far as the east is concerned," the Governor continued in his clipped, military manner, "I do not know about the legions there, but all soldiers who have been in the orient know about dynasties. They may prefer for the appointment to be made within a family which has experience of Imperial duties." He paused. "The army will, almost certainly, support your candidature."

"So the legions will probably support me," Claudius said, without obvious pleasure. "What do you think about the auxilliaries and the fleets?"

"What about the auxilliaries and the fleets? There are very few in them who are citizens. They have no political clout and, if any unit gives trouble, my ruffians in the legions would be very happy to sort them out. Oh, come on, Claudius, it's no good sitting there with a face like a spavined donkey. The Republic is gone. It's never coming back. Take control of the Empire. After all, what is the alternative?"

Claudius was obviously very tired but he straightened his back and re-draped his toga.

"Say I get appointed," he said. "What will the army expect of me, other than the usual cash bonus."

"An Emperor's job is to lead the forces of Rome in a glorious, and if at all possible, a successful, war. Preferably it should end in an expansion of the Empire. New resources for Rome. More land to settle time-expired soldiers."

"You have somewhere in mind." It was not a question from Claudius. I was trying not to be noticed.

"Not Germany," said Governor Galba. "I have been there long enough to know that the further you go into Germany, the more forests there are and the more Germans there are in them. I could never get my veterans to settle there after discharge and there is little enough of value to confiscate. The Danube command is in a similar position. In the east, you don't want to fight for a desert and simply provoke the Persians. To the south, in Africa, there is only desert and mountains beyond what we already hold."

"Britain," said Claudius, slyly, "has silver, I'm told."

"Which your mints badly need, and, yes, I would be interested in some of the Imperial contracts which would flow from a successful invasion. More than that, though, reputations are at stake here. Yours, your late nephew's, the army's, even the Praetorian Guard's. They all need to be made or repaired. Militarily, it will be an invasion of a region with clearly defined limits where no other forces can easily intervene. There is every chance that it will succeed."

"You would command the invasion force?"

"Absolutely not," said Galba briskly. "The objective is to consolidate your position, not mine. You will command."

"As you well know, I have no military experience. None."

"You know, for a historian, you haven't learned much from history. Times have changed. Emperors do not have to do the actual fighting any longer. There are plenty of experienced military men, with reputations to be made, who will clamour to do that for you. I will help you choose one and draw up a plan for him. You do know which end of a sword is the sharp bit? Well, there you are then."

Claudius laughed a little and then nodded.

"Britain it is, then."

"Good," said Governor Galba, with satisfaction, turning the glare of his round but not unfriendly eyes on me. "Which is why I asked for this young man to be present. Our Emperor has spoken of your exploits. Tell us about the personalities of the people at the British Palace."

CHAPTER 19

▼

BRITAIN

High on the windswept downs of south-east Britain, a chief of the Cantii sat on the tailgate of a halted chariot and fed her baby. Ena was in her mid-twenties but had married late and had only one other child, a boy of about six who sat next to her on the tailgate. Huddled in mutual comfort in the lee of her cloak, she looked south to the distant gleam of the Ocean. They had turned off the road behind them onto a relatively open stretch of grassy chalk. Segonax, a light bandage tied around his head, more as a reminder than as serious protection, cut and bent small bushes to create a tiny shelter. He dusted his hands and stood up.

"All finished, ma'am." Segonax was a chief's son himself but had been well brought up. Ena gently disengaged from the baby, who was nearly asleep, and slid off the tailgate. Taking her son by the hand, she went to Segonax and installed the baby, on her cloak, inside the shelter, with the little boy as its serious guardian. Segonax swung his cloak over the shelter and secured it to the thin branches. They straightened and looked at the simple course Segonax had marked with two saplings jabbed into the chalk.

"I do know the basics of driving, you know," she said. "My charioteer sometimes lets me drive."

"Well, yes," said Segonax politely. "The uneven ground distracted you last time. Had it been a tree you hit, you would have lost a wheel. This will be different. I've put out those two stakes. I want you to drive around them, turning left at the first one, right at the second one, left again at the first one, and so on"

"That sounds simple."

"Only one thing to remember. Do not turn as soon as the horses' heads pass the stake. Only turn when the chariot wheel is level with it."

"I know that."

"Good. Give it a try. Not too fast."

Ena stepped onto the platform and gathered the reins. Segonax stripped the hobbles from above the horses' knees and stood back. Ena awkwardly turned the horses to face the course. They sensed her uncertainty and became uneasy. With her tongue showing in the corner of her mouth, she looked at her sixteen year old instructor. He tied the hobbles round his waist and nodded encouragingly. She flapped the reins and the chariot began to move, axle squeaking faintly. At the first stake, she watched intently until the wheel drew level and then hauled on the left hand reins. The horses were surprised by the degree of force transmitted to their mouths and one gave a little bob. The chariot trundled close, but safely, around the first stake.

"Well done. Keep it going. Not too hard on their mouths."

She went around the second stake in a wide, right-handed turn and lined the team up on the first stake again. She had slackened the reins and the horses were now uncertain of her intentions. They, very slowly, walked over the first stake and flattened it.

"Don't worry. Keep going. I'll put it back." Segonax was sticking the sapling back into the ground when suddenly he turned and ran for the shelter. Ena jerked the surprised horses to a halt and ran after him.

Segonax had the red-faced little boy in his arms when Ena reached him.

"It's all right, it's all right," he soothed. "This brave boy thought he saw a wolf. It was actually a fox and it quickly ran off when he shouted, didn't it boy?"

They made admiring noises and replaced the diminutive guardian with the sleeping baby. They went back to the chariot and grazing horses.

The morning wore on. Ena was trembling with the strain of guiding the team around the saplings. Segonax felt he was going mindless with boredom.

"All right," he said. "I think you have got that. Bring them over here. We'll try something else." He was standing next to a wide, shallow depression in the chalk "Now, when you take your chariot over a shallow ditch, you must remember two things. Approach it at right angles if you can. Less chance of turning over. And, most important, remember that, when the horses climb out of the ditch on the far side, they think that their job is done. They relax at the very time when they must exert maximum effort to pull the chariot out. Be ready to flick the reins the moment they are up on the other side. Right, try that."

Ena did as she was instructed and the chariot rolled smoothly through the depression. She turned to smile at Segonax, but he had gone. He was running hard for the shelter, perhaps not quite as hard as the first time.

This time, though, he came back with a tall, unkempt stranger walking in front of his drawn sword. Ena had her own sword out as she ran up.

"The children are all right," shouted Segonax. "This man has news."

"I'm sorry, lady," said the man in a foreign accent. "I did not see the children until I nearly stumbled onto them."

"My cloak had blown off," confirmed Segonax.

"Who are you? What news?" demanded Ena.

"I need to speak to Ceri urgently. I'm from over there." He nodded in the direction of the sea. "I believe he is an important man in this area. Do you know him? Where is he?"

"I am a chief, this is a chief's son. You can speak to us."

"Yes. I can see that from your clothes and jewelry. And that vehicle."

"What news?" Ena put her sword away.

"Well. There is some activity at their old embarkation port that I will discuss in detail with him, but there is another thing. Everyone will know shortly. The Roman Emperor is dead. Murdered by his guards, apparently."

"I do not think that anyone in Britain is going to be pleased about that. What about a successor?"

"Already elected. His uncle, a man called Claudius."

"Claudius?" exclaimed Segonax. "But they say the man's a drooling idiot!"

"These Romans," said Ena dismissively. "We'll take you to Ceri. I'll get the children. Segonax, you will drive, please."

CHAPTER 20

▼

EUROPE

More than the unfamiliar scent of the sea, it was the lack of noise that woke Camp Commandant Anicius Maximus, third in command of Legion II Augusta. He knew immediately that he was no longer in the midst of his five and half thousand beloved armoured infantrymen nor about the same number of non-citizen auxiliaries which, together, made up the command he had left behind in Germany.

Instead, he looked at the moisture beading the underside of the leather roof of his tent and felt the cool air swirling over his half-closed eyelids. He automatically excluded the careful shifting of the sentry in the doorway and the quiet rasp of brickdust on metal outside, and relished the silence. In his twenty years of service, the one constant was not danger nor excitement nor even comradeship, it was noise. Noise on the drill square, on the march, in the battle line and, always, in camp. Until now.

Luxuriously, he stretched. Aches, and the occasional pain, in joints and limbs could not, unfortunately, be attributed to honourable battle injuries. For his age and length of service, he had remarkably few wounds. Scars on his right forearm, above the level of a wristguard, indicated that he was a right-handed infantryman accustomed to going into battle with shield and short, stabbing sword. Thin, white, horizontal scars on his forehead were from his helmet rim, mementoes of crushing blows absorbed by his helmet and skull in his front-line days. Otherwise, he had sustained no significant wounds. Any permanent physical discomfort was age-related arthritis, aggravated by the drear cold of Germany.

Well, this was not Syria, where he had been born, and it was not Germany either. It was spring and he was in Gaul. Nearby, beyond the unseen sea, was

Britain, the land of a different type of barbarian. The distant call of a cavalry trumpet roused him. Ala I Thracum was the only military unit deployed here. How many men in an auxiliary cavalry wing? Five hundred, and they were only getting out of bed now? Time he visited them, shook them up, made sure they knew who the new senior officer for the area was.

He swung his legs out of the narrow camp bed and, with an almost suppressed grunt, he stood up. His batman, Viridomar, immediately appeared in the doorway, with the helmet he had been burnishing in his hand. The sun was almost up.

"Your breakfast is on the table, Commandant, together with your writing things. You uniform is laid out and your armour nearly ready. Your new latrine is over there."

"What's wrong with the water supply here?" Maximus grumbled. "My bath last night was muddy."

"I will find out, Commandant. The decurion in charge of the cavalry sent a message that he will make a courtesy call mid-morning."

"What's the matter with these horse-soldiers? They spend half the day cleaning their horses and the other half putting them to bed. Get my horse ready. I'm going to visit him."

As he ate his bread and bacon and drank a cup of rough red wine, the Commandant started a list. 'Cavalry,' he wrote, followed by 'water supply.' Then he wrote the words 'lighthouse' and 'surveyors.'

Viridomar brought in clean breeches which he put on under his tunic. The familiar weight of the mail shirt settled onto his shoulders and he tied the girdle. As this was to be an official visit, the harness bearing his decorations went on next, and his sword over the top. He put on his silvered helmet with the horsehair plume and picked up the vinestick and tucked it into his girdle. He declined help, swinging into the saddle and suppressing another groan when his saddle-sore thighs settled against the leather.

To say that his appearance at the cavalry camp caused consternation would not be an over-statement. Fortunately for all concerned, the trooper on guard saw him in good time and managed to get both the decurion and a respectable mounted reception on parade before the Camp Commandant entered the gate.

He inspected the small parade of about forty men and horses and did not like what he saw. The troopers sat their horses easily, legs dangling, but too relaxed for a unit being inspected by a new senior officer. Several of the flat, oval shields tucked under the troopers' left knees needed paint. A speck of rust showed like blood on one mail shirt. Nail-heads standing proud of the horn of one hoof indicated a loose shoe. He pointed his vinestick, without speaking, at each flaw. At the end of the line, he dismounted and gave his reins to the disconcerted decurion. He picked up a fore hoof of a horse chosen at random. Several small stones were trapped between the frog and the horn.

"Hoof not picked out, Decurion."

He opened the mouth of a horse showing foam around its lips.

"Bit damage, Decurion."

He pointed his vinestick at one trooper now looking a lot more alert.

"You. Dismount. Off-saddle."

The man probably spoke Thracian in the mess but he understood the command, undid the girth and pulled off the saddle. A patch of sweat-stained and dusty hair appeared from under the saddle, in contrast to the rest of the animal's glossy coat.

"Horse groomed without removing the saddle, Decurion."

The Commandant looked at the mounted Decurion still holding the reins of his horse.

"Parade again in one hour," he said without emphasis. Then he turned on his heel and walked to the Decurion's quarters with that officer meekly following him like a mounted groom. An orderly tried to sweep away the remains of breakfast as the Commandant approached. Maximus kicked away a stray cup and seated himself in the Decurion's chair. The orderly gave up and led away the horses.

"I am Anicius Maximus, Camp Commandant of Legion II Augusta and now officer commanding this district. Who are you? No, salute first. Now, proceed."

"Rufus Sita, sir, Decurion of turma three of Ala I Thracum."

"Well Rufus Sita. Whether you remain Decurion or not depends on what happens in just under one hour from now. Where is the rest of your unit?"

"The Prefect and the other squadrons have deployed along the coast, checking the movement of fishing boats and inspecting roads, tracks and beaches for illegal crossings, sir. The Prefect is due back the day after tomorrow."

"Very well. On your superior's return, give him my compliments and say I wish him to report to me, at my quarters, at his earliest convenience. In the meantime, I need a local guide for a few days, I'll borrow that shifty-looking orderly of yours."

The Decurion nodded absently, his eyes drawn to the horse-lines and the parade ground.

"Say 'sir,' Decurion! One more thing. The water supply for my quarters was polluted yesterday. If any one of your men waters his horse or crosses the stream above my waterpoint again, he'll find himself walking back to Thrace. Clear? Good. You may go and see to your preparations."

It was late afternoon when the Camp Commandant halted his muddy horse outside his tent and slid out of the saddle. He did not try to suppress a groan as he straightened his back and handed his helmet to his batman. He slumped into his chair, drew a deep breath and pulled the list towards him. He scored through the words 'cavalry' and 'lighthouse.' He left the words 'water supply' and 'survey-ors.' He added the word 'farmers.' Then he undid the catch in the front of his baldric and allowed his sword to fall to the floor.

CHAPTER 21

▼

ROME

When the Senate confirmed Uncle Claudius as Emperor, Narcissus and Pallas both become even more important men. Most of the day-to-day business of Empire came to their desks. A lot of it, I suspected, should have been dealt with by the Senate or the bureaucracy. After the periodical purges which had swept the organs of state during the reigns of Emperors Tiberias and the late, barely-lamented, Gaius Caligula, there were far too many people in office who were not prepared to make decisions. Either they were simply incompetent or they were cowards. Either way, a river of work was diverted towards Claudius. His freedmen absorbed as much as they could, often making far-ranging decisions in the name of the new Emperor. I found it fairly sickening, Senators ignored the lowly freedmen in public and competed for their favour in private.

Claudius seemed to thrive on his changed circumstances. His stammering and twitching in public all but disappeared, although his limp and his lisp would probably always be with him. The huge volume of additional work did not disconcert him. He calmly allowed the freedmen to carry much of the additional load, frequently admonished Senators for moral cowardice, and, when only he could decide, he used his considerable experience in historical research and in the courts to establish the extent of the problem and to motivate his decision. I was impressed.

There was not much for me to do after the first few days. Hermann, the leader of the surviving German bodyguards, asked me to represent them to the Emperor. I recommended that Claudius send them home, they were hated by the public and that might reflect on him. He thought that I might wish to stay protecting him at the Palace but I told him truthfully that I would be very happy to go back to the Cohort. In the end, Claudius decided to keep the Germans. Their loyalty to the Emperor-in-office was not questioned and the Roman population had already revenged itself on their comrades. Claudius was very angry when Hermann prostrated himself before him, as he had been accustomed to do before the self-proclaimed god Caligula. The Germans quickly began to insinuate themselves back into their former close-protection role and we members of the Urban Cohort found less and less to do at the Palace.

There were many other dismissals and appointments as the new administration consolidated. I was no longer a member of the inner circle but Philip told me that the Prefect of the Misene Fleet had been replaced and, when the new Praetorian Prefect was told to report to the Palace, it was Rufrius Pollio who strode in on a wave of garlic. He had a long private meeting with the Emperor about Praetorian morale and came out looking pleased. The few Senators who had originally opposed Claudius' candidature were not punished. Even Asiaticus emerged into public life again. Narcissus confirmed what I could see. Claudius genuinely did not want a browbeaten, cowed Senate such as he had inherited and was trying to get the members to rouse themselves.

For all the work done in his name, Claudius still managed to find himself a little spare time. With me, he chatted about the British and about gladiatorial contests, having heard, probably from Titus, of my one ignominious appearance. Strange to say, talk of the arena turned my thoughts to the family I had not seen for so long. I was probably just getting bored.

Before Governor Galba returned to Upper Germany, he came to see the Emperor. Narcissus was there, of course, and I was called in right at the start. No one else was present.

"The question," said Galba, "is not whether we can land in Britain and defeat their field army. Our soldiers can handle that."

"Oh, yes?" Claudius interrupted immediately. "Are you sure of that?"

"Yes," he said, looking the Emperor in the eye. After a moment, Claudius blinked.

"Proceed," he said.

"The question is, rather, whether we can stay there. Julius Caesar twice landed armies in Britain and twice defeated their forces but he could not remain."

"There were political considerations," Claudius began.

"That's what Caesar would have had us believe," amended Galba. "In fact he made a number of miscalculations. Military miscalculations. He sent an army officer to survey the British coast for landing places. As a result he managed to land two large armies on nice open beaches where his soldiers could deploy and—on both occasions—half his fleet was wrecked. The Ocean is not the Mediterranean, there are huge tides and fierce storms all year round. He had a lot of trouble getting his people home because he did not have proper naval advice.

"Second miscalculation. He took the minimum in supplies with him, intending to live off the land. The Brits destroyed their crops and burned their granaries as they retired and Caesar could not send for more because…"

"…his fleets were wrecked," Claudius finished for him.

"Third miscalculation," continued Galba, smiling approval at his Imperial pupil. "He did not have enough troops…"

"Wait a minute," Claudius held up a large hand. "He had five legions on one occasion, with all the attached auxiliaries. You told me that I am going to struggle to release four."

"He did not have enough troops to hold the ground his legions had won. Four legions with auxiliaries will be enough to defeat the British in the field. We need to find garrison troops from British sources. Otherwise, our front-line legionaries are going to be frittered away guarding bridges."

Galba turned his wide-eyed stare on me.

"The people who can produce those support troops are in Rome. In the British Palace.

"So," said Claudius, summing up like an advocate. "We need information from a Navy perspective on Ocean conditions and safe landing places. We need a store of food for, what, fifty thousand men—and all their animals—ready to be transported across to Britain. We need confirmation that local British troops will be available to supplement the invasion force. That's all going to take time. Especially the food. It's got to last the invasion force until the next harvest, probably."

"There's plenty to do while the food is being assembled," said Governor Galba. "You cannot release four legions if the various threats on the borders are not dealt with first. Let Hosideus Geta tidy up in Mauretania. I will pacify Upper Germany—the Chatti have been getting above themselves—and Governor Gabienus Secundus has agreed to lead the army stationed in Lower Germany against the Chauci. He will clear the Rhine delta and the coast."

His eyes seemed almost incandescent with enthusiasm.

"When that's done, I think we can release, say, three legions from the Germanies. March them overland to the coast of north Gaul and send part of the Rhine Fleet down as well. Fill the ships with cut timber and we can build more ships at the embarkation port. Take the fourth legion from somewhere on the Danube. I take it you are still happy with Aulus Plautius as Task Force Commander? He can bring one of his legions with him."

"Which legions do you think," Narcissus was scribbling furiously.

"I'll confirm that with you later," said Galba. "Legion II Augusta though, certainly. I need a Legate to command that Legion. Have you anyone suitable and available?"

Claudius raised his eyebrows at Narcissus.

"I suppose you suggest Vespasian?" he said.

"Which one?" asked Galba quickly.

"The younger brother," said Narcissus.

"Agreed," said the Governor. Narcissus made another note.

"Speaking of that Legion," said Governor Galba. "I have sent its Camp Commandant to Gesoriacum on the north Gaul coast. I suppose it will be the embarkation port again. I will forward a copy of his preliminary report on the state of its facilities as soon as I receive it. If you wish, he can draw up contracts with the local corn-producers and start to fill the granaries."

"Have him do so," the Emperor was keeping up.

"I'll inform the local Governor," said Narcissus, mindful of protocol.

"It's most important that we appoint a seaman as soon as possible. He does not have to be Navy, necessarily, although a rank would be helpful. Get him down to the Ocean and he can start taking soundings or whatever it is that they do."

"Narcissus?"

"I recommend Titus Seleucus, sire."

"A freedman," the Governor sounded doubtful, "and born in Syria from his name."

"My freedman," emphasised the Emperor. "His full name is Titus Claudius Seleucus. We'll make him a Captain."

"Oh, very well. Coming from Syria he'll probably get on well with the Camp Commandant anyway. Now, as to the prospect of British support troops."

All eyes turned to me. I had been thinking hard in anticipation of this subject.

"Sire, all the refugees claim massive support among their previous subjects and associates. Old King Bericos might once have commanded considerable support amongst the Atrebates, but very few followed him into exile. That might be significant. Cogidumnos is very decisive and capable but is not of royal blood. He was a chief of the Atrebates. The others are family, or persons without influence from other British tribes. The exception is Adminios."

"What is he?" asked Governor Galba with interest. It crossed my mind that the brisk little soldier was probably an authority on dividing opposition along tribal lines.

"He's one of the sons of the British High King. Ran away after a family quarrel over the allocation of territory. Says he feels he has been badly treated. The other refugees dislike and distrust him because of his family connections. Most of them ran away because of some action of the High King or his family. I believe that Adminios has hopes of being the next High King with our help."

"What is his personality?" Galba pursued the subject.

"Complicated, devious, immature."

"Not our man," the Governor declared.

Claudius nodded. "It sounds more like Cogidumnos," he agreed.

I took another breath. I could see, on the one hand, a promotion, a decoration and a quiet career as a junior officer in the City's police service. For the rest of my working life. On the other hand, I could see profit and adventure beyond the last frontier of the Celtic world. My choice. Those three men could see the obvious requirement even though no one had yet voiced it.

"What we don't know," I said with gathering excitement, "is what support any one of them actually has in Britain. I do not have access to any impartial intelligence on the subject."

"Impartial intelligence is slight," said Narcissus, "a few merchant marine skippers, some traveling salesmen." He looked at Governor Galba but he remained expressionless. "Nothing like what we need."

"What we need," said the Emperor, with a hint of a smile, "is for someone to go down there and find out."

"Someone Cogidumnos will work with," said Galba.

"Someone who can speak the language," said Narcissus with a gleam of gold.

"Someone trained in single combat," said the Emperor.

I actually felt like laughing.

"When do I leave?" I said with a deep, mock sigh. "And can I take Titus with me?"

CHAPTER 22

▼

EUROPE

Camp Commandant Anicius Maximus was sitting at his camp table as the sun came up, eating breakfast with one hand and with a pen clenched in his other fist. A long shadow fell across his list and notes.

"Decurion Rufus Sita reporting as ordered, sir."

"Sit down, Sita."

Viridomar soundlessly appeared with another chair and moved off, with the sentry, out of earshot.

"I have had a long discussion with your Prefect about the condition of his unit and there are to be a number of changes in Ala I Thracum. He has indicated his wish to retire. As far as you are concerned, you are no longer a decurion."

The young horse-soldier swallowed but said nothing.

"You may wish to leave the service, should that be so, I shall grant the request. There will, of course, be no terminal benefits."

Sita remained silent. He was a family man as the Camp Commandant was aware.

"There is an option. I am told you are an excellent horseman and are literate I have a use for such a person, temporarily, on my staff. Are you interested?"

"Yes, sir."

"Should you do well, I shall ensure you a good posting elsewhere. If not, I shall make you aware that you have not done well. Clear? Good. Take this requisition to your former unit and have them send the extra tents and maps here. Bring your personal equipment and horse back with you and report to me here when I return this evening. You may go."

The Commandant worked on turning his notes on the serviceability of the lighthouse into a clear paragraph for his preliminary report. He had concluded the paragraph on the existing military forces in the area before his interview with Rufus Sita. Finished, he threw down his pen and walked stiffly to his horse. He hauled himself into the saddle and turned his horse's head towards the sites of the entrenchments thrown up by the so-called invasion force assembled by the late-Emperor, years before. Another long day lay ahead.

Just outside his headquarters area, the small mounted escort provided by Ala I Thracum fell in behind and he led the way to the faint outline of the entrenched camp from which the intended invasion force of the late Emperor dispersed after refusing to embark for Britain. Even the thought of it brought a faint flush of shame to his weathered cheeks. At least he had been spared being here then himself. The soldiers returning to the Rhine command could not wait to broadcast their excuses. Excuses he now had to investigate. Raging seas, they had said, filled with monsters; inadequate, rotting and leaking ships; shortages of everything, including food and replacement weapons; leadership whose sanity was suspect. All true, no doubt, but not the real reason.

The real reason lived in the informal settlements surrounding the great military encampments of the Rhine command. The soldiers' non-official families had to be left behind, at least for a while, during any invasion of Britain. No one was offering any guarantees that troops deployed to Britain would ever return to their families' homelands of Gaul and Germany nor that any military transport would ever be available for wives to join their husbands in Britain. Serving soldiers were not allowed to marry; therefore, there were no wives.

At least, thought the Commandant, the mutinous invasion force had destroyed its encampment when it dispersed, as Roman military practice demanded even in the case of an over-night camp. He was willing to bet a year's pay that it was the centurions and not the commanders who had enforced that, and that it was the centurions who successfully fought the insolence, disobedience and defiance of disgraced troops to bring them back as organised units to their parent command. The centurionate certainly earned its money that year.

If ever another invasion was contemplated, and it was to be mounted from here, the Camp Commandant silently promised his past colleagues that Roman order would prevail from the outset.

He inspected the remaining traces of the encampment. It was laid out close to communications and to several good water points and, as he had been expecting, it was vast. Not, however, as big as he had been expecting and not, to his mind, correctly aligned.

"What were they playing at?" he muttered aloud.

"Sir?" said a Thracian trooper of his escort.

"Nothing."

Anicius Maximus slid off his horse to their mutual relief. He would never claim to be a horseman. He plucked the legs of his breeches from his sore thighs and started to walk, relishing the warming and stretching of his leg muscles.

It would be impossible to be sure without a proper survey, but the encampment appeared to be laid out to the standard Roman military pattern. If so, it was not big enough for the number of units known to have been involved. Either the regulation gap between the walls and the accommodation had been drastically reduced to shorten the length of walls to be dug, or the legions had left supporting arms, such as the cavalry, special service units and detachments of the Fleet, outside to shift for themselves. Either way, it appeared to be a lasting indictment of the discipline of the Task Force.

The answer was to have the surveyors here now and to peg out the walls, gates, streets and accommodation properly. Another paragraph for his preliminary report started to take shape in his mind.

That afternoon, he met with the local farmers. The gathering took place in the open, outside the port. There were about a hundred men. He noticed with approval that there were very few women present. The Roman custom of men dealing with business and women with the home was, at last, beginning to take root. An interpreter was on hand. He would probably not be needed. Most of those attending spoke some Latin although the muttered conversations around the gathering were all in Celtic. The farmers looked relatively prosperous, which was good. Few property-owners become revolutionaries.

"Can you all hear me?" he called, stilling most of the private conversations.

"Good. I am Commandant Anicius Maximus, a senior army officer and the new military commander of this district of the Roman Empire."

This declaration did not seem to impress too many.

"I've called you here to discuss two important matters, one related to your security of tenure and the other concerning the profitability of your farming operations."

There were no private conversations now. They understood what he was saying all right.

"Firstly, your security of tenure. There is no such thing as a traditional right to land," there was a ripple around the crowd, "except in so far as it is ratified by the State. In other words, the State confirms your holdings and the State can withdraw that confirmation. If the security of the State is threatened by outside forces and you—any of you—is seen to be supporting that threat, the State will take away any right you may have to the land. For all practical purposes, in this area, I represent the State. I have determined that unofficial contact with Britain may constitute a threat to the State. Anyone participating in any way with such unofficial contacts will face the penalty."

An elderly man stepped forward. His respectable clothing hung on a large, bent frame. Work-worn hands dangled by his sides and dull eyes regarded the Commandant. Not opposition, thought Anicius, just a formal protest.

The interpreter had a high, nagging voice and translated every rambling twist of the spokesman's argument which he chose to deliver in Celtic. The Commandant waited him out.

"Thank you for your comments. What is your name? Right. Obviously your lack of the official language caused you to miss a very important point. I said that unofficial contact with Britain is forbidden. Contact is official when it is routed through the port authority in Gesoriacum or my office. All other contact is unofficial. Shall I have that translated for you?"

Many heads were shaken.

"Any more questions on that point? No? Good. Secondly, this has been designated an exercise and training area for the army. No, troops will not be billeted in your houses and proper precautions will be taken to limit any damage to your crops or livestock. The good news is that the army is in the market for grain, as much as you can produce."

It was as if the sun had risen over the gloomy gathering and lit up the faces of the crowd.

"Now, the army can bring in the grain from the big estates in southern Gaul, but I decide where it comes from and you will have the first opportunity. From tax records, I know how much you say you can produce, but people do not always tell the truth to tax officials."

There were a few bold grins and many shifty glances.

"I feel sure that you can produce more if you try. It will not affect your tax assessment, at least for the first year. Granaries must be built on sites I shall identify and the grain must be delivered there. Your tax liabilities will be written off against work done on the construction of the granaries and on part of the grain you deliver. Any grain delivered over and above your tax liability, will be paid for by the army in cash. I will take any questions."

When he got back to his headquarters, the Commandant was pleased to see that more tents had been erected and proper horselines had been set up in a stand of trees downstream of the accommodation. Viridomar took his tired mount and told him that a horse-soldier was waiting for him.

"Rufus Sita," said the Commandant, unclipping his baldric and laying his sword on the table. "I see you have made a start. Good. Your job is to run this headquarters, people, animals and equipment. Report to me every morning for orders before I leave and bring me the guard list every evening before you dismiss."

He took his chair and pulled his list towards him.

"You were a junior officer, do you know about sand tables? Good. Construct a model of the port and surrounding area under cover. Work on it whenever you have time and report to me when it is finished. Is that the guard list? Right. Dismissed."

CHAPTER 23

▼

ROME

My father died suddenly. Enos, his estate-manager and long-time friend, did his best to get word to me in time for me to get to the funeral. The messenger went to the administration offices of Urban Cohort XII and, of course, the pen-pushers sent him to the British Palace instead of to the Imperial Palace. When I did get the news, Narcissus arranged leave for me and Philip offered to get me a passage on a boat down to Pompeii.

Instead, I borrowed a horse and rode it to near-exhaustion to get there in time. I arrived, dirty and tear-stained, just as the pyre was to be lit. I was not really fit to be seen but my brother Marcus, plump and immaculate, put his arm round my shoulders and we stood together, throwing food and clothing into the flames for the use of our father's spirit. As Romans, we understood that his spirit was going either to heaven or to hell and Marcus had made sure that our father had a coin in his mouth to pay the ferryman on the River Styx. As Celtic Romans, however, we had a suspicion that he might have only entered the Celtic Otherworld and he would be back.

My sister, Letitia, had been betrothed to some vacuous aristocrat in southern Italy and had not been able to get back in time for the funeral. Enos, older and balder, was still sharp of eye and of nose. I was genuinely pleased to see him. The real surprise was to hear that Marcus was married and had a child. His wife was among the veiled women at the funeral and I did not meet her until we had gathered up the ashes to be later placed in a monument on the main road outside Pompeii.

First, Marcus led the way into our father's study, got out the wine and asked Enos to excuse us. We sat, side by side, on our father's desk, something we had never been allowed to do when he was alive. We each poured a few drops on the floor and then emptied our cups down our throats.

"He was bewildered, at first, when you left, you know," Marcus said, "and astonished when he heard you were intending to earn your living in the arena scuffling with criminals."

"There aren't as many criminals as you might think. Most of them just need the money, and the excitement."

"Did you kill anyone?"

I told him about my first and only contest which he must have already heard about from Enos. He listened and laughed in the expected places but his eyes were vague. There was something else to be said.

"How did you get into gladiator-school in the first place?"

"Enos arranged it."

"Enos?" That surprised him.

"Yes. He organised the contract—and later bought it back again when father found out."

"Why?" My brother's eyes were now very focused and I could see, behind that smooth exterior, an inherited business talent.

"I created a major problem for my father and the Chief Engineer. Specifically for the Chief Engineer's daughter."

"So you ran away into the arena, probably to get killed. Was she so repulsive?"

"No she was lovely. It—it was just impossible."

"Did you love her?"

I looked at the floor.

"No, but I made her pregnant."

"No you didn't."

The shock nearly strained my neck muscles. I looked into his face and my expression made him smile.

"No," he said. "I did. She's my wife."

"The baby…" I managed to say.

"The baby is mine," he said without any particular emphasis. "Anyone who were to say otherwise would be a liar."

He slid off the table and went out leaving me to my thoughts which were many and varied. He returned with a young girl, wavy dark hair, luminous dark eyes.

"My wife," he said, and left the room.

I turned to her and opened my mouth just in time to get my head jolted by a slap which made my eyes water.

The door opened again and Marcus looked in.

"Is all well, Livia?" he said sharply.

"Oh, yes," said the girl sweetly. "Everything is perfect. Shall we join our guests, dear. Your little brother has something in his eye."

After a bath and a fraught afternoon meal, I walked away from the old house to the top of the hill as I had done as a boy. The spring air was cool but the sun had warmed the dry crumbly earth and the new grass. I lay and looked at the high clouds we called mares' tails streamed across a pale blue sky. There was little bird-song, just the quiet rushing of the air.

I thought of my father a little and of Enos quite a lot. I thought of cowardice. As a boy I had sometimes worried that I might be a coward, not a physical coward but the sort of moral coward that Uncle Claudius railed about. In one action, abandoning Livia for gladiator school, I had proved my worries correct. In a sense, it did not matter if the baby were Marcus's or mine, I had thought it to be mine and I had run away, run away to danger as if to prove that I was not a physical coward even if I was a moral one. I had proved both. Well, half an apple was better than no apple and I could work on growing the other half. Tiberias the boy had finally died with the death of my father. Aurelius Victorinus, stage-name for a gladiator, had gained worth as the name of policeman and I would grow into it.

Livia was standing next to me, her matron's stola making her look almost tall. She looked down at me, neither of us moving.

"I really love him," she said, and walked away.

"Livia," I called after her, "thank you." She did not reply.

Before I left the following morning, Marcus called me again into the study, his study now I supposed. He wanted to talk about our father's bequests. I did not. He insisted. After the bequests willed to the Emperor, to Enos and to several of the household staff, my father had left everything else to Marcus as new head of the family.

"I am not a farmer and I do not aspire to becoming a nobleman," said Marcus, "at least, not yet. You are not a farmer either, so the estate goes half to Enos, as father wanted, and the other half towards Letitia's dowry, agreed?"

"I told you…"

"Which leaves you and I. I know how to run the business and I enjoy it. What do you say I give you your share in cash? I'll pay you some now and the rest in installments."

"I'll tell you what. I don't want any cash now; I have hardly touched my pay. Keep the money in the business and give me a sack of nails."

Marcus mouth hung open.

"I want a sack of copper nails and another sack of ships' fittings, bronze cleats, pintles, things like that. I want a letter of authority to sign contracts on behalf of the business and I want a contract with you granting me half of any profit I generate for the business."

Marcus burst out laughing.

"I thought I was the businessman. Where are you going to look for these sales."

"Give me authority to sign contracts anywhere outside Italy."

"All right."

I owe Marcus a lot.

CHAPTER 24

▼

ROME

"Well," said Emperor Tiberias Drusus Nero Germanicus Claudius, "if that is what passes for a debate in the assembly of the leading men of Rome, you might as well get all the Senators to give you a blank proxy vote and send them all home. I have never seen such a collection of distinguished men mouthing meaningless words. Not a genuine idea expressed between them—all of them waiting for a lead from someone else and none of them prepared to face the risk of being contradicted."

"They were waiting for you," said Sentius Saturninus, one of the two Consuls.

"Exactly my point. Where is the independence of thought? Where is the passionate support of different ideas? Where are the orators? Do they have no personalities, no ambition?"

"You have to be fair. There have been many times in the recent past where a Senator has expressed views dissenting from that of the Emperor and he has been denounced, convicted and executed by his very own colleagues on the instigation of that same Emperor."

"Do you think I would do that? Do they think that they were the only ones whose hides have been in danger? My family, the adults to whom I looked for protection, were cut down all around me and those that remained despised me. I was a crippled, solitary child, threatened on all sides from within my own family. The citizens look to the Senate for protection but what they have is an assembly of yes-men, frightened by their own shadows."

Claudius' frustration was turning into real anger. The Consul had to stop this.

"You have survived those threats. Circumstances saved you. Vocal, independent thinkers have been routinely executed by your predecessors, even while the

Emperors themselves were publicly proclaiming their subservience to the will of the Senate. The Senators don't yet know that you are different. You are going to have to show them."

"Show them? How?"

"Slowly. Don't reward everyone who disagrees with you. Look for a well-argued point of dissent and reward that. Keep your temper. Take a few personal criticisms, even insults. I know you can do that, you have in the past."

"You are supposed to be leading the Senate," argued Claudius. "You must stimulate it into a proper debating forum. I am the Emperor, I report to the Senate on the military affairs of the Empire…"

Claudius stopped and grinned ruefully. "I think you just said that."

"Yes," said the Consul. "What I have also said before, is that the Republic is over. Like it or not, you are the most important person in the Empire. The Senate is full of able men, most of whom want to help you. Your reporting to them is a fiction. But you can and you should consult with them. They can add value to your decisions and we will all benefit."

Claudius slowly relaxed. They were sitting alone in his study in the Palace. He seemed to change the subject.

"Have you thought about what you would like to do after your year is up?"

Sentius Saturninus studied the Emperor.

"Not specifically. I will not be officially able to stand for Consul again for ten years and a lot may happen in that time. You may have disbanded the Senate by then."

"Not likely." Claudius laughed. "Who would I have to vent my anger on then? You don't seem the sort of man to just leave office and retire to your estates."

"No. Perhaps a Governorship or an appointment as one of the Censors."

"The Censors' appointments for the next census are officially still open, as you know, but I would be grateful if you did not accept if one were offered to you. It would be an appointment of great prestige, vital to the functioning of the Senate, but actually amounting to little more than counting of heads. I have a much more challenging job in mind for someone like you."

The Consul thought for a moment.

"I have heard rumours of Britain?"

"Good." The Emperor did not seem pleased that the Consul was not surprised. "The Governor-designate has been decided upon. It had to be a man with current military experience. An invasion across the Ocean will not be the same as a landing from the sea in the Mediterranean. There are unique military problems."

Claudius sounded as if he had been solving unique military problems all his life.

"Who will the Governor be? Galba? Or, Hosideus Geta?"

"Galba has his hands full in Upper Germany and Hosideus Geta will not be available early enough in the planning stage. It is Aulus Plautius from the Danube."

There was a long pause before the Consul responded.

"Aulus Plautius is not very well known to the general public."

"No," Claudius said with a grin. "He is a distant relative of mine and I think it would be accurate to describe him as competent but not colourful. This is as it should be. The Governor-designate will lead Imperial forces in the occupation of a new Roman Province. He will be seen to act under the guiding hand of the Emperor."

"I see," said the Consul "Does the same description apply to me?"

"Never," Claudius' good humour was restored. "The job I have in mind will require someone used to deciding competing priorities. He will also be a person who has the stature to make strong men accept that decision. It will seem to the general public to be a boring administrative function, in fact, it will be critical to the enterprise. I think you are the man to do it. When you succeed, all the able men in the service of the state will know that you are the best of them."

Claudius accepted a cup of wine from Narcissus who had, almost silently, joined them.

"Imperial resources will be sent from Italy across Gaul. Others will be deployed from the Danube and the Rhine commands. Still others from Gaul itself and from Spain. All will be funnelled through a single embarkation port, across part of the Ocean and onto a hostile coast. It will be your job to marshal the resources, decide the priorities, to allocate shipping and to keep Plautius supplied. Initially anyway, your duty will be done when Plautius' requirements land in Britain. Later, as he moves forward, your jurisdiction might extend."

"British support?" Narcissus reminded quietly.

"Yes, there will not be enough soldiers to sit on conquered ground, guarding it. If Plautius tries that, his advance will soon peter out. The sooner we can activate reliable British levies to hold ground, the sooner Plautius can move on."

"They will have to be very reliable," Sentius Saturninus said, reflectively sipping his wine. "If not, the British levies are going to be sitting between Plautius and any Roman support."

"Quite right. We have thought of that. We have several dissident British leaders who have appealed to Rome for support. They will be available to be placed in control of British levies under our command. The only chance they have of survival in the British environment is to co-operate fully with us. They know this. Introduce them into the captured territories as rapidly as possible to take charge of the levies and release regular troops."

"What we need to know Consul,' said Narcissus. "Is whether our dissidents command sufficient support to raise the manpower for the levies. Research is being undertaken into this. A man called Aurelius Victorinus will report to you on his return."

"It would also be helpful to know in advance how good these dissidents are in identifying reliability among the levies."

"I don't think we can assess that at this stage, Consul. If they make a mistake when they are committed, they will undoubtedly die. We can assume that they will be particularly attentive to that aspect."

"However," said the Emperor. "They are useless in Rome. Let's get them back to Britain and see what they can do. What do you think? Do you want the job at the end of your term?"

"Absolutely."

After Consul Saturninus had left, Narcissus cleared away the cups.

"Titus Seleucus is here."

"Good," Claudius said, pleased. "Have I made him a Captain yet?"

"Fleet headquarter at Misenum has been notified. I do not know if he has been officially appointed yet. Communications take time. When you send him down to Gesoriacum to look at naval requirements, I think Philip should go with him. There is nothing special he can do for us now in the Fleet Communications Division here in Rome. He is a trained intelligence specialist and a sailor. He can go as Captain Seleucus' aid."

"Good idea," approved Claudius. "Communications between the embarkation port and Rome need to be seriously upgraded for the invasion. Have him report on that."

"Right. I have also been thinking about whether the British will fight. We all assume that they will and, certainly, Julius Caesar was not disappointed in that regard. But what if they don't? What if we go to all the trouble of mounting an invasion to add territory to the Empire and glory to the Emperor and they just cave in?"

"They must fight," said Claudius seriously. "I will not have sufficient resources to mount another invasion elsewhere and you have all convinced me that I need a military triumph."

"Do you know anything about the tribute that Caesar says he extorted from the conquered Britons?"

"I don't think he said how much it was or whether it was to be a single payment or an annual one. As far as I know, nothing has been paid."

"I'll check the public records office and prepare a claim for all the money due. That claim should guarantee a fight if we need to use it."

"Do that," said Claudius. "Make sure that you add the interest."

"Before I call Captain Seleucus in," there was something in Narcissus' voice which focussed the Emperor's attention, "there is one more, unrelated matter I would like your decision on."

"Go on."

"Incitatus. The late-Emperor's horse was a candidate for a Consulship and you know about the controversy concerning possible—er—deification."

"So?" Claudius was enjoying Narcissus' delicacy.

"Incitatus is still on the premises and being treated with quite extraordinary respect. This is causing scandal among the religious and irritation among the Palace staff. The only people who are happy are those grooms employed to clean and feed it. It gets virtually no exercise as no one wishes to climb onto the back of a god."

"Understandable."

"So, does the god stay or the horse go?"

"You are asking me this as an animal-lover or as the Pontiff of Rome?"

"As the Pontiff."

"Find an Elysian field and retire the horse to it."

CHAPTER 25

▼

EUROPE

We embarked on the warship 'Sol' at Ostia on a wet spring morning. The few gulls around stood in stick-legged, sodden lumps over their reflections on the shining paving. The harbour did not appear to be crowded although there was a considerable bustle around our ship. Rumour had it that we were going to Sardinia first, before heading north for Gaul. My knowledge of the sea so far comprised only of day-trips, always within sight of land. I was excited about a deep-sea cruise.

Philip, looking quite professional in his sailor suit and with his damaged ear, took charge of the baggage arrangements for his superior, a swarthy Captain of the Misene Fleet called Seleucus, and us. He examined the bundles of baggage not required on the voyage, checking the stitching on the, hopefully, waterproof covering. He had thoughtfully brought luggage labels with him. He inscribed our names and destinations on the lead with an awl and then used it to attach the labels to the bundles with twine. He looked at me questioningly when he dealt with my two heavy sacks of ship's fittings but he made no comment.

I stood, with a wad of documents under my arm, beside Cogidumnos and Scota while we watched the seemingly casual but continuous activity of a highly-trained crew making the final arrangements before putting out to sea. Scota showed disturbing signs of wanting to tell the crew how to make those preparations and I could see that even Cogidumnos was getting nervous about the black looks that sailors and marines were directing at her. Scota had, like Cogidumnos, made at least two deep-sea voyages during her flight from Britain and this seemed to make her an authority on all things nautical. I had made none and could not contradict her. I was quite relieved when Titus appeared, splashing through the puddles towards the ship.

The sea was extremely rough as we left the shelter of the land, at least it seemed so to me. The thump of the oars, the twittering of the flute and the strange smells hanging around the hull in spite of the howling gale were all totally alien. Captain Seleucus was talking to the ship's Captain and beckoned me over. The heaving wet deck made the short walk to the rear hazardous. I nearly staggered into the pit where the oarsmen laboured.

Captain Seleucus kindly told me that the weather was expected to freshen a little later and that I should shepherd the passengers into the shelter at the rear end of the ship. The warship's Captain did not introduce himself to a mere mortal but did lend me a well-worn document case and offer me a few words of advice on shipboard etiquette. They included the need to keep nosey, red-headed foreign women from interfering with the crew and the necessity for lumbering flat-foots who wished to vomit to do so down-wind of the ship. I actually thought he was speaking of me until I heard Titus retching desperately behind me and the shouts of anger from the rowing benches.

Even under the leather shelter, the wind and the wet penetrated. The hull groaned alarmingly and rain and spray clattered on the roof. Scota sat on our baggage with damp hair hanging around her face and made acid comments on the whole enterprise. Cogidumnos wedged himself into a corner and closed his eyes. Titus composed himself for death on the heeling wet floor. I sat like a prim matron with my document case on my knees. Philip occasionally put his head through the curtains, an expression of dripping nobility on his countenance, but was soon driven away by the wet fug developing in our refuge.

The ship's motion where we were, close to the stern, seemed exaggerated and I am sure that, more than once, I was lifted clear of the bundle I was sitting on. I promised myself that, if I could entice Philip in, I would get him to sit on my nails. I looked out once or twice, carefully keeping my eyes away from the heaving desert of black and white water that surrounded us. The day wore on, punctuated by the sound of the oars, the flute and Scota. Sometime in mid-afternoon, Cogidumnos sat bolt upright, his mouth close to Scota's ear and roared "Quiet!" She gave him a look that would have split oak and they simultaneously turned their backs on one another and pretended to go to sleep.

Suddenly, it was the end of the day. The beat of the oars slowed and the wind died as the warship moved into a wind shadow. Looking out again, I saw land right in front, in the drizzle, and close. Sailors were clustered up in the front holding poles and ladders. There was a shout. The oars ceased altogether and there was a heavy rumble from underfoot. The ship stopped. The deck was suddenly thronged with men, stretching and groaning, laughing and talking, and, with bundles and tools in their hands, heading for the front of the ship and the beach. I checked my traveling companions. No one had actually died. We had survived the first day of the voyage.

Sitting on the damp beach, huddled around a small fire of driftwood, we passengers recovered quickly. Even Titus showed signs of returning good humour, pretending to become nauseous whenever one of the ship's crew came too close and insisting on treating me with exaggerated respect. I had been notified of my promotion to optio just prior to departure. We were both now officially members of Legion VIII Augusta, wherever that might be.

Steam rising from my clothing, I looked around the campsite, for that is what it had rapidly become. Marines were on guard at the perimeter and their colleagues hammered and strained a flimsy palisade fence to mark the boundary. Heavy bundles were being thrown onto the beach and rapidly transformed into standing tents. The small area swarmed with activity. Before nightfall, we had all engulfed a huge meal of hot porridge and disposed of several cups of Navy wine which was probably also used to scour ships' bottoms. We had faced the perils of the sea and were, we thought, well on the way to becoming tarry old salts.

We put in at Carales in Sardinia where a Fleet detachment managed the timber supply to Fleet headquarters at Misenum. We also called at Forum Julii on a lagoon of the Argenteus River in southern Gaul. The Base facilities were huge, but the Misene Fleet detachment had been much reduced. It had formerly been the Fleet's headquarters but it was too far from Rome. Typical military, build a huge Base and then find it is in the wrong place. When I commented on this, Philip, who was becoming something of a pain on naval matters considering that his job was in the Communications Division, protested that the colony of retired soldiers was now under no threat, the former Greek colony of Massilia was now fully Romanised and the rationalisation of the opposing Roman Fleets after Actium had long ago been completed. The Base and its staff had successfully fulfilled all the functions for which it had been founded. Round of applause for the Navy.

The weather improved as 'Sol's' hull rode lower on the freshwater current of the River Rhone. Driving northwards upriver, the warship provided a moving vantage point for the passengers to survey the square, ploughed fields and the armies of slaves on the big estates of the Province.

There were now more passengers. At Forum Julii we had embarked twenty recently recruited legionaries of Legion II Augusta who had just finished basic training and were on their way to join their unit on the Rhine. They were under the command of an old legionary with a sagging belly and no front teeth known to everyone as Fangs. The young soldiers were very biddable and totally inexperienced. It would be a few years yet before they would become the terror of the Germans. They had been issued with the newest in military equipment. Only Fangs wore chain mail armour. The youngsters had all been issued with modern loricated armour, curved metal plates enclosed the soldier's torso and sets of smaller plates curved over each shoulder. They had infantry helmets with much improved protection for the wearer's cheeks and back of his neck. They knew what an optio is and behaved in a very respectful manner to me even though I was nominally from a different legion.

The seamen treated the new legionaries with a sort of fond contempt, frequently pointing out the impossibility of swimming in armour. Only once did the crew display genuine anger towards the soldiers. Two horsemen were having a private race along the riverbank and the young soldiers surged to that side to see. The entire ship tilted alarmingly to the left and more people, equipment and baggage began sliding to that side. The Captain hung onto one of the helmsmen who, in turn, hung onto the handle of his oar. Cogidumnos and Titus were taken by surprise and slid away. Frightened shouts echoed from below deck and the oars on the right of the ship rose in a straggling frieze out of the water. The mast swayed across the sky. I clung to the edge of the deck with one hand, and the back of Scota's clothing with the other. I thought that we were going to turn over. I had no idea what to do, nor if anything could be done.

What saved us was that the sail was not set and the warship was being rowed up river. The two banks of oars on the 'downhill' side acted against the water as a sort of outrigger and the rowers in the lower bank did not panic and abandon their oars when half the Rhone came in through their ports. The marines below deck, almost as experienced on the water as the sailors, clawed their way 'uphill' over benches and frightened oarsmen until their combined weight provided a counterbalance. 'Sol', grudgingly at first, then faster, heaved itself upright, the oars on the right smacking back onto the surface of the water. Something smashed below deck, there were a few quiet curses, a lot of heavy breathing and then a kind of silence.

The anger started to build almost visibly. The Captain released his hold on the helmsman, tugged down his tunic and roared a series of questions and commands at his officers. There was a scramble of movement and a stream of reports in different voices directed to the Captain and then, again, a kind of silence. In it, I could actually hear heavy breathing from the crowded and dripping rowing benches. I pulled Scota to her feet and put my hand over her mouth, she had just drawn a deep breath and I did not feel that her opinion, uttered loudly in a foreign accent, would contribute to the management of the near-disaster.

The Captain beckoned a stricken Fangs and the Centurion of the ship's marines to the stern. After a moment, he summoned me too. The Captain was white-faced with fury, the ship's Centurion stood with pursed lips and blazing eyes focused on the elderly legionary who seemed incapable of speech. Captain Seleucus appeared at my elbow. 'Sol's' Captain pointed a finger at Fangs.

"You!" he shouted, and Fangs flinched. "You are supposed to be responsible for those baby soldiers. They are supposed to be going to destroy Rome's enemies, god help us. Not to be doing their best to destroy an Imperial warship and to kill its crew. Your Legion is not going to be pleased with you, your Provincial Governor is not going to be pleased and the Emperor himself will most probably have you executed."

Fangs gaped. The Captain's finger swiveled until it was pointed at me.

"You!" he said, and I flinched. "You are the senior foot-soldier on board. What are you going to do about it?"

That was a good question. Everyone in earshot turned to me, and that meant most of the crew. The spaces between the decking and the sides of the ship were jammed with the heads and shoulders of angry crewmembers. It was no good telling them that I was only a policeman, that I had only just been allocated to a legion and that the miscreant soldiers were not even going to that legion. If I renounced responsibility for them, I could be stripped of my new rank and the Centurion of marines would then feel free to have the youngsters flogged or keel-hauled or whatever they do in the Navy. To have those youngsters physically scarred by punishment before they even joined their unit would be the finish of some of them. They were watching me, aghast.

"I will teach them a lesson, sir," I said firmly to the Captain.

"Do so!" he said immediately.

I turned to the young legionaries and told them to take off their equipment and stow it properly. Standing with their tunics fluttering in the slight river-breeze, they looked very young and vulnerable. The two horsemen on the riverbank had abandoned their race and were watching with interest from the saddle. The warship, oars trailing, had started to slide gently downstream. I turned to the Captain.

"Would you please order the lower rowing benches to be cleared, sir. The Army will row the ship today as part of their continuation training."

There was a complement of one hundred and eight rowers on the liburnian 'Sol', seventy-two actually rowing at any one time.

"Very well," said the Captain with a glint in his eye. "I am going to limit accidental damage to my oars to a minimum. The only people rowing, until they have reached an acceptable standard, will be the soldiers. The twenty trainees will do the work of seventy two experienced oarsmen until I say otherwise or until you conclude the day's training."

There were cheers and jeers, but with a few smiles, from the audience.

"Now," said the Captain, the hard lines of his face relaxing slightly, "what about their leader?"

I could not put the elderly legionary alongside the recruits for 'continuation training'. He probably deserved greater punishment than they, as the measure of the responsibility he carried, but he could have a heart attack on the rowing benches.

"As he is an experienced soldier," I said, "and the river is getting shallower, I shall station him at water level to report underwater dangers to the ship. He will stand on the ship's ram until further notice."

"Make it so," said the Captain.

At first, the crew enjoyed the Army's training hugely. Sitting about in exaggeratedly relaxed poses, the sailors, oarsmen and marines commented loudly on style and timing of the rowing. They exercised their combined sense of humour to the detriment of the sweating infantry. They compared Fangs unfavourably with the existing ship's figurehead and they pointed out that the warship was hardly keeping pace with the horsemen walking their mounts on the bank. Eventually, however, they got bored with their inaction. One or two crewmembers slipped below to offer advice to the trainees and to keep them company. The timekeeper assisted the novices to keep their stroke with notes on his flute. The soldiers sweated and grunted but they did not complain. Water was taken to them by the crew. Some crew even offered to take over from the soldiers. I was pleased to see that none accepted. Towards evening I reported to the Captain that Army continuation training was concluded.

"Good," he said. "I was concerned that we were going to be back at sea by this evening. Well done."

The head of navigation on the River Rhone is not a strictly accurate Navy description. Lighters, barges and fishing boats do operate further up stream but warships do not go any further than this, the most northerly of the Misene Fleet

Bases. From here, we were going to go by road. Captain Seleucus and Philip would take the good military highway to the headquarters of the Rhine Fleet at Bonna. Titus and I would escort Cogidumnos and Scota north to the port of Gesoriacum on the edge of the Ocean opposite Britain. We would attach ourselves to any military formation going in that direction, or so we thought. On arrival at the port, I was to report to a Camp Commandant Maximus of Legion II Augusta.

I handed in my credentials and the mail I had brought from Rome at the Fleet Base. I was immediately shown into the Navarch's office. I had learned from Philip that this rank, in the Navy, was superior to that of Captain.

"Welcome, Optio Victorinus," said the Navarch, beaming on me. "This is Rufus Sita of Commandant Maximus's staff. He has been waiting with six cavalrymen to escort you to Gesoriacum. I understand you are a water engineer? Splendid. You and your people can leave as soon as your staff collect and load the pack animals Sita has arranged. You have further instructions from the Commandant, Sita?"

The naval officer turned to the Thracian staff man.

"The Commandant has instructed that a detachment of legionary replacements for Legion II Augusta does not go on to the Rhine as originally intended, but marches north with us. It was on board the same ship with you I believe, Optio?"

I thought of Fangs and the blistered trainee-oarsmen and nodded.

"Good," said the Navarch. "As an optio in the legions, you are the senior officer of the party and will command. Any questions? Leave as soon as you are ready, and give my compliments to Camp Commandant Maximus. Anything the Navy can do to assist, he only has to ask."

CHAPTER 26

▼

EUROPE

To say that I was out of my depth would be to put a very positive slant on my mental condition after disembarking my new command from the warship. The Captain and crew had lined the sides of the berthed ship to watch the departure of the passengers they had safely conveyed halfway up the Rhone. They knew that the navy element was heading by road, which was bad enough, for the Rhine Fleet Base. They had also heard that the army contingent, under the newest optio in the Roman army, would be marching north off the edge of the world. That was something to tell their wives about.

Loading pack mules had obviously not been on the syllabus of basic training for infantrymen of Legion II Augusta. Most of the young soldiers were sons of colonists, military veterans retired to groups of land allotments in various parts of the Empire. Had they been experts at animal management, they would probably have stayed on in the colonies, but most of them had left their families precisely because they did not want to spend their lives dealing with intractable animals. Now they were faced with loading their immense amounts of new gear on flop-eared, wall-eyed bundles of muscle with yellow teeth, sharp hooves, bad breath and an attitude.

Fortunately, there were a few sons of peasant farmers in the ranks who had handled the beasts before. They automatically took charge and shrugged off the half-hearted offers from the six troopers with Rufus Sita. No citizen-soldier, how-ever new, admits he cannot do things as well as an auxiliary, except ride a horse, and who would want to do that? The normal allocation of pack animals in the legions is one mule for every eight-man section. Rufus Sita had organised one mule for my immediate party of Titus, Cogidumnos, Scota and myself. He had brought one mule with his cavalry contingent and had requisitioned three mules for Fangs and his twenty new legionaries.

The cavalrymen of Ala I Thracum had loaded their mule and sat and watched the fun. Several young legionaries were kicked and one had a substantial bite on his shoulder before two things happened. The colonists' sons grabbed the mule that had been too free with its teeth, whipped away its legs and sat on its head until all its two sets of legs were tied together. It was then propped on its feet, dusty and shaken, and its allocated load was then fastened on it so tightly as to threaten breathing. Two legionaries took a firm grip on the head-collar and Fangs stood in front of it with a substantial piece of wood; then the hobbles were cast off from its legs. At its first attempt to buck, Fangs brought his baton forcefully down on the mule's head. As an intelligent animal, it then decided to co-operate while, no doubt, plotting its revenge. One legionary mule down, two to go.

While this was going on, Cogidumnos led forward the mule allocated to us. It also displayed some defiance until Scota stepped forward to the mule's head. She took a furry ear in each of her small hands and gently bent them double. The animal snorted but stood stock-still while Cogidumnos and Titus, almost at leisure, loaded it with our bedding and rations. My two heavy sacks went on top. When Scota released it, the mule snorted again, waggled its ears furiously and had a little bob to satisfy itself that both the load and its ears were firmly in place. Then it bent its neck and pretended to graze. It was probably trying to work out its next move.

The legionaries had learned their first animal management lesson. The two remaining mules were quickly loaded and I placed all the pack animals in the centre of our little column. I looked at the sun—it was already mid-morning. I had been learning some legionary drill and thought that the time had come to practice it. At the top of my voice I shouted "Are you ready?" The horses were a bit startled but the young soldiers responded immediately, "We are ready!" I repeated the question twice more and twice more received a resounding response. Then with my cavalry in advance, I led my miniature legion out onto the road to the north.

A start had been made to upgrade it to military standard for heavy equipment but the construction crews had not yet progressed very far. Soldiers make roads, under the direction of surveyors and specialist construction engineers. It seemed that there were not many soldiers available for road-making duties in this part of Gaul and work at the road-head seemed to me to be lethargic. I was happy to put the noise, dust and squalor behind us. Pillars of smoke rose at various distances in front of us as the surveyors corrected the alignment of the new road which was following, generally, the more meandering line of the original native trackway as improved by Julius Caesar.

The hobnails of the infantry crunched confidently on the wide Gallic road. The legionaries just out of basic training might not know much about loading a mule but they had learned a great deal about marching. Helmets slung on chests, and each shouldering his regulation two javelins and two fencing stakes, the foot-soldiers seemed indifferent to weight they were carrying: only their bedding, entrenching tools and rations were carried on their allocated mules. The red of their clothing and shields glowed against the green backdrop of vegetation. They looked around with interest, perhaps imagining themselves as the all-conquering legionaries of Julius Caesar ninety years ago.

I had not had a chance to speak much with the staff man. Rufus Sita, I gathered, was from the Balkans, as were all the cavalryman. He had recently transferred to the staff of the military commander at Gesoriacum from the Thracian cavalry stationed there. I did not know anything about cavalry and very little about army customs but I could see, from the sideways looks the cavalrymen directed at him when he gave orders, that his transfer might not have been a happy one. Fangs later told me that he had been demoted for some military offence and his previous subordinates in the cavalry were now pretty much his equals. Sita did not say much, but Fangs thought that he blamed his men for letting him down. It was a situation that needed to be watched.

Beside the road, a wagon drawn by mules waited to go with us to the Ocean. The load bed of the vehicle was fitted with a huge bladder made of sewn oxhides. There was a cheer from the legionaries when they saw the monstrous vehicle. The Camp Commandant at Gesoriacum had obviously no intention of operating without a proper supply of wine for his troops. It gave me a good excuse to reorganise the column.

I put the dray, with its civilian driver, in the centre of the column with the pack mules and placed Rufus Sita in charge of all transport. The undergrowth had not yet been properly cleared back and, in places, the route ran through defiles which would need to be made good before ordinary businessmen could travel alone. There was no danger of bandits to a convoy of our size but several civilian travellers did try to attach themselves to the rear of the column. They were kept at a distance by the mounted rearguard, while oncoming traffic was turned off the road by the lead scouts. We made good time.

It seemed to me quite early in the day when Fangs, marching beside me, began looking at the sky, clearing his throat and nodding towards the shadows. I knew that we were supposed to entrench every overnight camp but I had no idea how it was done nor how long it took. Perhaps, on the first day, it would be wiser to stop sooner rather than later. One of the cavalrymen came trotting back and saluted me, which took me by surprise. He reported that we were approaching a campsite and he slid off the horse and handed the reins to me. I could, I suppose, have sent Fangs. The temptation to act publicly as the commander, making what should have been a simple decision, was strong.

Despite my lack of riding breeches, I swung into the warm saddle and rode forward about a mile. There was a clearing sufficiently far off the roadway to offer a degree of privacy at the headwaters of a small stream. It had been used before, the outline of the entrenchments still visible. After a brief inspection, I decided that it would do. I waited on the road and directed the column where to turn off. The horsemen drifted through the trees onto the campsite and the legionaries marched in behind Fangs in good order. The elderly legionary was looking around dubiously but said nothing. The mules trotted by and Scota gave me a smile. The dray, with its vital load of wine, lurched off the roadway and ground its way down the slight incline to the campsite. Titus came and stood next to me as Fangs' hoarse voice ordered the column to halt. I was feeling good. Perhaps I was descended from Caesar.

The column had not been ordered to break ranks. Fangs marched back to me. He did not salute.

"Bad decision, Optio," he said. To give him his due, he did not emphasise my brand-new rank. "The ground is soft, makes for easy entrenching, but, if it rains, we are going to have a hell of a job getting the dray back on the road. If you put it back on the road now, though, either it will be empty by the morning or we'll have to put a separate guard on it. And even then it might be empty by the morning."

"The campsite has been used before, though."

I tried to keep the defensive note out of my voice.

"That's the other problem," he said. "Whoever was here did not bury their rubbish properly. It's too close to the stream and animals have dug it up and scattered the stuff around. It was some bloody cavalry unit I'm sure. A broken harness pendant in the rubbish and old horse manure all over. Luckily they put the latrine in the right place and filled it in properly."

"Good here, isn't it?" said Titus, looking around with wide innocent eyes. I was beginning to doubt that I was descended from Caesar.

"What is your recommendation?" I asked Fangs. "Move on?"

"Our credibility would be gone," said the old soldier and we all knew that he did not have to say "our". "I'll tell the lads that this is how not to leave campsite. It can be part of their continuation training. They'll put it to rights and entrench it properly."

"I'll get hold of the cavalry," said Titus. "Their friends left this mess. They can dig a new rubbish pit and move the old one. Collect what the horses left behind."

"Do it," I said, trying to retain a vestige of authority. "What's your proper name?" I asked the legionary.

"Just call me Fangs, Optio," he said, baring his gums. "Everyone does."

The young legionaries had put up many practice camps before. They knew the layout and the dimensions required for any particular occupancy, things I did not. They put out guards and stacked their shields and javelins. Fangs cut them measuring-sticks and watched with approval as they pegged out wall-corners, gates and internal roadways, ignoring the relics of previous occupants. Then they took their entrenching tools from the pack mules and attacked the soft ground with a will.

The cavalrymen were much less enthusiastic about their task but, under the supervision of Titus, the clearing up was getting done. Cogidumnos and Scota were offloading the mules, feeding them barley and taking them to water below the campsite. They would be tethered within the walls for the night.

When the ditches were dug and the embankments were up and the palisade erected on top, the dray was driven inside and parked, at Rufus Sita's direction, next to where I was sleep. My bedspace, in the standard design, corresponded with the position of the Praetorium in a full-sized legionary camp. Everyone in a Roman military camp always knows where everything important is because they are all always in the same place from one camp to another. The entire convoy was now inside and a guard placed on each gate.

Rufus Sita had got the pack animals settled down and a few of the legionaries were trying their hands at grooming them. The big cavalry horses were tethered nearby, nosing at large bundles of cut grass, the Thracians cleaning tack beside them. The smell of bacon frying in its own fat was making me salivate. I turned towards my bedspace, Rufus and Fangs following. Titus was there already and I beckoned Cogidumnos to join us. Scota insisted on coming too, much to the silent indignation of the old legionary.

My bedding had been unrolled on the grass and I sat on it. The others sat on the ground or leaned against the wagon with its load of wine.

"Tonight, I'll be guard commander," I started. "After tonight, we'll take turns. The guards report to me. Tell them." Fangs nodded. "Stand-to at first light."

"What about breakfast?" intervened Scota sweetly.

All of us stirred uncomfortably. None of us, other than Cogidumnos, was used to having a woman present at a business meeting, never mind making a contribution.

"Well, my dear," said Fangs, visibly fighting down his indignation again and smiling horribly, "the cooks usually make enough at this time of the day for the troops to keep for the next day."

"No need though, now," said Scota, aged all of seventeen. "These boys need something hot in their stomachs before going out. I'll have the guards wake me early and make bread and mulled wine while everyone else is busy."

"Now, look here…" started Fangs.

"What a good idea," said Titus.

"They'll work all the better for it," said Cogidumnos.

"I suppose so," said Rufus Sita and then smiled.

"That's settled then," I said quickly while Fangs was drawing breath.

Several young soldiers arrived with plates of sizzling bacon, lumps of coarse bread and cups of Army wine. They bestowed special smiles on Scota. Whatever the official recruiting age, I was sure that most of them were not much older than she was. We ate where we were. I found I was ravenous.

As it was getting dark, I went around the guards. Whatever their training instructor's conservative views, he had given them a good military grounding. They all had their helmets on and their eyes wide open. One of them had had his upper arm firmly bandaged. I had seen what sort of a bite a malevolent mule can give and could imagine that he was in a lot of pain. It was a measure of the keenness of the young soldiers that he had not had himself legitimately excused guard duty. I relieved him, softening the blow by immediately appointing him as my personal orderly, and sent him off-duty with orders to wake me early the following morning. I then went down to check on Cogidumnos and Scota.

I could understand why King Bericos wanted her to be on this operation. He was no longer young enough himself for military operations and he probably wanted to build on his political connections in Rome. He had thrown himself on the mercy of the previous Emperor and would want to make contact with the new one. He, apparently, had no living sons and Scota was his eldest surviving daughter. She should have been married long ago, of course, but now her marriage would be critical to the continuation of his family's claim to the throne of the Atrebates. She needed to refurbish her own contacts in Britain on behalf of her father and even, odd thought, if she was ever going to claim the throne herself.

She was not at her bedspace and Cogidumnos was not nearby either. A trace of suspicion hovered at the back of my mind. I made my way between the straight lines of bedrolls and the chatting off-duty soldiers. I needed to make a routine call at the latrines.

I noticed that someone, with a sense of delicacy unusual among the military, had screened the facility with cut bushes. I found Cogidumnos standing outside.

"Are you waiting?" I said foolishly. "Who is in there?"

"I am!" shouted the unmistakable voice of Scota from within. "And I would appreciate a little privacy."

Fangs had come up behind me to join the little queue. He had his head lowered and was shaking it slowly from side to side. He, at least, believed that military life would never be quite the same.

CHAPTER 27

▼

EUROPE

Captain Seleucus and Philip had been well received by the commander of the legion based at Bonna on the Rhine. He had not, however, had much time to spend with naval officers from the Misene Fleet. Legion I Germanica was preparing to support the legions based downstream in a major effort to clear the enemy from the mouths of the Rhine and the coasts of the Ocean beyond. Naval officers from the Misene Fleet were very welcome, but he believed that they could best supplement their expertise from the Fleet headquarters at Colonia. It was a short passage downstream. The warship 'Pietas' was waiting.

Hustled on board the liburnian, the sailors from the Mediterranean looked with awe at the sheer volume of brown water sweeping silently through the dark green landscape. The sky was purple, with distant curtains of dark rain hanging from the low clouds.

"Doesn't look much like the Euphrates, Captain," said Philip.

"Nor much like the Nile either, I would imagine," responded the freedman from Syria.

The bowels of the ship and its wet decks were crammed with military stores and people and the crew were struggling to manage the ship in the crush. Captain Seleucus went off to introduce himself to the ship's Captain and Philip wormed his way slowly towards the bow where a small group of yellow-haired Germans had cleared a space for themselves between the two artillery pieces. A voice like a bull's proclaimed from the stern that no one was to move about during the passage and everyone was to remain in place until the ship was securely tied up at Fleet headquarters. Passengers were to keep the noise down so that orders could be heard.

The ship was boomed off from the quay and oars, extended from either side of the ship, settled into alignment. The current suddenly gave the ship a gigantic push and the oars were heaved to give the helmsman some steering leverage. 'Pietas' accelerated downstream. The left bank of the Rhine seemed to start to flow past the ship and a cold wind swooped over the bow.

The space appropriated by the Germans was out of the direct wind although frequent eddies stirred the ends of their braided hair. These were not the murderous athletes of the Imperial bodyguard but true aboriginal tribesmen dressed mainly in leather and wet fur. Their sharp little spears had been taken off them for the passage but they still had their knives which they fingered as they glowered at the other passengers and grunted together in their strange language. There was a strong smell of unwashed bodies in the air. No one seemed inclined to encroach on their space.

An intelligence man does not gather intelligence by not speaking to people and Philip was on this journey to gather intelligence. His verbal overtures to the German group elicited no response. They watched him with disturbingly light-coloured eyes and made no comment, not even to each other. Philip persisted until one or two of them began to look bored and turned their heads away. The only slight spark of interest he could detect was when he turned his head and they noticed the damage to his ear. Several of them had visible wounds. In Latin, supported by much miming, Philip described how he had been struck by the spear of a noble German defender of the Roman Emperor. There was a stirring. An older tribesman, with amber beads round his neck and an old wound to his chin, cleared his throat and grunted one word.

"Why?"

Progress.

Philip launched into a long description of the recruitment, training and function of the Imperial bodyguard. They all seemed to listen carefully, no one said anything. He explained how a mistake had been made during his attempt to save the Emperor and a noble German of the bodyguard had wounded him, thinking him one of the assassins. There were a few hoarse chuckles at this and tension relaxed slightly. The man with the amber beads moved his feet and graciously indicated a place on someone else's deck where Philip could seat himself.

It seemed that they were trackers and interpreters on their way from Bonna to join Legion XV Primigenia to fight the Chauci. At the mention of the enemy's name, one of them spat on the deck, not far from Philip's feet. To test them, Philip asked if they did not mean Legion XXII Primigenia. Oh no, they said, pointing, that legion was upstream.

They were going to Legion XV Primigenia, pointing again, which was downstream.

The Chauci, they said, to another discharge of spittle, were their blood-enemies and they would enjoy bringing those coastal marauders and mother-rapers down. There was a growl of agreement. Conversation was hard going but, by the time he elaborately took his leave of the Empire's allies, Philip thought it was time usefully spent. The Germans seemed to have a good grasp of Imperial military deployment, and the reasons for it.

Still pushed by the current, 'Pietas' edged into the protecting arms of the Rhine Fleet headquarters. It was about three kilometers short of Colonia and comprised an administrative area about two hundred paces a side, walled and topped with a palisade fence. Very few passengers disembarked and only dispatches were landed and collected. The signaller who dealt with the dispatches told Seleucus and Philip that they were expected by the Prefect but, unfortunately he had been called to a liaison meeting with the Governor who was with Legion XV Primigenia. The signaller took them to the Fleet's main office block, a substantial, brick-built structure.

"Welcome Captain," the Navarch greeted Seleucus and bestowed a nod on Philip. "The Prefect presents his apologies but a major campaign is starting and he must be with the Governor at Noviomagus." He noted a blank look on their faces. "It's one of our Bases, but a pivotal one in this campaign. Look here."

On the wall map, they could see how a campaign against an enemy based in the swamps, islands and coastal areas of the Rhine would pivot on Noviomagus. It was built at the beginning of the Rhine delta with access to the various mouths of the Rhine by river and by canal.

"Tough fighting and easy drowning," supplemented the Navarch. "Fortunately, we have strong allies with critical skills and local knowledge of river crossings in tidal waters."

"Germans?" Philip could not help but sound dubious.

"Of a sort," said the Navarch looking properly at Philip for the first time. "Actually they are Batavians. They live mainly on this big island between the principal mouths of the Rhine. Give them an inflated goat's bladder or a bundle of reeds and they'll get across the River Styx in full flood—and fight a pitched battle on the other side. Amazing."

He turned back to his desk. "Now, you need to get to Gesoriacum and you need to do it before the main fighting starts or you might find yourself stranded here. There is a ship available for you now, but all shipping will be at a premium in the very near future. I dare say you wanted to have a better look at the way we do things on the Rhine, but I think you would be wise to get to the Ocean sooner rather than later."

"What do you think, Philip?"

"No choice Captain. I would like to see the amphibious operations but we have a time table."

"Right," said Captain Seleucus. "What ship is it?"

"It's not a warship as such," said the Navarch. "We have liburnians but they are not good Ocean-going vessels, too long and narrow. In any case they are already committed. The Prefect has allocated you the 'Justitia', a Rhine Fleet transport. About the same size but much more solidly built than a liburnian, if slower. You can convey the ship-building timber that Camp Commandant Maximus has been screaming for at Gesoriacum."

"Sounds good," said Seleucus. "I suppose there is no shortage of timber in Germany."

"That, and rain, we have plenty of. All the transports are made here of German oak. It only takes legionaries about a month to build one and they certainly prefer shipbuilding to making roads. It's the felling and extraction of the timber. We have plenty of prisoners-of-war as labour and, god knows, we have plenty of trees, but you have to be careful giving an axe to a German prisoner, we lose more guards that way. I'll keep them at it, and stockpile the planks and frames here. I'll send them down to you as shipping permits."

"What about mail, sir?" asked Philip.

"Same thing," said the Rhine Fleet officer. "Although there might not be much shipping coming to you until this campaign is over. I think it might be quicker for you to communicate by road to the Misene Fleet Base on the Rhone. They get dispatches to Rome from there quick-time."

He stood up, and the others took the hint.

"When you see Maximus," said the Navarch, "give him my regards. Have a safe voyage, Captain. And you too, Philip."

CHAPTER 28

▼

EUROPE

Marching north from the Rhone, my little command settled down while I became more comfortable with my rank until I found I was not looking forward to handing it over when we arrived at Gesoriacum. Also, Scota fell in love.

Titus, Rufus Sita, even old Fangs, tried to impress her, and the young legionaries of Legion II Augusta would willingly have swum in the Ocean to please her. She had only eyes for Cogidumnos. I had always thought of him as a cold fish, even though he was a fine-looking man, but he had changed a lot since leaving Rome. He had shed his toga in the City and now, striding along the native trackway in his woollen trousers and cloak, he seemed to better fit the surroundings than he ever did in Rome. He had let his hair grow and no longer shaved his upper lip where the shadow of a respectable Celtic moustache was becoming noticeable.

Scota had outwardly changed less. She was still intelligent, athletic and combative but, the further north we went, the more exhilarated she became, the more lustrous her auburn hair and the more dazzling her green eyes. It was no wonder that even the morose Thracian troopers found every excuse to drift past the transport animals where she could be found joking and arguing as we marched. I felt more than a pang myself when she turned her white smile on the British renegade.

For me, the best time of the day was just before the afternoon meal, the walls up, the guards posted and the smells of newly turned earth, horses, woodsmoke and sizzling bacon in the air. The senior people would assemble and sit, lean or lie around my bedspace to consider that day and the next. Scota's opinion had become not merely accepted but, quite often, sought, except, of course, by the arch-conservative, geriatric legionary. As a military orders group, it was far from formal. It always took place around a meal together in the open. The only concession to rain, and to our seniority, was that, in any downpour, we would huddle together under the wine-wagon. The soldiers made do with ramshackle structures cobbled together with their shields and javelins.

Seventeen days spun past like a chariot wheel. The lead-grey of the Ocean showed on the horizon. We started to descend beside a north-flowing stream. I called an early halt. Rocks were jammed in front of the wagon wheels and I ordered everyone to tidy up.

As usual, the young legionaries went at the task with a will, shouldering each other for a place at the stream's edge and splashing water like schoolboys. The horse-soldiers off-saddled and groomed their horses with wisps of straw, picked out their hooves and casually checked their teeth. The startled mules got similar, if more circumspect, treatment. The Celts, in addition to a cold-water wash, shook out their clothing and combed their hair. The rest of us, comb-less, flattened our hair with stream water. Then we picked up our equipment, kicked away the brakes from in front of the wagon wheels and marched on to Gesoriacum.

Less than two kilometers further on, a formidable figure in silvered armour sat his charger under a tree. Anicius Maximus, Camp Commandant of Legion II Augusta and military commander of Gesoriacum, had come to see what we had done with his wine.

I saluted and reported who we were, where we had come from and where we were going. He did not tell me who he was, but then, he did not need to. I often think that dark eyes tend to soften an appearance. In his case the eyes were as bright and sharp as black, polished stones. He inspected my command on horseback, nodding at Fangs whom he seemed to know, staring disapprovingly at Cogidumnos who stared impassively back, and pushing against the oxskin bladder on the wagon as if to gauge how much wine was left. He then told one of the troopers to dismount and give me his horse. The man looked puzzled and hesitated. Perhaps he did not understand Latin very well. Before Rufus Sita could intervene, the Commandant made things clear. As quick and accurate as a Roman pickpocket, he plucked his vinestick out of his girdle and backhanded the cavalryman across the upper arm. The Thracian tumbled out of the saddle and I snatched the reins from his hand before the Commandant practiced his forehand on his other arm. He was more startled than hurt, but he was paying a lot more attention.

I was not wearing riding breeches but I swung into the saddle with as much dignity as I could muster. Scota covered her eyes in pretended embarrassment and returned the Commandant's stare with a sweet smile. He turned his magnificent horse and I jogged on after him, ahead of the convoy.

That evening, as instructed, I reported, with Fangs, to his tent. He had hardly spoken on the last few kilometers to Gesoriacum, through the farmlands and down towards the Ocean. Although I strained my eyes, I had not been able to see any sign of Britain on the horizon. Now, I thought we would be getting down to business. Fangs told me that he had gone through recruit training with the Commandant but, after they had emerged as new legionaries, their careers had soon separated. Maximus had risen to the highest level in the Legion while he had, without resentment, remained an ordinary soldier.

Outside the tent a big old ruffian of a batman waited for us. He and Fangs exchanged coarse insults in hoarse whispers, then the man held back the tent flap and announced us in a loud voice.

"Optio Aurelius Victorinus of Legion VIII Augusta, and Fangs, the most Fearsome Figurehead in the Fleet."

The batman clearly kept his ear to the ground.

"Viridomar," said the Commandant, pleasantly. "Bring wine and then get out of our sight. Sit gentlemen. Welcome Optio. Nice to see you again Fangs"

They chatted a while about the doings and the personalities associated with their Legion, II Augusta. Fangs was encouraged to talk about the twenty recruits he had brought through basic training and he did so, very thoroughly. With cup in hand, he provided a clear verbal picture of each man. He concluded, as if by formula, that, promising as they were, they were not a patch on the recruits of his youth. The Commandant appeared to be uncomfortable and eased his backside in the chair as if he had had a lot of riding to do.

"Good, Fangs. Get your youngsters settled down and entrenched for the night. Keep an eye on those two Brits. You are going to stay here with me for a while. I need to have a talk with the Optio about his orders and intentions. I understand that the orders are from high level and we will need to provide support. In the meantime, depending on the Optio's needs, you can lay out a full sized legionary encampment to include this headquarters and the cavalry wing. Allow for four times the usual number of granaries. Tomorrow, I want a list of craftsmen in your unit. See Viridomar, he has got an amphora of the good stuff for you. My present. Would you excuse us now?"

The legionary saluted and left, rubbing his hands.

"Now, then," said the senior officer, turning to me. "What is your real connection with Legion VIII Augusta?"

"None, sir, I have no idea even where it is."

"It's on the Danube, so, if you are hoping for some pay you may have to wait a while. If you are officially on their books, I can pay you from here and recharge the costs to them. I'll have Rufus sort that out. In the meantime, draw rations for your party from here. What are you tasked to do?"

I told him.

"What you need is a fishing boat. I'll requisition one for you but I do not recommend a local crew. They may have sympathies with the other side and an accident in the Ocean is easy to arrange. There are Roman mariners here in plenty but they are merchant seamen and loose-mouthed when drunk. It would be better to use disciplined military men"

I mentioned Captain Seleucus and Philip.

"Yes, I saw their itinerary in the mail you brought. The Fleet on the Rhine is committed now but they should be here shortly. Better for you to wait for a reliable Navy crew, I think." He did not wait for agreement. "How was the road from the Rhone?"

I told him of the lack of urgency among the road construction workers. The sharp eyes narrowed and the Commandant made a note. His stylus dug deep into the wax.

"Incompetents," he closed the tablet. "I understand you know something about surveying."

This was not idle conversation. I could see the threat to my independence.

"I am not a surveyor, sir. I trained as a water engineer so I do know my way around surveying instruments. My orders, though, are concerned only with the evaluation of our allies' support base in Britain."

My voice, even to me, sounded hoarse and feeble. I did manage to meet his stare as he considered me.

"You know what is going to happen here," he said. "The building and filling of granaries is critical. Anyone wanting to disrupt the invasion plans has only to attack the granaries. They must be sited properly from the outset or they may be outside the fortifications when the Task Force assembles. You do see that?"

The trouble was, I did see that. I was not going to give in so easily.

"Cogidumnos may have contacts on this side of the Ocean whom I must meet and evaluate before the crossing."

"*May?*" said the Commandant, while I groaned inwardly at my mistake. "Don't you know yet whether he has any contacts on this side? I see. Well, I have.

So, while we wait for the Navy, I will introduce you to one of my contacts from over there and you will do a little surveying, agreed?"

"I don't have any instruments," I said weakly, and felt even worse as his forbidding features broke into a beaming smile.

"That, at least, is not a problem. I have a groma in stock and you can improvise the rest. See Viridomar on your way out."

CHAPTER 29

▼

BRITAIN

"It's Legion II Augusta and Legion VIII Augusta so far," said the High King, sitting with his brother and his adviser in the otherwise empty hall in Kaleoua. "That means, with their attached auxiliaries, about twenty two thousand men. We'll eat them for breakfast."

The fire burned low and the remains of their three meals still littered the long table. No servant had been allowed back in to clear away.

"That can't be all, surely," Caratacos was shaking his head "Professional soldiers or not, they would be crazy to try it unless they had double that number."

"Unfortunately you are right." High King Togodumnos leaned back and loosened his belt a notch. "Ceri's information is that the road to the south is being improved. That means more soldiers on the way."

"Also," said Fox, "the Romans are buying up corn that hasn't even been planted yet. They are definitely getting ready. We have done nothing so far that could be considered a provocation so I would anticipate a demand for that fictional tribute again."

"Not that old nonsense. Do we look like a charitable institution?"

"That's the only excuse they've got for the moment, other than the whinings of our traitors there."

"Well," said the Druid, Fox. "The Romans do claim to be offended by our sacrificial burning of criminals."

"What have they got against religion?" the High King was only partially joking. "And, in any case, what's it got to do with them?"

"They have selective sensibilities," said Fox. "Their state religion approves and encourages the public slaughter of fighting-men, wild beasts and their victims in

the name of religious holidays. Their methods of official execution include stran-
gulation and the throwing off cliffs. No, this is nothing more than an excuse."

Caratacos' mind was on another track.

"Where are they going to store this corn they are buying?" he asked Togodumnos. "Can Ceri find out?"

"I say we are probably looking at four or five legions with their auxiliaries, say
about fifty thousand snails in round figures." The High King was following his
own line of thought. "We know that they can find or make the ships but, firstly,
will those cowardly troops embark this time and, secondly, if they do, where will
they land?"

"If we accept fifty thousand as a working figure," Fox calculated, "we far outnumber them. The Catuvellauni alone, we know, can field 60 000 warriors, the
Trinovantes probably 50 000, and the Cantii in the south east about 22 000
between them. How many from the Atrebates, Caratacos? About 11 000? And I
think that even King Buduoc should be able to field 6 000 northern Dobunni. In
round figures, from the tribes directly acknowledging the High King, we can
expect roughly three times the force levels that the Romans can commit. That
does not include smaller contingents from other British, and perhaps even Irish,
tribes."

"What it also does not include," said Caratacos, "is the fact that we cannot
keep those force levels in the field for longer than a month, depending on the
time of the year. The Romans, as long as they have supplies, can stay in the field
indefinitely. Can Ceri find out where that corn from Gaul is going to be stored?"

"Well, if we cannot stay in the field as long as the Romans, we shall have to
beat them quickly." Togodumnos laughed. "No, I'm not being flippant. Knowledge of the timing of the invasion, if it does come, is going to be critical. I intend
to use all our forces in a massive, all-out assault before the Romans can get inland
and while we are still at full-strength."

"But if we don't beat them conclusively at the landing point," Caratacos was
getting irritated. "It will become a matter of supplies. Tell Ceri to find out about
the corn over there, will you."

"Alright, alright," Togodumnos soothed his younger brother. "I'll task our
nephew to do just that. Now, we cannot predict if the Roman troops will mutiny
again when ordered to embark…"

"No, but we might be able to influence them," Caratacos' firm assertion
stopped the High King in his verbal tracks.

"How?" he demanded.

"We must find out why the snails object to crossing the Channel. It's not that they are afraid of falling off the edge of the world or being attacked by sea monsters. Romans cross the Ocean in all directions all the time. We must find the real reason and use it. Get Ceri on to it."

"I agree." Fox's support of Caratacos surprised Togodumnos but, after a moment he nodded.

"Right. I'll do it. Now, as to the possible landing place. They have twice landed in the south-east, Cantii-country. They have twice had a difficult time of it and retired. Do you think they will land there again?"

"No," said Fox.

"Yes," said Caratacos.

"You first, Fox."

"They know we will be expecting them there and they know that the Cantii have twice resisted Roman invasions and burned their own crops rather than leave them for the invaders. That, admittedly, was a long time ago. More recently they know that the Cantii chased out the traitor Adminios because of his Roman sympathies. There is no local support whatsoever for the Romans in the south-east. They will land somewhere else and hope we have our forces concentrated in Cantii-country. I believe they will land here, on the coast of the Atrebates and push north for Lud Dun. They might be able to seal off most of our forces in the south-east peninsular while they take Kaleoua, Lud Dun and Camelodunon in succession."

The two brothers silently tested the proposition against their own military experience.

"No." The High King was emphatic. "Even if they thought I would put all my eggs in one basket before being sure where the landing was taking place, they would know that they could not land sufficient manpower to seal off the army of Britain in the south-east and, at the same time, reduce our three principal cities."

"Added to which," said Caratacos, "they cannot rely on that much local support here among the Atrebates, either. Ex-King Bericos has been gone a long time and there is not much opposition left. They would have to measure the possible advantage of any local support against a much longer sea-crossing. They won't want to land on a hostile beach with half their army scattered in ships all over the Ocean. For the same reasons, they won't try to land at Camulodunon itself, where there will be no local support at all. No, I think they will land in the south-east again."

"So," the High King of Britain summed up his strategy. "What we want from Ceri's intelligence network is, more than anything, the Roman embarkation date so that I can mobilise the army of Britain at the latest possible stage. The Cantii and the Atrebates will assemble locally. All other contingents will assemble at Lud Dun where the good road system will enable me to deploy rapidly either to the south-east or the south. Ceri will command the Cantii, you will remain in command of the Atrebates. I will command the bulk of the army assembling at Lud Dun."

Fox and Caratacos considered the command structure. Caratacos was a soldier experienced in British warfare but Ceri was not experienced and was allocated a vital function. What Togodumnos had also said, however, was true. The High King could reinforce and take command of the Cantii very quickly from the main army assembly point at Lud Dun.

"I agree," said Caratacos, "and I also agree that we must make every effort to defeat them on the beach."

"If they do get ashore?" enquired Fox.

"Then," said Togodumnos, "we'll smash them on the Medu River."

CHAPTER 30

▼

EUROPE

Philip showed me over the 'Justitia' when it docked. It looked more like a huge bundle of firewood than a military fighting ship. I knew that it was carrying a full load of timber for shipbuilding purposes but it was hard to see where the load ended and the ship began. They had apparently had a slow, rough passage and room for such trivialities as crewmembers had been very limited. As stevedores craned untidy bundles of planks out of the ship at Gesoriacum, I took a good look at it.

The only warship I could compare it with was the liburnian 'Sol'. 'Justitia' was much broader in the beam and much higher at the bow and the stern. Having seen the size of the rollers coming in from the Ocean, I could see the reason for this. It was probably also the reason for the massive timbers used in its construction, fastened together with huge iron nails. Philip told me it had a flat bottom for grounding if required and the thick sides could resist floating ice which could be encountered on the Rhine where it had been built.

I asked him about the nails. In the construction of the liburnians, planks were laid edge to edge and were fastened to one another by wooden mortice joints. The frame of the ship was inserted at a later stage and the planking secured to it by wooden dowels. The below-water part of the hull was then sheathed with lead to provide ballast, assist in water-proofing and to repel borers. The lead was nailed on with copper nails.

The transport 'Justitia' was built to a different philosophy. It had no ram and fewer rowing ports, higher up the hull. It was designed to operate in cold waters where borers are not so active and, on the Rhine, lead is scarcer anyway. Ballast was provided by a layer of rocks laid on the inside of the hull and a good deal of water supplemented it. Such waterproofing as there was, was provided by caulking of the spaces between the planks with seaweed, which naturally swells when wet. The pumps are usually very busy on a Fleet transport.

The nails do rust and eventually fall out, but the transports are for rough usage and do not have a long life anyway. Even a major leak, developing on a river surrounded by forest, is not considered by the military to be major problem as long as tools and spare nails are carried on board. The ship's carpenter would have no need to do a nail-by-nail survey on any transport destined for an Ocean crossing with me on board. I would gladly do it for him. With my sack of copper nails in mind, I resolved to convince Captain Seleucus as soon as possible of the need to launch several proper warships to protect the leaky transports.

As we walked up to where Legion II Augusta, in the shape of Fangs and his men, were digging in, Philip told me about the Rhine and what they had seen there. The campaign in the Rhine delta had commenced as they turned into the canal connecting the river to the Ocean and they had passed through in convoy with a number of troopships going to deal with coastal marauders. He told me what he had heard of the Batavian allies and their prowess at crossing rivers and flooded areas. I told him of the state of the road south to the Rhone and that, given the character of the Commandant, it was about to change for the better.

When we reached headquarters, Rufus Sita was packing up for the move to within the new Camp. I gathered he was unhappy about having to destroy a half-finished sand table, whatever that might be. Viridomar was still on duty outside the Commandant's tent. He was unusually polite as he asked Philip about a village on the left bank of the Rhine, his home. It seemed that he was a Celt, a blood-enemy of the Germans to hear him speak of it. Given the history of the Rhine, this would not have been surprising. The surviving Celtic communities in the Rhineland were natural allies of the Romans against the Germans. Philip did his best, but I could see he had no idea where Viridomar's village was, nor anything about the local conditions there. The batman did not hide his disappointment as he announced us to the Commandant.

Captain Seleucus was still with him, chatting in Greek. The small table was covered in calculations of manpower, rations, numbers of animals and shipping requirements. The clutter was removed and replaced with a map I did not recognise.

"This is the south coast of Britain," said the Commandant, switching to Latin for my benefit and fixing me with his sharp black eyes. "See that large island just off the coast? And the bay behind it? Cogidumnos claims it is a heavily populated part of the coastline with a lot of support for King Bericos. I have checked his story and it is true in so far as the King's predecessors once ruled Atrebates on both sides of the Ocean. The remnants of the tribe on this side no longer owe any official allegiance to him, of course, but there is still some unofficial contact across the water."

"One or two agents have been developed from among the Atrebates on this side," put in Seleucus pleasantly.

"And one or two of those agents have come to a sudden end on the other side." The Commandant was not well-pleased with the interruption. "My information is that there is no significant support for King Bericos here. There is, however, a small number of Continental Atrebates who might be useful to a new administration in the Atrebatan territory of Britain. Cogidumnos and that woman, King Bericos' daughter, are to make every effort to generate support among them. At the end of the day, however, the only way to assess the support potential for the King's possible return is to canvass the British."

The Commandant got to his feet and moved stiffly about the small confines of his crowded tent. We turned in unison to watch him.

"I will introduce you to one of my agents, a man called Ambon. He has made several crossings and you can trust him. We have usually used a fishing boat in the past but, since the embargo on cross-Channel movement, this may now be too obvious. Roman merchantmen are required to report direct to Lud Dun or to the British capital, Camelodunon, and are not allowed to call at the south coast ports. The Captain has a possible solution."

Seleucus ignored the slightly patronising tone, as a freedman he was probably used to it.

"The answer is 'Justicia'. It looks more like a merchant ship than a warship and the British are used to Roman merchant vessels in the Channel. I need to look at their coastline in detail so I'll land you at night in a small boat from 'Justitia'. Two birds with one stone."

"We may be detected," said Philip to his superior. "Will that not endanger your work?"

"Hold on!" I felt we were going too fast. "I decide who goes ashore. Philip doesn't even speak the language."

"Nor does Titus," responded the Greek sailor from Egypt, "and I'm sure you are going to want him in the party."

"Titus and I were given specific responsibility for this task. He goes. You do not."

"Enough!" The Commandant stamped and a spasm of pain crossed his face. Seleucus smoothly interjected.

"Philip is a good intelligence-gatherer and I need him with me. I want him to handle the small boat to drop off and collect the shore party. If we are discovered, it will not be fatal to what I have to do." He turned to me with a smile. "It might well be fatal for you of course. Who do you want to take?"

Commandant Maximus could not leave it alone. He leaned on the table and tried to sum up without waiting for my reply.

"Optio Victorinus leads the shore party. His colleague, Titus, and my agent, Ambon, go too. They take Cogidumnos. The woman stays here."

"Her name is Scota." It was really foolish to argue with this experienced and senior army officer but I felt an irresistible surge of anger. I did my best to keep my tone level and reasonable. "She is the King's daughter. He will want her insight as much was we do."

"We do not work for any King. This particular King works for us, and the information we are going to all this trouble to collect is for our use, not his. Ambon will tell you, it is dangerous over there. You might all be captured or killed. With her still alive and with me, I can mount another reconnaissance. Without her, I cannot. She stays."

Seleucus, who seemed a remarkably nice man, decided again to relieve my embarrassment.

"Optio, I really think it is best that she—Scota—remains behind in this instance. She can continue to canvass support among the Continental Atrebates and this will allow us to mount the operation, with Cogidumnos, all the earlier."

There was no denying the force of the argument. I had stumbled into a quagmire because I had been given broad instructions from the highest authority in the Empire and I had assumed everyone would accept my decisions automatically. The lack of thought invested in those decisions had been exposed in a few sentences by the military men. They could have been much harsher than they were, but that was not because I did not deserve a tongue-lashing. It was because I had been sponsored by the Emperor. I had better not let him down again.

Philip was, perhaps, still smarting at my quick rejection of his services. His question was loaded accordingly.

"How are you going to evaluate King Bericos' support?"

"Not alone," I had the belated sense to say. "Cogidumnos, Ambon and I will each see and hear the same things but will consider our impressions jointly. I will not compile any report without hearing them out in full. Where we disagree, that will be noted in the report. I would appreciate your help at the compilation stage."

CHAPTER 31

▼

EUROPE

Senator Asiaticus rode down the familiar tree-lined driveway, through bars of shadow, towards his country home. White wisps of cloud gave perspective to the towering blue of the sky. Bird and insect sound surrounded him in the warm evening air. The horse moved easily despite the distance they had covered, blowing gently on occasion to clear its nostrils of the fine dust stirred by its own plodding hooves. Other than for a bearded slave limping beside the horse's head, Asiaticus was unattended. A few farm hands waved from the fields. Southern Gaul was at peace.

The long, low, red-tiled roofs of his villa came into sight and several members of staff came running. He smiled and patted hands, shoulders and heads but what he really wanted to see was the house and his wife, in that order. His horse waggled its ears and bucked slightly. He told the manager, without anger, to have the bee-hives moved away from the driveway onto the other side of the house.

He learned more from what his manager and staff did not tell him than from what they did. The pigs and the sheep were thriving. The goat's milk was plentiful and the oxen were in good health. From his position in the saddle, he could see a donkey turning a flourmill and the women hoeing the big vegetable patches. The large white house gleamed among verdant plenty.

He gripped the reins, iron signet ring digging into the fingers of his right hand.

The manager, who had been watching his face, hastened to explain that the Army had collected all the horses due in terms of the contract but had requisitioned all the other horses as well. They had been taken away north. Asiaticus had been paid, but nothing, other than the slenderest of breeding stock, was left. Also, a large number of slaves had been requisitioned, with ox carts, to carry stone for road-making. His estates were not any less wealthy than they had been; he had been paid.

He had plenty of money, always had had. The wealth he savoured in middle-age was living livestock, and of this he felt he had been plundered.

His young wife stood in front of the pillared entrance at the far end of the gardens, formal with statuary, trimmed hedges and geometrically sited ponds. She was dressed in a long formal stola. Her dark hair was covered with an expensive silk scarf. He sat his horse. She bowed slightly and made a short formal speech of welcome while he looked over her head. One of the roof tiles was askew. The pigeons had whitened the copingstones.

Sliding from his horse, he embraced his wife. He pulled his folded toga from behind the saddle and threw it over his shoulder, then he led the way inside. He walked straight through to the house across the central courtyard, house servants, gardeners and clerks bowing and getting out of the way. He turned and dismissed the manager until the following day and then strode across the mosaic into his office. He had not been here for many months and looked at and touched his possessions with pleasure. He threw down his toga, sat in his chair and looked about.

His wife glided into the room with a jug of his estate wine and a silver strainer. A small loaf of bread—made from wheat grown on the estate, ground into flour here and baked in this house in an oven heated by wood cut from his trees—also lay on the tray. It tasted very good.

She had thrown back the silk scarf from her hair which had been dyed a fashionable dull blonde and contrasted with her brown eyes. She looked directly at him and smiled with pink lips.

"Welcome home, Valerius," she said softly.

He walked around her and closed the door gently. Then, he deliberately tore her fine Indian cotton stola from neck to hem.

CHAPTER 32

▼

BRITAIN

I did not like the look of Ambon. It was not his appearance, bulky, bristly and red-eyed though it was. It was his direct stare and knowing, yellow-toothed smile that seemed to threaten imminent violence. I had known such men in gladiator school. Some displayed the attitude like a mask to hide the ravening worms of fear. Some were truly unhinged and killed constantly so that no enemies were left alive. I had a deep reluctance to turn my back when he was present. Still, no one said that being an Imperial intelligence agent meant being in sheltered employment. Cogidumnos and Titus did not seem to have any qualms, themselves. I decided to keep Ambon always in my sight and wear my chain mail vest.

We took our swords, Titus and I opting for the standard legionary pattern, Cogidumnos taking a long Celtic sword with a decorated hilt. Ambon bemoaned the loss of an implement called a falcata until Viridomar found him one from somewhere. The heavy, single-edged blade with its straight wooden handle looked impossible to carry comfortably, but he improvised a sort of scabbard which he slung over his back. We were dressed as Celts, complete with woollen trousers. Cogidumnos wore a silver torc as befitted his status. Neither Titus nor I could ever pass as Britons but, perhaps, we might be accepted as Gallic Celts, at least until we opened our mouths.

We went over 'Justitia's' side quite far out to sea. The night was very still and sound carries a long way over water. There was a moon but also a lot of diffuse cloud. The water was just a few shades lighter than the hills of Britain and in almost a flat calm. The fragile hide and wicker boat rocked alarmingly, and Philip hissed quite unnecessary warnings, as we settled into the small, smelly hull. Ambon had indicated the landing point from the 'Justitia's' deck but, from the slightly lower level of the boat, I could not pick out the headland he had been using as a marker. He confidently pointed a direction to Philip and the seamen started to paddle, a quieter option than the oars. The vapour of our breathing seemed to hang in the cold air over the boat. It seemed almost as if we were not moving but, when I turned, 'Justitia' had gone.

A pinpoint of red light appeared at the edge of the sea like a hole poked in a fire screen. The seamen laboured on, small sounds of gasped breath and swirling water seemingly loud in the boat. The faint murmur of sea on the shore could now be heard. There was a smell of seaweed.

About a hundred meters from the water's edge we stopped. We were beyond javelin range but an arrow could reach out this far. The red glow disappeared. Ambon clapped his hands in a short rhythm and a faint response echoed from the shoreline. On Philip's order, the paddles dipped again and a moment later the hull grated on pebbles. Ambon called softly.

"Phylus?"

"Here." A tall figure moved forward.

"How's the eye-lotion business?" Ambon snorted at his own humour.

"Good enough for me to be able to see you, unfortunately. Who is going back to the ship? What's your name? All right Philip, this bundle goes back with you, give it to Maximus and tell him it is for Governor Galba, got that? Galba. Right, let's get off this beach. Walk on the rocks. Tide's coming in."

As the man placed in charge of the shore party, I felt I was being uncomfortably propelled along by events, but an exposed beach was certainly not the place to stand and discuss the issue. Philip just caught my sleeve and confirmed the pickup details, then I followed the rapidly disappearing shore party into the shadows of the undergrowth fringing the beach. I had to move quickly to catch up, vegetation scratching my ankles and catching my clothing. I almost blundered into the rest of the group sitting in a tight circle in a waist-high clump of bushes.

"Glad you could make it," Ambon was apparently enjoying himself.

"I'm Phylus. You are...?"

I told him.

"Right," said Phylus. "I've arranged the meeting with sympathisers at a homestead three kilometers from here. They are there now. Ambon knows where it is. Which one is Cogidumnos? Right. You have not got long. They will want to be gone by dawn. You, on the other hand, will have to hide for the rest of today if your pick up is tomorrow."

"Wait." I did not want to interrupt the flow but this arrangement pointed to disaster. "The so-called sympathisers, are to be allowed to leave before we do?

What is to stop them from reporting to the local authorities while we are waiting for the boat?"

"Nothing, my Roman friend. And nothing will have prevented them from doing so before they even came to the meeting. The local authorities might be waiting around the homestead even as we speak. I don't think so, but I cannot be positive."

Ambon drew a breath for some witticism at my expense but I cut him off.

"Time for us to earn our money, then," I got to my feet. "Lead on."

Phylus did not move. "I leave you here."

"Very well." I tried not to show disappointment. "Thank you. Lead on, Ambon."

He shambled to his feet and burrowed into the undergrowth like a huge, sway-backed boar. I followed him with Cogidumnos behind me. Titus brought up the rear.

I had not counted the number of men with Phylus but, whatever the number was, far too many people outside my control were already aware that a party of Romans was ashore in southern Britain. The High King's warriors might even now be galloping towards the beach. The three kilometers to our destination seemed more like five.

The vegetation was not forest or woodland but seemed to be farmland which had been abandoned. We passed a ruined building with the naked spars of a previously thatched roof pointing at the night sky. Cultivated land reverting to woodland goes through a stage of dense regrowth. It does not provide firewood or shelter from the weather but is useful cover from view. It was through this form of undergrowth that we made our way in almost total darkness.

Ambon halted at the edge of ploughed land. I could not see the homestead but I could smell smoke. Perspiration quickly cooled and cold started to gnaw the ears. There was no sound except for our breathing.

"Go around," I told Ambon. "Stop when you get to the track to the farmhouse."

"We might bump into one of them," protested Ambon, his breath enough to make a strong man flinch. "They will have put out a sentry, maybe several."

"Swing wide and we take that chance," I told him. "If the High King's men are here, they will ambush the approach from the seaward side."

There was no guarantee of that, but it seemed likely. If the High King's men had not arrived, then a position on the track to the homestead would give us advance warning.

We reached the track and nearly walked over it in the dark. I left Ambon with Titus near, but not under, a prominent tree, allocated our rally point if anything went noisy as the derelict building we had passed, and then set off down the track to the farmhouse with Cogidumnos. We walked quite openly with our hands away from our weapons. The slight ambient light occasionally gleamed on my companion's torc.

Unusually, no dog barked as we approached the farmhouse. A foot scuffed on the track behind us and we ignored the sound. We walked straight up to the porch, knocked on the door and walked in. The fire in the centre of the round room illuminated several moustached faces and the smoke, or the tension, caught in my throat. There was a pause while I blinked my watering eyes and then a growl of welcome rose from the half dozen men around the fire. Cogidumnos was hauled close to the fire and a place was pointed out for me. The door closed out the cold night.

I was not insulted to be more or less ignored, in fact it suited me. I could follow the conversation only with difficulty, the local dialect coming through very strongly. It was more important for me to form some sort of assessment as to the standing of these men as well as to their degree of commitment. Cogidumnos was certainly made welcome enough and enquiries about family and states of health were rapidly exchanged.

Cogidumnos' mention of the name Bericos caught my attention. The response to the name of the former King was muted and unenthusiastic. On the other hand, their reaction to a question about local relations with the administration at a place called Kaleoua was vociferous. They were discriminated against, it seemed, victimized and oppressed. Foreign Britons, Catuvellauni mainly, had migrated into the lands of the Atrebates and were taking the best jobs in the administration and were being allocated land accordingly. The resources of the Atrebates' territory were being raped by Kaleoua which was where the only real development was taking place. The courts were controlled from Kaleoua. Kaleoua was run by a representative of the High King.

I gathered that one, at least, of the company was a fisherman who had been disappointed in a court decision on a dispute over a fishing right. Interestingly, the disputant who had been successful had also been a local man. Another had been dispossessed of his farm to pay compensation to the family of a man he had killed in a drunken brawl. Still another had been unfairly downgraded in citizenship status, and forced to pay a fine, for simply beating his wife.

The conversation began to bore me and I became dangerously sleepy. No food was offered and I could not take out my own and eat it alone. Beer was passed around but I drank as little as was polite.

Eventually, the door was opened again and I was surprised to see the faintest lightening of the sky. Farewells were exchanged and our hosts, one moderately drunk, hurried out to make their various ways home. The owner of the farm, a grizzled little widower, attached himself to me and I took the opportunity to gossip, in my faltering Celtic, about the affairs of the district. He told me that there were thirty farmers' homesteads within a day's walk and most of them were part-time fishermen as well. It had been a well-populated area once but now several families had moved closer to Kaleoua where there were more opportunities. Some, he said, with a wink, had gone overseas. Perhaps two or three families. I thanked him for his hospitality and walked away up the track with Cogidumnos.

I hoped our colleagues had positioned themselves as far from the prominent tree as I had instructed because, when we reached it, several of the dissidents were urinating on its base. We did the same until they were out of earshot along the track. We then turned off the track and the other two, luckily dry, joined us. Before it was full light we had withdrawn into the regrowth beyond the ploughed land on the seaward side of the farmhouse.

We settled down amongst the waist-high bushes and small trees in a small depression just outside the ploughed land. The hazy, rising sun had no warmth and we could not build a fire. We did have food. I left the others to eat and crawled to the edge of cover where I could watch the farmhouse. I was tired and cold but strangely content. For all I knew, I was the most northerly Roman in the world.

Titus crawled up and lay shoulder-to-shoulder. I chewed a grass stalk and, while Ambon and Cogidumnos slept, I told him about the meeting. The taste of the farmer's beer faded. The old man came out of the house late in the morning, chopped some wood, milked the goat, went back inside. There was no sound except for a slight breeze and gulls in the distance. It was really quite pleasant. I turned on my back and went to sleep.

The settling of Ambon's bulk beside me woke me. It was early afternoon. The weak sun, low on the horizon, was beginning to decline to the west. Leaving them, I slid backwards to where Cogidumnos lounged in the depression. He looked rested and pensive. Without being asked, he reminded me that the people we had met comprised only a sample of the support he could call on. I pointed out that they represented, together, only a small coastal area of the High king's domains. Furthermore, they had appeared to be more aggrieved with administrative decisions which had gone against them, rather than responding with loyalty to King Bericos. After a pause, he agreed but asked what more could we Romans expect, or want. If those men were prepared to listen to him while he was an exile, how many more would follow him when he arrived to take up residence?

With a frantic rustling, Ambon appeared through the undergrowth, crawling rapidly on toes and elbows. He said the word I did not want to hear.

"Horses! I woke Titus. He's watching."

"Get ready to move." I was already crawling back along his route.

I could hear the hoofbeats as I joined Titus and shrank to the ground. Six horsemen, horses blowing, were riding at a canter down the track to the farm-house.

"Hide or fight?" said Titus with a grin.

"Neither. We run bravely away. This brush will not hide us from a man on a horse. We may possibly beat six of them, but there will be more. Tell the others."

He went.

The horsemen had the farmer out in his yard and he was shaking his grey head emphatically. Two of them dismounted and strode into the house, swords drawn. Time we were gone. When I crawled back, only Titus was there. Out Celtic allies had carried out a tactical withdrawal. At least, I hoped so. They could just have easily taken it into their heads to attack the cavalrymen on their own.

Running fast through clinging undergrowth while bending double is a true test of fitness. We had to stop from time to time to check direction but, by the time we reached the derelict farm buildings, I was not certain whether it was fatigue or the gathering dusk that was clouding my eyes. A tall clump of dry grass had been gathered at the top and tied into a knot, indicating that our Celtic friends had been here and were still running. Titus carefully untied the knot and we imitated them.

We were now running upright, and the going was correspondingly easier, downhill to the sea. A flicker of white slightly to our right summoned us into a small, low wood on the edge of the beach. It would be a very brave cavalryman to ride his horse in among these close-packed trees. Cogidumnos or Ambon had chosen well. While we panted against the rough bark, they watched the darkening country behind us.

It became progressively darker and cold enfolded us. I shivered and looked out to sea. No sign of 'Justitia', it was much too early. We were in good shape. We still had some food, weapons, a good defensive position and no one was injured. There was no sign yet of pursuit and darkness was almost complete. All we needed now was a smelly oxhide boat and an argumentative Greek sailor, and those assets were, hopefully, on their way.

Five days later, 'Justitia', with us on board, was still at sea. Five days while the weather had got progressively worse and five days while the ship plodded slowly east along Britain's south coast. They were days of extreme tension and effort for the crew of the Fleet transport and of uncomfortable boredom, for the most part, for the returned landing party. Titus, had been comprehensively sea sick for the first two days but was now showing signs of becoming an irritating old salt.

The pick-up from the beach had gone smoothly. Philip had been out by only a hundred meters or so, which, I could understand, was good small-boat navigation at night on an almost unknown coast. It did provide the opportunity for sustained criticism from brand-new seamen such as myself. The opportunity, once he had delivered me to the safety of 'Justitia' was duly taken.

Captain Seleucus had welcomed us back, briefly congratulated us, and told us we were now going to get some real work done. From then on he seemed to be either up the mast, prowling about in a small boat with a lead-line or annotating charts. In the meantime, the wind whistled threateningly in the rigging to the scream of sea birds and we watched surf exploding on beaches as we crept along the south British coastline. Philip was always, it seemed, with the Captain. Cogidumnos was often in a huddle with Ambon and Titus, initially anyway, was on his deathbed.

I had mentally composed my report. I could have given it to the ship's clerk to write but decided to do it myself when the desk was planted on solid ground. I had time on my hands to wander around the ship and get in the way of the busy crew.

I located a marine willing to show me the ship's artillery. There were two pieces, both arrow-shooting machines he called catapults, mounted one on either side of the bow and covered against the weather. The Captain, happy to get me out from underfoot, gave the marine permission to demonstrate. The marine pulled the cover off one of them.

A catapult is like a short sturdy bow laid horizontally. The two arms of the bow are separated by a long channel down which the iron-headed arrow or bolt is launched. Each of the arms is inserted in a vertical roll of sinew which is kept tight by a screw at the top of the roll. The tension in the tightened sinew tends to force the outer ends of the arms forward against the frame of the weapon. The outer ends of the arms are linked by the bowstring.

When the catapult was to shoot, an artillerymen would adjust the elevation by raising or lowering the rear end of the arrow-channel. My marine pointed out a sort of shuttle that runs in the channel. He demonstrated how the shuttle is hooked to the centre of the bowstring and then drawn to the rear by a small windlass at the end of the channel. The windlass hauls in the shuttle, which tows the bowstring backwards, pulling back the arms of the bow against the torsion of the sinew in which they are embedded.

When the bowstring is fully stretched, a sear is engaged to hold it in position and the shuttle is disconnected. The bolt, with its sharp iron tip and wooden shaft, is positioned in the channel and its shaft fitted to the taut bowstring. Pressure on the trigger then drops the sear, releasing the bowstring to hurl the bolt along the channel and away towards the enemy.

"All very simple, really," said the young marine. I had more questions.

"Range?" he said. "About three hundred meters on the Rhine. We've never practiced with them on the Ocean, not in this ship anyway."

"Yes," he continued. "The legions do have them, although they don't give them to auxiliaries, no mechanical aptitude you see. I believe the legions allocate them one to each century of eighty men. They have bigger ones too. Of course, legionaries have it easy, they have a stable platform to shoot from."

Nuisance or not, I could not persuade Captain Seleucus to allow me to shoot his catapult. Catapult-bolts cost money and I might break something. Anyway, his crew did not have time for amusing me. The answer was no.

On the fourth day, our lookout spotted a sail crossing our track. It was identified as a Roman merchantman out of Lud Dun. We had entered the shipping lane connecting Gesoriacum on the Continent with the Thames estuary and we turned north as if to round the North Foreland into the estuary. That was not, however, the route we took.

A natural channel cuts through between the Ocean and the estuary, separating out a small island from the British mainland. Many Roman skippers who know its shallow, tidal waters prefer to use this shortcut rather than to go around the small island into the turbulent water where the estuary and the Ocean meet. A small, navigable river, the Stura, empties into this channel from the mainland side.

The Captain ordered most of the oar ports to be closed and hidden, and all the crew, except for the helmsman and a few sail-handlers, were sent out of sight. My catapults remained covered. To a non-seaman, I suppose that the lightly disguised Fleet transport could look like a Roman merchantman. We waited off-shore until the following morning when the tide, wind and current were moving to the Captain's satisfaction and then 'Justitia' nosed in towards the channel.

The side of the entrance to our right seemed to particularly interest Seleucus. It consisted of a long pebbly bank stretching out about three kilometers from the edge of the island. The top of it would be well exposed, he said, even at high water. The other side of the entrance, the British mainland, was much higher, the beach much narrower. The entrance of the channel was narrow, perhaps less than a kilometer wide, and shallow, but soon opened out as the ship edged north and north-westwards, pushed by the tide. Two shepherds and a dog watched us from the mainland.

The channel was about sixteen kilometers long, becoming wider as we went further north. About half way along, a guard boat sat watchfully, on our left, in the mouth of the Stura River but did not approach. Roman ships, we knew, were not an uncommon sight on passage to the Thames. It was, nevertheless, a relief to see the channel opening out and to sail slowly out into the sea again.

Instead of turning west for the Thames and Lud Dun, 'Justitia' continued almost due north, as if for the British capital, Camulodunon, until it was unlikely that any of the watchers would still have an interest and we were out of the main-stream of British coastal shipping. We did meet a Roman merchant ship coming up from Camelodunon but managed to stay outside hailing distance. When the shipping had thinned out to a few distant sails, the disguised Fleet transport turned in its track.

Captain Seleucus did not re-enter the channel but went around the island on the seaward side, arriving off the long bank at the southern mouth of the channel as dusk was settling. Time for a law-abiding merchantman to stop for the night and far enough away from the Stura River guard boat. Waves were breaking on the seaward side of the bank but the sea was nowhere near as rough as we had seen it further back along the south coast. It was low tide. The anchor was dropped from the stern and 'Justicia' slid up onto the pebbles with a tired groan which was almost human.

Philip, who had spent all day with chart and ruler, departed over the side with lead line and a wax tablet. For form's sake, I went over the bows with a few sea-men and two hawsers. We made the ship fast and lit a cooking fire in a hole on the bank while Philip bobbed about in the ship's boat. The seamen tightened the ship's hawsers as the tide came in. I was mildly surprised at how often this had to be done. No one came along the bank or from the channel to challenge us.

Long before midnight, Philip, red-eyed and wet through, came ashore from a water-logged boat and gratefully accepted some hot wine at our little fire. While he and his men drank, we emptied out his boat in the darkness and carried it over the bank and launched it in the channel. Groaning theatrically, he made his way to the boat with the dry seamen from my party, leaving his own men to steam in relative comfort. Before dawn we were finished.

Captain Seleucus had the crew below deck haul in gradually on the anchor cable as the tide ebbed, and 'Justitia' slid finally off the bank with a minimum of effort. With Philip almost out on his feet and our Captain exclaiming in satisfaction over his voluminous notes, our ship pointed its blunt bows south across the choppy grey sea towards Gesoriacum and a motionless bed.

CHAPTER 33

▼

EUROPE

Gesoriacum should have been like returning home but a lot had changed in the ten days we had been away. The little contingent of replacements for Legion II Augusta, with the reluctant help of the five hundred cavalrymen of Ala I Thracum, had dug a low, rectangular perimeter bank, 400 meters by 600 meters, for the Camp which would one day house the entire Legion, or one of them.

The palisade fence which should top the embankment had, as yet, not been begun but cavalrymen already stood guard at the gap in each wall where gateways had been designated. Units had been moved inside. The cavalry tents and horse-lines were packed closely at the south of the Camp, on either side of the Praetorian Street. Far away, in the centre, Rufus Sita and his small staff occupied the large area pegged out for the Legion's headquarters. Close by, in another large empty area, the Commandant's single tent squatted on the ground allocated to the commander's residence. Between the Commandant's tent and those of the cavalry, where, one day, ranks and files of tents would stand, stood the four tents of the legionaries of Legion II Augusta, Legionary Fangs commanding.

Rufus Sita was waiting for us at the Praetorian Gate in the north wall. This was an impressive title for a gap in a long, low embankment with one dismounted cavalryman as its custodian. Still, I could see the point. The Camp had been laid out exactly like every other legionary camp in the Roman army. When the Legion marched in, every section would know where it had to go and every legionary would know where every facility of the Camp was to be found.

Sita was looking harassed and clutched a stylus in one hand like a badge of office. He managed a smile of welcome but did not indulge in any chitchat.

"Captain Seleucus and Navy personnel over there."

He indicated a largely empty space to the west, or left, of Praetorian Street. There was one large and one small tent there. I could hazard a guess as to which one was Philip's.

"Optio Victorinus and the special service section over there."

One small tent stood alone to the east, or right, of Praetorian Street.

"Just a minute!" I was indignant. "Where's my tent?"

Sita's brow furrowed as he recalled standing instructions.

"Centurions and above, large tents," he recited. "Optio's and below, small tents. Small tents accommodate eight men." His brow cleared. "One tent for Titus, Cogidumnos, Ambon and yourself, Optio. Plenty of room."

My temper was not improved by Titus and the horrible Ambon visibly suppressing their amusement.

Cogidumnos was, if anything, more annoyed than I was, but about something else.

"Where's Scota?" he demanded.

"The woman?" Sita's brow furrowed again. "No women allowed in Camp," he recited. His brow cleared. "She was sent to find accommodation in town. I have the address somewhere."

"Listen, you idiot," Cogidumnos was speaking quite calmly. "That woman, as you call her, is important. She is the daughter of a king and a target for assassination. She had better be safe."

"You'll have to discuss that with the Commandant," said Rufus Sita loftily. "He wants to see the Captain, the Optio and you, all separately, when you have been to your quarters."

I was the last one to be interviewed. Philip, who was not required, gave me the bundle Phylus had entrusted to him on the dark beach in Britain. It felt like a bundle of wax tablets stitched into a leather, water-resistant, covering.

The Commandant listened to my verbal report in silence. The hard, gleaming black eyes never left my face. When I had finished, he told me to sit down. Viridomar was told to bring another cup and then he turned and asked me if the bundle I had with me was the written version. I told him that the bundle I had was from an agent in Britain for Governor Galba and that I would complete my written report in two days. He told me, without any particular emphasis, that my written report would be ready tomorrow and to a standard fit to be seen at the Imperial Palace. The day after tomorrow I was going to Rome. I could take Governor Galba's mail with me.

When I had regained my breath, I asked about the rest of my party. A faint smile crossed the grim face.

"They all stay here," he said. "I'll send an escort with you as far as the Rhone. Before you go, collect a letter from Captain Seleucus to the naval officer commanding the Misene Fleet detachment there."

"I hope I'll be returning here, sir?" I ventured.

"You'll get your orders in Rome. When you see Governor Galba, you may give him my compliments."

As we seemed to have run out of small talk, I threw back my wine and took my leave.

On my way to my tent, I saw Cogidumnos standing at the gap in the north wall, the Praetorian Gate I must remember to call it. As I ambled up, I noticed that he was standing tensely with his fists clenched, staring at a tent which was being erected just outside the Gate.

"What's happening?"

"I think all those blows on his helmet have rattled his brains loose!"

"What do you mean?" I was puzzled, although Cogidumnos' words did seem to strike a resonance somewhere.

"The Commandant," he said angrily. "I told that military numbskull that Princess Scota was important to the expedition and that there was no way I was going to allow him to isolate her, without protection, in what may be a hostile town."

"And he listened to your sound advice, did he?" I asked innocently.

"He's had that tent put up outside the Camp, in front of the gate guard, and he's given Scota instructions to come back here and move into it."

"Well," I said. "I hope I am around to hear your explanation to Scota."

I went off to work on my report.

CHAPTER 34

▼

BRITAIN

Uncle and nephew sat together on the high ground overlooking the Medu River from the east, the way an invader would see it. To their right, the river wound its way northwards, past the guard boat station, to the wide tidal flats of the Thames estuary. In front of them lay the smoky settlement from where the big, vehicle ferries crossed the river. To their left, the river wound down from the high ground to the south.

"I don't think they would try to cross here," said Ceri, small, bright eyes darting. He gathered his knees in long arms. "The approach road is too narrow and muddy. The Medu gets even wider to our right, where we can't see it, and becomes tidal. If they did get across here, they would have to face superior numbers charging down on them across that open ground. It would commit them to our sort of battle and they would get thrown back into the river. No, I don't think so."

"Go on," said the High King, leaning back on his hands with his legs splayed out on the grass in front of him. His mouth twisted under the very fair moustache as he politely suppressed a yawn. Ceri looked left and nodded upstream.

"If I were the Roman commander trying to get to Lud Dun and then north to our capital I would cross much higher up. I would approach along the main trackway on the Downs for Lud Dun and a Thames crossing there."

"We both know that even large bodies of troops can get across the Thames at low tide from the mouth of the Medu. They don't have to go as far upstream as the bridge at Lud Dun. They would need local guides, of course."

They looked at each other with grim expressions. Local guides could always be coerced even from a patriotic population, but the Romans had the principal local guide already in their hands. Adminios, brother and uncle to the two on the hill-side, was poised to guide the alien forces should they embark from Occupied Europe.

They turned their heads as a slow-moving chariot was pulled to an abrupt halt behind them.

"I thought that Ena was getting driving lessons from young Segonax," mumbled the High King. "She still handles the reins like a ferryman in a flood."

"I heard that!" shouted Ena, frightening her horses. The chariot jolted forward and she just managed to step down with dignity.

She dropped onto the grass next to Togodumnos and casually plucked a stem. Her horses, seeing that they were safe, settled down to graze.

"So," she said. "What are the High King of Britain and his Regional Governor discussing on this beautiful hillside? Or is it just the view?"

"The view as seen by a possible short-arsed invader," said Ceri with a grin.

"The Romans are not going to get ashore, are they?" she said fiercely, "even if they come."

"They are going to leave their bones on the beach with the skeletons of their ships," growled the High King of Britain. "But, if anything goes wrong and they manage to get a footing, then we must have a plan."

"Well," said Chief Ena, "my people have burned their crops and driven away their livestock willingly before, and they will do so again. I will give orders to have all boats and ferries removed and secured on the west bank of the Medu. If they do come and if they do get ashore, we'll pen them in between the Medu and the sea and they can starve there."

"That's what we'll do," said Togodumnos. "They will come. Tell her, Ceri."

"Chief Ena knows most of this already. Roman skippers report a noticeable increase in military activity in Gesoriacum. Old camps being reoccupied. New facilities being measured out. More troops have arrived, only a handful so far, but they are legionaries not auxiliaries. Corn is being gathered, a lot of it. Also a vessel of their Fleet has arrived with a load of planks."

"Maybe for ship-building," mused Ena. "Although it could be for putting up threshing-floor roofs for the corn they are getting in. No, they could use any old local wood for that. It's ship-building. They're coming."

"Also," continued Ceri, "I hear that a strange ship has been seen sniffing about the south coast, into the Thames estuary. It headed towards Camelodunon."

"That reminds me," said Ena, reaching down the neck of her tunic. "The guard-boat crew on the Stura River saw that strange ship go north through the channel. They had not seen this type before."

She produced a folded piece of old leather with a charcoal drawing on it.

"This is why I wanted to see you. One of the crew drew the sketch. I have made copies for you."

"I don't know," said Togodumnos, peering at the sketch. "It does look longer and flatter than the usual merchantmen. Are those supposed to be oar ports? I haven't seen so many before."

"I wonder..." began Ceri.

"Yes, exactly," said the High King, dusting fragments of dry grass from his hands. "I'll take one copy and see if it docked at Camelodunon. You, do the same at Lud Dun, Ceri. If possible, get another copy over to Gesoriacum and see if it is that military ship."

"I'll send other copies round the other guard boat stations and to the headmen of fishing villages," put in Ena.

"I've just come from Caratacos," the High King told Ena. "His man, that Silurian, Bivan? Yes, Bivan, was supposed to be watching a Gallic eye-doctor but the so-called medico got away from him. The same night, Ceri got word that there had been a landing at a fishing village on the coast down there, although that has not been confirmed."

"It could be that this ship was involved, then."

"It's possible. I want you to feed all information through to Ceri; he will keep me informed. Above all, I want to know which part of the coastline the ship spends most time at, got it?"

"Got it," Chief Ena mimicked, looking directly at Togodumnos with suppressed amusement.

The High King of Britain looked over her shoulder and, in a very bored voice said, "Chief Ena, is that your unsupervised chariot trundling away downhill?"

She sprang to her feet and was seriously annoyed to see that the chariot had only been moved a meter or so by its grazing team. After a fairly brief farewell, she stepped onto the vehicle's platform and drove waveringly away.

The two men walked back to their mounts. The two beautiful horses had been tethered by tying the shortened reins of each to the saddle of the other.

"Give me a leg up will you, Ceri."

Togodumnos was really getting quite portly. He would have to do something about his weight if he did not want to become an object of ridicule amongst the Celts.

"Let's go upstream."

Their mounted escort drifted out of the trees and followed at a distance.

"I remember that man Bivan, he was the river pilot. Did uncle Caratacos execute him?"

"No," said the High King with a snort. "I told him to, but he declined. Apparently that Bivan is an expert on river routes both on the Thames and in the far west. He goes up to Camulodunon quite frequently. I've seen him there myself. Anyway, Caratacos decided that he must be punished. He is sending him to you."

"What for?"

"He wants you to deploy him to the marshes on the south side of the Thames. He does not know that area nor the crossing place. You could put him at the guard boat station at the mouth of the Medu. They should know those tidal flats like the backs of their hands."

"Not as well as they think they do. I'll put him with some wild-fowlers. They hunt those areas in flat punts which will float on wet grass. He's in for an uncomfortable time. Serve him right."

They had to go several miles upstream before they could take their horses across the river.

"Yes," said Togodumnos. "I think the Romans will come along the high ground and cross the Medu up here somewhere then they'll head north west for Lud Dun. How quickly can you demolish the Thames bridge there?"

"It's fairly solid and it won't burn easily. Perhaps half a day."

"Give that job to Grainne. How is she?"

"For the first time, she is looking a little frailer. The spirit is not diminished though, you can see it in her eyes."

"All right," said the High King, reining in. "I suppose you are going back to Lud Dun now. I must get back to the capital."

"You are not going to tour the coast?" Ceri was surprised.

"Not this time. I've seen all those beaches before but, in any case, I can't spare the time. The Iceni have got a boundary dispute with their neighbours, the Coritani, and King Prasutagos has asked me to arbitrate. The Coritani have agreed."

"Great news. Both tribes are effectively accepting your authority."

"Nothing is settled yet, but it is promising." Togodumnos tried not to look too smug, as Ceri grinned at him.

"Which way are you going?" Ceri asked his uncle.

"I'll take the direct route across the Thames here. I'll collect some local guides from among your wild-fowlers and we'll see how passable it is at this time of the year."

"Safe journey, uncle. Watch out for the tide."

CHAPTER 35

▼

ROME

The Imperial Palace seemed almost deserted and, at the same time, in some disarray. There were Praetorians on duty, behaving in their familiarly arrogant way, but none of the almost-silent scurry of organised activity which usually formed a background to the impressive spaces within the Palace. There were a few dry August leaves on the mosaic within the entrance and the shards of a broken pot had been pushed behind a pillar rather than being properly cleared away.

No one was around to show me where I was supposed to go. One of the Guardsmen condescended to go and find someone, grumbling about non-believing slaves taking advantage of State religious holidays and women looking for any excuse to go off and wash their hair. It seemed that the goddess Diana's one feast day of the year was enough to cause significant dislocation at the Palace. No wonder that she was only allocated one day. The heavy document case dragged at my arm, I reminded myself that I must return it to that ship's captain sometime.

Narcissus padded into view, resplendent in new wig and silk robe. He gave me a golden smile, which seemed quite genuine, and hustled me into the depths of the Palace. He kept up a running flow of light conversation. The Emperor was most pleased I had arrived safely, particularly when the Palace was at its most private. Governor Galba was with the Emperor. His soldiers had been most successful in Upper Germany. We were to go right in.

Galba did not stop speaking as we entered.

"...so the Chatti are finished as a serious threat," he was saying, "and Governor Secundus is doing a great job in Lower Germany burning out those pirates' nests. The Rhine is clear from end to end. Time for the next phase."

Emperor Claudius, forearms on his wide desk and hands clasped, looked at me and smiled a welcome. He looked well, eyes clear and good colour in his cheeks. Someone had made him brush his hair.

"Aurelius Victorinus. Put down that case, we will look at official dispatches later. Tell us about Britain."

The three of them watched me intently as I did so. I was most conscious of Galba's wide-eyed stare and wondered if he was actually hearing what I was saying, or just waiting until he could take over the conversation again.

"What about the army's supplies?" he snapped when I had paused.

"One complete harvest is in. This year's is coming in to the granaries now."

"I understand that we nearly lost the stored grain," he demanded, almost before I had finished.

"Not exactly," I said carefully. "Commandant Anicius Maximus insisted from the start that the granaries be built within the fortifications he had constructed. Initially, we had to thatch the roofs. An attempt was made to set them on fire and we lost one granary. The Navy now has its tile-works in production and that won't happen again.

I could see him drawing breath and continued quickly.

"And there was an attempt to poison the military water supply using fish sauce which had been allowed to rot. I have altered the water reticulation to the Camp and that won't happen again either."

"What reprisals have been conducted?" Governor Galba wanted to know.

"Commandant Maximus had several known dissidents from the area put to death."

"Good."

The Emperor nodded and turned to my questioner.

"What is the next phase, Galba?"

The Governor pointedly looked at me and then back at Emperor Claudius.

Without looking at me, and without any emphasis, the Emperor repeated his question. I was beginning to like Uncle Claudius quite a lot. Galba cleared his throat.

"In addition to Legion II Augusta, I recommend the following as the backbone of the Invasion Task Force. Legion XIV Gemina and Legion XX Valeria from Germany and Legion IX Hispana, with the Governor-designate, from the Danube. Vespasian now has command of Legion II Augusta. I suggest that the commanders of the other legions remain in place."

"No," said the Emperor. Galba stopped. "Governor-designate Aulus Plautius, as you yourself noted at an earlier meeting, is not well known and he needs a second in command. Hosideus Geta is a famous soldier and should get his chance. One of the other legionary commanders will have to make way for him. Which legion do you recommend?"

Galba slowly closed his mouth.

"Legion XX Valeria," he said.

"So be it," said our Emperor.

A lot had changed in the management of the Empire since I was last in Rome.

"Why did you select those four legions in particular?" asked Claudius in his not unattractive lisp.

"Ah," said Galba, recovering his brisk manner. "They each contain a high proportion of men approaching the end of their enlistment. Some have even served more than their twenty years. When they have captured Britain, we can give them their discharges there in the form of British land that they can farm as colonists."

Galba smiled in appreciation of the elegance of his plan.

"The colonies of ex-soldiers will help to secure the conquered areas and the treasury will not have to pay them out in cash."

"Do you mean," said Narcissus, quite indignant, "that you intend allocating to the most critical military operation of this reign, four units of elderly invalids?"

"Elderly invalids," said the Emperor Claudius, mildly, "often show remarkable resilience. But my friend has a point, Galba. Invading a hostile country across the Ocean requires fit soldiers at least as much as it requires experienced ones."

"Now that the German campaigns are almost over, the medically unfit, of whatever length of service, will all be discharged in Germany. We will have to pay them something. After that, though, there will still be a lot of fit men coming up for retirement and entitled to full benefits. We need to make provision for them. British land will be that provision, and they will fight all the harder for it."

There was some element in this plan that was worrying me but I could not identify it. Galba was still in full flow.

"I've had a private word with the Camp Commandants of the various legions," he said, "except in the case of Legion II Augusta where I spoke to the Chief Centurion. The legions that are staying will exchange suitable personnel with the legions that are going to Britain. I estimate that the three legions from Germany going to Britain will be built up to about one third of men approaching retirement."

He turned to face Narcissus directly.

"You don't need to worry. The invalids are all being discharged medically unfit before this process starts. No soldiers who are not fit will be included in the drafts from other legions because the Camp Commandants, or the Chief Centurion, would not accept any of them anyway."

"The chief centurion of a legion," said the Emperor, displaying a new knowledge of barrack-room lore, "isn't he the officer the soldiers call the 'first spear'?"

"Yes," said Governor Galba. "That's the officially accepted nickname. The unofficial nickname has a lot more to do with his genitalia than with any military hardware. Although 'military hardware' does seem very appropriate too, come to think of it!"

The Governor and his Commander in Chief roared with laughter while Narcissus and I looked worriedly at each other. Suddenly, what had been troubling me came into sharp focus.

"The families," I said, sharply.

"Yes!" said Narcissus.

"What?" demanded Galba.

The Emperor was still wiping his eyes.

"Those legions have been in Germany a long time, right, Governor?"

"More than thirty years, yes." Galba was looking closely at me.

"And the men we are talking about, about a third of all the legionaries, are close to the end of their service. They must be married, have children?"

"Legionaries are not allowed to marry, son."

"But they do have unofficial families," interjected Narcissus, "local women mainly, I would suppose, and their children, born in Germany."

"The women are mainly local Celts, a very few Romans and almost no Germans," Governor Galba answered slowly, looking as if he was not sure what we were getting at. Emperor Claudius was looking thoughtful. I decided to take the plunge.

"What arrangements, Governor, are there for the many unofficial families the legions will be leaving behind?"

"The short answer, son, is none. It is not an Army problem. Each such relationship is a private arrangement between an individual soldier and the woman concerned. Every soldier knows the situation before he enlists. He may not marry while in service. They all accept this. When they retire, then they can marry or have any unofficial relationship legitimised."

"In this case, though," said Narcissus, "their unofficial husbands and fathers are going to be marched away across Europe, over the Ocean and retired in a land outside the known world. How are they ever going to rejoin them?"

Galba's face was getting red and his eyes even rounder.

"Many of them will not want to. Look, what do you think happens when a soldier is killed? His unofficial wife, and any children, simply form a similar relationship with another soldier. That's what happens. It's not only in the Army, either. I really do not want to give offence, Narcissus, but what happens when an owner wants to sell a slave? He sells the man off and the so-called wife, as often as not, forms a similar relationship with another slave. Isn't that what happens?"

Narcissus, mouth compressed in a hard white line in a grim face, simply nodded.

"Yes," went on Galba, in a quieter voice. "That is what happens. When the legions have conquered Britain, the surviving legionaries who are eligible will be given an honourable discharge and will receive British land as their retirement bonus. The law will recognise any existing relationship. It will then be up to the individual to make arrangements for his family to join him if that is his wish. Or he can marry a local British girl if that suits him better. It probably will. It will be a lot cheaper for him anyway. Either way, it will be his decision, his problem, not the Army's."

I think it was the mental picture of a Celtic woman standing watching a Roman legion marching away from her for ever, but I could not keep quiet.

"Governor Galba," I said quietly, "could it be, though, that quite large numbers of those legionaries might be so attached to their unofficial families that they might refuse to go?"

"Son, I…"

"Galba," said the Emperor, mildly. "You keep calling the Optio, 'son'."

"Optio Victorinus," amended the Governor, "you are thinking of that disgraceful incident under our previous Emperor. Let me tell you something. No one ever believed that that so-called invasion was ever going to take place. It was a farce, a pretence right from the start and the soldiers just played their part in the game, like the officers and like the Emperor."

I was impressed that this illustrious soldier, businessman and administrator of the Empire, was making such an effort to explain this to me, the second-lowest form of life in the legionary structure. Perhaps he was trying to explain it to himself?

"You are an optio, you have seen service in the Urban Cohorts but you have little to no experience in the life of a front-line legion. That will come. I have commanded military units for the best part of twenty years and I am reckoned to be a severe disciplinarian. I am telling you, Optio, that compared to the centurions of a Rhine legion, I am a wilting flower. If the Emperor orders the invasion, the centurions will order the men to embark and the men will embark. No question."

There was a silence. The air seemed to be faintly ringing. The Emperor cleared his throat.

"Well, thank you everyone. Aurelius, please leave the dispatches and address where you can be reached with Narcissus."

Narcissus walked with me through the echoing halls of the Palace.

"What do you think about that?" he asked, directly.

"At school, my teacher always complained about my sums. I understand that there are about five and a half thousand men in a legion and there will be three legions from Germany, say sixteen and a half thousand men, not counting the legion from the Danube. Galba calculates that about a third of the men from Germany will be due for retirement, say…"

"Five and half thousand men," said Narcissus, not smiling. "One legion's worth. One man in three."

"They will be in their late thirties or early forties, experienced and valuable, or they would have been discharged early on medical or other grounds. Except for their years, they could be considered the best men in every unit. Their children will be growing up. I can accept that there might be soldiers in any legion who would abandon their families, but not these men. I forsee trouble."

"The Imperial treasury is virtually empty after the waste of the last Emperor and the money the present one has had to pay out on his accession. We cannot afford to pay them out their terminal benefits in cash and yet it is critical for the present Emperor that the invasion be a success. Will the centurions' grip on the discipline of the soldiers be enough carry the legions into Britain?"

"I am an optio, nominally a member of a legion, but I have no first-hand experience of legionary life. I understand that there are about sixty centurions in a legion, ranging from the most junior, in command of a century of eighty men, to the chief centurion of the legion, the 'first spear'."

"So they probably cannot affect the issue by numbers alone, I understand that. But, what about their prestige and the discipline they are responsible for?"

"I can only go by what I have seen. Anicius Maximus, at Gesoriacum, joined as an ordinary legionary and rose through every level of the centurionate. He was promoted from 'first spear' of a legion to being its Commandant, third-in-command. I was present when he ordered those ten dissidents to be rounded up for reprisal for the sabotage there."

"Those men were not soldiers, though, were they?"

"No, they were local Celts, and one of them was a woman."

"What did he do to them?"

"Celts, you know Narcissus, believe that the human spirit resides in a person's head. He had their heads crushed under the wheels of a loaded wagon. There has been no sabotage since."

We had stopped and I could feel the cold of the marble floor seeping through the soles of my shoes. Narcissus looked searchingly into my face. His eyes, like mine, had seen steaming human entrails hanging from the jaws of wild beasts in the arena. He swallowed convulsively.

"The centurions, they will be mostly married men themselves?"

"Their situation is different," I told him. "They do not serve a fixed term of enlistment and even the most junior of centurions gets paid thirty two times more than an ordinary legionary. They can afford to make private provision for their families."

"I see. So. This enterprise must succeed. The centurions alone, however, ah, resolute, may not be able to make it happen. Numbers are against them."

"Numbers and quality. And we have not taken into account married soldiers who are not due for retirement. They will also be leaving their families behind."

We started to walk again, side-by-side, through the almost empty Palace.

"There will be further discussion about this," said the freedman. "Whatever happens, keep me informed."

Going down the steps of the Imperial Palace into the sunlight, I was conscious of a small, warm breeze and a lot of noise. The streets were busy. Not with the movement of officials, nor with the bustle of commerce, but with feminine laughter and crowds of ambling slaves. It was the holiday of the goddess Diana and hair-washing water was being thrown out of windows in every block of flats, working males below being the preferred targets. The wet streets were no places for free, male citizens to linger. I made good time to the sanctuary of the Praetorian Camp.

If the City's streets, on this holiday, were hazardous for free males, they were ten times worse for any member of the Urban Cohorts brave enough to venture onto them. It was not unknown on this day for the content of the hair-washing bowl to transform itself into the content of a chamber pot while still in mid-air over the head of an unsuspecting patrolman. It was not surprising to find that the Urban Cohorts' part of the Camp was still well-populated with members who had urgent business back in barracks.

I burst into my old quarters with a roar of: "Got you, you loafers!"

The counters of a board-game went flying, a pair of dice were palmed with lightning rapidity while one of my ex-colleagues, with pretensions of being an intellectual, tried to hide a bundle of dirty pictures under his mattress. Inevitably, one member of the section, stretched out in contemplation of the inside of his eyelids, sat up too rapidly and almost damaged the bunk above him with his head.

There followed a formal round of curses, insults and threats. They were moderately pleased to see me and listened with some interest to my story, asking politely about Titus. Almost in passing, they told me that the slave Domitilla, Titus' long-time girlfriend and lover, had been freed, had married an olive-oil merchant and was now pregnant with their first child. This was the first I had heard of this. Titus, if he knew, had not said anything.

"Of course," said the intellectual of the dirty pictures, "Titus should have got her well and truly pregnant before he left."

"Some chance," scoffed another, fingering the bump on his head. "You wouldn't catch a girl like Domitilla like that. Titus was a sponge-diver."

This was a reference to the contraceptive device used by nice slave-girls receiving the attention of hairy policemen.

The door burst open.

"Got you, you loafers! Oh, god, no! Not again. Victorinus come back from among the barbarians to bring Rome to its knees."

"Good morning, Centurion," I said politely.

"Good morning, my arse," he said coarsely. "You lot. Get out on patrol now. Worried about a little scented water? You are all wet behind the ears anyway. Move!" He aimed a violent but ineffective kick at the last man through the door and turned to me, a beatific smile illuminating his blunt features.

"That's better. Now, you come to my quarters, have a decent cup of wine and tell me about this Britain place. I understand you are an optio now? Obviously some dementia in the higher ranks."

It was towards midday when I got away from the old Centurion, several cups of wine to the better and with a promise from him to get my letter to brother Marcus by the quickest means possible. I needed Marcus to review the production schedule of ship's fittings in the light of improved communications from Italy to the Ocean-coast and the ship-building potential at Gesoriacum. I would have liked to travel the relatively short distance to Pompeii to see the family but dare not leave the City while waiting for the Imperial summons.

Holiday or not, the taverns were doing a roaring business, the off-duty slaves as customers, harassed citizens serving them. It was almost like slave-owners waiting on their slaves at Saturnalia all over again. The only difference was that, during Saturnalia, the slaves wear their master's clothing. Diana does not insist on that. The streets were less busy, hunger and thirst drawing people indoors, and the danger of getting wet through seemed to have decreased. All the hair-washing must have been done by now and the women attending their secret rituals.

I was staying at the British Palace, although I could have bunked-in at the Praetorian Camp. I recognised the porter as a pair of suspicious eyes framed by the peephole in the front door. When he recognised me, the door swung open and he greeted me as if I had not spent the previous night there. King Bericos, who was a late riser, wanted to see me. He was in the study and, surprisingly, Adminios was sitting with him. I was quite touched when the big old barbarian embraced me. Adminios contented himself with a friendly nod. The scar on his forehead had almost disappeared.

They both watched me hungrily as I described what was happening on both sides of the Ocean, nodding and making encouraging sounds. I told them about the state of health and the doings of Cogidumnos and of Scota and about the meeting with the Roman sympathisers in the territory of the Atrebates. I did not tell them of the 'Justitia's' cruise along the south and east coasts afterwards. Bericos did not ask the question I had been dreading but I decided to go ahead and tell him anyway.

When I had finished, he hid his disappointment well and nodded gravely behind his huge white moustache.

"So, there was not much visible sign of local support for my return," he mused. "It's been several years now, and your relatives, Adminios, have been busy subverting my subjects. It's not surprising. All that will change again when they see their King back in Britain."

I was not so sure. Cogidumnos and Scota, together, might form a focus for Atrebates' nationalism. Resistence to Britain's High King was possible, but not without leading the people straight into the Roman fold. The cause of Atrebates' independence was lost. King Bericos' time was past.

Adminios was asking me for news of the south-east, the Cantii. Apart from the possible landing place we had surveyed, and I was not going to even mention that, there was little I could tell him. I had gathered from Ambon that Adminios' name was hated in the fiercely anti-Roman south-east.

Although they put a brave face on it, the two renegade Britons were profoundly disappointed that their former countrymen were not anxiously waiting for their return to place them back in their seats of power. They were on the verge of becoming nonentities. Their barely-concealed gloom soon began to affect the other residents of the British Palace and the evening meal developed into a fairly maudlin drinking party which continuously seemed to be on the brink of violence. I was happy to escape to bed.

The following morning I walked to the Imperial Palace through streets filled with hung-over slaves, slipping as unobtrusively as possible through the crowds, and bright-eyed women with shining hair. I have always enjoyed walking the streets of the City and this morning, it seemed as if everything was back as it should be. Many more women, even outdoors, appeared to be wearing silk and there was none of the feverish anxiety that was common everywhere during the previous Emperor's reign.

Narcissus received me in his own large office. Early though it was, a number of Senators and military officers waited outside and there were not enough marble benches to go around. I was called straight in. The tremor in his hands was as noticeable as ever and his voice was hoarse.

"Optio Victorinus. Your orders are to take these dispatches to Gesoriacum, immediately. They are for the eyes of Commandant Anicius Maximus and Captain Titus Seleucus only."

He rose and walked rapidly around his office. He had not dismissed me and I sat still. He stopped and stared at me.

"A decision has been made," he said. "We are going to go with Governor Galba's recommendations. All of them. Good luck and a safe journey."

CHAPTER 36

▼

BRITAIN

"Do you know what they did?" Ceri demanded in the High King's hall in Camelodunon.

The doors and shutters had been opened while it was being swept out and to allow the smoke from the newly-laid fire to blow away. It was bitterly cold and the draught sent sparks from the fire and lifted the High King's thin hair. He huddled in his chair, his very fair moustache buried in the thick wool of his chequered cloak.

"No," he grumbled. "What did they do now?"

Ceri's eyes glittered in the pale winter sunlight carpeting part of the interior of the hall. A servant coughed as she carried ash outside.

"They burned that fishing village we were using as a landing place and killed every tenth person. Put them out naked on a frozen pond overnight."

Togodumnos shuddered delicately inside his cloak.

"We've always known they were savages pretending to be civilized men," he said. "And nobody ever said they are not determined. They remind me of our Silurians. What happened to the rest of the villagers?"

"Ran away to relatives. Some crossed here—in a fishing boat. Ena's taken them over and settled them on the south coast."

"What's happening at that port of theirs?"

Ceri walked about closing shutters and doors just as Fox walked in, pushing back the hood of his cloak. His face was ruddy with the cold, contrasting oddly with his bristly ginger hair. He nodded to the High King and warmed his hands at the fire.

"They have one completed legionary fortification, as we know," said Ceri, sitting again, with his feet pointed at the fire. "They have started on a second. Our friends say there are at least two more pegged out. The shipyard is fully operational. They've put up shipbuilding sheds so that their carpenters do not get frozen fingers. They are launching four ships a month with the skilled workers they have there now and they are expecting more. The new ships are being beached in river mouths along the coast. They are under guard. Cavalry. You should see those horses. The upgrade of the main road south is nearly complete."

"We can expect an impossible demand shortly," remarked Fox.

The door burst open again, letting in a draught that caused the fire to whirl. Caratacos strode in, smelling of horses and cold air. He grinned at Togodumnos whose head had been starting to emerge from the folds of his cloak but which had now been withdrawn again. He pushed Ceri's feet to one side and jostled Fox for space at the fire.

"What impossible demand are we talking about?" he asked cheerfully.

The Druid straightened his clothes. "I think they are going to ask for back payment on that figment of Julius Caesar's imagination, the tribute he claimed to have extracted from the then High King."

"That piece of nonsense is ninety years old," growled Togodumnos. "No one believes in it."

"It doesn't matter," said Caratacos. "Politically, you cannot pay it and, even if you did, their Senate would just think up some other impossible demand. No point in worrying about it, just think of a way of refusing that will be the most embarrassing for them. Demand that they return our runaway criminals, like Adminios and Bericos."

"Yes," said Fox, "we have always returned their shipwrecked sailors safely."

"Think up some revolting charges against them," Ceri was enthusiastic. "Adminios is a wife-beater and King Bericos a child molester. We want them back to stand trial before our criminal courts."

The High King's head again rose out of the folds of his cloak, this time in indignation.

"Be careful what you say about your uncle Adminios, young man. You don't want to get on the wrong side of your aunt. And Bericos is no longer a King."

"What's wrong with you?" said Caratacos. "That white face and red nose is not a pretty sight."

"I've got a cold," complained Togodumnos, sniffing in emphasis and standing up to his full height, "but that does not mean I can't put you on the ground two throws out of three."

"Go for it," said Ceri, leaping to his feet. "I'll see fair play."

"Wait, wait," intervened Fox. "Meeting first, wrestling after. Sit. Sit down, or I'll take you both on myself."

The brothers sat down with sidelong grins at each other and at the slight, bristling figure of the Druid.

"Anyway," said Caratacos. "To the Romans, wife-beaters and child-molesters are probably model citizens."

"All right," said the disappointed Ceri. "Cavalry, how many horses have we got now?"

"About four thousand, now, not counting the breeding stock." Fox was pleased with the change of subject but not with his figures. "We lost too many foals from the last crop."

"So we'll still have to rely on the chariot force."

"What's wrong with the chariots?" demanded Ceri defensively. He really knew the answer.

"Not enough roads where you want them. Too many natural obstacles, usually where you want to fight battles. Too many brutal men in enemy ranks quite prepared to kill a team rather than fight a warrior." Caratacos listed the drawbacks. "Still, we have no choice. The senior men like them. They are good platforms from which to direct a battle and they give the infantry confidence."

"I certainly don't want to fight without my chariot," affirmed Ceri.

"See what I mean?" said Caratacos.

"Well, at least, the road system in the south east is well-developed," Fox put in. "And the Downs are good chariot-country."

"Can you get at those ships?" Caratacos asked Ceri. "Burn them at their moorings. Or the woodyards? Or the shipbuilding-sheds, maybe? What about the shipyard workers—some more rotten fish-sauce?"

"I'm trying all those things, but they've tightened their security a lot, and the reprisals, even for an attempt, are very heavy. Our friends in Gaul are not as welcoming for our agents as they were."

Fox grimaced.

"They are becoming fat on the business the preparations for our destruction is bringing. They are becoming collaborators. Use them while you can, Ceri, by next year you won't be able to tell them apart from the Romans."

"What about any new allies here?" Caratacos was asking his brother.

Togodumnos pursed his lips under his fair moustache.

"King Prasutagos and the Iceni have always been reasonably well disposed. He and the Coritani were happy with the border dispute I mediated between them, but they are not yet committed. I think that young Queen Cartimandua wants to support us, but that domain of hers is always in such a ferment of in-fighting I don't think we can rely on any practical help from the Brigantes. I know you think that she might have secret contact with the Romans, Caratacos, but I have not seen any real evidence of it, and neither have you."

"No, I have no hard evidence. That girl is very hard to tie down. No wonder her parents called her 'sleek pony'."

"So, I do not anticipate immediate help from those tribes. Until we win a major battle, that is, and then help will pour in. The Durotriges, southern Dobunni, Silures, no they would not be unhappy to see us do their fighting for them. The Durotriges think that they can retire into those huge hill forts for a few days and the Romans will go away. They have no idea."

"What about the Irish?"

"I would have thought you would have had a better idea of their standpoint than I, Caratacos. No? I have been in touch with High King Conaire Mor on several occasions. His Druid, Niall, has been here twice and Fox has just got back. Tell them, Fox."

"Yes," said Ceri. "What's it like, Fox?"

"A beautiful, verdant country, full of fighting musicians. The only thing that they are frightened of is a snake. Perhaps because they don't have any. Our horses are doing well and are multiplying satisfactorily." He turned to Caratacos. "I did not see Brigit. She had been wounded in fighting in the north. Not life-threatening I understand."

"The High King, Fox," reminded Togodumnos, gruffly.

"Yes. Conaire Mor promised a lot of moral support, and a cessation of raiding if it is going to be helpful. But…but, he will not directly antagonise or oppose the Romans."

"As I said," said the British High King. "Everyone is very happy that we are going to do the fighting for them."

"So," said Fox, speaking mainly to Togodumnos, "it is agreed that we make every effort to destroy the Romans on the beaches or, at least inflict a serious reverse on them. Failing that, we defeat them on the Medu River."

"We must not be pushed further back," insisted Ceri. "We would be giving up Cantii territory and they hate the Romans more than we do. Also we would be giving up good chariot country for the thickets and swamps of the Thames valley."

"If I cannot hold them on the Medu," the High King stood up, "I will fall back north of the Thames and defend Camulodunum. Don't ask me what happens if I lose the capital. The question does not concern me. If that happens, I shall be dead."

CHAPTER 37

▼

EUROPE

Gesoriacum was almost unrecognisable. The completed legionary entrenchment was now topped with a proper palisade fence and more tents were planted in the spaces which had been allocated to them, particularly in the area designated for the Navy.

I had overtaken several bodies of replacement soldiers marching north along the improved main road from the Rhone, and a lot of wagons loaded with supplies and equipment. These were being marshaled and directed into the legionary Camp and its storerooms. Roofed threshing floors had been erected and were doubling as bad-weather drill halls. By the sea, the shipyard was busy every day, all day, and the coastline and river mouths were jammed with brand-new ships, mainly transports of the Rhine Fleet pattern. Digging had started on a second entrenchment. I had surveyed a total of four.

The cavalry of Ala I Thracum provided guards for ships and shore facilities as well as trying to fit in the required amount of coastal patrolling. All members of the Navy made ships; in any spare time, they also made roof tiles. The young replacement legionaries were required to do just two things. Practice their close order battle drill and dig. In the centre of this whirlwind, sat the formidable figure of Anicius Maximus, Camp Commandant, in a single, large tent pitched centrally in the space pegged out for the legionary commander's house. I stood in front of his littered table.

"I am not satisfied," he said.

"With what, sir?" I tried not to gulp like a guilty recruit. "The Emperor did not have any adverse comments on my report."

"The Emperor has his priorities. I have mine. This is not about reports, Imperial or otherwise." He slapped his vinestick down on his table. I did not jump.

"I am not satisfied with the training status of the young replacement soldiers I am getting. I now have one hundred and fifty of them waiting for their legions, nearly two centuries of new men without an officer between them. That pot-bellied, toothless legionary does his best and so does that insubordinate colleague of yours from the Urban Cohorts. The young soldiers have completed their basic training but they need a proper continuation-training program or the Celts are going to eat them alive, not to mention the centurions of their legions when they arrive."

Saying nothing seemed to be the best policy. He knew that I had only a little knowledge of legionary drill, learned mainly from a book and from Fangs.

"You were trained in a gladiator school."

Did everyone in the Army know that?

"And the Celts prefer to fight with a mad charge and then to indulge in single combat if they can break our ranks. These youngsters do not know what they are going to face. Teach them. Report to me what you are doing every day."

I had a quick word with Fangs and Titus. I did not mention Domitilla. If Titus knew about her marriage, he had not discussed it, and probably did not want to. If he did not know about it, I did not need to tell him. They were both supervising muddy legionaries, digging like badgers, and were tired of the task. They brightened when I told them about the continuation-training program I intended to commence that afternoon. The diggers were pretending not to listen.

"These legionaries are mainly earmarked for Legion II Augusta," said Fangs. "The others are replacements for two other Rhine legions. We have divided them into two provisional centuries for administration. Titus teaches one and I the other."

He continued in a much quieter voice.

"They are getting bored and stale. Any new slant on training will be welcome."

"We'll use that threshing floor," said Titus. "The granaries are full and it is available."

"Parade them there at midday," I told them. "One century in full armour with practice swords and standard shields." Practice swords are much heavier but less lethal than the standard variety. "The other century without armour or shields. Have them cut long sticks, the heavier, the better. I'll see you there."

I had just enough time to go and give Philip his mail. He was in the Navy area of the Camp, feeding birds.

"Thought I'd find you toying with your lunch," I greeted him, " but those are the smallest chickens I've ever seen."

"Pigeons, Aurelius, they are pigeons, and you a country-boy."

"So you have finally been demoted to the keeper of the sacrificial animals, is that it?"

"The British Fleet is experimenting," he replied solemnly. "These birds carry messages over long distances at high speed. I am having them released from fishing boats quite a long way out to see if they will fly over the Ocean and find their way back to their coops here."

"Do they?"

I was not surprised at the new official designation of the ships and men gathering at Gesoriacum. I was not paying much attention to his pigeons.

"About half of them. Gallic hawks are very efficient or the birds are traitors."

"I've brought your mail."

Philip took the letter eagerly and opened it with his service knife. It was from his father in Alexandria so I left him to read it in peace.

Fangs and Titus had the legionaries divided into two centuries outside the former threshing floor which was now to be the drill hall. The young soldiers looked alert and happy to be doing anything rather than digging. Fangs was giving them an opening lecture on the standard legionary shield in an impressively clipped, professional manner.

He had removed the heavy bronze boss from the centre of a shield, revealing the handgrip at the rear. He had also taken off the bronze binding from its edge. He peeled back the beautiful red and gold linen front of the shield, followed by the leather panel, to expose the curved, three-layered plywood below. The soldiers nodded they understood that gluing the three layers with the grain running in different directions, meant that there was less likelihood that the shield could be split by a single heavy blow. Fangs dealt with questions and then handed over to me.

I told the men in armour to discard their practice swords and form up in battle line. I then had the other century, armed only with long sticks, charge into them as fast as they could run. Although the battle line was ready and braced, the unimpeded weight of the charge broke through in the place where an armoured legionary slipped and fell under the force of the impact. The rest of the attackers poured through, widening the breach and several more of the defenders went down before they stablised their formation into two shortened battle lines, almost facing one another. The attackers stood in the middle, panting and laughing over the scattered, fallen defenders. The legionaries were used to this drill. I sent them back to their start points.

"How did the attackers break through?" I demanded, watching Titus and Fangs wheeling up two odiferous handcarts behind the reformed battle line.

"They were running together, sir, and hit us all at once," complained one of the fallen.

"Correct, soldier. Don't call me sir, I'm an optio. Now how do you prevent that happening?"

"Javelins, Optio. We throw them into them as they charge."

"Correct. Although any missile will do to break up the force of the charge. Try it again. Charge!"

The attackers had seen something suspicious taking place behind the shields of the defenders and, although they charged enthusiastically, their eyes were wide open. At about ten paces, the defenders took one pace forward and hurled hand-fuls of the smelliest manure obtainable by their trainers, courtesy of the horses of Ala I Thracum. While the volley was in the air, some of the attackers hesitated, others ducked or swerved and the defenders, still on balance, braced themselves. The impact of the charge, although still considerable, was weaker and delivered sporadically. The battle line held.

I allowed a few moments for laughing and cursing. Then I sent them back to their start points and had a private word with the attackers. They nodded, eyes gleaming with anticipation.

"Charge!"

The attackers bore down again on the battle line, ducked their heads under the missile shower and kept going. Instead of colliding with uniform force all along the line of shields, the attackers grouped into several small parties, each one targeting individual defenders. These were grabbed by the shields and plucked out of the battle line like feathers out of a chicken, and then rolled in the manure. One of the defenders released his shield and ducked behind his colleagues, who tried to close up, but there were now too many holes in the defenders' line. It had become a series of little groups of individuals waiting to be picked off.

"Stop! Look around you. This is where a battle can become a rout. What must you do now?"

The answers were immediate.

"Close up."

"Reform the battle line, Optio."

"Suppose," I raised my voice, "suppose that there are a lot of barbarians—and, generally, there are always a lot of barbarians—and they are streaming through the gaps. What do you do now?"

There was a pause.

"Each group must fight back-to-back, Optio."

"Until?"

There was a longer pause.

"Er, until reinforcements come, Optio."

"Let's see how long you have got." I said. "Each group of defenders get back-to-back." They shuffled into position. "Attackers. Take them on."

By concentrating on individual defenders, the attackers quickly started pulling defenders out of their positions or taking their shields from them. It was soon over. All the young soldiers, attackers as well as defenders, were starting to look bemused.

"Stop! Look around you. A rout. Of course, this exercise was not, strictly speaking, fair. The defenders did not have their swords and so their neighbours could not assist the individuals attacked." The young faces brightened. "Remember, the individual was overwhelmed because his neighbours could not assist."

I looked along the row of faces until I saw a face I recognised. They smiled as I made the old joke.

"I want a volunteer. You."

It was the legionary replacement who had been bitten by a mule on the way to Gesoriacum. His first wound in the army.

"Pick up your shield and sword. All of you do the same, and then into the drill hall and stand against the walls."

I stood in the open space with a long stick in my hand. The 'volunteer' watched me warily.

"You all saw outside that small groups of soldiers can be individually pulled apart by attackers working together to a system. Is that form of defence the only one? Here is a fully armoured Roman soldier facing me with his shield and sword. Here am I, a big old barbarian, with this stick representing my long sword. I have no shield, no helmet, no armour. It's no contest, really, is it?"

"You can move about a lot faster, Optio."

"And you can wound him at a longer range than he can hit you."

"Both true," I said. "Let's see. Attack me."

The legionary got set, raising his shield until only his eyes were visible between the rim of his helmet and the top of his shield, his short sword held horizontally at belt level. Only his legs, from knees downwards, were visible. He advanced in a quick shuffle, punching out at me with his shield and stabbing with his practice sword, as he had been trained. He was right handed so I moved to his left, away from the jabs of his short sword. I kept this up long enough to make the point to the watchers. He could not reach me, provided I did not trip over something on the battlefield. The question was now, could I reach him?

I feinted at his head to make him keep his shield up, ducked below his line of sight and rapped him on the ankle then straightened immediately, as he hopped backwards, and hit him hard over the helmet. There were shouts of surprise and of support from his colleagues.

With a hiss, he collected himself and shuffled forward, favouring one leg. I continued to circle to his left, keeping away from his sword. Suddenly, I jumped towards him and poked at his face with the end of my stick. He got his shield up to protect his eyes and I kicked him in the exposed knee.

"Enough!" I held up one hand as he gamely struggled forward. "Two injuries to the legs in single combat usually means only one ending. You could still win, but only if I slipped or if one of your colleagues came to your assistance. Still that was a very creditable performance."

"Well done, lad," said Fangs.

"Now. You have seen that a battle line can be broken. You have also seen that, in single combat, a barbarian has at least an equal chance with an armoured Roman soldier if...If what?"

There was a long pause before my erstwhile opponent found the answer.

"If...if the soldier continues to fight as if he was in the battle line."

"Correct! I knew you were an intelligent lot. If the line is broken, the civilised soldier is reduced to the same level as the barbarian—in fact, he may be even worse off—unless he changes his method of fighting. What must he do? The barbarian is circling around him, out of reach, looking for a chance to use his long sword. His surviving colleagues from the battle line are in the same situation, what do they do?"

"Think bar-fighting," prompted Fangs, although most of these youngsters had probably never been in a bar-fight, "think dirty."

Suddenly, one of the replacements slammed his hand down on top of his shield.

"I stab my friend's opponent."

"Yes! You fend off your opponent with your shield and stab your friend's opponent while he isn't looking. And your friend does the same for you. Don't lose sight of your own opponent, but kill any other barbarian within reach who has his back turned. Watch this one, Fangs, I see definite signs of a misspent youth."

They laughed.

"The barbarians will try and do the same to you, if they can, but now the advantage is back with you. You are wearing armour and a helmet, you have a shield. The barbarian does not have this protection. He is much more vulnerable to a stab from an unexpected direction, and he knows it. His enthusiasm will disappear like a fire in a rainstorm."

I put my stick aside and looked at the smiling faces.

"You are now going to practise this. Wait, wait. Remember that even in a practice mass of single combats, people can get hurt. If you hurt one of your colleagues, you will have to do his digging for him tomorrow. The only touches that count are those with a weapon which does not land on another weapon, shield, helmet or armour. Those touches do not count. All others represent wounds. Titus and Fangs are the judges as to which combatants' wounds are disabling. Their decisions are final. We'll start off with ten men from each century."

At the end of the day, I went to the Commandant's tent. He wrinkled his nose as I saluted and made an adverse comment about cavalrymen allowing their horses to stale outside his tent. I gathered he had caught a whiff of manure from somewhere. I reported on the first day's continuation-training. He seemed moderately satisfied.

Before I left, he instructed me to expedite the training and to make it as realistic as possible. The Emperor had issued an "Execute" order. I knew what that meant.

CHAPTER 38

▼

EUROPE

On the Danube, where it had been based, and from which it had fought, for almost forty years, a giant stirred. Legion IX Hispana was about to move.

The headquarters had already been handed over to elements of Legion VIII Augusta and the headquarters staff had relocated to the huge new Camp constructed nearby. Detachments in the field had handed over to their reliefs and had marched in to join them. For the first time in many years, all of the five and a half thousand men of Legion IX Hispana were together, in tents, in the same Camp. Two wings of cavalry auxilliaries, recruited from the Danube area, were also accommodated with their one thousand horses in the same Camp. Ala I Sabiniana and Ala I Tampiana were going to travel, with the Legion, a long way from their homes, probably for ever. They would pick up other additional auxilliary units, cavalry and infantry and mixed, on the way.

The moon was full and the stone surface of the road to the west shone like oiled steel. Yellow watch-fires broke the crowded gloom of the Camp, with the ridges of hundreds upon hundreds of tents illuminated by the moon. To the east lay a vast sprawl of darkened huts and houses, the accommodation of the soldiers' unrecognised wives and children. It was here that the first stirrings became evident. A rash of small cooking fires broke out, cocks began to crow and the barking of a few dogs seemed to echo in the still air.

In the Camp, as the light of the moon weakened, there was a rising hum of male voices and movement, pierced by the occasional clatter of equipment, the neighing of horses and the hysterical braying of a mule.

As the first line of light appeared in the east, trumpets pealed across the camp and the lines of tents collapsed and vanished. Wailing cries immediately rose from the family accommodation and dark figures began to move from the mass of huts. They rounded the Camp to gather on the north side of the road. A few figures in uniform, spectators from the incoming legion, gathered opposite them on the south side of the road.

The trumpets sounded a second time. The flow of figures from the family accommodation increased. The crowd of dark figures on the north edge of the road spread like spilled ink. From inside the Camp, thousands of animals groaned and protested as the weight of their loads settled on their backs. The palisade fencing on the walls surrounding the Camp appeared to vanish.

A horseman appeared at the Praetorian Gate of the Camp and walked his mount out onto the stone road. A sigh rose from the spectators. Then rank after rank of cavalry walked out, the grey light from the east reflecting dully from helmets and chain mail, shod hooves clattering on the road surface. Several figures on the north of the road held up parcels of food to the troopers. Some were accepted, most were not. The advance guard of the five hundred men of Ala I Sabiniana rode slowly into the dark of the west.

The tops of the entrenchment walls were suddenly fringed with hundreds of human heads outlined against the lightening eastern sky. To the sound of fast, systematic digging, the walls sank into the ditches in front of them, revealing the standing men and loaded animals of the army.

A single horseman walked his magnificent charger out onto the road. He turned aside up a slight rise and stopped among the military spectators overlooking the road from the south. They quickly made space for the Governor-designate of Britain. Aulus Plautius' conventionally handsome features were half illuminated by the pink light from the east. He faced the silent families across the stone road.

A huge, distant voice asked a question within the Campsite and thousands of male voices responded. The question was asked a second and a third time. The third reply was a full-throated roar. Legion IX Hispana was ready. Aulus Plautius' tense posture relaxed fractionally.

A small group of tall men topped by standards and the eagle marched onto the road and the mass of men and pack animals began to unwind behind them. Aulus Plautius saluted as the Legion's eagle, backlit by the first rays of the rising sun, passed by him.

The Chief Centurion led out Cohort I, the double-strength cohort comprising the eight hundred most reputable soldiers in the Legion. A Senior Centurion led each of its five large centuries. At their appearance, a long wail, interspersed with piercing cries, rose from the mass of families thronging the north side of the road. File after file of armoured men, laden with weapons, tools and rations, crunched past with hobnails grinding the stone surface of the road.

The heads of the soldiers, now half-illuminated by the sun at their backs, were all turned to their right, away from where their commander sat his horse and towards the tear-streaked faces of their families.

Aulus Plautius watched the contingent of sappers march past with their bags of tools and then his own personal baggage on pack mules. There followed a gap ahead of an escort of cavalry from Ala I Tampiana which was allocated to him but he did not immediately move to take his place. Instead, he watched the hundred and twenty horsemen of the Legionary cavalry clatter past followed by the horse-drawn artillery and a group of senior officers. Cohorts II to X followed, each cohort led by a Senior Centurion, each century led by a Centurion. Some of the Centurions looked to their left, at him. Every other soldier looked to his right. Loaded pack mules, allocated at a scale of one to every eight-man section, trotted past with the cohorts.

Suddenly, the road was emptying, its surface scratched by hobnails and horse-shoes and dotted with hot manure. The Governor-designate and the families looked at each other silently for a last time. Then he turned his horse's head to the twilight in the west. He kicked his horse into a canter on the soft ground beside the road, his shadow stretching long in front of him.

CHAPTER 39

▼

EUROPE

Cogidumnos had not been able to persuade the Commandant to allow Scota to stay in the Camp and he had found that he could not browbeat him either. He had, foolishly, tried to threaten Anicius Maximus with compiling an adverse report to send to the Emperor. The Commandant had offered him an escort and a fast passage back to Rome to deliver the report in person. Cogidumnos had subsided; he was a more important man on the edge of the Ocean than he ever was in the shadow of King Bericos in Rome. I had been very pleased to hear all this. Even for a British barbarian, Cogidumnos had an extraordinarily high opinion of his own importance.

Scota had refused to stay in her tent outside the Camp Gate and so Cogidumnos had rented a small house in the port. I found them there. It was a small, poor place compared with the British Palace, and not in the best part of the town. The town itself was booming with additional trade of every sort flowing from the assembling of the invasion Task Force. Cogidumnos had managed, nevertheless, to find a small area of quiet. There were no petitioners or supporters gathered outside the door and the only other person inside was a local girl they had taken on to keep the place clean.

I had brought letters for both Cogidumnos and Scota from King Bericos. The Celts do not have a written language so the King had written in Greek which I cannot read. Philip, of course, had no such problem and I had left the letters with him overnight for copying and resealing before I delivered the originals. I got a fairly haughty reception, at least from Cogidumnos, when I arrived with four young legionaries and a cart loaded with new roof tiles stamped "CL BR", denoting that they had been made by the British Fleet.

"Cogidumnos," I said as kindly as I could. "You are behaving like a fool. Every Celt in this town knows who you are and who Scota is. You have said yourself that Scota is a target for assassination and so are you. It's no good sulking here because you cannot bully the Commandant. While you are out of sight of the Roman military, your influence is waning and you will soon be forgotten."

He looked at me almost without expression.

"I must return to the Camp," he said. "Scota must be protected. What are you going to do about it?"

She had been reading her father's letter, looking very pretty in a long woollen stola, and now looked up in indignation at Cogidumnos.

"What do you mean 'Scota must be protected'? Go on back to the Camp. Nobody asked you to come here in the first place. Just leave me your sword and go."

It seemed as if domestic bliss did not necessarily prevail. Run to an accident, walk to a fight.

"These four soldiers," I said. "are also skilled in roof-tiling. They did the granaries in the Camp and they are going to replace the thatch on this house with fireproof tiles. They will sleep next door and kill anyone who tries to attack Scota."

Cogidumnos looked at Scota, who ignored him, and back at me. He said nothing.

"You can go now," I said.

He turned suddenly, threw some things into a bag and strode out of the door, slamming it behind him.

Scota looked up.

"Has he gone?" she asked with a smile. "How is my father?"

I gave her a brief account of the doings at the British Palace and that her father was disappointed by my assessment of the support he was likely to receive in Britain.

"Yes," she said. "He writes some quite nice things about you. Of, course you would know that already if only you could read Greek."

I was embarrassed to feel my ears going red.

"I won't tell you what he says," she rubbed it in. "Just ask the person who opened my letter and sealed it up again so professionally. Goodbye."

Back at the Navy section of the Camp, I managed to get some time with Captain Seleucus. Now that the British Fleet had been formally constituted, I had expected that he would have received a promotion but this had not come through. As an Imperial appointee with a direct reporting line to Emperor Claudius, I suppose an official promotion was really immaterial. I had come to talk business but he had other ideas, at least at first.

He told the marine sentry to allow no one into his command tent. With Philip helping, he uncovered a large sand-table model of a broad peninsular with an island just off-shore at the end. A blue line, representing a river, flowed down the peninsular and into the channel separating the peninsular from the island. The bottom end of the island terminated in a sort of tail, narrowing the channel entrance. I recognised the place.

"Britain," he said.

"The landing place, Captain?"

"Could be."

We all looked at the model. The tent flapped once. I could hear their breathing and Fangs' voice shouting a command in the distance. They looked up at me.

"Special forces seize ground on the mainland side of the channel," I said. "Main force lands on the island, clears it of enemy and re-organises. Main force crosses the channel, picks up the special forces and advances along the peninsular."

Captain Seleucus smiled and signaled to Philip to cover the model again.

"I've got something for you," he said and placed a neatly rolled square of parchment in front of me. It was a contract for me to supply ship fittings to the British Fleet and it was signed by Camp Commandant Anicius Maximus, military commander at Gesoriacum. Seleucus and Philip grinned at what must have been a fairly amusing look on my face.

"Congratulations. He wants to see you. We are going to have a visitor."

A very large tent was being erected next to that of the Camp Commandant. Whoever the visitor was to be, he was important. I decided that thanking the Commandant would be inappropriate—and probably premature anyway. He would find a way for me pay the military back for the award of the contract. I might well be about to start paying.

For once, the Commandant was not working his way through masses of documents in his tent or rapping out verbal solutions to problems brought to him by Rufus Sita. He was standing over the working party erecting the new tent, sailors, judging by their sleeveless tunics. The leather was new and stiff, and working under the critical gaze of the area's military commander was distracting them. They looked around hopefully as I approached.

I followed him away out of earshot but not out of sight of their endeavours. The breeze ruffled his hair, exposing the white scars on his forehead. I was surprised to note that he was shorter than me.

"The Emperor has a message for the High King of Britain", he said. I felt my skin tingle. "A former Consul will be the envoy. He is on his way here now."

He nodded towards the Fleet working party.

"He will be staying with us for a few days—if those webbed footed mariners ever get his tent up—and he will go on to Britain to deliver the message. It is important that the message is placed in the High King's hands."

I could see that. The message must be a declaration of war or, at least, an ultimatum with war as the alternative. News of all the shipbuilding and entrenching must have already reached the Britons, both from their cousins in Gaul and through talkative Roman merchant seamen. They would be expecting a demand. Would the High King deliberately avoid receiving the envoy? What would that do to his prestige among his own people? Maximus was watching me thinking about it.

"There must be no doubt that the High King is aware that the envoy is on his way. His people must know that he knows it. That will ensure that he cannot find a way to avoid the messenger. Someone must go to Britain privately and, in the capital, publicly announce that an Imperial envoy is on his way. The High King must be given notice in writing, if possible. An attempt must be made to get him him to commit to a specific date to receive the envoy. Now, as to who is to do it."

I had no doubt as to whom he had in mind.

"Cogidumnos is, in their eyes, nothing but a traitor. At best, they would simply turn him away. At worst, for us, they would execute him out of hand and say that they had no idea that the Empire employs criminals as its messengers. That would give all the Celts a good laugh."

His sharp black eyes were watching me closely without a trace of humour.

"May I volunteer, sir?" I asked as innocently as I could.

The crowsfeet deepened slightly around the unwavering eyes.

"Yes. The Fleet has prepared a Greek translation of the message I wrote for the High King. Collect it from Philip. The Captain has arranged a passage for you on a Roman merchantman sailing for Camelodunon tomorrow. Don't talk to anyone else here about this. Has Captain Seleucus shown you the sand-table model? Is it accurate? You will be going through the channel again. Watch our for any changes in their security there, especially on your return voyage."

The situation on the return journey might well be different. On the whole though, if I managed my task correctly and the High King was committed to receive the envoy, I should get back with an unperforated hide and a tale to tell my grandchildren.

With a shout of triumph, the sailors got the tent upright, in the right alignment, and began tensioning the stays. The Commandant slapped his vinestick against his leg.

"About time," he said, thinking about the next problem. "What do elephants eat?"

CHAPTER 40

▼

BRITAIN

Ports are ports all over the world, noisy and smelly for the most part, with polluted waters and cluttered quays. They have an over-abundance of dogs given to barking and sea gulls addicted to screaming. They are peopled by self-important petty officials and would-be seamen who do not know one end of an oar from the other. Exciting enough places to visit as a child, they are frequently frustrating enough to break a real sailor's heart. Fortunately, I am not a real sailor.

I vaulted over the side with 'my' document case in my hand almost before the worn timbers of the merchant ship kissed the quay in Camulodunon. I ignored the shout of the guard boat commander who had clambered aboard on the river approach to the port and I set off uphill at a fast walk. I did not know where the palace of the High King of Britain was located but, unless he was a raving insomniac with no sense of smell, it certainly was not down by the harbour. I had no intention of being trapped in the stuffy office of some port official until he could think of a good excuse to put me on the next ship leaving port. Like any well-informed messenger to foreign parts, I was properly dressed in my best civilian clothes with my sword worn openly and my mail vest under my tunic.

The streets quickly became cleaner and less crowded although there were many wheeled vehicles causing clots of congestion. I could see no sign of pursuit. My foreign clothes and shaved upper lip drew no interest at all. Like all capitals, its busy population has a cosmopolitan element and I heard several different languages being spoken. The buildings were mainly of wood or of wattle and daub and some were quite large with more than one storey. They all seemed to be thatched and I could imagine the sort of fire hazard this presented. The city authority had, however, laid out the cobbled streets in straight lines and made them wide enough to act in some way as fire breaks. The generally damp weather in Britain and some sort of municipal Vigiles organisation probably provided adequate safeguards for the citizens.

It might not yet have occurred to the guard boat commander that I was heading for the High King's palace, certainly no one on the merchant ship knew my real mission, but news of my sudden disappearance as my ship docked would already be filtering upwards through the levels of British authority. I stretched my legs through the rustic capital.

There was no obvious sign of a mains water supply, in fact, if the number of women carrying large pots was anything to go by, such a system did not exist. I did see a cart loaded with rubbish but the streets seemed to be cleaned mainly by the rain and open drains running downhill towards the habour.

I was now on a wide street, still walking uphill and with a large, thatched building in view. The pedestrians here were more prosperous in appearance and dressed in brighter and less worn clothing. One of the men, heading in the same direction as myself, was wearing a fine gold torc.

There was a small group of idlers around the gate and a large, red-moustached man who was apparently the only external guard the establishment needed. I walked straight up to him and demanded, in my best Celtic, if the High King was in. He glared at me and rudely asked who wanted to know. I was at the right place. I announced in a loud voice that I needed to report urgently to the High King that an envoy from the Roman Emperor was on his way. The little crowd had stopped talking and was now openly eavesdropping. I repeated my declaration in a slightly different form to make sure everyone got it.

The guard obviously wanted to tell me to wait in line with the others but his little blue eyes flickered towards the crowd of bystanders. Some of the idlers, armed with my sensational news, were already edging away, anxious to spread the word to their own cronies. That word would soon be all over the capital and the High King, I was sure, would not be impressed if he were to be among the last to hear. The guard thought so too. To prompt him, I made a move to take off my sword. He gestured to me to keep it and hustled me inside, closing the gate firmly on the interested faces. Two or three of the bystanders were already walking rapidly away.

We were in a large, paved courtyard with the doors to the main building under a porch at the far end. In front of those doors stood another guard. They shouted back and forth in Celtic too full of local dialect for me to follow. The second guard disappeared inside. I took a step towards the door, following my luck, but I was brought up short by a large hand placed on my chest. The guard's eyes narrowed as he registered the feel of chain mail under my tunic. He glanced about and then set a stool in front of me, gesturing for me to sit down. It was not politeness. I would be much slower taking decisive action from a sitting position. I sat, placing the document case between my feet and keeping my hands in view. All was quiet, except for the gulls.

For a long time, nothing much happened. Several more guards drifted out of the door but remained under the porch. Someone banged on the gate behind me, making me jump. The guard grinned at me and shouted at whoever it was to go away. He remained alert and unthreatening, professional. I was feeling fairly relaxed. Part of my mission was already done. I was close to the High King and the rumour of the coming of the Roman envoy was already launched into the general population.

A smaller man with bristling ginger hair hurried out and beckoned to me. My guard took a step away from me but did not turn his back. I stood up carefully and picked up my case. He followed me as we crossed the courtyard.

"I understand you speak our language," said the little man, beady eyes assessing me. "Call me Fox. Who sent you?"

"The Roman administrator at Gesoriacum."

"Are you a soldier?"

"Just a messenger, now. I am Aurelius Victorinus."

"You can give me your message, then."

"My instructions are to notify the High King in person. I understand he is here."

"Wait."

I waited. He returned after a short time. The building I took to be a palace was, in fact a huge hall with a broad table running down the centre. At the far end, a corpulent old man sat looking along the length of the table at me. My footsteps on the stone floor sounded loud in my ears. He was not so old, his fair, almost white, moustache and his thin hair, coupled with his girth, gave that impression at a distance. The eyes were disturbing. Incredibly, he was alone.

Fox, behind me, said "Sire, this is the messenger. Aurelius Victorinus from Gesoriacum."

A large mastiff, lying under the table, yawned loudly. The air was still and smelled of woodsmoke.

"What is your message?"

I took out the bronze plates inscribed in Latin and in Greek and laid them in front of him. He ignored them.

"What is your message?" he repeated.

"An envoy of the highest rank is on his way from Rome to present to Your Majesty a personal communication from Emperor Claudius. I am instructed to learn from you a suitable date and place."

"And to make sure that everyone knows he is coming, no doubt. I have been expecting such an envoy. The whole country has been expecting such an envoy. Tell him that he is welcome to present himself before me at his earliest convenience provided he brings with him the criminals Adminios and Bericos to stand trial before a British court of law."

"He has already left Rome, as I understand it. Those men remained behind."

"You will tell him what I have said."

"I will tell him."

"Perhaps I can save him a dangerous voyage on our Ocean. As you will know, it is a hungry Ocean which is the unmarked grave of many Romans and their ships," said Togodumnos.

He put something on the table and flicked it towards me. A gold coin gleamed on the surface. I pretended to misunderstand.

"I have already been paid for my duty." I said.

"It is not for you, messenger. You people believe that when you die you need a coin to pay the ferryman of the dead to take your shade over the River Styx. Is that not so? For Roman armies, our Ocean is the River Styx. Tell your envoy that that is the only money he is going to get from me."

The dog sighed deeply.

After a moment, I picked up the gold coin.

"You may go," said the High King of Britain.

Outside in the clean air, I walked downhill, on loose knees, towards the stink of the harbour. I carried the empty document case in one hand and the gold coin lay in the other. Everybody watched me go.

CHAPTER 41

▼

EUROPE

Senator Sentius Saturninus had occupied the tent erected at Gesoriacum with such effort by the British Fleet. As this was deemed to be an official conference, he was dressed in the toga with the broad purple stripe. Anicius Maximus, in full regimentals, sat on his left with Captain Seleucus, in armour but without decorations, sitting beside him. On the Senator's right sat a burly, ruddy-cheeked young man with thinning, tightly curled hair. If it were not for the expensive armour, I would have taken him for a local farmer. Flavius Vespasian is originally a countryman but was then the newly appointed Legate commanding Legion II Augusta, Maximus' boss. I faced this galaxy of talent.

"Optio Aurelius Victorinus of Legion VIII Augusta, Senator." I introduced myself in case anyone was wondering what I was doing there. Strange to say, I was not feeling a bit nervous. The atmosphere was very different from the menacing gloom of the hall of the High King of Britain.

"Optio Victorinus," the Senator, although a small man, had a very resonant voice. "Your military rank does not reflect the importance of the mission from which you have just returned." Maximus stiffened. "I understand, however, that you have special qualifications that, in the opinion of your superiors, uniquely fitted you for the task you were given. Present your report."

If I had not done well, it seemed that the Commandant was in trouble, not me. That made me feel a whole lot more cheerful. I gave my account well, I thought, and they did not interrupt. If anything, Maximus seemed to relax a little. When I came to the High King's final message, I was able to repeat it word for word. I then laid the single British gold coin on the table and stopped. The Senator's eyes seemed to have glazed slightly. Then they cleared.

"You are certain of those words?"

"I am certain." I was. I had repeated them many times to myself on the voyage back.

"How complete is your grasp of Celtic?"

"It is good. Local dialects differ and are sometimes difficult but I have been in northern Gaul some time now. The High King is an educated man and his use of language is precise and clear. There is no doubt as to what he was saying."

"Very well." The Senator looked around the table. Vespasian stirred.

"If I may, Senator?" He turned his square jaw and clear eyes towards me.

"Why didn't you kill him?" he asked pleasantly.

I took a moment to think about that. I had been armed and he had been alone except for the skinny, ginger-headed Fox.

"I know very little about High King Togodumnos," I said, avoiding stumbling over the name, "had I killed him, he would have been replaced by someone we would probably know nothing about and I would have united the British behind the new King. Besides…"

"Besides…" prompted Vespasian.

"Besides, it might not have been so easy. Despite his physical appearance, the British High King is a fighting man."

"I see," said Vespasian with a sudden grin.

Maximus was murmuring to the Senator. To my embarrassment, I heard the words 'gladiator school'.

"I see," said the Senator and looked directly at me again. "You have executed your task well Optio. No, leave the coin. I may need it, yet."

The others laughed. The Senator was going to see the High King of Britain, however menacing his attitude. The Empire did not go to war on conversations reported by optios, apparently.

"Aurelius Victorinus may yet be required here by Rome." I gathered that the Senator, an ex-Consul, might well consider himself to represent Rome. "How complicated would it be to have him transferred from the books of Legion VIII Augusta to your Legion, Vespasian?"

Everyone looked at the Commandant, even Vespasian.

"A fairly simple administrative matter, Senator. I would suggest that his colleague from the Urban Cohorts be included in the procedure."

Maximus was pleased with me.

"Do so then," said the Senator, turning again to Vespasian. "Perhaps his rank should also be reviewed if he is to be employed again as an emissary?"

Vespasian nodded and looked at me with a smile.

I did not mind being kept waiting outside the tent for much of the rest of the day. Sitting on a bench in the weak spring sunshine, I found it very relaxing to watch the scurrying to and fro of dispatch riders and staff officers. Rufus Sita was much in demand. His face had taken on a permanent worried expression and I thought idly that there was a hint of grey in his hair. I could guess at how demanding working directly under the gaze of Commandant Anicius Maximus could be. It was time Rufus Sita escaped back to the cavalry where he could bully his horse.

Philip put in a rushed appearance on the orders of Captain Seleucus. He was excited. He had orders to lay on a proper warship, suitable to carry an Imperial envoy to Britain. More importantly, it seemed, his father was coming to visit him. Towards evening, Cogidumnos was called in. Most of the interviewees during the day had looked excited or, at least, tense; the renegade Briton looked, as usual, cool as a trout.

Viridomar, the Commandant's batman, had brought food around earlier during the day but, as dusk gathered, I was bored and was looking forward to a drink and a gossip with Titus. Preferably with a large lump of Army bread and a slab of hot bacon in my grip. It was a relief when Cogidumnos glided out of the tent and told me that I was dismissed for the day. As I walked stiffly over to the special service section tents, I heard someone shouting for Viridomar to bring lamps. The conference was not over yet.

"Here he comes. Here he comes, the valiant Imperial soldier twice chased out of Britain by the barbarians. The only optio in the army who can run faster than a chariot. Did those female warriors frighten you, then?"

Titus' cheerful insults were like a welcome home. Philip was visiting and raised a full cup as I ducked into the lamplit tent. Rufus Sita was also there but the ever-busy staff man was almost immediately called away to do something about the lighting of the conference tent. A hot plate of food landed in my lap as I sat and a cup found its way into my hand as if by magic.

"Come on then," said Titus. "Tell us your lies. How was Britain?"

"Britain!" Philip exclaimed, leapt to his feet and vanished through the tent flaps.

"He's heard your stories before," remarked Titus, emptying his cup.

Fangs stamped in with a steaming plate and a wineskin in his hands, sat down without invitation, and started in on his supper.

Philip was back a moment later with a triumphant look on his face and a small grey head showing from between his cupped hands.

"Hello," said Fangs. "The Navy's in. And he's brought us an appetizer."

Philip gave him a look of distaste. The sight of Fangs engulfing his food was not for the faint-hearted.

"This pigeon," he said proudly. "Was released just off the British coast and has just made its way back to its coop."

"Must have been a hard flight," said Titus, refilling every cup within reach. "I think it's dead."

"Yes," I added. "Take it outside and bury it. Did you bring any wine?"

"It's not dead," Philip exclaimed indignantly. "It's only resting. I'll get some wine when I've finished yours."

"We don't want any of the Fleet's fermented bilge water, anyway," said Fangs, the Army's wine expert. "It's no wonder the bird's on its last legs. Open its beak and I'll give it a squirt from my wineskin. Soon have it back on its pins."

Philip snatched away his pigeon and, hovering protectively over it started making cootchy-coo noises.

"Disgusting," commented Fangs, accurately aiming a stream of wine between his front gums.

"Look out! The enemy!" Titus greeted Cogidumnos as he stooped into the tent, looked around coolly and sat on his bedroll.

"If you think I'm the enemy," said the Celt with dignity, "you won't want any of this." He tugged a stone jar from under his bed. "Mead, a liquor made from honey. I'll drink it by myself."

"You know," said Rufus Sita, reappearing with more wine. "I think that all those blows on the Commandant's head have done some permanent damage."

Later, there was a lot of singing.

CHAPTER 42

▼

EUROPE

The British assault team had landed before dawn on the incoming tide. They had carried their leaky boats over the pebbles and hidden them before it was light enough for either villagers or military patrols to see. It was their information that the patrols had been drastically reduced due to other commitments. The tide should obliterate traces before villagers were about. For now, the priority was to make ground towards the target and to find a safe place to lie up for the day. The meeting with the local agent was arranged for dusk.

The team leader had taken the chance of landing close to the target based on local intelligence. This was still flowing intermittently despite savage reprisals. The landing had been later than he had hoped and it was now essential to move inland and find cover soon. At a quick, silent walk, the team flowed over open pastureland which could not be avoided and, careful not to break twigs, faded into a dense thicket on a rise in the ground. The last man replaced disturbed foliage and straightened flattened grass. Pigs had rooted in the thicket but there was no smell of recent feeding there. Grey light showed in patches through the low undergrowth and the team burrowed deeper. The leader crawled to the other side of the thicket and stared through the twigs.

A stubby finger of masonry showed black against the lightening sky. The port lay just a few miles to the east. He was closer than he had thought. He slowly exhaled a long breath. The sweat cooled on the back of his neck. No sign of cavalry patrols and thankfully no sheep or goats, which would mean dogs. At least not yet.

The day was spent mainly watching and sleeping. The men came to the leader's observation point one at a time and he pointed out to them the route of advance he had chosen. Whatever happened that night, they were in for a strenuous time, a long return walk and, if all went well, a lot of rowing.

As soon as the first star showed, they moved, darting individually between scattered spots of cover, gliding together over the ground like cloud shadow in more open areas. They reached the meeting place well ahead of time. The agent, visibly quaking, was already there.

"I could not get word to you," he muttered. "Cogidumnos is out of reach."

In the dark, he rightly sensed himself to be surrounded by tense and violent men. For a moment, he was poised between this world and the Otherworld. The leader exhaled softly.

"You are a brave man. You need not have come. Where is he?"

Tension subsided slightly.

"Inside an army fortification, surrounded by soldiers, hundreds of them."

"What else?" the leader had heard the faintest of intonations in the agent's voice.

"The girl is in a house in town. Only one or two soldiers with her. It's Scota, the daughter of your King Bericos."

"The daughter of the traitor Bericos you mean."

The team leader looked around at the faintly gleaming eyes.

"We've come all this way," he whispered and watched for any sign of dissent. There was none."

Take us to this house," he told the agent.

"Only if I go back with you," said the agent, daringly. "I'm probably known to Scota's guards. You have no idea what will happen to me if I am discovered."

"No one is going to survive our visit except the girl, and she will be returning with us. Now, we go."

The streets were dark but not entirely deserted. A cool wind searched the corners and shifted litter. Lamplight still showed under a few doors. A distant shout of a watchman in the town streets was answered by an even more distant one down by the harbour.

The young legionary on guard shifted to a more comfortable position on the large bundle of used thatching grass discarded from the house he was guarding. He wedged his back against the wall of the house opposite, causing the iron plates of his armour to grate faintly on the plaster. Leaning against the wall of his colleagues' sleeping quarters, he looked at Scota's newly-tiled house across the narrow street. No lamplight showed from under her door. A quiet snore came from the house behind him. He did not envy them. There was still something quite exciting about being one of the few people awake in a sleeping town.

There was no sign of the moon yet. He would wake his relief when it started to make its appearance. In the meantime, he was getting too comfortable on the musty-smelling thatch, time to check the back of the house. He left his helmet where he had been sitting and clambered to his feet, being careful not to scrape against the wall of the legionaries' sleeping quarters. He managed to restrain a curse as the stiff, unseen edge of the roof thatch combed his short hair and scratched his scalp.

His civilian shoes were without hobnails and he moved silently around the house under his care, placing his hand within the deeper shadow of each window to check that each shutter was closed and secure. Returning to his seat, he did not immediately sit down but turned to face the damp breeze. There had been a slight noise, perhaps claws on stone.

Stray dogs often haunted the streets at night, nosing for rubbish around the houses. He gently felt around with his foot until he located the broken piece of roofing tile he kept specially for the odd cur. He was becoming quite a good shot. As he bent slowly to pick up the tile, a British falcata smashed through the edge of the thatch above him, clanged on the backplates of his armour and bit deeply into the back of his skull. They tried to lessen the noise of his fall but he was a husky young man in heavy armour and his upper body weight was too much to hold. Despite the cushioning effect of the discarded thatch, the noise of his fall woke someone in the guards' house.

The legionaries inside managed to get their swords from their scabbards but could not get properly clear of their bedding before torches flared outside and the door burst open. Although they shouted and flailed, they died quickly under the flickering blades.

The assault team was on the verge of getting out of control. Several of them had sustained minor wounds in the killing of the guards, not all of those wounds were from the legionaries' swords. The team leader savagely punched a man preparing to throw his burning torch into the thatched roof. The fire would have lit up the streets for several blocks around. He caught a wild-eyed man by the arm and pointed at the door of the tiled house across the street.

"Take that down," he ordered.

The man swung his falcata and the heavy blade spilt the door from top to bottom, wrenching the planks out by using his weapon as a lever. A woman screamed something from inside. The man tore out the wreck of the door and threw it into the street. One of the torchbearers shouldered him to one side and charged into the doorway where he halted with a sound like a cough, swayed and toppled outwards into the street. His torch lay burning in the doorway.

"Windows," ordered the team leader.

Shouts of alarm were rising from nearby houses and time was beginning to run out. The shutters of two windows were smashed in, broken wood clattering into the room which was filled with smoky light from the torch. A second burning torch was tossed in through a window and some bedding or clothing caught fire.

The leader led a small rush for the doorway and managed to fend off a short sword that stabbed at him from the right. He was too close to the naked man and punched him in the face with the hilt of his sword; his feet, tangled in burning fabric and broken wood, still churning, still driving him forward, trying to drive his attacker against the wall. A blade stung agonisingly across the back of his neck but he could not deal with that. A woman screamed again and men grunted and cursed, the room filling with smoke, orange light and gigantic shadows.

He had the naked man pinned against the wall, so close as to smell him, but neither was able to bring his weapon to bear. The team leader head-butted him and tried to stamp on his bare feet. There were the sounds of several heavy punches behind him and the woman whimpered. His opponent kicked and bucked, trying to use the wall for leverage, but an arm reached through the window and clamped itself round the Roman's neck, pinning him against the wall. The team leader jerked backwards, just managing to retain his balance on the cluttered floor, and drove his long sword upwards into the man's ribcage.

Coughing, with warm blood trickling down his back, the team leader stumbled out of the house following the small, limp feet of the naked woman who was being dragged unceremoniously outside. The air in the street was cold, the paving lit fitfully by the flickering glare from the broken doorway.

The team leader glared about. From what he could see, many of his surviving men were injured and the woman appeared to be unconscious, perhaps dead. Military reaction would not be long delayed. He looked for the agent.

"Viridomar," he ordered. "Lead the way, the quickest way out of here. Now. Cover the woman," he ordered someone else, "that white body shows up like a beacon. Quickly, now. Follow him."

He counted his men as they turned into a side street, checked that the fallen team-member down in the doorway was indeed dead, and then hurried after them.

Scota had never been in such pain and discomfort. She was conscious first of a terrible fear that she was going to drown in her own blood. The swathe of pain across her nose and side of her face and the intolerable jolting against her bruised abdomen was nothing compared to the difficulty in drawing a breath. She was hanging, head down, over a broad, moving shoulder that was covered with a rough textile. Her legs were clamped against a male chest. Her feet were cold. She could not see.

In near-panic, she gritted her teeth against the pain below her ribs and raised her head. She managed to gather the blood and snot in one place and satisfactorily managed to spit the whole mess down her porter's back. She drew a shuddering and unimpeded breath but a violent jolt to her midriff drove the hard-won air from her aching lungs with nothing louder than a thin whine. She was dropped onto her bare feet on the cold paving and, despite the arm painfully wrapped around her waist, she felt much better for having her head up. She coughed and spat again, avoiding her own hair and feet.

In silence, they tried to gag her, giving rise to real panic that she would not be able to breath through her damaged nose. They compromised by tying her inside the cloak like a wriggling parcel, just her naked feet and legs visible to the knees. She checked her teeth with her tongue. Nothing missing. It was stuffy under the cloak but she could breathe and the pain in her middle was bearable. Her nose might be broken and it certainly felt as if her eye was closing but, otherwise, she was in good shape. Time to think about escape. She was jerked into motion again.

Stumbling along, with rough hands guiding her, her bare feet signaled the change from paving to gravel to rough grass. She winced as she trod on a sharp twig but did not cry out. After a long time, she was bundled deep into undergrowth and then was leaned, like a plank, up against a tree. Even through the cloak, she could hear heavy breathing around her. Otherwise, there was silence.

"No pursuit, yet."

"There will be. They have cavalry and plenty of ships. We move on. Everyone bandaged up? Let's go."

She was pushed forward and she deliberately collided with the tree, making sure her face stayed back out of harm's way. She gave a moan that was not entirely contrived. She received a cuff over the back of her head for her trouble.

"Stop that! Scota, we are going to let you see. If you make a noise like that again, you will be killed."

The fresh night air was a blessing. One eye was almost closed and the strands of hair sticking to her face irritated her but at least she could breathe and, up to a point, see. They had simply pulled down the part of the cloak covering her face into a deep collar around her neck. They had not untied her and retied the wrappings. This was just as well. By dint of much wriggling, she had eased the bonds upwards on her body to the level of her elbows. It might be possible to slip them over her head although that might entail the loss of the cloak as well. She was embarrassingly aware of her nakedness beneath. The problem of her own hair in her face was resolved by one of her captors who took hold of a large handful and started to tow her along by it.

Her feet hurt and her legs hurt. She had a headache to go with the bruises of the original assault, and now she was having her hair pulled out by the roots, it seemed. I could easily get tired of this, she thought.

The occasional mutter of voices in familiar Celtic dialect, and the knowledge that they had not gone to all this trouble to kill her out-of-hand, was somehow comforting although, physically, she knew she was weakening. She struggled to keep up to avoid losing her hair. Inevitably, she frequently stubbed her toes and sustained minor cuts from unseen obstacles in the dark. A thin sliver of moon provided almost no additional light. There was the sound of the sea not very far away. She found that she had to fight off the thought that it might be quite nice to die in Britain, close to home.

"Take her down to the beach," said the young team leader's voice. A man of few words. "Get the boats."

At the top of the low cliff above the beach, her silent escort altered his grip, winding her hair more firmly around his fist and pushing her in front of him. Her injured eye was streaming but she could just see the faint sheen on the sea and clearly hear the small breakers below. She was fairly sure that he would not kill her if she did not hurt him too badly.

He was prepared for her sudden deliberate collapse and had a good grip on her hair. He was not unbalanced and did not lose his hold. Her scalp on fire, she twisted to face him and saw him grin with satisfaction. His free hand bunched into a fist destined for her immobilised head. The grin vanished abruptly as she drew his sword from his scabbard.

He was quick. He threw himself sideways, releasing her hair. She went after him as he slid heavily down the cliff but she tripped over the cloak, as she was shrugging it off, and tumbled onto the soft sand of the beach. He was up and coming and saw the whirling sword only at the last minute. It hit him, hilt first, on the nose and Scota took off, naked as an eel, for the sea.

It was like running full tilt into a wall. The team leader did shudder with the impact but Scota flopped backwards, breathless, onto the wet sand. The leader bent over her and, to her, the starlit sky seemed to revolve slightly around the black bulk of his head. He spoke in a quiet, kindly voice.

"I suppose a quickie is out of the question?"

Her bruised lips nearly framed a smile as she lapsed into unconsciousness. It seemed that it was to be Britain after all.

CHAPTER 43

▼

EUROPE

It was a shambles. Thanks to the tiled roof, the neighbours had managed to put out the fire before the house burned down but the bodies were badly damaged. Not that they were in a position to feel anything, the legionary inside and the Celtic assassin in the doorway were both long dead. The two legionaries in their sleeping quarters had been killed in their beds. There was a wisp of life still in the legionary struck down on guard duty, but he expired soon after I arrived. Some of the attackers were probably wounded according to the neighbours. Scota had gone.

There was nothing I could do for the dead. While waiting for support, I used a torch to examine the streets around the edges of the scene. I had quite a long time in which to work on my own but there was no danger. The attackers had got what they wanted and they would be making long strides out of the area. The only danger would be from any wounded member of the group who had been left behind and wanted to die a hero's death. I made sure that I stayed out of sword's reach of any dark corner my torchlight did not penetrate.

I had established a line of flight from the blood spots on the ground long before the clattering of hooves announced the arrival of the stand-by turma of Ala I Thracum. When they did arrive, they filled the street with noisy bustle designed to disguise the fact that they were waiting for someone to tell them what to do.

I have always found that, however slowly a policeman walks to an unexpected situation, he will get there before a group of soldiers. Soldiers are trained to meticulously gather intelligence before action, to prepare in the minutest detail and to get into motion only when quite large groups of people are fully ready. Their response may be flexible but only between courses of action which have already been anticipated, planned for and practiced. The cavalry, the first to arrive, had not planned for, nor practised, the art of pursuing an armed group with a valuable hostage at night in city streets.

Unfortunately, I was far from blameless. I had presented an ultimatum, in person, to the High King of Britain and he had personally rejected it with contempt. Sentius Saturninus' official presentation of the ultimatum, if it now went ahead, would just be a formality. The High King had no intention of caving in to Roman demands and now that Roman intentions were out in the open, he had no reason to refrain from his own offensive action either. I should have been preparing for that, not sitting around in the sun outside the conference tent or drinking with my friends.

Rufus Sita had arrived at the same time as the horsemen and we had a quick conference with the cavalry decurion. He had somehow got it into his head that his duty involved a brisk canter through streets of admiring residents, followed by a successful charge on a group of witless fugitives and back home in time for breakfast with the rescued maiden over his saddle bow. Well, perhaps maiden might be the wrong word. He had a long face and a habit of nodding emphatically to confirm his own statements. He reminded me of one of his own horses bothered by horseflies.

There would be no reason to carry away Scota's dead body, so she must still be alive. If they wanted Scota alive, then they would want to display her somewhere. That had to be Britain. The blood spots I had found, and followed, indicated an escape route to the east. Tracking would be a slow process before daylight and the first priority was to prevent them getting Scota off the Continent.

It took a while, but first Rufus and then the decurion agreed that the cavalry should go directly to the sea shore east of the port and check for exit signs. I would follow the tracks with the first foot soldiers to arrive and Rufus would remain at the scene to deal with a certain senior officer who, I was sure, was even now rubbing the sleep from his eyes and bawling for Viridomar.

"That won't be the only thing irritating the Commandant," said Rufus with a sly smile as the decurion nodded away towards his men. "First his batman disappears, then the Brits turn his newly-tiled house into a fire-blackened slaughterhouse."

"His house?"

"Yes. The good Commandant has invested in a lot of property in the poorer parts of the town. Advance knowledge you see. Must have made a fortune already. Why do you think he was so happy for you to requisition tiles and to use military labour to re-roof his house? He certainly fooled you, didn't he?"

The cavalry departed with a lot of unnecessary noise.

"Speaking of missing batmen," I said. "If Viridomar's disappearance has anything to do with the appearance of a British raiding party, your boss will not be a happy Camp Commandant. I would give serious consideration to your future career path."

"What do you mean? If that loud-mouthed barbarian has turned traitor, that's not my problem. The Commandant employed him long before he appointed me."

"You are in charge of the headquarters staff, he will need a scapegoat. I do not think he will see it your way."

He thought about it for a moment and then turned sadly away. I called after him.

"Can Viridomar read Latin?"

"Yes," he answered faintly and kept walking.

Titus arrived with the fitter members of his century. Sensibly they had left their heavy armour behind.

"Optio," shouted Titus, a little breathlessly. "Have you left any enemy for us?"

"No," I said. "They've all died of old age. What took you so long?"

His men did not laugh. Four of their comrades had died that night and they had thoughts only of evening the score.

Following the blood spots by torchlight to the edge of the town was laborious and was even slower over the vegetable patches and pastures on its outskirts. There came a point at which neither the torches nor the increasing light of dawn was adequate to track by. The young legionaries wanted to go rushing off in the general direction we had established and, truth to tell, the raiding party did not appear to be taking any anti-tracking precautions. I decided to stick to the original plan and got them to stop and sit on the tracks. There was much fidgeting and muttering while I waited for the ambient natural light to improve.

We heard the horseman long before we saw him and the decurion arrived, guided by our shouts. Had it been any other sort of news, he would have sent one of his men as messenger. He had, he said with a nod, found the point where an outgoing party had crossed the beach and he handed me a Roman military cloak he had found on the sand. The light was now good enough to see the bloodstains on the red material and the several long auburn hairs sticking to it. Scota and the raiding party were out of our reach. Now it was up to the Fleet.

CHAPTER 44

▼

EUROPE

"Commandant Anicius Maximus," Captain Seleucus formally reported. "I regret to have to tell you that the British raiding party with their captive has eluded the ships of the Fleet. I sent three units to sea as soon as I heard the news. They had orders to row directly away from land until it became light to try and stay ahead of the fugitives but at dawn nothing was in sight. Sweeps along the British coast failed to locate any sign of them."

He thought that it was the first time the Commandant had looked anything but in total control. The military commander was as white-faced and immobile as marble.

"Fortunately," the Captain continued, kindly, "Cogidumnos is still safe."

"Yes. It was only the woman." Maximus' voice was almost hesitant but then gained strength. "I shall notify Senator Saturninus, it may have a bearing on his proposed expedition to the British High King. He is, I know, determined to go. Please keep his ship in readiness."

Captain Seleucus made a move to leave but the Commandant raised a hand. His eyes had brightened and a little colour had entered his cheeks.

"Legion II Augusta will arrive today with the cavalry of Ala Indiana Gallorum and several units of auxiliary infantry under command. Legate Vespasian will receive his command in the new Camp here. I shall be with him and I would be obliged if you were also present to represent the British Fleet."

Titus Seleucus, Captain in the Navy, and appointee of the Emperor but, nevertheless, only a freedman, was deeply conscious of the honour extended by a professional soldier who had, more importantly, been a citizen from birth. The

- 264 -

Commandant could, without giving offence, have represented the function as being a purely Army event.

"Thank you, sir. I shall, of course, be present. The cavalry wing, its name suggests…"

"They are recruited mainly from southern Gaul. The unit was formed twenty years ago and has been stationed in Upper Germany ever since. They are Celts, which is why I mentioned them, but they have worked for me before. They are good soldiers."

Celts being good soldiers in Germany did not necessarily guarantee that they would be good soldiers against fellow Celts, particularly if viewed against the rumours circulating about the Commandant's own Celtic batman, Viridomar. Celts had, however, fought well for Julius Caesar against other Celts, and southern Gaul had been Romanised for a very long time. They would probably be all right.

"Do they have experience in amphibious operations, sir?"

"That's another thing. They have frequently been part of such operations with the Rhine Fleet. Loading and unloading horses on Fleet transports is nothing new to them. They usually crane the horses over the side and swim them ashore, but the horses themselves are not frightened by unloading and can be walked down brows when the ships can be beached."

"It might be better that way if they are not used to salt water. Quicker anyway. I look forward to meeting their Prefect and planning some exercises with him."

"Prefect, yes. I have also to inform you, Captain, that a Prefect for the British Fleet has been appointed and is on his way here from the Rhone now. You are being superseded by a more senior officer, as I am, but both of us are vital to the success of the Task Force. We have laid the foundations and we are going to see it through."

"We are going to see it through," echoed the Captain. "Thank you, sir."

After the Captain had left, the Commandant placed both hands on the table and heaved himself to his feet. His arthritis was bad this morning. He was not used to the feeling of dread. In his decades of soldiering on the most active frontiers of the Empire, he was comfortable with his own mortality. When he died, whether he succumbed to the red spears of a German horde or expired in his own bed with his family around him, he knew he would do so with courage and dignity and in honour. He had lived a long, hard and profitable life and he hoped to leave it with his family secure in the financial provisions he had made for it and in the reputation he left behind. He dreaded confirmation that his long-time batman, Viridomar, was a British spy. In his own mind he could dismiss the probability that it was so, and, as the raiding party had escaped to Britain he might never have that confirmation, but there was a hot ember of conviction in his chest. Viridomar was a traitor and, whether publicly or privately, a part of Anicius Maximus was disgraced.

The Senator received the news of the escape of the British with their hostage with equanimity.

"It changes little, Commandant, except to give me a further demand from the Emperor to make of the High King. I shall demand that he return the girl— what's her name? I shall also demand that he hand over the murderers who killed Scota's protectors, four of them I think?"

"He is committed now, Senator. Not by the abduction, but by the insulting message he sent back with the coin. He might keep you as a hostage."

"I think not. He is a Celt, not an oriental, they usually respect the status of an envoy. All his people will know that I am coming, thanks to that optio of yours, and all he can do, really, is to meet me and be fairly unpleasant about it." Saturninus laughed. "After my years in the Senate and one term as Consul, I can stand a little unpleasantness. Have you got a ship ready?"

"Captain Seleucus has 'Mercurius' ready. A liburnian transferred from the Rhine Fleet."

"Very appropriate. Messenger of the gods, hey? I'll leave today, whenever the tide is right, and be off Britain tomorrow morning. They won't be expecting me so soon."

"The first legion, with supporting troops, arrives today."

"I know, but it is a purely Army function. Legate Vespasian can do the honours. It's his unit after all. I want to get the envoy-duty behind me. Its already spring and these northern summers are short. As soon as I get back, I will need to have a conference with Governor-designate Aulus Plautius. I will meet him wherever he is at that time. Will you make the arrangement? The subject will be the support he will require from the rear areas under my control at each phase of his operations."

"Senator, there is a further matter I wish to report."

"Your batman? Commandant, thank your good fortune that you have never lived in Rome. Since I was a child, I have been aware that there were spies in my home. Some of them were even spying on each other. The ones I have not detected are still there. If you catch him, crucify him. If not, forget about him. Whatever he learned, the High King is going to know about soon enough anyway."

Anicius Maximus walked to the new Camp. The pain in his knee joint seemed to have eased slightly but riding, this morning, was not on the agenda. His escort from Ala I Thracum walked behind him, leading their horses. The sentry on duty at Main Gate Left was a cavalryman from a different unit. The advance party from Ala Indiana Gallorum had arrived. Thracian horsemen exchanged a few whispered insults with the Gallic cavalryman as they were admitted into the Camp. The Commandant ignored the exchange.

In the vast expanse of the Camp's empty interior there was only one tent. It was pitched centrally in the space allocated to the Legion's commander's accommodation. Flavius Vespasian stood outside his tent with his hands on his hips and surveyed the few small groups of dismounted cavalrymen straightening the rows of surveyors' pegs, checking the palisade fencing on top of the walls and picking up almost non-existant litter. They glanced at the new arrivals without a great deal of interest.

The Commandant marched stiffly up to Vespasian who turned his healthy, smiling farmer's face to him and returned his salute.

"Our Legion and supporting troops are making good time. The Senior Tribune has sent a message that Legion II Augusta will be here by midday."

Of the six tribunes in each legion, only one was of magisterial rank and was therefore effectively the second in command of the legion. The other five tribunes ranked below the camp commandant in the legionary command structure.

The Commandant stared around at the desultory preparations taking place. Without being asked anything, Vespasian grinned and said.

"Permission granted, Commandant," and stepped inside his tent.

Anicius Maximus inflated his deep chest and emitted a roar which frightened the horses and caused one bow-legged cavalryman to stumble down the embankment.

"That man there!"

Every man in the Camp turned to the source of the impressive noise to see if he was its target. There was an inflationary pause while the Commandant pointed with his vinestick at a point ten paces in front of him and then loosed another resounding bellow.

"Fall in there!"

Tentatively at first, then at a trot, escalating into a sprint, men converged across the empty spaces to the indicated point.

In the gloom of the tent, Vespasian listened with an appreciative smile to his Commandant's picturesque description of the troopers' preparations so far, and their certain fate if the pace and purpose of the preparations did not immediately improve.

"You!" bawled the Commandant, and Vespasian could imagine the unfortunate trooper pointing tentatively at his own chest and raising his eyebrows in a silent question. "Yes, you! You squinty vole. Never mind the fencing, it's been erected by experts. Get your party over to the first Camp and bring back firewood, lots of it. Light cooking fires. Move!"

Vespasian winced sympathetically at the sound of a vinestick being vigorously applied to a slow-moving rump.

"You! Go to the headquarters. Find Rufus Sita. Got that? Rufus Sita. Tell him to issue one day's wine ration for ten thousand men. Bring it back here and guard it. Are you still here? That's better.

"You! Get your horse. That's the funny looking thing on four legs. Ride to the Legion. My compliments to the Senior Tribune and would he send forward the cohort and century standard bearers. When the Legion turns in the south Gate I want the standard already planted at the end of each unit's accommodation. Go!

"Who else? Right! You four look like intelligent men. Probably don't need your toes to count to twenty. Go and locate the watering points. If you cannot read the signboards, it's men upstream, horses and mules downstream and washing below. When you have seen them all, one of you stand at each gate to point them out to the soldiers. If anyone washes his dirty mule in the soldiers' drinking water I will know who is to blame."

Vespasian sighed and settled contentedly to his documentation. It was good to hear a professional at work.

From before midday, all faces seem to be drawn to the road terminating in the south Gate of the new Camp. Vespasian remained seated in his tent, leaning against a pole with a booted foot on a stool. He caught the excitement in the few voices outside and detected a slight trembling of the floor underfoot. He restrained himself and stayed seated as the voices outside were raised. A trooper of Ala Indiana Gallorum rushed up to the tent door to make a report. Vespasian merely nodded. Trumpets tore the air outside the south Gate and the Commandant's shadow fell across the tent's doorway. With feigned reluctance, Vespasian got to his feet and tugged down his tunic. His batman swung the long end of his baldric over the right shoulder of his silvered cuirass and clipped it to the shorter end so that his sword hung correctly on his left hip. He walked bareheaded out of the tent and the Commandant, his many decorations reflecting the weak spring sunshine, took up position slightly to his left rear. Captain Seleucus, glancing sideways to make sure he was not commiting a breach in military protocol, took up a position beside the Commandant. His cuirass did the Navy credit even though it was not yet adorned with any decorations.

Vespasian looked down the long straight Praetorian street to the south Gate, deserted except for surveyors' pegs and and the planted unit standards with their individual custodians. The aquilfer of Legion II Augusta turned into the south Gate bearing the golden eagle, symbol of the spirit of the Legion. He was followed by the tall, thin figure of the Chief Centurion, proudly leading the professional citizen-soldiers of the First Cohort of the Legion. Rank after rank of grey metal and red cloth, of dark heads and bright javelin points, turned into the Gate without pause and advanced behind their eagle towards their distant Legate and their Commandant whom they had not seen for two years. They did not recognise the Captain. The rows of eyes in the dusty, mature faces sought those of the Commandant as the First Cohort closed the distance. More and more units turned in the south Gate.

As the leading ranks of the First Cohort came level with its planted unit standards, the aquilfer and the Chief Centurion halted facing Vespasian. The eight hundred legionaries of the First Cohort turned left and right into the lines allocated to them. Cohort after cohort did the same, halted and faced front. The Senior Tribune, with the junior tribunes and the prefects of the auxiliaries rode slowly up the Praetorian street as it cleared. The auxiliary units filed into place, the cavalry and the pack animals and the transport filling up the rear, next to the rising smoke of the cooking fires. Dust sifted down. With a single shout, thousands of men saluted.

Vespasian stepped up to the tribunal, the commander's platform, to address his men. Countryman or not, Flavius Vespasian was an experienced politician as well as a soldier of repute. His voice carried far over the heads of the troops, rising and falling in practiced oratory. The Commandant, his face a mask of concentration, did not consciously listen to a word. He closely scanned the faces of the legionaries he could see in the foremost ranks, ignoring those of the officers. The men of the First Cohort, all veterans and the best of the Legion, which, of course, was the best legion in the Army, were all known to him. To his internal consternation, they were not looking back at him with happiness or with interest or, even, with hatred. Their eyes were sliding away from his as if to conceal their thoughts and they only seemed to look at their commander when he was speaking towards a different section of the military formation in front of him.

The senior officers, tribunes and prefects, all part-time soldiers, listened to Vespasian with exemplary intentness. The Commandant, however, looked at the

Chief Centurion, standing beside the aquilfer. The embodiment of military expertise stood alongside the custodian of the spirit of the Legion. They both stared back at him with unblinking eyes, not a shadow of expression on their faces. It was disturbing.

Vespasian concluded his address, stepped down from the tribunal and turned towards his tent. The trumpets shivered the air within the walled Camp. The aquilfer carried the eagle onto the ground allocated for the headquarters and where the eagle would remain under guard. The soldiers lowered their weapons and equipment to the ground where they stood. The mules were led forward with their loads of tentage and off-loading began. Iron tent pegs were driven in and tent poles fitted into leather on the ground. Centurions checked distances and alignments with measuring sticks. Senior officers, led by the Senior Tribune, lined up at Vespasian's tent to pay their respects. The Commandant watched the soldiers work They worked quickly and accurately but the noise level was low. There was something fundamental missing.

At the third command of the massed trumpets, all the legionaries' tents were raised simultaneously. From a flat plain crowded with men and animals, a tent city materialised, hiding most of them from sight. Streams of men began to throng the streets. Messengers headed for the space allocated to the headquarters to present guard lists for approval and receive the password allocated for the night. Duty cooks for each section hurried towards the ration wagons and cooking fires. Mules and horses were led in strings out of the Gates for watering. Doctors and the sick made their way to the space allocated for the Camp hospital.

The Commandant excused the Captain, who wished to see Senator Saturninus off, and walked to the headquarters area, returning respectful greetings offered on the way. He saw shy grins but the eyes did not quite meet his. Administration tents were being erected to the fixed pattern and clerks and staff-men were claiming their spaces. The tent acting as shrine for the eagle was already up and guarded.

They were expecting him as he knew they would be. The Chief Centurion was watching as the aquilfer checked and set the guard over the money chests. This was more important than Army money. It was the savings of legionaries themselves and the bequests of deceased soldiers to be paid out as soon as their beneficiaries could be reached. The aquilfer in every legion was its banker as well as being acknowledged as its most respectable man.

They greeted him respectfully, without boisterousness. He had known them both for many years, seen their careers develop, fought several battles in their company. He could not mistake their guardedness. They courteously accepted his invitation to supper at his quarters in the other Camp. This was not the place to talk.

CHAPTER 45

▼

EUROPE

The following morning, light strengthened in deep pink with stripes of dark grey clouds. The horse snorted in the cold air as it trampled the wet grass. Despite his discomfort, the Commandant, riding alone, enjoyed the quiet, knowing it would not last. Long lines of horses, colours not yet distinguishable, moved almost silently towards the watering places, their few custodians muffled against the cold. A thin haze of smoke rose above the walls of his destination, the pink light glinting on something metallic above the points of the palisade fence. A sentry, grey in the gloom of the gateway, challenged him more loudly than necessary, alerting his colleagues.

The horse raised its head, blew through its nostrils and pricked its ears at the mix of warmth, smells and noise filling the crowded interior beyond the gateway. It trod forward delicately as if being urged into deep water, the strange environment closing around it. Crossing the open space beween the walls and the serried ranks of dark tents its eyes rolled in an attempt to piece the gloom and a quiver ran under the hairy hide of its withers. Between and around the closely aligned lines, half-seen movement surged and eddied. A persistent, low-level grumble of noise surrounded horse and man as they paced the crowded length of the Praetorian street.

Sentries stepped forward to hold the horse outside the large tent, still lamp-lit, where Vespasian had his quarters. He would still be conducting his morning meeting with the senior offices in the headquarters area. Maximus controlled a grunt as he slid from the saddle and took a moment to steady himself and look around. The sentries respected his moment's silence. When he nodded, the horse was led away and a batman appeared at his elbow offering a cup of hot wine. The noise level and the activity in the Camp increased with the light.

Vespasian's burly figure, gilded by the strengthening sunlight, appeared to tow a small tail of followers across the space surrounding his quarters. He dismissed them courteously and cheerfully greeted his Legion's Commandant. They sat, steaming cups in hand, in the tent doorway, the sentries moving silently away.

"How was your supper party?" Vespasian was nothing if not direct.

"The men are, apparently, fit, well-trained and equipped. They coped well with the march and the specialist training program is ready. Co-ordination with the Fleet is still to be done. I have introduced Captain Seleucus to the Chief Centurion."

Vespasian nodded, said nothing.

"They tell me that morale is good."

"What do you think?" Vespasian smiled. "You have had several hours to form an opinion."

"Good but brittle."

"I think I see."

"What were they told when they left Germany?"

Vespasian thought for a moment.

"They were told the truth. What they believed, of course, is the important thing and it might not be the same thing."

"And soldiers sometimes believe what they want to happen."

"Like everyone else."

The Commandant shifted in his chair. His discomfort was not only physical.

"Whatever they believed in Germany, they will see here the full granaries, the hundreds of new ships, they will go through the training program and practice with the Fleet, they will hear of the ultimatum being delivered in Britain by an ex-Consul. We will circulate the High King's insulting reply—whatever he says. They will know that we are going. No doubt.

"The last Emperor got this far but did not cross the Ocean."

"The last Emperor brought the soldiers this far, but nothing else was ready. We are going. They will know."

"Family ties, even unofficial ones, are strong." Vespasian had to be the one to raise the subject. "The families believed what their husbands and fathers told them in Germany. It was not necessarily the official, true, version. Very few of them have tried to follow the Legion, so far. That tells me that the families believe that this is another pretence, that the invasion will not happen. The soldiers, I'm sure, told them this. When the men see the preparations and understand that we are indeed going, the families will believe that as well. Many of them will start to follow. There will be a lot of hardship."

"The women should stay with their parents on the border."

"It won't happen. Very few Celtic parents on the Rhine are reconciled to their daughters living with Roman soldiers, especially since we refuse to acknowledge the arrangement as a proper marriage. In any case, most of the women are not teenagers any longer. Many of them have teenagers of their own. They won't go back to their parents."

"They must realise that some of the men, perhaps many of them, will die on the beaches or in battles inland. The Ocean will be between them and the Legion. They must also know that the aquilfer might take months to find them and pay them out, especially if they are on the move. They should realise that they would be better off to stay where they are."

"What?" said Vespasian, pleasantly, "and let the old man run off and marry a British girl over there? I don't think so. We are talking about long-term relationships here, with soldiers on the verge of retirement in many cases. When the families are convinced that the invasion is really going to take place, they will follow."

Vespasian stood up and leaned against a tent pole, looking out at the Camp.

"The legionaries know that, if they die in Britain, their women and children will probably be homeless and destitute, at least for months. If they don't die in Britain, they will be expected to take their retirement there. Either way, they are not coming back. We are going to ask them to fight their way to retirement outside the known world."

"It may sound heartless," said Anicius Maximus, uncomfortably, still thinking of the families, "but, is it an Army problem? The Army expressly forbids serving soldiers to marry. I know many fine women have good relationships with the legionaries, but legions have to go where the need is. We cannot run military operations based on the needs of a horde of camp-followers."

"It is the need of the soldiers that I am thinking about."

They were silent for a while as the light grew and the Camp emptied.

"The Army will not facilitate the movement of the families." The Commandant made it a statement.

"How can it?" Vespasian said rhetorically. "It does not recognise the marriages, therefore families do not exist."

"The men will embark when ordered to do so." The Commandant was emphatic, bumping his fist gently on his diseased knee. "They are experienced and disciplined soldiers, whatever their other commitments. They will be honourably discharged when we have conquered Britain and can make their own arrangements for their legitimised wives to join them then."

"Yes?"

"Yes. Any womenfolk following the Legion before that will have to make their own way. The legionaries can see that. I think that the women will also see that, and stay where they are."

"Are you married, Anicius?"

"Yes. She's at home. In Syria."

"So am I. She is also at home. But the Celts, you know, are different."

CHAPTER 46

▼

EUROPE

I took my report to Narcissus over to Philip's tent for inclusion in the next Rome mail. He was with a powerfully built old cove with a silver beard and a southern tan. Several pictures and a wrapped parcel lay on the table in front of them and Philip was examining a framed bronze tablet. They were both smiling.

"Just the man I was looking for." Philip turned to his older companion. "Father, meet Optio Aurelius Victorinus, the man who got me speared by a German in a Roman theatre two years ago. My father."

"Just call me Pytheas, lad."

"Not Antoninus Maximus?" queried Philip, squinting at the bronze inscription.

"Just Pytheas," said the old man, who had a grip like iron.

Philip thrust the bronze diploma in front of me. The lettering certified that Antoninus Maximus, having completed his contractual service in the Alexandrine Fleet, had been honourably discharged and he and his descendants were now provincial citizens of the Empire of Rome. Philip was a Roman citizen.

"Congratulations Phillipus Maximus," I joked. "I'll bring you the enlistment forms for Legion II Augusta. We'll soon make a man of you."

"Forget it," said Philip, his eyes alight. "Any legion that accepted you is obviously below my new status. In any case, I'm a web-foot like my father and that's what I'm going to stay."

He sorted through the pictures and held up a miniature painting of a ship. Miniature it might be, but its scale against other vessels incorporated by the artist indicated that it was colossal.

"This is your ship, sir? The, er, the 'Cleopatra'?"

"Just call me Pytheas," rumbled the older man. "No 'Cleopatra's' voyage was a success but we learned a lot and this is the new one, 'Indus' we call her. Just launched in the Red Sea." He turned to his son. "Alexander was there, the old money bags. We are partners now."

"My brother is going to sail in her," Philip sounded almost wistful and held up a tiny portrait of a young man. "That's him, lucky peasant."

"Silk, isn't it—Pytheas?"

"Silk and spices. Silk is the big earner. As long as the Empire can produce gold, we can get the silk. The ladies and gentlemen of Rome love silk. The demand is huge and growing, I don't think we have more than touched the surface yet."

"Look," said Philip, "I'm sorry but I've got to get this mail together. The dispatch rider is waiting."

"You carry on, lad. I'll find the house and we can meet again after work. Bring some friends, we'll have dinner together. I hope you rented one with central heating."

"Just a minute, Philip," I intervened. "You said I was just the man you were looking for. What is it?"

"I'll explain," said Pytheas.

"All right," said the harried, newest citizen in the Roman Empire, "but, you are forgetting your parcel."

"No I'm not," said the old sailor, with a chuckle. "It's a present. Your first toga. Wear it tonight if you like."

We walked together out of the Navy area. Many more tents had gone up and a lot of unfamiliar faces were about.

"I am looking for an introduction," said Pytheas without further preamble. "I wrote to Legate Vespasian as suggested by Narcissus. Yes, I know Narcissus, or rather, my partner, Alexander the banker, knows him. Anyway, I sent the letter to Germany but Vespasian must have already left and I did not get a reply. Philip tells me it will be redirected here but I don't have much time. If it will be a problem for you, don't worry, I'll try a direct approach."

I assured him that I would make the appointment on his behalf. Outside the Camp he looked towards the sea.

"I believe that you can see Britain from here. I am named after the Greek sailor who sailed around Britain hundreds of years ago. Oh, yes. It is an island, or rather a group of islands, whatever the armchair-navigators say. He called them the Cassiterides."

"Interesting. The High King's family is sometimes known as the Cassi. I wonder…"

"You've been there? You must tell me all about it. This evening. Come to the house with Philip." He smiled almost grimly. "Wear a toga if you like."

I left Fangs and Titus to coach single-combat revision with the two centuries of replacements. I had expected that the replacements for Legion II Augusta, at least, would have been sent to their parent formation now that it had arrived. The Commandant had been very clear that this was not yet to take place. Come to that, there was no suggestion either that Titus or myself should be absorbed into the Legion we now officially belonged to. He often lectured us on contingency planning, perhaps this was to be a practical demonstration.

Down at the lower watering-point allocated to the Legion, I chatted to troopers of the Gallic cavalry. I had become almost accustomed to the British pronunciation. They, however, used a more familiar form of Celtic although it was well-laced with German words, all of which sounded, to me, like curses. Their unit had been on the German frontier for more then twenty years and some had married there unofficially. Most of them, though, had married girls from their home villages in southern Gaul who had happily stayed with their parents there. With their clean-shaven faces, their German curses and their subtle air of servility, they bore little resemblance to the wild Celts of Britain.

Further downstream, a large number of Roman legionaries were washing themselves and their clothing. They were almost all older than me, with white muscular torsos and brown, scarred arms and legs. I caught a number of sidelong glances in my direction and a number of muttered comments passed between them. They were civil and responded to conversational gambits, but I was a stranger, probably inexperienced in their terms and my motives were suspect. All of which was true. I gleaned very little until I was able to drop the fact that I had been to Britain myself, twice. Then I was the subject of a polite, intensive interrogation. Of all things, the questions which most often came up concerned the types of farming country I had seen. As I had been rapidly stalking through a native city on the one occasion and running for my life through abandoned farmland for most of the other, I could only provide limited insight. Over all, they got slightly more information from me than I did from them but, at least, they would remember my name and discuss my doings. It might be better next time.

CHAPTER 47

▼

BRITAIN

The high country north of the river Trent was not much like the Britain Scota grew up in. To her, it sometimes seemed beautiful in a treeless, unploughed, underpopulated way. She was not used to standing in an endless, airy landscape where she was the tallest object in sight and the only noises were the wind, the clicking of insects and distant cries of curlew and golden plover, where the only visible movement was her clothing, the tops of the knee-high undergrowth and the clouds. It was hard to believe that she was not alone in the lands of the Brigantes.

There were people there, in the swathe of country extending between the Irish Sea and the North Sea, but most of them lived on the lower ground, in the river valleys and on the plains towards the coasts. In the central moors and hills a few hardy farmers fought ceaselessly to clear back the resistant undergrowth for the plough and some inquisitive shepherds with their rail-thin dogs walked their flocks, competing with the red deer and alert for the rare wolf. Their habitations huddled almost unseen in folds of the ground, the thin smoke of their cooking fires flicked away by the clean wind.

Scota's home now was such a structure. Hardly bigger than her bed had been in the British Palace in Rome, it was of piled rocks and turves with a wood and turf roof that kept off most of the rain. It was out of the wind and had both an outside cooking place and a little stream of strong-tasting water just below it. Fortunately it was spring and the air coming in through the walls was not cold in the daytime. To be in exile here in the winter would be at a doorway to the Otherworld.

It was not customary to execute Celtic women, even those considered to be traitors, and exile was the most severe punishment usually meted out. No one decreed, though, that the exile had to be comfortable and Scota had almost cried when she had been left with a small bundle of clothing, an iron cooking pot and a meager supply of food outside her little house on the moor. That first night had been the worst. Her face had ached where her nose had been reset, her stomach had been upset from the strange water, she was cold, damp and hungry and, above all, she was alone. She had felt a strong impulse then to curl into a ball, to wrap her cloak over her tangled hair and to cry herself to sleep.

What saved her was the mental picture of the malice on the face of that evil, simpering witch, Cartimandua, Queen of all the Brigantes, when she gave the orders to her smirking charioteer. She must have been deeply pleased by the High King's request that she accept a former princess as a helpless exile. She had visibly relished the sight of Scota's bruised face and had searched her eyes for reaction to the conditions of her exile. There was no way that Scota, princess of the Atrebates, was going to let that fat, posturing, excuse-for-royalty, destroy her.

She had thrown back her cloak and forced herself to create a little smoky fire in the open. She had cooked herself a large helping of porridge in her iron pot. Her attention had faltered as she peeled a stick to stir the food and it was a bit burnt. She did not eat much but she felt better. Confidence and determination flickered and brightened. She had pulled the rotten, musty bracken, the bed of a previous resident, from her new home and, crouching, swept out the stony floor as well as she could. Provided there was no overnight rain, the bracken would be useful for restarting the fire in the morning.

She had installed her few possessions inside the hut, laying out her good wool cloak as a thin bed on the bare floor. It had been getting dark when she urinated in the low undergrowth, looking about to detect any observers in that deserted place. She had collected several fist-sized rocks from the stream and placed them ready as weapons inside the hut. Then she had closed the narrow entrance with the bracken as a flimsy curtain and lay down on the hard floor. Cold air eddied about her face. Her cloak comforted her skin and the residual warmth of the burnt porridge supplemented the deepening glow of her determination.

Tomorrow, she decided, she would burn the old bracken and tear up new for a fresh bed, she would find and uproot thorn bushes for her doorway. She would have a proper wash in the stream and scrub her teeth with the ashes of her fire. She would somehow make herself a comb. Then she would work out how she would get south across the broad, brown water of the river Trent.

CHAPTER 48

▼

EUROPE

The legionaries of Legion II Augusta had had contacts many times over the years with the legionaries of Legion XIV Gemina and Legion XX Valeria. Those three legions had been in Germany for decades and, although the German frontier is a big place, divided into two military regions, combined campaigning was the rule rather than the exception.

Legion IX Hispana was different. It had a long history of military service in Spain and, when it had been transferred to the Empire's northern borders some forty years before, it was to the Danube, not to the Rhine, that it was sent. Its structure and methods of operation were identical with the other three legions of the gathered Invasion Task Force but its culture was unknown to them and its personnel were strangers.

While the legion he had led from the Danube was settling into its new Camp at Gesoriacum, the Commander of the Invasion Task Force, Aulus Plautius, sat with Vespasian of Legion II Augusta to listen to the little Senator with the impressive voice.

"I am completing a written report on my mission," Sentius Saturninus said. "It must be addressed to the Emperor, of course, but I will have it copied to yourself."

Vespasian thought that Aulus Plautius looked tired. He had had the longest distance to march and had not yet had a chance to rest. Hosideus Geta was still on his way to take over command of Legion XX Valeria and to become effectively the Task Force's second in command. Vespasian would fill that function until he arrived.

"Please continue, Senator." Plautius' voice was quiet, almost soft.

"In brief, Governor, rejection. The High King met me formally, in his hall, surrounded by members of his family and leaders of subject peoples. A very haughty individual, I thought, but not entirely lacking in humour. He welcomed me and congratulated me on a safe passage over his Ocean. Asked me if I had a coin in case of accidents on the way back. I told him that the Roman people felt he owed far more than just one coin. He said that he did not respond well to extortion but that he would willingly assist the Roman Empire to bury its soldiers appropriately. One British coin for each Roman mouth. And so on. It was a formality, each side already being decided on its position. Anyway, it's done. Britain will not pay its just tribute to Rome."

"What is your position, now, Senator?"

"My duty as the Emperor's envoy is over as soon as my report is dispatched. My instructions from him are that I now become responsible for marshalling all resources in northern Gaul and to funnel them through Gesoriacum to support your Task Force. When you become established in Britain it will be my responsibility to use British refugees to recruit local levies to assist in guarding your communications. At that stage, it might be more efficient to move my base to Britain."

"I intend to use the Fleet to cover my flanks."

"Obviously. After your successful landing of the army—a completely military operation—shipping will be needed for two different tasks. To cover your flanks, as you say, and to keep supplies from the Continent reaching the army. I think, at that point, I could assist you best by taking control of the flow of supplies across the Ocean in the Fleet transports. The custom-built warships would remain under your direct control for close-support operations."

Aulus Plautius looked at Vespasian who nodded without hesitation.

"I agree, with one proviso."

This time, the Senator and the Governor looked at one another like men sharing a secret. Aulus Plautius turned once more to Vespasian.

"If the Task Force is checked at any stage in its operations, the Emperor has graciously indicated his willingness to lead a force to Britain to break the deadlock. Fleet transports would then have to revert to their troop-carrying role for a time."

"I see." Vespasian did not require any time to absorb the implications. He had already calculated that, politically, Emperor Claudius needed a military victory. Any genuine setbacks in the landings and expansion of the bridgehead would be laid at Plautius's door. Any imaginary difficulties, thereafter, could be resolved personally by the Emperor to his great public credit.

The Governor and the Senator, both travel-weary, shuffled their feet as if to rise.

"There is one thing," said Vespasian diffidently. "Morale in the legions, at least the legions from Germany, is not what it should be."

They both settled back in their chairs but more tensely than before.

"What do you mean?" The Governor's voice took an edge. Whatever the Senator's standing, this was Army business.

"They say they are unhappy about crossing the Ocean."

"They will do what they are told." Aulus Plautius was definitely tired. Vespasian was sorry he had brought it up when Plautius had only just arrived. Too late now.

"The camp commandants and the centurions are concerned. We are much better prepared this time, but the men remember only too well that the previous Emperor himself could not get the soldiers to embark. Perhaps if the Emperor Claudius..."

"Impossible!" snapped Aulus Plautius. "There is no need to trouble the Emperor at this stage. The Emperor may possibly decide to assist me later, but the army will embark when I order it to do so, no question."

Vespasian could see that he had, indeed, been about to make an impossible proposal. If Emperor Claudius personally ordered the men to embark and they refused, the whole enterprise would be a political disaster as well as a military farce. Still, Vespasian did not intend to be part of any military farce either.

"Perhaps if you were to sound out the camp commandants, sir..." Vespasian disliked the wheedling tone in his own voice.

"Not necessary. If there are disciplinary problems in the legions from Germany, the camp commandants will deal with them appropriately and I will be notified by legates such as yourself Vespasian. As far as rumours are concerned, you are right to bring them to my attention. I will continue to test them against my own judgement."

"Ah," the Senator's interruption was excessively polite. "What do the tribunes say, Vespasian? I know they are not as close to the soldiers as the centurions but the senior tribunes, anyway, are men of some experience?"

Vespasian could not point out that the tribunes were all temporarily in the army to further their political careers. If that were true then both he and Plautius could be accused of the same thing.

"They believe the camp commandants' concern is excessive, Senator. They are confident that they can ensure that the embarkation order is carried out."

Aulus Plautius nodded emphatically but made no further comment.

"Perhaps, sir, I could probe the reasons for this reported reluctance and report back to you?"

"Do so, by all means." The Governor was dismissive. The Senator caught Vespasian's eye and he subsided. That permission from the commander of the Invasion Task Force was as much as Vespasian was going to get.

CHAPTER 49

▼

EUROPE

There were now forty thousand soldiers of the four legions and their auxiliary units around Gesoriacum. There were also ten thousand sailors, some permanently posted to the new British Fleet and others on loan from the Rhine Fleet and the Fleet at Misenum. Civilian businessmen and would-be contractors, with their employees, swarmed around the Invasion Task Force, filled the eating-houses, baths, taverns and accommodation in the port. Property prices had become incredible. The port authorities and their electorate were fast becoming very rich men. They had also become inveterate complainers about noise, property damage and rape attributed to the vast crowds of off-duty soldiers and sailors spending their money in the port.

Camp Commandant Anicius Maximus, of Legion II Augusta but still military commander of the embarkation port area, as usual, had a plan. He transferred his right to sign military contracts to the rear areas commander, Senator Sentius Saturninus. This halved his still-growing daily workload and the Senator accepted, with relish, the challenge of dealing with contracts and contractors. Then the Commandant created a military police force.

Each of the four legions was required to provide, at all times, a century of its legionaries, under arms, on the outskirts of the port. The Fleet, similarly, provided a strong shore-patrol based at the foot of the lighthouse. A stockade for defaulters was built in the military area, military courts were established by the tribunes of the legions and the Commandant sent for me.

"I have noted the progress of the replacement legionaries under your tuition with satisfaction. The time has, however, come for them to move on in their careers. Send away the replacements to their legions today except for those allocated to Legion II Augusta. Those remain under your command. You and your trainers remain under mine."

I said nothing. He described the structure of the military police and military justice system he had instigated.

"There are many instances of friction between the military and the civilian population in the town which are too minor to justify mobilising the legionary contingents. A soldier has a dispute with a shopkeeper over the price of something, a girl complains that a sailor made an improper suggestion to her and we have eighty armed men storming into the town. That might create a riot where none would otherwise have occurred. The city fathers do have a sort of watchman force but it is totally inadequate."

"What is needed is a City police force?"

He did not like my stealing his punch line. His black eyes gleamed like arrow points.

"A town-curfew is in being for all ranks below centurion from dusk to dawn. You will see that the curfew is effective and patrol the streets during the day. Small groups, preferably pairs, of policemen. Sort out minor friction, call for the legionary contingents or the shore-patrol if there is anything you cannot handle. Clear?"

"Clear." I was thinking of something else.

"Clear, sir!" He reminded me, the arrow points were even sharper.

"Clear, sir. We need to be identifiable or half-drunk military may claim they did not know we had any authority. City police wear the old fashioned model helmet."

"Yes, I see. Well we don't have those helmets. Senior officers often wear a red sash around their waists. Your men can wear their red scarves as a sash over the right shoulder, the sword baldric over the left as it is now. I'll notify the legions."

"And the Fleet, sir, please."

"Of course, the Fleet as well. You may have eighty men of the replacements and both your trainers. Your jurisdiction is within the port city limits and any military functions attended by the townspeople outside. Report to me daily. Questions?"

"No questions, sir."

"Good luck."

I often felt a bit breathless after a meeting with the Camp Commandant but he did get through a lot of work.

The Army had finally resolved my pay situation but was still calculating and recalculating my bonus due on the new Emperor's accession. The precise date of my promotion to optio was now the focus of serious military attention. Long-serving front line soldiers may have had their faculties dulled by repeated blows on their helmets, but equal damage was done by butting their heads against the legionary pay offices. I was not worried about finances, the ship-fittings contract had worked out very well while it lasted and my bank account in Pompeii was looking good. My brother still wrote pressing me to take a cash-share in the business but I was quite happy with the existing arrangement. I had my military pay, free rations and the prospect of taking part in the biggest enterprise of the Empire. There might be even more profitable business opportunities in the offing.

The auxiliary cavalry had a sports day. A lot of townspeople went along and so did I, with a contingent of my red-sashed soldiers courteously patrolling, in pairs, through the crowds of spectators.

Thirty horsemen of Ala I Thracum were on the field, facing thirty of Ala Indiana Gallorum. The horses were without saddles and the men were naked except for loincloths and a large letter T or G painted on their chests and backs. In most cases, the unit identification letter was hardly necessary. The Gauls might have been civilized for a hundred years but they still shaved their entire bodies like their wild cousins in Britain. Unlike the British, they shaved their upper lips as well.

Off duty cavalrymen around the field were jumping up and down with excitement and explaining what was about to happen to townspeople and foot-soldiers alike. It did not take long to explain.

At the signal, with a mighty shout, the two teams launched themselves at each other from opposite ends of the field and met with an audible thump in the centre of the ground. Many men were unhorsed at the outset and had to scramble clear of flailing hooves and whirling bodies. Two mounted decurions used their sticks freely to prevent some of the fallen trying to remount illegally. Riderless horses and unhorsed cavalrymen were led and sent off the ground. The competition was only getting started.

The objective and the rules were simple. The objective for each team was to unhorse all the members of the opposing team. The only rule was that men on the ground were out of contention.

Professional methods for separating men from horses only became apparent as the field thinned out. The crowd particularly liked the sight of Thracian cavalrymen leaving their horses but were prepared to applaud almost anything They quickly became aware that two of the Balkan horsemen were working together in a very efficient system. They would circle around the outskirts of the swirling mass until, at some sort of signal, they would settle on one particular victim. One would ride directly at the Gallic horseman making it very obvious that he was the intended target and demonstrating various elaborate preparations for wrestling grips. Once the Gaul had become focused and braced for the approaching opponent, the other Thracian, who had been sidling closer but not looking at the Gaul, would suddenly kick his horse into a gallop, grab a fistful of Gallic hair and drag him over his horse's rump.

It was at the height of the laughter, roars of approval and shrieked warnings from the crowd that a hoarse voice spoke into my ear.

"A word with you, Optio."

More than a little annoyed, I followed. In a little clump of deserted wagons and carts, my companion stopped and sat on a bale of hay. After a moment, I kicked away a leather bucket and did the same.

He had the transverse crest of a centurion mounted on his helmet, the silvered chain-mail armour of a well-to-do one and the decorations of a brave one. He was no longer young, probably more than forty, with black eyes, deep lines in his cheeks and a long blue chin which would need shaving twice a day. I had suffered at the hands of the public barbers in the City, insolent and reckless with their perpetually blunt blades. There were very few occasions when a civilian customer would escape without a nick on his shaven face and some had even been permanently scarred. In the legions, careless barbers were in a high-risk occupation. There were no nicks on the well-shaven face of this elderly centurion.

He shifted his sword and rested his hands on the top of his stick.

"My soldiers tell me you have been inside Britain."

"I did not see much of the farm land."

"So they said. You have been there twice. I have spent my whole service on the Rhine. I know almost nothing about Britain other than what I have read in Caesar. He crossed the Ocean overnight but it is obviously dangerous. Ships sink, get wrecked."

"He crossed at the narrowest point, many crossings take longer. There are sometimes storms and the navigators have to watch the tides. Look Centurion, how can I help you?"

He swallowed. He had an old scar on his throat, an arrow or a German spear point, not a razor.

"If the Invasion takes place, I shall want to bring my family over," he said. "I am not going to leave them alone on the German frontier. I want you to put me in touch with a trustworthy private shipowner here."

"Willingly, but you said 'if the Invasion takes place.' Do you seriously doubt it?"

"Yes." He stared at me until I knew that I was not going to get further on that tack.

"You have children?" I asked, to keep the conversation going.

"Five, four now, one died of pneumonia. The eldest boy is almost old enough to enlist."

"Wants to be a centurion?"

"Yes. There will be six passengers. My wife and her father as well. He is quite old but we cannot leave him behind."

"I understand. Assuming the army goes to Britain, will you retire there."

"Centurions of whatever level do not have a fixed term of service. Retirement for us is at the discretion of the Emperor. I have applied for retirement already, my eyesight is not good, and it has been rejected already."

I gave this some thought. Applying for a medical discharge on the verge of a military campaign was a risky business from a career point of view, but this man was approaching the end of his career and the silver medals inlayed with gold on his chest denied any thought of cowardice. I decided to probe in a different direction.

"Passages over the Ocean in privately-owned ships are likely to be expensive. I think that lower prices could probably be negotiated if the number of passengers was higher."

"If the army goes," he said, with a grim smile, "I will guarantee a full ship of passengers."

"I need to talk to someone, but I would think that there would need to be payment in advance."

"His money would be safe. I am thinking about the families of colleagues, centurions like me. We would want to be assured that the shipmaster is competent and the vessel sound."

"Of course. How about this? We both consult and you locate me in the port area anytime tomorrow. Any of the military police will know where I am. We'll go to the shipmaster's office together."

The crowd roared nearby.

The following day, we walked together through the port's streets. A group of off-duty sailors nudged one another as they caught sight of my red sash. The house Pytheas had rented at ruinous cost was small but had sufficient space for him to meet his clients and it had a narrow view of the harbour. He had made his own preparations for the meeting. His sleeveless tunic showed off his brown, oarsman's arms as well as the faded tattoo of a steering oar on his bicep. His silver hair and straight gaze invited confidence. His little painting of his huge ship, 'Indus,' was in evidence. His framed bronze diploma, attesting to his twenty-six years of efficient service at sea, was on the wall. I nearly booked a passage with him myself.

Pytheas gravely inspected the list of centurions' families wishing to travel to Britain after the army invaded.

"Yes," he said slowly, "this passenger manifest would almost fill a ship."

"There are plenty more," said the Centurion quickly.

"Quite so," agreed the old sailor turned businessman. "We will agree a price based on a full shipload, if that suits you. One stipulation only, payment in advance in gold coin. No bulky bags of copper or bronze, please."

The Centurion smiled.

"No problem," he said. "From our side, we want to know about shipmaster and the ship. Will you be on board?"

He squinted at the inscribed lettering on the bronze diploma.

"I will certainly be on board one of the ships," said Pytheas, which jerked the Centurion's head towards him. "All the skippers will have been chosen by myself from among competent and experienced men. You have my guarantee."

The Centurion looked again at the diploma and nodded.

"As for the ships," Pytheas went on in an even voice. "The coastline is full of shipping to lift the army and their supplies. The army will not be coming back any time soon and a lot of the shipping will be redundant after the first week. It was built with that in mind. Some of those vessels were just thrown together. Many shipmasters will be buying those ships on the cheap. I will not."

The Centurion was all attention.

"I am negotiating an agreement to lease properly-built Fleet transports, such as you have on the Rhine." This was the first I had heard of this. "There is one down in the harbour now, 'Justitia'. My son can arrange for you to look it over if you wish."

"I know the Fleet transport design, they have served us well. They will not be new, though, and will certainly have had hard service?"

"True. I will not lease any vessel that is suspect but I expect a certificate of sea-worthiness from a serving naval officer might set your mind at rest?"

The Centurion nodded emphatically. I wondered if Pytheas had arranged an appointment with Captain Seleucus yet.

After the Centurion had gone and I stood with a cup of my new business associate's wine in my hand, I asked him about that.

"Appointments?" he said. "Leases? That is the fourth firm agreement this week."

"All centurions?" I queried.

"Centurions, standard bearers, a few wealthy legionaries."

"That sound like a lot of gold," I remarked quietly.

"It's needed, lad. On the Red Sea. The 'Indus' is waiting."

CHAPTER 50

▼

ROME

Emperor Claudius eventually found Narcissus in his wife's apartment. Anywhere else and he would have received a truthful reply from the messengers he had sent out looking for him. The messengers said that they could not find Narcissus, so the Emperor knew he would have to go and look for himself. Messalina did not like being disturbed when preparations were under way for her to start her official day. Other than for her husband, occasionally, she would only ever allow Narcissus to interrupt.

She could not rise to greet her husband properly, hampered by the protective sheet over her dress and with her yellow-wigged hairdresser only half-way through building her elaborate coiffeur. She did irritably wave away the slaves darkening her eyelids and whitening her arms so that she could, at least, see the Emperor. Other members of the household, holding open jewelry boxes and displaying a wide selection of flimsy sandals, backed rapidly out of the room. The clerk with her list of engagements for the day left more sedately. Narcissus stayed where he was.

At the Emperor's glare, the hairdresser tried to secure her unfinished work with a mouthful of pins and then left. She surreptitiously took the handmirrors to limit later fury on the part of her mistress. Being the leader of fashion in Rome was sometimes a burden.

Messalina was a lot younger than her husband even though she had had two children by him. She was by no means in awe of him, being of noble birth on both sides herself. If she was not his intellectual equal, no one could deny that, as a pair of physical specimens, she was by far the more beautiful. Her dismissive treatment of the most powerful man in the world was well-known and her frequent tantrums were legendary. Claudius did not usually find this objectionable and sometimes, wearied by the cloying servility of Senate and Court, it seemed downright refreshing.

Sitting bolt upright amidst the litter of her daily preparations, with her hair half-done, anger simmered close to the surface. It cooled slightly into a sort of amusement as her husband lurched across the room. He was heading for the racks where brilliant swatches of material were draped.

"Don't finger the silk, Claudius," she snapped. "Please. You will mark it."

"I don't think so," he said mildly watching the lights in the material as it slid over his muscular forearm. "Where does this come from?" He asked Narcissus but Messalina replied first.

"From India."

"Through the Red Sea, this consignment," added Narcissus. "Your lady-wife and I were just discussing the route."

"Yes," said Messalina. "Brave Romans have found a new sea route direct to India from the Red Sea, Claudius. It avoids those greedy Greeks at Palmyra. I'm only going to buy Roman in future."

"Good," said Claudius, not looking at Narcissus. "Greeks are everywhere and are, most of them, greedy. You have to watch them."

Messalina caught the inference and giggled. Despite the half-finished make-up, Claudius thought her very attractive. They had both been married before, both were entirely aware that theirs was a political marriage and that neither was particularly faithful to the other. Nevertheless, there was a comradeship in the isolation of power.

"You must not make fun of Narcissus," she said. "It has been many years since he has seen Greece."

"Only because the Celts have already stolen everything from the Oracle at Delphi."

"That was hundreds of years ago," protested Narcissus good-naturedly. "We've been piling up treasure again ever since, and, don't forget, the Celts then came around and sacked Rome. We had to move in to make Rome a paying proposition again. We just pretended to lose to the Roman army at Pydna."

"Well, we've got them cornered in Britain now," said the Emperor, referring to the Celts.

"Do you think, the Celts have got any of that Delphi treasure left, Claudius?" asked his wife.

"Doubtful," the middle-aged historian shook his head. "A lot was recovered in Spain and there have been a number of stories about hoards squirreled away by the most respectable Roman families involved in defeating Celtic armies. I doubt there will be much, if anything, left in Celtic hands."

"Well, you go on over there and find out. Keep me some of the best pieces."

They left her in a good humour to finish her preparations for the day. Their footsteps echoed on the mosaic and the full-length wall portraits seems to slide past like naked figures on a ship.

"The lady Messalina seems well?" the Emperor made it a sort of question.

"It goes with the position," said Narcissus, carefully, "but I think she is lonely."

"This preoccupation with silk worries me."

"Hers, or mine?" Narcissus smiled.

"Rome's. Relish for competition has always been part of the Roman make up, so enjoyment of the fruits of successful competition should not be surprising. Rome was built on competition and self-sacrifice and, when there were profits, they were returned to the State. Nowadays, competition is stronger than ever but self-sacrifice is not a valued virtue. Profits are hoarded by individuals or spent on trivialities. They are not returned to the State."

"In taxes you mean?"

"No. In the voluntary funding of public works and in bequests to public benefits. Now, most of the funding of public works is done by the Emperor and any bequests are made to him in case he confiscates the entire wealth of the deceased. Any disposable income left over is spent on private extravagances. There was a time when hair was just cut, not dressed, when wool and linen was sufficient to clothe even the most wealthy of men. Senators were proud to wear iron signet rings not gold. Successful men became very wealthy, but they did not flaunt it. Any disposable income was ploughed back to the public benefit. Voluntarily."

"And now," said the Imperial freedman, smoothing his wig and adjusting his silk robe, "it's all wigs and gold teeth. Silk clothing and teams of under-employed slaves."

"We are becoming almost oriental."

"It has been said before in your presence, sire. Rome is no longer a Republic. The Roman Empire has absorbed a good part of the orient, why should Romans be surprised that it has become a bit oriental."

"Because we need those Republican qualities to extend and to survive. Oriental dynasties rise through enterprise and quickly fall through extravagance. It will almost be a relief to deal with uncomplicated blue-painted Celts. They haven't got anything we want, except territory and raw materials."

"Both of which," said Narcissus, evenly, "the Emperor needs to stay in office."

Claudius stopped and looked at his freedman for a while. Narcissus did not drop his gaze.

"Right," the Emperor said shortly. Narcissus gently exhaled. "The Emperor needs to stay in office and his freedmen had better make sure to keep him there. I have a task for you. First, get Rufrius Pollio over to the Palace with his plan for deployment of the Praetorian Guard when I take the field. Tell him I want details on the matter of elephants. Then we need to discuss these reports of army disaffection in Gaul."

Narcissus had known Claudius for many years, when he had been an embarrassment to his family and a bad joke to the citizens. He had shared the continuous, energy-sapping danger of sudden murder or execution. He had tried to take on himself some of the mocking and ridicule. He had been close beside Claudius when he had been made Emperor, supported his tentative steps when he reluctantly gathered the reins of power into his hands. With him, he had stood all these years. For the first time now, Narcissus saw Claudius as truly Emperor. With him, when it happened, he would also fall.

CHAPTER 51

▼

EUROPE

You cannot be a policeman for any length of time without developing a feeling of community with the population you work for. It is not just a matter of animal survival, policemen generally work alone or in pairs and anyone, other than a complete fool, can find a quiet place to hide if he really wants to. Danger is, though, part of the equation. Policemen are specifically employed to go to dangerous situations, often alone, and to reduce or eliminate the danger to the population and, if at all possible, to themselves as well. Policemen who are slow to become aware of danger are quickly in deep trouble. Being part of the community, provides a policeman with early warning of danger and confidence in facing it. He is not so alone.

Awareness is a sense that develops with exposure. Even in a crowded street, I often feel I can see further and hear better than anyone else in view. If I have been in a particular street before, I will have greeted, spoken to or, at least, nodded at, business people, tradesmen, idlers and small boys. Small girls do not report to policemen. They run home and tell their parents. The more often I go to that street, the more links I try to weave in my safety net.

Business people fall into two categories in this regard. There are those whose businesses are not going well and so they have time on their hands to watch what is happening and to gossip. Then there are those who operate busy premises where, as day follows night, they are going to need a policeman's help one day. Tavern owners form a substantial part of this category. The drawback for them is that they cannot be too openly friendly without scaring away customers. The drawback for the policeman is that he risks becoming suspected of being on the take.

I was quite proud of my century of young military policemen. They had never been completely integrated into the Legion and did not believe, as some of the older, frontier legionaries did, that they were a garrison in conquered territory. They treated the locals and their property with respect and it was reciprocated. Because the prostitutes offered their favours, the grannies tried to give them cakes and the small boys knew their names, they each felt it was likely that community support would be on their side in a dangerous situation. This is a big confidence-booster.

They also started passing on a useful trickle of information from the townspeople, information that would not have found its way into official channels. One item was very disturbing. The off-duty legionaries had stopped going to the taverns.

This seemed so against nature that I had difficulty crediting the report at first. A lengthy prowl about the many drinking places which had sprung up over the previous few months tended to show me that the report was, in fact, correct. They were still crowded during the day with the sailors and the many soldiers of the auxilliary units. I saw cavalrymen and conventional native infantry soldiers, and I also saw representatives of specialist units such as the archers of Cohort I Hamiorum and the river-crossing experts from the 8 000 strong contingent of Batavians. What I did not see was any single representative of the four legions which formed the backbone of the Invasion Task Force.

However long the legionaries' working day, however taxing the route marches, close quarter battle drills, the digging of practice entrenchments, the camp fatigues, it was totally incredible that not one of the twenty two thousand legionaries could find time or inclination to swagger into town for a drink.

I found Rufus Sita at headquarters packing his kit with a face as long as his horse's. I was not too preoccupied not to poke fun at his mournful expression and eventually raised a glimmer of a smile. He was apparently on transfer from the Commandant's staff, but not back to Ala I Thracum where he had formerly been a decurion. Clearly, he was not going to get his rank back, but the Commandant was sparing him the embarrassment of returning to his previous unit as a trooper where he had once been a junior officer. I pointed the obvious out to him and he cheered up a bit. He was posted to Legion XX Valeria, now under the command of the famous soldier Hosideus Geta, hero of Mauretania. There should be plenty of opportunities for promotion there.

Even though I was early, he got me in to see the Commandant straight away. For once, the only item on Anicius Maximus' desk was his stick. It was just as well. It turned out to be a busy afternoon. His black eyes bored into mine as I made my report. When I had finished, he picked up his stick and walked out. By which, I gathered, I was expected to follow him.

He strode stiffly over to the huge tent now occupied by the commander of the Invasion Task Force and Governor-designate of Britain. The sentry saw the Commandant coming and wisely got out of the way. He was not so circumspect when he saw me following and I had to wait briefly outside. A shout from within changed the sentry's mind.

I had not met Aulus Plautius before and I had heard little of him. The legionaries from the Rhine command did not appear to know much about him, although those from Legion IX Hispana seemed to quite like him. He was a youngish man with dark curly hair, comfortably seated in the large, well-furnished part of the tent partitioned off as his office. With him was a smaller, older man with an orator's voice, Senator Sentius Saturninus, commander of the rear areas.

"Optio," Plautius said after the Commandant said who I was, "repeat the report you have just made to your superior officer."

I did so. He still did not have any discernible expression on his face. After a moment, the Senator stirred.

"Something I forgot to tell you, Plautius. Could be relevant. An ex-colleague of mine with estates in southern Gaul is here to renew his army wine contract. He tells me that his private sales to taverns in Gesoriacum are falling off. Asiaticus is quite worried. He is only making half a fortune every day. What's the matter, Optio?"

"Nothing, Senator."

Still, the Governor said nothing. The Commandant cleared his throat.

"Sir, the three other commandants tell me that legionaries are not leaving the camps at all except for work and fatigues. The Chief Centurion of my Legion confirms it."

Either the Governor was calculating furiously behind those shuttered eyes or he was about to doze off.

"Seems a bit unusual," prompted the Senator. "Almost unprecedented isn't it?"

"Shit!" said the Governor suddenly.

"I beg your pardon?" said the Senator, who was probably hard of hearing. After all those years in the Senate, it would not be surprising.

"The legionaries are saving their money," said Plautius.

The Senator did not remark that that it was very commendable.

"They are saving their money," went on the Governor, "and they are not depositing it with the aquilfers of the legions, are they Commandant?"

Anicius Maximus looked a bit startled and did not reply.

"They are not," stated the Governor, as if he had not asked the question. "In fact, many of them have withdrawn their savings from the aquilfers. They want ready cash on hand. Why?"

"They are finally convinced that the Invasion is going to take place?" hazarded the Senator.

"Yes, they certainly are convinced of that. So why are they not in the taverns? There is precious little to spend their money on in Britain by all accounts."

"Because," I ventured, "they are going to refuse to go, and need the money for when we cut off their rations. Or they are going to agree to go, provided they can bring their families."

"No!" said the Commandant, glaring at me.

"Yes," I gritted my teeth. "I think so, sir."

There was a pause.

"It really is the only explanation, isn't it?" the Senator remarked quietly.

"Shit," the Governor said again.

"But the centurions have said nothing about…" began the Commandant and stopped.

"And that, in itself," said the Governor, with great emphasis, "tells us a great deal, don't you agree, Commandant?"

Anicius Maximus looked stunned.

"We need to know," I said, daring, "whether they are going to simply refuse to go or whether they are only going to refuse to go without the families."

"Yes?" said the Senator encouragingly.

"If the families, particularly the families in Germany, start to move in this direction, we will know that the men will go if their families follow them. If the families don't move, we can expect an outright refusal to embark."

"All right," said the Governor. "That makes sense. I'll contact Governors Galba and Secundus. What else?"

"I've had an application to lease ships from one Pytheas," said the Senator, "for after the Invasion. You know him, I believe, Optio. Ask him to come and see me again would you?"

"Very well," said the young Governor. "Thank you Optio. You may go. Keep your superiors informed. Commandant, would give us a little more of your time."

I looked at the Commandant, uncertain as to whether to wait for him outside. He appeared to have recovered his poise and made go-away motions with his hand.

The reactions of Titus and Fangs were totally different and the opposite of what I expected. Titus, former City policeman and inveterate eavesdropper, was astounded that the famed legions were again contemplating mutiny. Fangs said that it served them right, that they never considered the effect of decisions on the hard life of ordinary soldiers and if the legionaries marched off back home without their part-time officers it would be just too bad. I realised, for the first time, that I had no idea if Fangs had a family.

"Yes," he said with a little gleam of paternal pride. "I was married before I enlisted but kept it quiet. The kids have all died or grown up now and so it's a little easier. But the old woman really had to struggle on a legionary's pay. Had to grow and sell vegetables to make ends meet sometimes, and in those winters, in Germany, you wouldn't believe the cold. She comes from the south of Spain, you see."

We did, indeed, see. Now, on the verge of retirement, perhaps with the thought of settling somewhere with his retirement bonus in the blessed sun, Fangs was being told by 'them' to march away from his long-suffering wife and retire to a patch of wet ground in Britain, assuming he survived. The bland assumption that he would abandon his old wife to selling vegetables in Germany for the sake of a 'proper' marriage to some surly British girl was sickening in its arrogance.

"The legionaries say they are frightened of crossing the Ocean," offered Titus, the unmarried man, still not totally convinced.

"Frightened of crossing the Ocean," scoffed Fangs. "They are no more frightened of crossing the Ocean than you would be afraid of patrolling the backstreets of some strange town."

Titus and I thought about that, but Fangs had not finished.

"They've seen really frightening things. You go to the Teutoburger Forest in Germany. Before my time, Governor Varus—he came from Syria so he knew a whole lot about soldiering in Germany—he took three good legions, with their auxiliaries and all the soldiers' families, on a tour through enemy country and he got them all slaughtered, day after day, men, women and children. There were precious few officers' families with them and, when things were at their most desperate, do you know what those officers did?"

We did, in fact, know what they did.

"They committed suicide, that's what they did. They deserted their men and the women and children. Rome's heroes, those officers. As if it is harder to kill yourself than it is to die doing your job. Walk through that forest. I have. Mile after mile of the bones of the real heroes and heroines. Black trees and white bones, some of them little. No, the legionaries are not frightened of any old Ocean."

There was a fairly long silence. I felt that I had to break it.

"Right. What we need to do now, though, is to find out how much of the Fleet and the auxiliary units think the same way. That means visiting the taverns. We'll divide the town between us. Try not to alarm anyone."

"Optio," Fangs cleared his throat and spoke respectfully. "The auxiliaries are not really a problem, you know. If they join in any mutiny they'll just be additional numbers. If they mutiny separately, or refuse to return to duty after a settlement, the legions will simply destroy them. It's the legions we have to worry about."

"What about the Fleet?" Titus was feeling left out.

"I don't know much about sailors," said the old legionary, "but their base will most probably be here. Their families can settle outside Gesoriacum and there is no word of any of the crews being retired in Britain."

"And there is no word of the crews being excessively frightened of the Ocean, either," I added with a nod at Fangs. "I agree. It's the legions we have to worry about."

"Well, why worry?" said Titus, brightening up. "We have a complete century of juvenile military policemen to prevent four frontier legions from mutinying. The Invasion is safe. What about those tavern visits, then?"

"We'll do them anyway. That's where the gossip is. I am open to any other suggestions, though. Nothing? Give it some thought and let me know."

Down in the town, visiting the patrolmen and the tavern owners, I thought I could now detect a thinning of the usual crowds of military. It could have been imagination. There were a lot of tired cavalrymen and sailors in town and I knew from Philip that practicing the loading and unloading of horses and mules went on every day now. Some of those animals must now be very bored with looking down past their dangling feet at the salt water below.

I had just come out of a hole-in-the-wall type of tavern where I had been well received by a friendly if distracted publican, perspiring happily in busy afternoon trade, when a small, shock-headed girl tugged at my hand.

"Come," she piped in Celtic, "come."

"What's the matter, darling?" She squinted up at me in the pale sunshine, tattered dress, barefoot.

"Mummy has fallen down," she said.

"Where?"

She pointed a small arm down the crowded street. I could see nothing out of place. Walk to a fight, run to an accident. I scooped up the little body and, trying not to use her as a ram, I dodged across the street.

"Where? Where's Mummy?"

She pointed into a shadowed alleyway. Her small body was tense, her face close to mine. Something was tickling at the back of my neck as I swung into the alley. Her eyes were huge and fixed on my face, her small mouth pursed. The shadow of the high walls fell across us. No tears on those dirty cheeks. I stopped.

A tremendous blow impacted between my shoulder blades. I staggered forward, clutching the screaming child, pain streaming like sparks up my neck and down my arms. There was another blow on its way but my legs seemed to be wading through water. I collided into ranks of empty clay vessels, several of them shattering. I could not get out of reach of my assailant nor put down the little limpet fastened onto my left shoulder. Clay shards broke under my feet and I started to fall.

I had to use my sword arm to break our fall, but the back of my tunic was ripped out by the second blow, not my cringing skin. I released her onto the littered ground and bracing both hands either side of her, I kicked backwards like a frenzied mule. It landed with a satisfactory thump and drove out a hoarse gasp. I swung back to my feet, my back on fire but free of the little body. A shaggy figure was outlined against the sunlit street behind him. I had neither space nor time to draw my sword and I could not see where the knife was in front of the backlit figure.

I got my hands out of the knife's way, behind my head, and kicked out again, and again satisfactorily landed on his lower body. Fire streaked across my thigh. My assailant lurched to one side and avoided my thrown helmet which sailed out of the alley into the crowded street. The little girl had gone quiet. I had no idea where she was in relation to me. My hobnails skidded off some obstruction and I went down on one knee. My opponent was breathing heavily as he lurched towards me and I scrambled backwards on my knees, my still-sheathed sword dragging on the dirt.

The only way I could free my weapon, I unclipped the baldric and got both my hands on the sheathed sword, jabbing it towards the would-be assassin, stopping him in his tracks. I coughed but saw no blood and got my feet under me. I could not guess how badly I had been hurt. He took a pace backwards. I freed the blade of my sword and took a pace forwards, scabbard in the other hand, baldric dangling. I coughed again and spat, took another step forward.

With a shriek, a little scrambling figure brushed past my legs and headed for the street. The bulky, shadowed figure of the attacker whirled to flee but his injured leg betrayed him and he went down on one knee. Without the slightest compunction, I drove my sword into his back and he toppled forward with a thump. He gave a long sigh and lay still.

As I leaned against the wall, deep pain radiated from between my shoulder-blades and warmth slid down my leg from a gash in my thigh. I looked at the body. I was taken back in my mind to a rainswept street in Rome. My assailant was no longer bearded but there was no doubt. He was the slave—now the deceased slave, thankfully—of the good Senator Asiaticus. With an effort, I straightened up and wiped my sword on the slave's clothing before sheathing it. It was just too painful to get the baldric back over my shoulder so I carried the weapon in my hand.

Various spectators were peering into the alley. One, braver than the rest, held out my dusty helmet to me. I could not have been a pretty sight as I stepped out of the alleyway but, at least, I was a lot prettier than the one I had left behind. I straightened my shaking legs and took a few deep breaths, then I carefully straightened my shoulders. I now, no doubt, had damaged links in my chain mail shirt at the back to balance similar damage to the front. Narcissus, I owe you, twice.

Two young military policemen came running. One appeared, at first sight, to be saturated with blood but ran easily, eyes alert. He and I, almost simulta-neously, asked each other what had happened. What had happened to me was quite easily told. The little girl had vanished. The assassin's spirit would be on the banks of the Styx.

What had happened to the wine-soaked young policeman was told at more length by his unsympathetic colleague.

"It was those puddle-jumpers, the Batavians," he said irreverently.

They had apparently been called to deal with a fight in a tavern and had hur-ried there—big mistake. Having been unable to break up the fight which had only just got started, and everyone was apparently enjoying, they had decided to close the premises. The damp one had trapped himself behind the bar as he tried to close the shutters—bigger mistake. The fun-loving patrons had then seized their heaven-sent opportunity, forgotten their differences, and thrown dozens of cupfuls of wine over the helpless policeman.

I could not help laughing as I patted him on a wet shoulder. The same shoulder which had been bitten by an angry mule at the Rhone River. There are some young men who are just accident-prone.

"Lots of lessons learned today." We all nodded wisely.

I was really hurting by the time I stumbled back to my quarters in Camp, looking forward to a bath and an examination of the damage. The slave had really made a determined effort to bore a hole through the back of my chest and the skirts of my tunic were sticking to my thigh. Of course, there was an urgent message for me to report to the Commandant immediately. I had a feeling he had not been pleased by my contradicting him in front of the commander of the Invasion Task Force. There had also been an ex-Consul present but I doubted that that counted for much in the Commandant's own personal hierarchy. It seemed I was about to benefit from an attitude-readjustment session.

Titus was out so I borrowed his clean tunic, gave my leg a quick wash and a cursory bandage, dusted my helmet on the hem of my cloak and hobbled over to the Commandant's tent. He looked at me closely, his gaze pausing at the bloodstains I had not had time to get off one of my shoes.

"I hope," he said, "that the other party looks worse than you."

"Much worse."

"Much worse, sir!"

"Much worse, sir."

"Good. I have two jobs for you but luckily you can combine them. Rome is sending down a pack of British refugees led by a King Verica or somesuch. Senator Saturninus wants them met on the Rhone and escorted here without getting lost or running away, he has a use for them apparently. Think you can manage that?"

"King Bericos? Yes, sir."

"The other job. A freedman," the Commandant's lip curled slightly, "a personal emissary of the Emperor, apparently, is also on his way to see the Governor-designate. Bring him back with your party. Safely. Take a turma of cavalry. Not from Ala Indiana Gallorum. Clear?"

"I am to take a turma from Ala I Thracum. Yes, sir."

I mentally agreed that it might be stretching loyalty too far to have Gallic cavalry guarding British refugees. I was looking forward to seeing the old barbarian king again.

"Right. One of your two reprobates will run the military police century. What about that long-service legionary of yours?"

"Ah. I think not."

The Commandant said nothing, just stared.

"He is sympathetic with his colleagues in the legions. Understandably. But, in this climate? Besides, he is a good man but does not know a lot about policing."

"Yes. I see. Titus then. Tell him to report to me. Tell him he is now an Optio and he had better not let you down."

I felt my face stretch in a very wide grin. The Commandant was looking down, fiddling with a red clothes brush.

"Go and see the doctor," he said. "Have a good rest and be on your way by dawn tomorrow."

He tossed the object onto his table in front of me. It was not a clothes brush but a helmet-crest.

"You are now a junior centurion," said the Commandant. "Congratulations. Don't let me down. No, come back here, Centurion, and salute. That's better. You are dismissed."

Now all I had to do before limping over to the Camp hospital was to break the news to Fangs.

CHAPTER 52

▼

EUROPE

Going up to the Rhone was a painful business. The doctor had been very efficient in his stitching and one of the medics among the thirty Thracian cavalry changed my dressing most evenings. A lot of transport traffic, wheeled and hoofed, was heading for Gesoriacum. The stone road surface was already chipped and scarred, well padded with dried manure in places. For the sake of our horses' hooves, and my own comfort, we generally kept to the softer ground beside the road.

It should have been a real pleasure, leading my little cavalcade, with the transverse crest of a centurion decorating my helmet for the first time. I wore my sword on the left hip now, as is the custom for centurions, but I kept my sash draped over my right shoulder, under the baldric. The journey was not, for me, so much a pleasure as a trial. Many of the faces of the on-coming drivers and muleteers on the road displayed some astonishment at the sight of a white-faced centurion leading his horse south on foot. My main consolation was that Asiaticus' slave had recently made an even more uncomfortable journey.

Army medical care and a moderate pace saved my leg from blood poisoning. By the time we reached the Misene Fleet Base on the Rhone, the stitches had held and the wound was healing healthily.

I had left my loricated plate armour behind. I had tried riding in it before and found it almost impossible to do so comfortably. Either it had to be fitted tightly or the weight pressing down on the hips threatened to trap the lower abdomen against the saddle, endangering future generations. If it was fitted too tightly, though, it was inclined to ride upwards, progressively restricting breathing. It is ideal for infantry, perhaps, but is clearly one of the reasons why you rarely see a legionary on a horse.

My troopers of Ala I Thracum wore chain mail armour which was more accommodating to the body, and I had earlier seen the auxiliary archers wear armour of bronze scales. Many senior officers wear expensive cuirasses, specially made to fit their bodies exactly. They are fairly comfortable when riding. I had none of these, and made do with the welcome weight of my chain mail vest worn under Titus' tunic. I would have to start spending some money soon, before my troopers became too embarrassed by my appearance to follow me anywhere.

The Fleet Base on the Rhone had grown enormously since I had been there last and seethed with activity. Several ships and barges were being off loaded and more waited on the river. The military road had been extended down the banks so that further unloading could take place directly from ship to roadway. I got directions from a harassed clerk—is there any other kind?—in the Fleet office and found a large, colourful camp of tents, marquees and pavilions sprawling on a slight rise outside the Base. Sitting at his ease in a chair outside one of the tents, with his armour shining in the sun and his cloak thrown casually back, was an officer of the Praetorian Guard.

"Yes, decurion?" he asked languidly of the leader of the cavalry troop riding beside me. He obviously did not think the sickly looking-person in the travel-stained tunic next to the decurion was worthy of much attention. I unhooked my helmet from one of the front pommels and carefully lowered myself to the ground. The decurion took my reins. I passed the Praetorian as he was struggling to get out of his chair and I headed for the largest and most colourful tent in sight.

Before I reached it, I was grabbed in a hairy embrace and a king roared his welcome in my ear. Ex-residents of the British Palace arrived from several directions, faces lit up by wide grins. Almost all the men had regrown their moustaches and both men and women were in Celtic woollens despite the warm weather. My abused body sustained much pounding and hugging, but all in a good cause. The noise died away abruptly as a slight figure in brilliant clothing appeared at the doorway of the big tent. With hands extended and gold showing in his smile, the bald-headed little freedman trotted across the grass.

"Welcome, Aurelius Victorinus, welcome," gushed Narcissus. "What's this, a centurion now? Congratulations, indeed."

"This fellow…," complained the Praetorian behind me. Narcissus looked over my shoulder and his face froze. The Praetorian's voice stopped as if his throat had been cut.

"…is a friend," finished Narcissus for him. "Stop your whining and go and show his men where to camp."

The officer, small by Praetorian standards, still dwarfed the freedman but he immediately turned away to do what he was told.

"Come inside," said Narcissus, eyes lighting up again with goodwill. "Have you been ill? Here, take a seat. Don't worry about that Praetorian, all he knows about is elephants."

It was like getting into a hot bath after a route march. Tiredness and niggling pain faded away. The wine was very good but the welcome was better. After assuring me of the Emperor's health, Narcissus did not say a great deal except to ask the occasional question. I found that I talked a lot without feeling uncomfortable about dominating the conversation. I described the personalities and the undercurrents within the Invasion Task Force and went into detail about the surging groundswell of feeling among the family men of the legions.

"They have not, though, actually mutinied, have they? There has been no outright refusal to obey orders?"

He was, as usual, watching me intently as he listened.

"No. No order to embark had been given at the time I left Gesoriacum, but it must have been imminent. The campaigning season is short in the north and we are already into it. I brought mail," I remembered belatedly and struggled to get up."

"Leave it. I shall look at it later. How were you injured."

I told him about the fight in the alleyway and the death of the slave. I did not need to remind him about my earlier encounter with the man.

"Senator Asiaticus," he mused quietly. "He has estates in this region. Well, well."

He did not pursue this line of thought with me but expressed his delight that his gift of the mail vest had served me so well. He insisted that I take it off and show him. I pointed at the flattened links on the front of the vest.

"That was Pallas. An accident but could have been a fatal one for me." I pointed at the back. "That was the assassination attempt. It would have certainly finished me off without the vest."

"Yes, I see." He was actually looking at the fading bruising on my back. "Determined man, wasn't he, that slave? Where is the Senator at the moment, do you know?"

"I hear he was in Gesoriacum when I was attacked. Something about a wine contract with the army."

He nodded as if in confirmation of something. He invited me to have supper with him later, which was my cue to leave him with his dispatches.

The food was excellent and the company better. It included port officials from the Fleet, a king, a shy decurion of cavalry from Thrace, owners of local estates, a Praetorian who knew all about elephants, and myself. It was masterfully hosted by an ex-slave, one of the most powerful men in the Empire. After his other guests had noisily departed, he poured me a last cup.

"Interesting fellow, that elephant man," said Narcissus, seriously. "By the way, I happen to know he's short of ready funds. He wants to sell some spare armour, silvered chain mail, I believe. Why don't you make him an offer?"

While I was searching for something to say, he went off on another tack.

"When I was a slave, we used to enjoy dinner parties like the one tonight. Plenty of different types of people, the more outrageous the better. Carry off the unconscious to bed and then have our own party on the leftovers. I wonder why leftovers always taste better than just-cooked food? The worst were the gatherings of Senators, all looking for an advantage over the others and scared to put a foot wrong. Pompous, empty drivel, hardly worth eavesdropping."

He laughed suddenly.

"I remember once. We were entertaining some supercilious orientals from somewhere east of the Black Sea. They thought they could drink anything and that slaves crawled out from under stones. We made up some special wine for them, spiked to give it a kick like a donkey. Every time one of these guests held out his cup he got full measure of the fortified wine. Everyone else got the normal drink. By the end of the evening there were snoring Armenians draped over the furniture everywhere, other guests stepping carefully over those prone on the floor. They couldn't work out why the slaves were falling about laughing."

I was laughing myself. Narcissus leaned back.

"Those dispatches," he said more seriously. "The order for the Invasion Task Force to embark will be given seven days from today. Will they do it?"

"Not unless there is provision for the families."

"I see. I gather that there are some negotiations going on with private ship-owners. To transport the families later."

"Most of the ordinary legionaries cannot afford the fares. Centurions can, and they are certainly making their own arrangements, but they will not be able to force the troops to embark if they refuse. It may work. I don't know."

"Well, we shall soon see. Until that time, there is much forward planning to do. Dealing with a mutiny, if it happens, is one thing. Getting ready to exploit the successful landing in Britain can't wait."

"Elephants and Praetorians?"

"Just so."

"Praetorians mean the Emperor."

"Yes. If necessary."

We thought about that for a moment.

"Tomorrow," said Narcissus. "We break camp early, say, mid-morning. We are going to identify and survey the site of the main transit camp for the Praetorian Guard."

"The landowner may not be pleased."

"I think you may be right."

The following morning I had a brief discussion with the Praetorian, examined the silvered chain mail of his surplus armour and agreed a very reasonable price. I thought he would not be happy with my draft on my bank in Pompeii but Narcissus stood guarantee for it and his frown disappeared. My thirty cavalrymen appeared pleased that their boss was now properly dressed.

The Camp was dismantled with more enthusiasm than skill by the Palace servants Narcissus had brought with him. They were obviously more used to mosaic floors and marble pillars than with leather roofs and wooden poles. With much delay, but without too much damage, we managed to get our accommodation, furniture and supplies stowed on huge Gallic wagons, and into uncertain motion, before midday. It was lucky we were not going far.

It was early afternoon when the entire caravan rumbled to a stop under an immense pall of dust in the forecourt of a large, country house set within the wide fields of its estate. The tall, wide-hipped figure of the owner stood in front of his house, his eyes glittering under a long forehead, the dull gleam of an iron signet ring showing on his right fist. Senator Valerius Asiaticus was not obviously pleased to see us.

He did not come forward to greet a mere freedman. I walked behind Narcissus to where the man stood. His glance at me was contemptuous.

"What can I do for you?" he said without moving.

"You can invite us into your office," said Narcissus and strolled past him. "This way, is it?" and he kept on walking past the decorative vine trees in the entrance. Asiaticus had no choice but to follow, just like the Praetorian had had to follow me the previous day.

There was deep guffaw from King Bericos beside the wagons. He had forgiven me for losing his daughter to the British raiders. He knew that she had been alive when she left the Continent and she was unlikely to be executed by any British authority. In exile, she could be found and even, perhaps, freed.

A wax-faced clerk fled from the office as we entered closely followed by a moderately-furious Asiaticus. Narcissus sat behind the great man's desk. I closed the door and leaned on it. Seeing who was standing, armed, behind him seemed to cause the Senator a sudden twinge of anxiety. He shifted so he could see us both.

"Senator," said Narcissus, at his most affable. "You are privileged."

"I am?"

"Yes. In fact, you are doubly privileged. You are going to host my party on your estate here for a few days. No, we will not move into your house. I absolutely refuse. We will set up our own accommodation fairly close by so that you do not have to go to the trouble of building us a separate bathhouse. We'll just use yours. I do not intend to cause you any inconvenience at all, so my own staff will cook all meals for my party. Just have your steward send over sufficient wine for us all. And the uncooked food. Now, the second reason you are privileged."

He beamed upon the open-mouthed Senator.

"I have decided that your estate is ideal for the transit camp of the Praetorian Guard on their way north. There will be about six thousand of them. Plus about twenty elephants."

"Elephants!" The Senator's voice came out in the form of a squeak.

"Yes. Their manure is very good for young vine trees I believe. Keep the urine away from your vegetables though, much too strong, you see. Now, we are going to survey and lay out the camp and I am not going to accept your help to dig the walls. Absolutely not. We do not wish to be a bother. Just have your people build a bathhouse for six thousand dirty soldiers, and latrines for them, and that will be more than enough hospitality. Make sure that you lay on water to the camp so that they do not inconvenience your household. You have at least three weeks before they arrive."

Narcissus spread his palms and smiled with friendliness at the stunned Senator.

"Was there anything else, Centurion?"

"No," I said, slowly. "I think you have said it all."

He sprang to his feet and headed past me out of the door. I followed with the Senator stumbling along behind.

"Centurion?" the Senator squeaked in disbelief. "They've made you a centurion?"

I ignored him. We reached the entrance. Horses and people outside looked at us with interest.

"Centurion?" he roared, having at last managed to take a breath. "You are not a proper centurion's backside. Why—why, you haven't even got a centurion's stick."

"Now, that is true," I said coming to a halt. I tore off a largish branch from one of his ornamental vine trees, laid it on the plinth of a nearby statue and chopped off both ends with my sword. I held up the slightly crooked length of green wood admiringly.

"That's better. Now I've got one. Thanks very much."

I put my vinestick through my girdle and got onto my horse.

CHAPTER 53

▼

BRITAIN

The coming of the warmer weather to the high British moor was a real comfort to Scota. The piled stone walls of her tiny dwelling now let in fewer drafts. She made it part of her daily routine to mould mud from the bed of the little upland stream to plug the gaps as she located them. The wind now hardly penetrated the walls at all, although she could not do much about the low, narrow doorway. She still blocked it with a thornbush at night but the wind still found its way into the shelter of the fold in the ground where the hut had been made, seeped in through the doorway and stirred the ends of the bracken bed on which she slept. Now, though, the stirring of the air, even at night, was not cold.

Over the days of solitary exile, she had narrowed her life's objectives to just two. She was going to survive and she was going to escape. Although she rarely saw another human figure, she was, nevertheless, conscious that semi-wild shepherds, with their flocks and savage dogs, haunted the hills. They would have had their instructions from the servants of the Queen of the Brigantes, instructions backed up by the prospect of severe penalties should they fail to report any unusual movement on Scota's part. Surprisingly, none of them had even come near her little campsite, far less made any attempt to molest her. She suspected that the instructions from the young and jealous Queen Cartimandua covered that as well.

From the first night, she had kept stones beside her at night for use as weapons. These she had now supplemented with a short, thick stick which she had slowly sharpened to a point against a boulder and had hardened in her outside fireplace. This stabbing implement she had hidden in the turf roof of the hut along with the stick for cleaning her teeth, her improvised comb and the stick for stirring and eating her porridge.

As part of her self-protection plan, she carefully hid small piles of rocks at a short distances outside her campsite in every direction If she were surprised and had to run away, she could do so in any direction and still collect some weapons in flight. In due course, she would supplement each of these weapon reserves with sharpened sticks as she found time to make them.

She had made a simple sundial with a vertical stick and stones implanted in the ground and, from its indications, confirmed the direction of her intended escape. Whatever the weather, if she left the hut, she always took her cloak, her shoes, her iron cooking pot and her little reserve of food. Those she could not make or replace. She actually wore the shoes as little as possible, saving the soles for the long flight ahead.

The lazy oaf she knew as Queen Cartimandua's current charioteer delivered her ration. He was always alone and on foot. If he had had a vehicle or a horse, he left the transport far away. Attuned now to her surroundings, she invariably heard him coming long before his arrival, and made sure she was within sight but far out of reach when he reached her dwelling. He usually now just threw down her next ration of meal, poked around inside her campsite, urinated on the wall of her home and then wandered off without trying to catch her. He had tried that only once and he would have a permanent scar on his forehead to remind him of it.

She tried every day to save a little of the ground wheat. The gathering of a reserve of food was excruciatingly slow. She had hoped to catch fish or trap small animals to replace her ration but this was proving very difficult. She had become used to the strong taste of the water that had originally so upset her stomach, but it must also actively repel any fish from her stream. She never saw any.

Her knowledge of trap-building was limited but, while quartering the ground outside her campsite looking for edible greens and mushrooms, she also looked out for the tracks of hares and smaller mammals. She stripped flexible bark from the tough undergrowth and made nooses that she anchored over the tiny game trails she found. In an attempt at something more sophisticated, she scraped a pit and planted the bottom of it with pointed sticks before covering the top with bracken. It would definitely incapacitate any small animal falling through the bracken. No small animal had, so far, obliged.

She had seen plenty of birds about and no nearby trees in which they could nest or roost. They must nest on the ground. It was probably already too late in the year for bird's eggs anyway, and she doubted that, determined though she was, she would have the resolution to eat any hatchlings she found in a ground nest. Adult birds were, of course a different matter, assuming she could find and catch any. Unfortunately, she did not appear to have that nest-finding instinct inherent in the grubby small boys she had grown up with in the kingdom of the Atrebates, so far to the south.

Despite her lack of success as a hunter, and her limited success as a gatherer, her little reserve of food gradually grew as she, herself, became thinner and harder. It was only the start of summer. There was time.

She awoke with a slight start and gripped her pointed stick beside her under the cloak. The night was still, a corner of latticed moonlight shone through the thornbush in her doorway. It might have been the yelp of a fox. She sometimes found their small pawmarks around the stones of the cooking place. Unlucky foxes. Never was anything to eat left unguarded in this place. She raised her head, trying not to rustle the bracken mattress, and turned slowly towards the doorway. The comfortable cloak impeded her, trapped under the slight weight of her hips. The noise it made as the upper folds fell away onto the bracken caused her heart-beat to accelerate. There was no sound from outside. Her legs were still entangled in the cloak, she could not get them under her without making more noise in the narrow confines of her hut. The roof was too low to sit up properly anyway. She faced the doorway, her left hand braced on the floor and her weapon in her right hand. The thumping of her heart slowed down.

It was only momentary. The left arm was bearing most of the weight of her upper body and was starting to silently protest with a feeling like heated wires running from the palm of her hand to her armpit. Gently she subsided onto her right elbow, still aiming the pointed stick at the narrow doorway. Then she heard faint, but laboured breathing outside.

Her first thought was—a sheepdog. Some of them, she knew, ran wild and became killers and not protectors of the flocks. Her second thought was much worse. It could be a shepherd. She had never seen a shepherd near her hut and had never found any human tracks nearby, other than her own and those of the despicable charioteer. Any stranger approaching her campsite for the first time, even in daylight, would have difficulty in identifying her lair until right on top of it. It would be so much more difficult at night, even with a moon. Whoever was out there might know her approximate location but would not be able to see the outline of her tiny, huddled hut against any skyline.

The longer she stayed still and listened, the wider her range of awareness spread, even from inside the rocks and turf of her hut. A stone grated faintly amongst the gravel. It had not been displaced by a kick, no sound of it bouncing or rolling. It had been pressed down into the gravel by a substantial weight. The breathing came a little closer. A human being was outside. The moonlight was blotted out so suddenly that she nearly cried out. Her left arm was trembling with fatigue and numbness started to develop in the little finger of the hand holding her weapon. A few more moments and she was going to be in a palsy of fear and strain. Something tugged at the thornbush blocking the doorway.

Summoning all her resources, she screamed at the top of her voice and thrust the thornbush violently outwards. There was a grunt and the bush was pinned to the ground. She could not pull it back towards her. In the restored moonlight, a human leg and foot, standing on part of the bush, appeared in the doorway. She hurled herself towards the doorway, stabbing out with her weapon. A large hand descended and locked itself around her slim wrist, the first physical human contact she had had for weeks. She could not jerk or slip out of the grasp and the intruder, with much heavy breathing, started to apply considerable traction to her arm and shoulder. She screamed again in anger as much as fear. Her assailant muttered, grunted and swore in a form of Celtic.

Scota anchored her limbs and body inside the doorway and she could no more be pulled out of her refuge without damage, than a hermit crab can be pulled out of its shell. Unfortunately, damage to her or her hut did not appear to be high on her attacker's list of concerns. The stones around her doorway shifted and groaned, dust and bits of turf pattered down on her head from the straining roof. There was no doubt that, if her arm did not come out of its socket, the hut would surely begin to collapse. Screaming made her feel better, so she screamed again. The traction on her arm lessened slightly but the clamp around her wrist did not. The structure around her seemed to settle back into a form of stability.

A cultured voice outside asked, quite politely, "Are you Princess Scota?"

Her own voice sounded rusty to her, either from disuse or from the full-throated screaming she had tried to use as a weapon.

"Who, in the name of Bel, are you? And let go of my arm before I get really annoyed with you."

He assailant laughed. A quite attractive sound.

"Oh, no. I'm a friend, but I don't expect you to believe that. I let go of your arm and you'll retreat into your lair where, I have no doubt, you have an arsenal of nasty weapons. Then you'll refuse to come out until morning. I don't have that sort of time and neither have you."

"I don't have any other weapons," Scota said convincingly, while groping around for her stones. "And I'm not coming out. Let go. Go away."

"Are you going to come out?" His grip on her wrist tightened and her arm felt as if it was being stretched.

"No"

A lot of dust and turf fell on her and a patch of night sky suddenly appeared above her head. It widened suddenly as another slab of turf was torn off the roof. The grip on her arm extended through the doorway did not slacken but her assailant did not appear to be having any difficulty in using his other hand to remove the roof from over her head. More turf and some of the twigs used as rafters disappeared from above her. Showers of litter went down the neck of her tunic. Her little iron cooking pot bounced on her shoulder and fell somewhere into the bracken.

"All right, all right," she exclaimed crossly. "I'll come out."

"In a moment," he said, rapidly enlarging the gaping hole in her roof. "Now, give me your other hand through the roof."

Gritting her teeth in anger she allowed her other wrist to be imprisoned before his initial grip relaxed and she snatched her hand in through the doorway. He would not allow her to stand up until he had again secured that wrist through the roof. Then she stood, waist-deep in her house, with both wrists firmly grasped in the hands of the home wrecker.

"I said," repeated the stranger, calmly, "are you Princess Scota. But I don't think that there is much doubt about that now, is there?"

"Who are you? Let go of me."

"As I said, I am a friend. My name is Phylus. I've been looking everywhere for you. I was going to simply rescue you from the Brigantes, but now it's much more urgent. I now probably have to save your life."

"Do you work for my father? How is he? Where is Cogidumnos?"

"I could quite easily kill you now. You do see that? Right. I am going to let you go. Lift you out of this wreckage and then answer your questions. Behave yourself and I'll tell you."

"I want my cloak and other things."

"Hurry up."

Bending, Scota gathered up her property and then submitted to being swung out of the wrecked roof of her dwelling. She had been tempted to pick up her stones and to brain the man as he lifted her, but decided that the propect of news of the world outside and the promise of the word 'rescue' were sufficient to grant him a reprieve. Temporarily.

"How is my father, King Bericos?" She placed some emphasis on the title. Her present appearance might not do justice to her own title but she had no compunction about emphasising her important connections.

"As far as I am aware, he is in good health. Be careful with that name. As far as most of the people in Britain are concerned, he is a traitor. Also, understand this. I do not work for your father. He and I ultimately work for the same enterprise. I believe that your death would not be in the best interest of that enterprise."

"Death? Celts do not execute women." Scota wanted to sound less intelligent than she was.

"Not formally, no. Ask yourself this. How difficult would it be to ensure that you ate something which disagreed with you?"

No reply was necessary to this.

"All right," she acknowledged. "I could have been killed in the fight to capture me. I could have been dropped overboard on the crossing of the Ocean, with no questions asked, and I certainly could have been killed with little more political trouble in the so-called Court of Queen Cartimandua. What has changed? Why am I now likely to be killed?"

Phylus gestured for her to follow and limped past the fireplace and down the bed of her little stream.

"I don't know if the decision to kill you has, so far, been taken," he said. "The matter was being hotly debated with Cartimandua as I left. The queen's husband does not like Romans at all, and British royalty who lean towards the Romans are automatically his enemies. He wants you dead, immediately and, if possible, painfully."

"Queen Cartimandua does not want to kill me?" Scota was surprised.

"Queen Cartimandua would have had you killed in a heartbeat," was the discouraging reply. "You damaged her favourite charioteer." Phylus laughed. "But that would not be the real reason. She may be vain, but I think she is both intelligent and politically aware for her years. Even if it is contrary to civilized practice, there would be some approval of the sudden death of the daughter of a traitor. She has just not wanted to annoy the Romans nor the British High King. Up to now. Now that the Romans are not coming, and the High King and his cronies are busy celebrating, she may feel she can indulge herself."

"Hurry up Phylus," said Scota, her mind more on immediate matters. "Why are you walking so slowly? And what do you mean the Romans are not coming?"

"I am walking slowly because I put my foot in a hole on the way to your camp and something sharp came through the sole of my shoe. You can have a look at it in daylight. The Romans are not coming because their army has mutinied—again."

Scota stopped abruptly.

"Again," she repeated. "The spineless jellyfish. It's a wonder they can look their families in the faces. Where are we going? I must get back to the Continent."

"Two kilometers south of here, we'll pick up my two mules and my stock. By the beginning of tomorrow, patrols permitting, we should be at the River Trent. We'll cross as it gets dark. Behave yourself if we meet anyone and curb your tongue. You are supposed to be my daughter. I have my reputation to think of."

CHAPTER 54

▼

EUROPE

My leg wound had healed well and I hardly thought about it as I jogged along beside Narcissus' large, ornate carriage. Senator Asiaticus' ex-slave had, at least kept his blade clean. I was getting used to the new helmet-crest declaring I was now a centurion, the most junior in the Army, no doubt. Despite money in the bank, I was still wearing the tunic I had borrowed from Titus in his absence, a second hand, if very fine, chain-mail shirt and my old, legionary-pattern sword, now on my left hip. My vinestick, courtesy of Asiaticus, was new.

Narcissus had drawn the curtains and was either sleeping or thinking. There was plenty to think about. The Invasion Task Force had refused to embark for Britain. More specifically, the twenty-two thousand long-service, professional soldiers of the four legions ordered to embark had flatly refused to do so. Centurions and senior officers had apparently ordered, commanded, threatened, negotiated, pleaded and offered bribes. The men remained unmoved. The legionaries would not embark on the assembled ships. The junior ranks of the auxiliaries and the British Fleet had just stood back to watch the fun. They could not compel the legions to go, and they would certainly refuse to go alone if anyone was foolish enough to issue that order.

Messengers on exhausted horses had reached us in succession on the Rhone. As Narcissus had retired to study the written reports, I had lost no time in cornering the tired riders and interrogating them. In each instance we had compared notes. Every official and most unofficial communications stated that the soldiers resolutely refused to cross the Ocean and go to fight outside the boundaries of the known world. Either the senior officers of the Invasion Task Force actually believed this rubbish or they were trying to deceive us. The centurionate went along with the fiction. Its members knew the real reason but had undermined their own authority by making private arrangements for their own families, something most of the soldiers were unable to do. The soldiers had made known their determination not to go, maintained their solidarity with continuous rounds of meetings and rallies, and awaited their Commander in Chief's next move. They had consolidated Emperor Claudius in office despite his lamentable lack of military experience. Let him come and give the army the order himself, then they would see what to do. Maybe it was already time for a new Emperor.

Narcissus had refused to budge until the stream of messengers stopped coming. He had heard me quote the police slogan many times before and while he might have been prepared to run to limit accidental damage, he was too wise to run to a fight before the officers on the spot admitted that they were defeated. Many of those part-time soldiers of high military rank are experts at the art of sliding out from under responsibility while remaining immediately available for any credit that might be going.

When no more messengers arrived for two days, he wrote to the Emperor his first report on the subject and, even before dispatching it to Rome, he ordered us to break camp. We were not going to wait for a reply. We were going down to Gesoriacum.

Our arrival was in the late afternoon and we put on as good a show as we could. My little escort of thirty Thracian cavalrymen seemed to me almost an insult, in terms of numbers, to the status of the Imperial freedman in our care. The large staff of Palace functionaries he had brought with him added appropriate pomp and the colourful party of British refugees, in the most impressive of their jewelry, gave it an added touch of barbarian splendour. We still seemed to me to be a very small cavalcade.

No official party came out to greet us although crowds of unarmed soldiers silently thronged every vantage point and stared almost insolently at the curtained carriage. Narcissus drew back the curtains and stared impassively back, only the whiteness of his face betraying some of the strain he must be feeling. Some of the horses sensed the atmosphere and skittered sideways with eyes rolling and ears back. I gripped my vinestick tighter.

A sharp word of command close at hand startled me. The sudden measured tramp indicated troops stepping off under disciplined control. Two files of legionary soldiers in plate armour and red cloaks wheeled onto the roadway in front of us, leading us towards the Camp housing the Governor-designate of Britain. As the full century turned onto the roadway, I saw the red sashes over their right shoulders, recognised the voice of Titus giving the command, and that of

Legionary Fangs calling out the step. The military police century led freedman Narcissus and his party through the mutineers.

"Aurelius," Narcissus hardly moved his mouth. "Get up front. Don't stop for anything until we reach the most central point of the Camp, whatever it is called."

I trotted past the little vanguard of Thracian cavalry and alongside the solidly marching files of my century. Faces adorned with welcoming smiles did more for my morale than a seat in the Senate. Without breaking pace, Optio Titus gave me an extravagant salute and Fangs his usual gappy grin. I reined my horse to a walk and led the reinforced procession to the south Gate.

Belatedly, a mounted reception party of senior officers was gathering just within the sanctuary of the Gate. Gilt and silver flashed in the late afternoon sun. The walls were red with the tunics of spectators. Swallows flitted overhead. At a walk, I could sit my horse with dignity and the procession could keep closed up without straggling. The foot soldiers behind me shortened step to conform. Aulus Plautius was not with the reception party, in fact none of the legates were. It seemed that tribunes had been sent to escort the emissary from the Emperor. If I knew Narcissus, the Governor-designate was going to regret that.

One of the tribunes kneed his horse forward and raised his hand in greeting or in salute and opened his mouth. I took great care not to catch his eye and shortened the reins so my horse could neither shy right nor left, the pressure of my knees told it to keep moving. The measured tramp behind me did not falter and Fang's voice ground out the step. At the last moment, the tribune's horse shimmied out of the way, leaving him sitting his horse beside the roadway with his mouth still open and his hand half-raised. The files of marching legionaries filled the gateway with the tramp of hobnails. Horses backed and turned as tribunes lost their disdainful expressions and tried to get out of the way. There was a deep rumble of amusement from the spectators and I distinctly heard Titus snarl at some sprig of nobility to get his gilded backside out of the gateway.

The length of Praetorian street stretched in front of me to the Praetorium of the Camp. In front of the headquarters, a small group of figures sat watching my approach. I walked my horse steadily down the straight street, the grind of hobnails as regular as a liburnian's oar-stroke behind me. I did not look back but I could imagine the Tribunes' disorganised attempt to get beside the evenly rolling carriage of Narcissus, emissary of their Commander in Chief. Crowds of mutineers filled the cross-streets between the lines of tents.

The figure in the centre of the Praetorium group suddenly stood up, immediately followed by the others. Plautius had realised his mistake. Servants scurried out and whipped away the chairs leaving their previous occupiers standing. The Governor-designate took a step forward.

I ignored him and turned right, onto the ground surveyed for the legionary commander's accommodation and presently occupied only by the Commandant's quarters. Titus and Fangs turned their files right and left and marched steadily around the perimeter of the ground, dropping off legionaries every few paces until the area was surrounded by stationary military policeman. At their Optio's word of command, they faced outwards and stood still. I turned and faced the street and watched the horsemen walk their horses into the square followed by a visibly amused crowd of British looking back at the disconcerted group at the Praetorium. I expected the Palace servants and all the transport to turn in next. Instead, it was Narcissus' carriage with the curtains drawn again. He had decided not to stop to listen to Plautius. When it stopped and the remaining transport rolled onto the ground, there was a pause. It seemed to be up to me.

"Optio," I shouted in the most impressive voice I could muster. Out of the corner of my eye, I could see the pale faces of the senior officer craned towards us.

"Yes, sir!" he roared in return. The first time Titus had ever called me 'sir'. It might easily be the last.

"No one enters this perimeter without my personal permission." I pointed with my vinestick at the Commandant's tent, savouring the moment. "And have that obstruction removed." To the Palace servants. "Make camp."

When everyone except the sentries was satisfactorily scurrying about, I scanned the surroundings under my helmet brim. Crowds of mutineers drifted from their lines and stood watching what we were doing. There was indecision at the Praetorium, a state that had probably become permanent since the early days of the mutiny. Aulus Plautius had chosen not to greet Narcissus personally at the Gate. He could not bring himself to offer that courtesy to a freedman. It simply proved that the man was an idiot. Narcissus was the only chance he had of keeping his career. Now, he had put himself in an impossible position. To walk after Narcissus he must face the danger of being turned away by the military police. Even if he were allowed to the curtained windows of the stationary carriage, he might still be turned away. That would emphatically be the end of his career and, possibly, his life. Even the mutineers sensed this and looked with interest from the Praetorium to the emissary's carriage and back again. If nothing else, it was dawning on them that Narcissus had been empowered by their Commander in Chief to a degree to at least equal the authority of the Governor-designate.

When the tents were up and the furniture established, everyone was looking at me. The Celt in me certainly enjoyed the drama. I rode slowly over to the carriage keeping my face as impassive as possible. One curtain flicked open.

"What now?" I whispered to Narcissus.

"I was going to ask you the same question," he muttered with the barest hint of the old smile.

"The mutineers are a bit impressed. Plautius cannot move. How about I ride over to him and tell him to convene a proper conference which you will chair? Senior officers only. Then follow it up with a meeting with the centurions?"

"No meeting with the centurions. They have let the men get out of control. I will impress them more with not meeting with them. If necessary, I'll go over their heads, speak to the soldiers direct."

I was still struggling with this idea when Narcissus nodded inside the shadow of the carriage.

"Yes, give little Plautius the message about the senior officers' meeting. Do not say it is a conference. It is for me to receive their reports. Make that clear. And tell them I will be ready to hear from them mid-morning tomorrow. Not before."

I saluted him and meant it. Then I turned and rode slowly out past the stationary military police, turned right onto the cross street and walked my horse towards the Praetorium.

The crowds of mutineers were now quite dense and remarkably silent. I did not dignify them with a glance but I knew these were not exuberant young recruits but, for the most part, responsible, courageous adults at or near middle-age. Other than a few slight surges of movement due to congestion, they stood still and watched, trying to evaluate the threat or benefit to themselves and to their families that I represented.

The senior officers were still standing in a close group in front of the headquarters. I recognised Aulus Plautius, of course, and Vespasian was there, looking more like a healthy gentleman-farmer than ever. There was also a brown-faced officer I took for Hosideus Geta, the hero of Mauretania. They were all looking just a little bit anxious. They had failed to prevent or to control a mutiny in a very critical Imperial project. Worse, they had failed, so far, to lay the blame on anyone else. Worst of all, they had tried to recover some of their stature in front of their mutinous subordinates by treating the Imperial emissary as if he were just an ordinary freedman. I wondered if we had any chance of successfully invading Britain.

I saluted them with a sour taste in my mouth and delivered my message good and loud so that the mutineers could hear it too. I then turned my horse and walked it back to the emissary's encampment. No one spoke to me but, when I glanced across the spectators, one or two of the mutineers nodded.

CHAPTER 55

▼

EUROPE

His servants had spirited Narcissus from his carriage to his newly-erected tent.
The decurion and Optio Titus were waiting for instructions. I handed the reins
to a nearby trooper and walked past them into the huge tent. Narcissus was sitting in the gloom. Titus looked in the doorway and disappeared, shouting for the
staff to tighten the tent ropes properly and to find lamps. I told Narcissus what
had happened.

"Impressions?" he asked.

"The senior officers will either be very repentant tomorrow or even more arrogant. It was difficult to assess the mutineers with such a big crowd but I think
they are hopeful you can resolve this."

"I really hope those military asses are arrogant tomorrow. Tonight, I do not
want to see any soldier above the rank of legionary. Let the senior officers stew a
bit. I will definitely not see any centurion. If Senator Sentius Saturninus arrives. I
will see him."

"You need unofficial information from the rank and file." He nodded. "Some
of the more fervent mutineers might prevent the others from approaching you. I
suggest that I see what the military police and the cavalry can glean."

"There is, of course, a danger that they will decide to stay with the mutineers."

"I think not. The legionaries are more or less committed by their visible protection of you. The cavalry may defect but they are only auxiliaries and there will
not be the same pressure on them from the mutineers."

The entire tent shuddered and a tent pole straightened as the guy ropes were
tautened. The side-walls were raised and the flaps over the doorways were tied
back. Mellow afternoon light flooded the interior.

"That's better," said Narcissus, with a smile. "Yes, do it. Have supper with me if you have the time."

I went out to where Titus and the cavalry decurion watched the servants unloading the wagons. I waved Fangs over. Amidst the bustling staff and the immobile soldiers, and more distantly surrounded by thousands of spectators, we were, nevertheless, fairly private. I peered at the Thracian horseman, decided to take a chance.

"Narcissus sends me to thank you and your men for escorting him here. He will convey his appreciation to your Prefect. You may leave us now."

Titus and Fangs both stiffened. The decurion glanced sharply at me from deep-set eyes. He looked down and scraped his boot on the ground. Then he growled.

"We're staying."

"I said, you can go."

"I heard you. Did you hear me?"

He no longer appeared to be the deferential provincial horseman I had become used to. I decided to stop while I was ahead.

"Oh, very well. Set up your horseline here. Have your men take them to water after I leave. Let them report to you what they see and hear out there."

He nodded, grinned shyly at the others and marched away.

"Leave?" queried Titus. "After all the trouble we had in getting you in here?"

"How did you arrange that, by the way?"

"Commandant told us when you were due to arrive," put in Fangs. "He…" he nodded at Titus.

"We," said Titus.

"…did the rest." Fangs completed.

"Thanks," I said.

With the senior officers in a state of nervous inaction and the authority of the centurions spent, we discussed the possible centres of authority in the mutinous legions. Fangs had the answer.

"The aquilfers," he said. "They are the custodians of the spirit of the legions. Each one is the most respected man in his legion. Just now, the legionaries feel that they have been so casually treated that the spirits of the legions must be offended on their behalf. They are trying to make out that it is sacrilege to take the spirits out of the known world against their will. They want us to believe that it is not the legionaries refusing to cross the Ocean, you see, they are being denied permission to go."

"What rubbish," said the peasant from Etruria.

"Rubbish it may be," Fangs was quite annoyed with Titus, "but these men have followed the eagles into battles that would have turned your hair white, and won. They believe in loyalty to the unit and they believe that loyalty is a two-way thing. Why should the spirit of their legion not support them when they are in trouble?"

"All right," I had to intervene. "How do we get the aquilfers to a meeting?"

"You don't understand, Centurion," Fangs was at his most formal when explaining something that every recruit to a legion is taught in basic. "Aquilfers do not only have a rank in the legions, they are the spiritual core of the legions. They don't get called to meetings. People consult with them."

"Mutineers probably wouldn't let them come anyway," said Titus unfeelingly.

"Can you take me to them?" I asked Fangs.

"Now?"

"Well, I'm going to have a bath first."

The spectators had thinned out considerably by the time I walked out in my tunic with my towel slung over my shoulder and the bottle of oil and scrapers dangling from my hand. A lot of the mutineers were heading for the baths and smoke was rising from the furnace. Cooking fires also contributed to the atmosphere of a quite pleasant summer's evening. No one interfered with me nor took any intrusive notice. It was apparent that business was over, at least for today.

I deliberately walked past the Fleet's accommodation on my way to the gate nearest the washing point on the river. I had no intention of getting myself trapped in the bath-house if any tempers were ignited by the temperature. I had not gone far before Philip was walking beside me, obviously also on his way to wash.

"My father," he muttered without so much as a greeting, "needs to see Narcissus, urgently."

"He will want to see him. Can you get Pytheas to his tent? Narcissus cannot go out tonight."

"I'll arrange it. In case there is a hitch, there is something for you in my bottle."

While washing, we unobtrusively exchanged oil bottles. The legionaries took no particular notice of us. Several barbers were at work under the trees and I got a very acceptable shave. Unlike most of his kind, he hardly said a word, just thanked me for my business and palmed his fee as if I were any other legionary.

"Good luck," he said as I left.

My quarters comprised a single small tent. In it, my camp bed had already been installed. My polished helmet and fine mail shirt hung from an improvised clothes tree. Someone had cleaned my shoes and laid out clean clothes on my bed. With a small twinge of embarrassment, I recognised the tunic as being my own. The one I was wearing still belonged to Titus.

Inside Philip's clean oil-bottle was a short list of days and dates. Narcissus realised what it was immediately.

"A schedule of suitable sailing dates for the Fleet. Thank god for friends who understand the Ocean."

"It is from Philip, or maybe Captain Seleucus."

"I owe so many people so much," even in the lamplight, the tremor in his hands was noticeable.

"What they do," I said, "they do willingly."

"That's what I mean. Now, have something to eat while we wait for Pytheas."

After Pytheas had left, Fangs and I went to see the aquilfer of Legion II Augusta. He was seated in his tent next to the shrine housing the eagle and lesser standards of the Legion. He was a well-made man in his early forties, with black hair cut in a fringe and brightly oiled. He was unarmed and dressed, like us, in a simple red tunic. Fangs told him who we were, although I think that this formality was unnecessary. Two chairs had already been placed facing his.

"What can I do for you?" His voice was high and light. The white scars on his right forearm confirmed that he had served his apprenticeship in the front rank of the battle line.

"Tomorrow," I began. "The emissary of the Commander in Chief will hear from the senior officers of the Invasion Task Force why they think that the soldiers have refused the order to embark. They will tell him that the men are frightened to cross the Ocean. Is this true?"

"'Frightened?'" He drew the word out slowly. "No, not frightened of the Ocean."

"Some of the more intelligent may say that the spirit of the legion prohibits the soldiers from going outside the known world."

A grim smile showed on the aquilfer's face. "If that were to be the opinion of the more intelligent of the senior officers, then those senior officers do not know their history. Legions have always led the way out of the known world. It expands as they advance."

"So the spirit of the legion does not prohibit the crossing of the Ocean?"

"How many legions went to Britain with Caesar?"

"But they withdrew, and they were led by Caesar. Are those the factors."

He did not answer directly.

"Caesar's successor, Emperor the divine Augustus, recorded that the boundaries of the Empire should not be extended beyond those he handed down. His successors, by and large, have followed that advice. Until now. That could be a factor."

"Yet, it was only advice. Surely, if every Emperor were to be bound in every detail to the pronouncements of his predecessors, there would be no expansion, certainly no Emperors and, other than a few static border guards, no need for the Army either."

The aquilfer sat silent with pursed lips. He stirred.

"The spirit of the Legion is made up of the living members and the shades of those members who have died. It serves and is supported by the State. Individual members are served and supported by their families. So the families are, in a sense, part of the Legion's spirit."

"And so you believe that the State has a duty to support the families in some way?"

"It would only be just."

"Even though the State does not recognise that soldiers do have families?"

"It would, nevertheless, only be just."

"Say that some provision could be made for the families, short of recognition. Say some private benefactor was to provide free, or nearly free, passage across the Ocean. After the legions become established in Britain. For families of those about to retire."

A shadow of a frown appeared on his face, so I amended hastily.

"Or, for all families of legionaries whose marriages can be authenticated."

"If such a benefactor were to be found and if he were to make such a provision for all such marriages," the aquilfer smiled, "the spirits of the legions would be satisfied."

I caught his use of the plural but I needed to clarify one other aspect.

"The certification of the marriages, bearing in mind that the State still does not recognise them?"

"The aquilfers will make enquiries and certify those eligible."

"I need to see the other aquilfers, tonight."

"No, you do not." He smiled broadly for the first time. "I told you. We were expecting you."

I marched back, shoulder-to-shoulder with a middle-aged legionary with no front teeth. I reported to a strong, kindly little man with very little hair. Then I slept in my camp bed like a fallen log.

CHAPTER 56

▼

EUROPE

There was really no neutral ground for the meeting Narcissus had called with the Governor-designate and the four legionary commanders. They had not been happy about coming to him but he had made it very clear that he had no intention of going to them. I made sure I was outside his tent when the five of them marched up in their most impressive uniforms, armour and decorations.

Aulus Plautius, I thought, might have had some difficulty in convincing them that there was no future in treating their Commander in Chief's emissary with disdain. Certainly, his own regular features were white with strain. Hosideus Geta, of Mauretanian fame, stared hard at me and grinned with clenched teeth and upper lip lifted. I disliked him on sight. Vespasian nodded as he went into the tent. The other two legates did not even look at me. They were expecting a difficult meeting and, by the look of them when they came out, they had been right. Without looking right or left, they marched away to the headquarters area. The mutineers watched and did not jeer.

Narcissus was lying on a couch with his hands clasped on his stomach. He looked totally relaxed. He opened one eye.

"General meeting with the mutineers. Field of Mars, wherever that is. This afternoon before the main meal."

He closed the eye.

The Field of Mars, so-called after a vast drill and parade area outside Rome, had been cleared and flattened by the soldiers of the legions and the auxiliaries. On it, the senior officers had practiced manoeuvring large units of troops with different specialities. There had not been time, or need, for any formal parades. A high orator's platform, the tribunal, from which the commander could address the assembled Invasion Task Force, had been constructed at one end. Twenty two thousand mutinous legionaries could be easily accommodated on the Field of Mars and, if they packed closely around the tribunal, quite a lot of them would be able to hear what was being said to them.

In an easy and casual manner, Titus and Fangs, followed by the cavalry decurion and, later, Philip, drifted up and we had an informal meeting, shifting to stay out of range of alert ears. I made them make their reports first. On behalf of observers under their control, they reported a wide perspective of the mutineers from different stand-points. The most valuable was that of Fangs, long-term friend and colleague of many of the legionaries.

"Rumour is current that passages will be found for the families. The aquilfers are confirming it as quickly as they are being asked. It is not enough."

"What?" I was severely jolted. "What else do they want?"

"I've been in a mutiny before," said Fangs, "on the Rhine. And I have heard of others. It starts with a legitimate complaint and everyone gets behind it. It is defensible and respectable. Then individual grievances are brought up, legitimate or not. They are tacked onto the original complaint and use it as a vehicle, stealing some respectability."

"I understand, but what do they want."

"Some say they want all marriages to be recognised, some say they want some sort of cash bonus to help the families settle in Britain."

"They are getting free passages." I pointed out.

"In addition to free passages." Fangs' jaw set stubbornly.

"There is no such thing as a free passage, anyway," said Philip. "My father is arranging the passages with the aquilfers but someone is going to have to pay."

"What they are looking for," said Titus, glaring at Fangs as if it was his fault, "is a cash bribe."

"Some of them," agreed Fangs.

"Philip is right," I intervened. "The passages may be justifiable and free to the mutineers but someone will have to pay for them. There will be nothing over for bribes which are, anyway, not justifiable."

"Why not?" said Fangs.

"Because the mutineers receive the pay they are contracted for, and they have only recently received a bonus on top of it. From the Emperor on his accession."

"Anyway," the quiet decurion joined the discussion for the first time. "If there is to be any further mollycoddling of the legions, the auxiliaries will want a part of it."

"And the Fleet," said Philip.

"All right, then," said Fangs, by no means convinced. "The Governor-designate better be as persuasive when he speaks to the men."

"Persuasive?" Titus said dubiously. "He is so pale he is almost transparent. He couldn't persuade me that my name is Titus."

"He's had his chance," I said, without thinking. "Narcissus will speak to them this afternoon, from the tribunal."

"What!" Fangs was genuinely shocked. "But he's a freedman. They won't allow him anywhere near the commander's tribunal, never mind allow him to address them from it. It's not right. It's—it's sacrilegious. They are free citizen-soldiers not a bunch of…"

"Not a bunch of auxiliaries?" queried the decurion mildly.

"That's not what I mean. Only commanders speak from the tribunal. The spirits of the legions would be offended." Fangs concluded as if his final declaration settled the matter.

"Ah." Titus was nodding thoughtfully. "The spirits of the legions would, however, be happy at the soliciting of bribes. Is that it?"

"Narcissus may be a freedman," I said, mainly to the furious legionary, "but he is the personal emissary of the Commander in Chief of all the legions. He will speak to the mutineers and from the tribunal, too."

I was almost relieved when Fangs turned on his heel and stamped off. With knowing looks, the Thracian horseman and the Greek sailor drifted away leaving me to discuss security arrangements with my Optio.

The future of the Emperor and the Army hinged on the impact a small foreign freedman made on the mutinous citizen-soldiers of the Empire. Behind the scenes agreements might have addressed what Fangs had called the respectable and defensible concerns of the soldiers. What about the opportunistic demands of the vocal few? Could they drag the mutineers into endorsing ever more outrageous demands until the mutiny spiraled out of anyone's control? Or could the mature character and ingrained self-discipline of most of the long-service soldiers and family men be relied on to turn against the few greedy agitators? What would initiate that backlash? Perhaps, I could.

Rivers of red flowed out of the four legionary Camps and formed a huge, and growing, pool on the Field of Mars. I was dressed correctly, as a centurion of Legion II Augusta in full uniform and armour. My handpicked military policemen were dressed as were the mutineers, in the red tunics of legionaries but without arms or armour, and I could not see them, or Titus, amongst the crowd. When I had told them what I wanted them to do, their eyes had grown very large and the colour drained from their faces, but they had not flinched. Now it depended on their placement among the great undulating sea of red, on their courage and resolution. I could not see even one of them.

I had noticed before with this particular class and age of legionaries that there was surprisingly little noise generated by quite large crowds of them. There was the continuous rumble of quiet conversation and, even, laughter, but there was no jeering, name-calling or raised voices. This was a particularly formidable body of men. Interestingly, here and there among the shifting mass, like armoured islands in the sea of cloth, stood little knots of soldiers in full parade-order. As far as I could make out, they all wore the distinctive transverse crests on their helmets. The centurions had been disobeyed by the soldiers, and they perhaps sympathised with them up to a point, but they were not prepared to give up their hard-won status to melt entirely into the crowd of mutineers.

Movement from the Camps slowed to a trickle and ceased altogether. Even the rumble of quiet conversations on the Field of Mars died out. Birds could be heard overhead. The senior officers, resplendent in silver and gold, walked almost defiantly to stand around the tribunal. They scanned the multitude impassively. They were all from the highest levels of Roman society, most of them from old and famous families, and they did not show any fear of death. They did fear disgrace, not because suicide was considered the honourable response to disgrace, but because the stain of disgrace would not be entirely wiped away even by self-administered death. They were not career soldiers but, as military service is an essential component of Roman public life, they were trying to be the best soldiers they could be. To the mutineers, the senior officers were often inexperienced and always part-time soldiers. They accepted the Governor, the legates and, even, the tribunes because they were the representatives of the population, the Senate and, above all, the Emperor, not because they were individually expert soldiers. A legate did not have to be as good a soldier as his camp commandant. His military expertise was only part of the reason he held his command.

It was ironic that the noble families of the senior officers would be as concerned about the outcome of this day as would be the humblest unofficial family of an absent legionary in any shack in one of the huge encampments on the Rhine or the Danube.

It was hard to read the mood of the crowd. There was tension and anxiety, certainly, and, I thought, determination, in the set of the pale faces turned towards the tribunal. Eveyone knew what he was there for—it was about provision for his family. Everyone knew that that was the one subject which was not going to be officially debated. Had the unofficial efforts of so many quite junior people been enough to satisfy the mutineers? Had the aquilfers' prestige convinced where the centurions' had not? If not, the mutineers would simply maintain the fiction that the spirits of the legions would not permit permanent absence from the known world. They would refuse to embark. Their officers would be disgraced. The Emperor's authority would be publicly repudiated.

There was now barely any movement, and no noise. Without a fanfare and without an announcement, a little man walked with quick steps to the rear of the tribunal. A hissing sound swept over the crowd like a wind over wheat.

"Narcissus."

With care, but without a pause, he climbed the steps to the platform of the tribunal while the air seemed to me to vibrate with almost silent outrage. One of the mutineers close to me made a noise like a suppressed moan through clenched teeth. The figure gained the platform of the tribunal and faced the enormous, slightly shifting crowd. He was dressed, as was his right, in the plain, unbleached toga of a free man and a citizen. His head was bare. He was quite small.

Narcissus, I thought, forgive me. I took a very deep breath and howled over the heads of the silent crowd.

"Hey! Hey, hey! It's Saturnalia!"

Faces jerked towards me in fright and shock.

"Saturnalia!" yelled Titus' voice to my far left in the crowd. "It's Saturnalia!"

There was a whoop to my right, closer, as one of the braver military policemen shouted.

"He's dressed in his master's clothes. It must be Saturnalia."

Other voices rose from various parts of the crowd, accompanied in one case by uncontrolled nervous laughter.

"The slave is wearing his master's clothes."

"Saturnalia."

"It's Saturnalia.

The crowd heaved and eddied. I was surrounded by white faces and staring eyes. Over their heads I could see the little figure, frozen on the platform.

"Saturnalia!" I shouted again. "The slave is wearing his master's clothes. The little slave…"

I was jostled and pushed. Mouths were pursed, teeth were shown in something like a snarl. A burly, grizzled Senior Centurion ploughed his way towards me. Eyes glared under frowning brows.

"Saturnalia! It's Saturnalia."

The heavy-faced Centurion shoved his way through to me. I could see a patch of grey stubble on his chin.

"Shut your face!" he said inelegantly.

"He's rude," snarled a mutineer about me. "Chuck him out, Centurion."

"Yes, no manners, at all," added another. "Out. Go on. Get Out."

"Throw him out, Centurion."

"You!" said the Senior Centurion in my face, and getting a good grip on my sleeve, "you are insulting the Emperor's messenger."

"Saturnalia!" I managed one more time.

Other crested helmets were converging on me, mutineers urging the wearers on.

"Throw him out!"

"Get him, Centurion. Do you want a hand?"

"Insulted the Emperor."

"Heard him myself."

"Here, you. Out."

My feet were no longer on the ground and I was being swept over the crowd like a raft in a river. Fortunately they were packed too closely together to do much damage and I managed to prevent myself from sliding underfoot. I was ejected, breathless and disheveled at the crowd's edge and left to pick myself up behind a wall of red backs. I hoped the rest of my volunteers had got off as lightly. Even standing on tip-toe, I could not see Narcissus and I started to trot breathlessly towards the wall of the nearest Camp. With a run and a frantic scramble I got up the embankment and held onto the palisade fence at the top.

Narcissus was all right. He was still on the tribunal and appeared to be speaking to the crowd. I was too far away to hear what was being said but there was no crowd noise and the faces were all turned towards him. Several figures limped and stumbled away from the fringes of the crowd. I counted them and breathed a sigh of relief. The volunteers had, at least, survived. By some wild waving with one arm, I attracted their attention and they gathered in the wide ditch below me. Titus sat on the edge of the ditch, his nose bleeding, and grinned with red teeth.

"Have you got any more light duties for us, Centurion?"

It got a faint, breathy, laugh from the volunteers. One of them hugged his ribs and coughed.

"Well done," I said.

There was a sudden quiet rumble of crowd noise and then silence again. From my perch I could see small, glittery things floating over the heads of the front of the crowd. They drifted towards the tribunal and then hovered around it. There was a long, low roar from the crowd. The aquilfers had brought the legionary eagles from their shrines to the tribunal. The sacred metal birds surrounded Narcissus. They all looked towards Britain. The mutiny could be over.

The crowd started to grow larger and thinner. It reminded me of the end of the Games in the City, except here the crowd was all dressed alike. For a member of the Urban Cohorts outside the arena, this would be a typically dangerous moment with the supporters of the winners walking away, the supporters of the losers nearby. Often the losers would only be looking for a way to vent their frustrations. In this case, they should be focused on attacking the British. The British!

"Titus!" The alarm in my voice jerked his head upwards. "The British. Get back to the Camp. Guard Bericos. Keep them quiet. Don't let them react to insults."

"Where are you going?" Titus and the rest were on their feet. Even the youngster with damaged ribs.

"Cogidumnos is still in town. Go."

I slid down the embankment and, gripping my sheathed sword in one hand and my helmet in the other, I set off at a rapid trot towards the town. I had lost my vinestick somewhere in the crowd.

The fringes of the dispersing crowd were close but no one seemed intent on pursuing me or hurrying in the direction of the town. After a distance I glanced back again. It seemed that columns of red were moving towards the gateways of the four legionary Camps. I was running more slowly, my mail shirt heavy on my shoulders. By the time I reached the outskirts, I was walking. There was no sign of any out-of-control mutineers heading towards the town. The streets were quiet but a lot of residents were anxiously alert, and my appearance gave rise to a number of questions about the mass meeting of the legionaries. I ignored the questions, apart from making a few comforting noises, and put on my helmet as I walked. Outside Cogidumnos' house, two military policemen were posted. Standing in the doorway, totally in control, stood the relaxed figure of the legionary we all called Fangs.

CHAPTER 57

▼

BRITAIN

The doors and the shutters of the High King's hall were open. Motes of dust hung in the shafts of early morning sunlight streaming in. The air was cool but no fires were needed to warm the vast interior on a summer morning promising another hot day. The servants had finished their noisy, cheerful cleaning, the dogs had been chased outside and only the adult male members of the family were left to nurse their hangovers in peace.

"You know," said Caratacos. "I'm getting too old for this."

The High King was in his early morning mode, sunk in his chair, feet on the newly-cleaned table, glaring out over the folds of his woollen cloak with dull red eyes.

"You are thirty, little brother. Two years younger than me. Now when you get to my age, you will really understand about drinking in moderation."

"Not that you ever do, uncle," croaked Ceri. "For myself," he continued piously, "I drank little, went to bed early and, if it hadn't been for the sparrows stamping about on the roof, I would still have been sound asleep."

"Thank god we can stop celebrating," Caratacos licked his dry lips. "The warriors have gone home, the Romans aren't coming, we can get back to normal."

"The sooner you two go home the better," High King Togodumnos agreed ungraciously. "Providing hospitality for half of Britain is politics. Entertaining members of my family afterwards is likely to be the death of me."

"Is anyone alive in there?" a light, reedy voice sang out from outside.

Ceri shot to his feet, knocking over the bench. Caratacos still looked dazed. A shadow appeared in the sunlit doorway.

"The Romans have been and gone, have they? Left British casualties strewn all around the High King's hall?" the woman's voice, as always, carried the accent very attractively.

"Brigit!" roared Ceri, and winced at the impact of his own voice.

"Brigit Mong Ruadh," said Caratacos more quietly as he scrambled to his feet.

"Great Bel," said High King Togodumnos, wearily putting a hand over his eyes, "it's the Irish."

"And here we are," said Brigit easing herself out of Ceri's enthusiastic embrace, "come to give the British the benefit of our military expertise, and the Romans have not even stirred."

"Not coming," said Caratacos embracing her more carefully.

"Very wise," she said, smiling up at him.

"I heard you were wounded."

"A scratch. All better now."

She turned to the slumped figure at the head of the table and hugged the broad shoulders.

"And you, High King darling. How are you?"

Togodumnos did not answer; he simply placed a hairy kiss on her pale smooth cheek, then licked the ends of his fair moustache and winked lasciviously at her. She laughed at the smiling faces.

"Is there no breakfast at all in this house?"

They knew most of the Irish troopers of her escort. Only one of those who had been with her before had died in battle. The soldiers grinned shyly as they were greeted by the family. Niall, Brigit's adviser, was made particularly welcome and he put up with jokes about his horsemanship with dignified good nature. Fox, his counterpart in the British High King's court, arrived breathlessly and the two Druids each greeted the other with a small bow before their faces relaxed into wide smiles.

Togodumnos took his feet off the table, shouted for food and drink and ignored a theatrical groan from Ceri. He seated Brigit beside him and asked her about her brother, High King Conaire Mor of Ireland.

"He sent me," she said, "to see how the British defeat the Romans so that I can improve our own military techniques. It seems you have defeated them before they could even leave the Continent."

"Their cowardly soldiers mutinied." Ceri's face was flushed. "We raided right into their embarkation port."

Togodumnos was glaring at him.

"The Irish are experts at raiding overseas. Don't encourage them."

"Oh, no, High King," said Brigit, innocently, "we only raid where we are wanted," and she fluttered her eyelashes at him.

The hard-working servants, scurrying in with food and drink, were startled by the laughter.

"Speaking of raiding," said Brigit, after the food had been eaten. "On our way here, four of my heroes were watering our horses when they caught a woman trying to steal a horse. There was a campsite not far away, recently deserted."

One of the Irish troopers went out and returned with a small, dirty figure in tattered tunic and trousers.

"Scota," said Ceri immediately.

"Is that her name?" said Brigit. "And a fine Irish name, too. She pretends she is dumb, perhaps witless, but I can see she is a competent, determined woman. Only a very determined woman would try and steal a horse from the pride of the High King's army."

"Not Irish," said Caratacos. "She is the daughter of a traitor. The so-called King Bericos of the Atrebates. She was captured by Ceri's raiders, living with the Romans."

"She's supposed to be in exile isn't she?" Ceri was puzzled.

"Queen Cartimandua," Togodumnos intervened with weighty authority, "has clearly not had time to notify me of the fugitive's escape. My thanks to the soldiers of your escort."

"Cartimandua is an evil, vindictive witch," Scota spoke for the first time, "and my father, King Bericos, is no traitor but the true ruler of the Atrebates."

"Ah," said Brigit, "it speaks."

"The Atrebates would not agree with you," Caratacos spoke directly to the captive. "When were you last there?"

Scota was silent.

"Who helped you?" asked Niall.

"No one."

"There was at least one other person, a man, in that campsite."

She was silent again.

Togodumnos had, at last, thrown back his cloak in the increasing warmth of the hall.

"We do not execute, nor torture women here," he said. "You are lucky we are not your friends, the Romans. I am inclined, though, to send you back to young

Queen Cartimandua who, I am sure, will be extremely embarrassed and irritated by your escape, especially since she has not had time to notify me of it."

Togodumnos watched her carefully. He thought he saw a slight flicker cross her eyes.

"Who helped you?"

She remained silent.

"Very well. You will have a bath, some food, clean clothes. Then we will talk again about your return to Queen Cartimandua and the realm of the Brigantes."

After Scota had been taken away, High King Togodumnos looked around the table to make sure his guests had had enough to eat and drink and then said to Brigit.

"We have some business to discuss."

The Irish soldiers, without any further hint, stood up politely and made their way from the hall. The Druids, Niall and Fox, remained with the family and Brigit.

"I would like to discuss," began Togodumnos, "the further gift of cavalry horses to my friend, High King Conaire Mor of Ireland."

"My brother, Conaire Mor," said Brigit with a bright smile, "wishes me to discuss with you the resumption of Irish raiding on the British west coast. Outside the areas that acknowledge your authority, of course."

CHAPTER 58

▼

EUROPE

"Centurion," said Hosideus Geta one morning. "I want to see you."

I followed him into his tent and was surprised to find Captain Seleucus already there. The sand table model I had seen earlier occupied most of the floor space of the tent. I recognised the south-eastern peninsular of Britain with the island just off its tip. I recognised the river running down the peninsular and emptying into the channel between the mainland and the island. I remembered standing on the long pebbled bank extending from the south-western corner of the island and forming one side of the entrance to the channel.

I did not interrupt as Geta pointed out all these features to me as if I had never seen them before.

"Now," he said, his brown face appearing even darker against the roof of the tent. "Have you got all that?"

I said that I had absorbed all he had imparted.

"Good," he said. "What is necessary is that the high ground on the mainland at either end of the channel be occupied from the outset. Clear?"

I considered asking him whether he was talking about the invasion or whether he was just passing the time of day, but I suppressed that childish impulse.

"Clear," I said, instead.

"It is necessary that that ground be occupied to give cover to the ships off-loading onto the bank on the island-side of the channel mouth. The Fleet will need advance warning of the approach of the enemy by land from the west or, even, in boats from the Thames estuary. All right?"

"All right," I said.

"Later, ships might be able to anchor in the channel and off-load directly onto the mainland. All depends on enemy reaction. Got it?"

"Got it," I said.

I knew it was foolish to tread the line of insolence with a man who was second in command of the Invasion Task Force and the commander of Legion XX Valeria. I was quite thankful when Captain Seleucus interrupted the dangerous litany.

"You see, Victorinus. If the landing is opposed, it will be necessary to put the legions ashore first. If, on the other hand, no major enemy forces are close to the landing place, then a mainly cavalry force will be needed ashore to find and watch them. The sequence in which the ships are off-loaded will be my responsibility. I am to be the beachmaster and I will need proper information."

"So, the first landings are to be made by special forces to provide you with information."

"And through me, the Governor-designate and the Fleet," the Captain agreed.

I had little doubt as to which element of special forces was destined to undertake the most dangerous duty. I could see Hosideus Geta watching me with that contemptuous smile. His men were said to admire him greatly, I found that hard to understand.

"I have one excellent century of military policemen," I said.

"No," said Geta. "You have one century of fit, young legionaries who have had continuation training in single combat."

"And," I looked him in the eye, "those legionaries have not been involved in the mutiny."

"Your men are not expendable, if that's what you think," said Hosideus Geta. "They are a good example to the older legionaries. They will want to do better. That's why your century goes first. That's why they are going to land from a liburnian at the southern mouth of the channel, climb the cliffs and entrench at the top. They are going to stay there, whatever happens, and they are going to report what they see to the beachmaster, Captain Seleucus."

"I will be on the bank on the other side of the channel with my signalers," the sailor said. "Philip and three other signalers will go with you. They will pass your reports to me. I will signal the Fleet."

"What about the north end of the channel?"

"Your liburnian, 'Mercurius', will go in behind another warship and the Fleet transport 'Justitia'. While you are going ashore from 'Mercurius', the other warship will sink the British guard boat and bottle up any waterborne enemy forces in the river, the Stura? The Stura. 'Justitia' will carry on to the northern exit of the channel and will put its troops ashore on the mainland there. 'Justitia' will stay to prevent any interference coming up from the Thames estuary."

"Which unit will be going ashore from 'Justitia?'"

"Not legionaries," snapped Hosideus Geta. "I cannot spare any more of them. They will be marines drawn from the warships."

Yes, but you can spare us, I thought. And the Fleet's marines. What the second-in-command had said about my century being an example might be true, but what he had also said about our not being expendable was manifestly untrue. Neither my men, nor the marines, had been involved in the mutiny and we were being sent on shore first. As an example, perhaps. As a buffer, certainly. Still, any soldier, in the final analysis, is expendable and the job we would be doing was vital. Whatever happened to us, the Army could claim to have been first ashore because I would be landed before the marines and I was, notionally at least, part of Legion II Augusta. I could almost certainly predict the answer to my last question.

"What are your instructions," I asked the commander of Legion XX Valeria, directly, "if the enemy is present, in force, where I am to land?"

"'Mercurius' will withdraw after landing your force," Geta said, with the smile I was definitely beginning to hate. "You will act on your own initiative as circumstances dictate."

The air seemed a lot fresher outside. Rain was in the air and the wind was getting up. Narcissus was outside his tent, greeting a senator I recognised as Sentius Saturninus. He saw me and waved me over. I saluted them both. The wind tugged at the Senator's toga with its purple stripe. Narcissus took off his wig and tossed it behind him into the tent. Then he smiled widely.

"I just wanted to tell you both. We are receiving word from the Rhine, and from the Danube, that large crowds of women and children are leaving the frontier Provinces and are marching towards us here. It's time we got on with the invasion. The army will be ordered to embark at dusk the day after tomorrow. It will do so. The legions are receiving their instructions now."

Somehow, I did not doubt any part of what he had said. If Narcissus said that the army would embark, that is exactly what it would do. The Senator, very elegantly, offered his congratulations. I stood, nodding and grinning like an idiot.

When I turned to go, Narcissus called me back. He ducked into the tent and emerged with a battered, slightly crooked vinestick and held it out to me.

"Thank you," he said.

I briefed Titus and Fangs and then took as many of the century as possible to a quiet corner of the Field of Mars where I drew a copy of the sand table model I had seen in Hosideus Geta's tent and explained to the young soldiers what we were going to do. Not one of them had been into battle before. Come to that, neither had I. Fangs was the only exception. Our very first battle was probably going to be the biggest and most complex of the new Emperor's reign. We had two days to be ready. I left Titus and Fangs furiously updating the training schedule while the excited youngsters tried to assist. I went to see Pytheas.

The tough old sailor-businessman had somehow managed to get the town council to let some municipal offices to him. Even so, he was working surrounded by a frantically working swarm of contract clerks and merchant seamen. Messengers darted in and out of the offices, some civilian, some, I saw, were legionaries from the offices of the legionary aquilfers. Stacks of marriage certificates were being sorted and filed.

"They are coming." I said after the briefest of greetings.

"I know," he said, taking the wind out of my sails. "The aquilfers are getting reports from their opposite numbers on the Rhine and the Danube. Their offices have been overloaded with requests for marriages to be authenticated. They are just getting on top of it now."

"Who is paying for this?" I realised, after I had blurted it out, that it was quite a rude question. He did not take offence. He drew me out into the corridor which was marginally less busy than his offices.

"My partner in Egypt is a man called Alexander," he said. "He is very clever and very wealthy. He is subsidising the families' passages. Out of his own pocket. He is the Emperor's banker, did you know that?"

He noted my stunned look and his silver beard twitched as he smiled.

"I am telling you this for a reason," he said. "Alexander is a rich man and he can afford it. But he does not continue to get richer by behaving like a charity. He is also a very fortunate man. The Emperor has just granted him several years' monopoly on the silk trade through Egypt. On extremely favourable terms, I understand. I'll get the details when I'm finished here."

"So, the Emperor has granted him this monopoly," I was mentally groping here, "and this Alexander is subsidising the transport for the unrecognised families of the Emperor's soldiers. And these two facts are totally unconnected, right?"

"Right," he said, and smiled.

"All right," I said. "Why are you telling me, then?"

"Philip will be going with the Invasion Task Force," said the old man, "but he, like me, is a sailor. He probably won't get any further inland than the beach. Now, you and I have done business before and you are a soldier, a legionary. You will be where the action is."

Little did he know how true that was likely to be.

"Before I commit too much of Alexander's money," he went on, "and endanger the families, I will want to know that the Task Force is firmly ashore and that the intention is still to stay there. If the British army is decisively beaten, so much the better. There will of course be a consideration in it for you. Will you do it?"

Does an owl hoot?

CHAPTER 59

▼

EUROPE

When he had dismissed Captain Seleucus and the cheeky young centurion, Hosideus Geta walked over to the Governor-designate's quarters. The Legate of Legion II Augusta, Vespasian, was with Aulus Plautius. Also there, was the Senator, Sentius Saturninus. They were poring over yet another sand-table model of southern Britain. This one covered a lot more territory than the landing area alone.

"The High King will undoubtedly try and defeat us on the beaches. But he will know that his ancestor could not do that with Caesar's expeditions so he will have a fall-back plan." Plautius was summarising what they already well knew. "They fought Caesar on the River Thames but this High King can't do that. He cannot afford to give up much ground without losing the Cantii, his strongest support. If he cannot throw us back into the sea, he will fight us on the Medu River."

"It looks like three phases, then," murmured the Senator. "The Ocean crossing and the landing on the mainland and island in south east Britain, followed by an advance to the Medu where, hopefully, we defeat the main British army, and, finally, exploitation from there."

"'Hopefully'?" Vespasian raised his eyebrows.

"Hopefully they don't run away before we can destroy them," clarified the Senator grimly.

Plautius looked up at his second-in-command.

"How did your meeting go?"

"No problems."

"Good. I want to discuss the move up to the Medu and the exploitation beyond but first, a report of Legion II Augusta. Vespasian."

"My aquilfer is inundated with applications to have marriages certified. The men are busy packing heavy equipment."

"Good. How about Legion XX Valeria, Geta?"

"The same. The centurions have regained control."

"Legion IX Hispana, the same," remarked Governor-designate Plautius, "also, Legion XIV Gemina. The mutiny is over. Well done, everyone."

Senator Saturninus looked at the youngish faces of the senior officers.

"Of course we have a lot to be thankful for," he agreed mildly. "Narcissus's contribution was significant, don't you think?"

"The man was a laughing stock," declared Hosideus Geta, dismissively.

"Yes," said the Senator slowly, looking thoughtfully at the second-in-command. "Yes, I suppose he was."

"The advance to the Medu River," Plautius called the meeting to order. "The obvious route is along the native road which runs westwards along the high ground. It is a dry, well-travelled route but it is in good chariot country. I am not going to use it. There is another native trackway which runs parallel to it to the north. The going is not as good but it has the big advantage that it is close to the shoreline of the Thames estuary. The ships of the British Fleet will protect the army's right flank and bring forward bulk supplies from the landing beaches. This will also reduce the numbers of pack animals we have to take with us. I doubt that the Cantii will leave any around for us to requisition. Senator?"

"Fleet activities will be co-ordinated by Captain Seleucus as far as the Medu. Then, I suggest, warships be tasked by the army and supply ships be tasked by myself as rear areas commander. Agreed? Thank you, Governor. The Prefect of the British Fleet will sit with me in Gesoriacum until the army has cleared sufficient ground for us to relocate to Britain. The local defence of the landing point in Britain when the army moves forward?"

"I suggest my Camp Commandant," Vespasian spoke up. "He did some good preparatory work here before the legions arrived."

"Agreed," said Plautius. "What's his name? Right, instruct Anicius Maximus to report to the Senator, please. Now, Senator, what about these British allies of ours?"

"I have two distinct parties, Governor. One, led by Arminios, the High King's brother, is hated by the Cantii. I don't like the man myself, and I don't think he can be trusted in the recruitment of British levies. He may, perhaps, be useful as a replacement for the rest of the High King's family if we decide to execute them. I suggest he will be most useful, initially, as a source of local knowledge so that centres of resistance among the Cantii can be eliminated. I will keep him with me."

"Very well," Plautius agreed, again. "The other party?"

"Led by King Bericos and exclusively from the Atrebates tribe. They should be able to stimulate recruitment from that tribe and provide levies for the rear areas so that your front-line soldiers can be released. They have no particular love for the Cantii. They might even be helpful in rooting out anti-Roman elements there."

"I would see this King," the Governor used the title with an expression of distaste, "I would see him being attached to the military force tasked to clear the south coast of Britain. Now, anything else on the move forward to the River Medu?"

"Order of march, Governor," Vespasian reminded gently.

"Yes. Fleet on the right, in the estuary. Batavians with their river-crossing equipment on the shoreline. All eight cohorts of them. On their left, Legion XIV Gemina with Legion IX Hispana behind it. I plan to be with Legion IX Hispana. On their left, Legion II Augusta with Legion XX Valeria behind it. You, Geta, will remain with Legion XX Valeria. On the far left, on the high ground, the cavalry."

He looked around the intent faces.

"If I am killed, Legate Hosideus Geta will assume command. Questions?"

"Very well," Plautius continued. "After the crossing of the Medu and the destruction of the High King's army, the main objective will be the British capital at Camulodunum. The secondary objective will be yours, Vespasian."

"If I may, Governor?" the Senator asked. "There is a concern amongst Provincial officials on the Continent that armed parties of Britons, might flee to Gaul. There is also a remote possibility that Celts from Gaul might try to cross to Britain to fight against us there. There is also a pressing need for me to find British levies from among the Atrebates so that legionaries are not wasted on the control of conquered territories."

"I understand." Vespasian knew all this.

"Those problems are going to be resolved by Legion II Augusta," resumed Aulus Plautius. "After the crossing of the Medu River, you will strike westwards with your Legion and its auxiliaries to clear the area between the Thames and the south coast. Certain units of the British Fleet will be allocated to you. You are to prevent any unauthorised crossing of the Ocean in either direction, free the Atrebates to contribute to the conquest of Britain and reduce the fortifications of the Durotriges, particularly the one they call Mai Dun."

"I understand," said Vespasian again.

"When will you be able to present your plan to us?" Hosideus Geta considered Vespasian to be a rival.

"It's ready now," said the man who looked like a farmer.

CHAPTER 60

▼

BRITAIN

The fourth time I was to stand in British soil was the morning of the Invasion. Our small squadron comprised three warships and the Fleet transport. Ours was called 'Mercurius' which suggested a fleet-footed messenger of the gods, not a heaving, creaking, wet contraption, labouring over a choppy, grey and silver sea, laden with green-faced soldiers and aggressively cheerful sailors.

Titus, my Optio and long-time friend, astonished me by stubbornly refusing to get seasick. Fangs, on the other hand, displayed no such restraint. Most of the young legionaries followed his example.

Dawn revealed grayish cliffs close at hand on the left with surf sullenly detonating at their base. I found that watching the other ships swaying and dipping did not help my uneasy stomach and I concentrated on what was happening within our own vessel. The eighty legionaries and all their personal equipment were crammed below deck to assist in stabilising matters. The oarsmen had not been used during the night as the wind or tide, or whatever, was said to be in the right direction. As soon as light started to grow, however, the sails were taken down and the mast lowered. With a great deal of noise, the oars were got out and the flute started its monotonous and apparently unending stream of notes.

The men were not allowed on deck, even though the motion was definitely easier with the oars of the upper bank in action. The lower bank of oars was not used at first because of the amount of water coming through around the leather covers and through the ports. I was allowed on deck as the commander of the landing party and I managed to approach the Captain in the stern without actually stumbling over the side.

The sight past his wet shoulders was amazing. Right across the southern horizen, bulky grey shapes of transports, crammed with men and animals, rose and fell under their sails on the lumpy sea. A few leaner shapes, the warships, swooped and wallowed around them.

The Captain, eyes red and haggard cheeks covered in grey stubble, pointed over my shoulder toward the front of the ship. We were, it seemed, nearly there. I climbed forward, over piles of equipment sewn into waterproof coverings and marked with inscribed tin labels and bundles of palisade stakes. I squeezed into the narrow space between the two forward catapults. The artillerymen were in position and straining to look forward and upwards at the opening of the channel ahead.

I could make out Captain Seleucus on the stern of one of the warships as it veered to the east and rounded the tip of the long pebble bank forming one low arm of the mouth of the channel. 'Justitia', looking almost tubby against the narrow warship escorting it, turned into the channel ahead of us. Oars foamed in the water as both ships steadied in the wind-shadow of the low cliff of the mainland to our left. White sea birds flickered along the cliff face. Ragged clouds reflected the light of the rising sun.

Unbelievably, two men and a dog looked down on us from the mainland just as if they had not moved since my last visit. One of the men abruptly disappeared. The other shaded his eyes and patted his dog without otherwise moving. I felt the ship steady under my feet.

"Legion II Augusta," I bellowed. "On deck."

'Justitia' was picking up speed in the calmer water of the channel and I saw the glint of weapons on deck as the marines got ready. They still had several miles to go. We did not. My heavily-burdened soldiers scrambled from below deck, being careful not to injure one another with their javelins or entrenching tools, shields getting in the way. There was almost no room to stand except on top of equipment. The centre of gravity of 'Mercurius' was dramatically raised and the deck seemed to sway. The force of the oar strokes steadied the ship again. Philip had managed to get himself in the wrong position in the landing party so I ordered him off the deck until we had landed.

With a volley of orders, the Captain had the left-hand oars partially retracted and brought the length of the liburnian to a dead stop, broadside-on to the narrow rocky beach. Small waves tended to push the stern away from the shoreline and the helmsmen and the right hand oarsmen struggled to hold the heavily-laden warship in place. Sailors slid down the wet oars with hawsers to secure the ship. The brow was manhandled over the side. My soldiers struggled, slid and swore after me down the wet planking and onto Britain. Philip and his signalers followed.

No sooner had the signalers cleared the end of the brow than the sailors were using it as a chute to send down our bundles of valuable kit. I left a visibly pale Philip to deal with securing the equipment as it thumped unceremoniously onto the beach and I led off towards a steep path up the cliff. I was carrying less than anyone else, rank having its privileges, but even I was out of breath before I was half-way up. Out of the corner of my eye I saw 'Mercurius' turning out into the channel as I breasted the top of the cliff and looked straight into the muzzle of a large, damp dog.

Not being a dog-lover myself, I lashed out at the mastiff with my vinestick. Fortunately for me it easily skipped aside and, before it decided that I would make an acceptable breakfast, a distant whistle from its fast-departing master summoned it away.

I straightened up from my mastiff-fighting crouch, half expecting to find myself facing ranks of chariots lined up wheel-to-wheel and ready to charge. It was almost an anti-climax to find the bare, wind-swept ground totally devoid of any visible life. Still, there was no time to be lost. The shepherds, if that is what they were, had not rushed off to tell their wives the news.

One would have expected that the first of the men onto the cliff top would have been the fittest and most active of the younger men. Sea-sickness must have taken its toll because the first to emerge, admittedly being urged on from below and looking as if a heart attack was imminent, was none other than Fangs. The young soldier who appeared next was somehow managing to carry twice the regulation number of javelins and an additional entrenching tool. The youngsters liked Fangs.

As the middle-aged legionary seemed temporarily incapable of speech, I placed the younger legionaries as they appeared and gave them arcs of responsibility. Some of them sat on their haunches to catch their breath but most stuck their javelins in the ground beside their allocated positions, tightened their chinstraps and confidently drew their swords. It's a wonderful thing, youth. Titus, wrapped in a large coil of rope, brought up the last of the legionaries. I had eighty armed men on top of a cliff, come to capture Britain.

It appeared that Philip, down on the beach, had sustained the first war wound of the invasion. According to Titus, the hobnails of the shuffling legionaries had damaged the planking of the brow, raising a large sharp splinter. Philip had slipped on his way down and had been impaled in the buttock by the said splinter. He was currently receiving emergency surgery on the beach. I left Titus to organise the hoisting and carrying of kit up from the beach and went forward to scout with a recovered Fangs.

We cautiously, and then with more confidence, quartered the ground around our position on the cliff top. There was no sign of any native warriors. No recent wheel marks or hoofprints. No British army. To the north, I thought I could see some wisps of smoke, probably from some settlement on the Stura River. Otherwise, we seemed to be alone.

They had managed to get Philip up from the beach somehow. He and his signalers had moved along the cliff top to where they could see the beachmaster's position on the bank across the channel. They had begun to erect a mast and lay out flags of various colours. Titus had laid out a defensible area around it and set the soldiers to work with entrenching tools. They were embedding palisade stakes, each at an angle pointing outwards, to discourage mounted attackers. The last bundles of rations and tentage were being carried in.

"Ready," said Philip, limping over.

"Right," I said. "Tell your Captain to bring in the cavalry."

CHAPTER 61

▼

BRITAIN

The shepherd was running hard. His feet flattened yellow dandelions and the white daisies nestling in the strong summer grass and he hurdled the smaller bushes, scattering a few stray sheep. His breath rasped in his throat but he was young and fit and was driven on by the shining prospect of celebrity when he got to the chief with the news that the Ocean was full of ships. Beyond that, he did not think. The Romans were coming after all. So much the better. Battle is better than herding sheep.

Ena got the news when she was clearing away the breakfast things. She handed the baby to her mother, took down her sword, kissed her little boy and shouted for her chariot. Rolling over the grass behind her small ponies, she headed east for the cliffs south of the Stura River.

Men, and a few women, were converging on the same point from the farmlands and across the pastures, but only a few of them were mounted and most of them were not even armed. She waved them away, and shouted instructions, but only a few sensible ones turned back to prepare properly. The young boys were the worst, running the fastest and with a selective hearing which tuned out the instructions of their elders. She overtook a puffing village headman and turned him back to gather the armed people. He was very tempted to refuse but a look into her face told him what would happen to his status if he did. Grumbling, he turned around.

Standing as tall as she could, Ena could see that the few runners ahead of her had slowed to a stop and a man on a little horse was hurrying back towards her. He waved his arm, eyes wild with excitement, and told her that Romans were already on top of the cliffs and had erected a flagpole, the people were getting ready to attack. Ena could see that there were, at most, twelve adults present, only half of them armed. She used all her powers of persuasion to get them to stay where they were before she had the time to inspect the enemy. Fortunately, no more would-be heroes were arriving. The headman would be having his hands full.

Driving slowly forward, she first caught sight of several dabs of colour on the edge of the cliff. Her horses' ears were pricked forward and they walked tensely. Metal reflected the early morning sun. She wished she had thought to bring one of the unarmed adults as a horseholder but perhaps it was just as well. She did not have the time to settle the inevitable argument as to who should go with her and who should remain. She stopped, tied the reins to a wheel and climbed a tree, her sword banging against the trunk.

The tree was small and bent but gave her a sufficient increase in elevation. She was about three hundred paces away from the enemy. They were hiding behind a row of sharpened stakes and their red and gold shields were bright against the green grass at the cliff edge. There appeared to be about a hundred of them, unmoving, in a cluster around their flags. Beyond their position, far out to sea, there were ships, masses of them. It was, without any doubt, the Invasion.

Her horses whickered and shifted. A small boy stood below her. She was shocked that she had not heard him arrive. It could just have easily been a Roman soldier with a long spear.

"Where are they?" The boy's mother had washed his face before he had left home and his eyes lit up the freckled countenance. He had a slingshot wound around a small fist. "Where are the snails, then?"

Ena was all the more furious because of the fright he had given her.

"Get, away! Go back to the others, at once."

"No," he said, "they sent me. Some men are coming from the Stura. They are all wet. You are wanted."

Of course she was wanted. She was the chief and she was sitting up a tree waiting to get caught by the enemy. There were things to do. She slid ungracefully down the tree. The small boy had gone.

Her driving had improved marginally under Segonax's tuition, but turning the vehicle while trying to watch the Romans was taxing. The hub of one wheel almost lodged against the trunk of the tree but jerked free in a shower of bark and she sucessfully got the horses lined up for the return trip. A final look over her shoulder and then she set off at walking pace, heart pounding at the near-disgrace.

The little crowd had grown. The headman was back, reporting that the local militia was gathering about a kilometer to the rear and about a hundred had so far reported, properly armed but without food or water. In addition to the six armed adults waiting for her, two ashen-faced men in drying clothing reported that there was a huge ship in the mouth of the Stura River and that they had had to swim for their lives when their boat had been rammed. They wanted to tell her in detail of the fierce fight that they had put up and to convince her that it was not their fault that they had lost her guard boat. She, though, wanted details from them of other shipping movements in the channel. They had seen another, even larger, ship moving past the Stura and heading north up the channel. In fact, they had been rowing out to challenge it, they said, when the warship had pounced on them. The other members of their crew? Undoubtedly all dead. They were the only survivors.

Somehow, Ena doubted the last statement. In her short experience of warfare, soldiers claiming to be the only survivors of a disaster tended to be only the fastest runners. Other "only survivors" were probably forming a queue across the landscape.

Another distraction. A furious mother demanded to know what Ena had done with her son. She wished to make it clear that she was a true patriot and her son a paragon but he had rushed out of the house without finishing his breakfast to go and fight the Romans and she wanted to know what her chief had done with him. In truth, the little boy with the slingshot was nowhere to be seen and Ena had a dreadful instinct as to what the little fiend was probably up to.

She turned her chariot, scattering the small crowd, and drove cautiously back to where she had last seen him. Alerted by her horses' raised heads and pricked ears, Ena drew back on the reins and tried the professional charioteers' trick. She ran out along the vehicle's draw bar and tried to retain her balance between the horses' shoulders as she scanned the open countryside ahead. A small body with a red head could be seen apparently bounding like a ball towards her. More frighteningly, there was a large male figure, in the armour and red cloth of the enemy, in pursuit. The Roman appeared to have discarded helmet, shield and javelins to run faster and he was overhauling the fast-moving defender of Britain.

Ena scurried back along the drawbar, putting one foot on the back of an indignant horse in the process, and flapped the reins. The horses jolted the chariot into motion but appeared to be reluctant to rush towards the approaching pair before being sure what was happening. They condescended to move in a slow trot with heads raised and senses focused ahead. They took no particular notice of Ena's shrill commands and slapping reins. She drew her sword, more with the intent of stimulating her horses than of attacking the Roman, and waved it about.

The Roman heard her, and saw the chariot lumbering towards him with an armed warrior on board, turned around and bolted back the way he had come. The little boy also saw her and, sensing how unpredictable adults can be about small boys doing what adults said they were going to do, he gave the chariot plenty of room, circling out of Ena's reach as he hurried homewards. Ena and her horses were left on a deserted field.

Not for long. With a harsh shout, a small body of Roman foot soldiers appeared, accompanied by their fugitive colleague. Helmets on, shields raised and javelins poised, they jogged towards where Ena's team had unilaterally come to a halt. Perversely, the horses now appeared to find the approaching Roman soldiers fascinating and were very reluctant to turn. With much slapping of reins, screaming and other unseemly behaviour, the region's chief managed to get her team to turn. Once facing in the right direction, however, the team understood what was expected and fled the scene.

The headman had gathered his little armed party, which was cautiously advancing when they were confronted by a galloping, wild-eyed team and a bouncing chariot with their leader, scarcely less wild-eyed, in it ordering them to fall back. They reformed where the chariot came to a halt and faced the Roman soldiers over about half a kilometer of otherwise deserted country. The British offered a volley of insults and abuse. After a pause, the Romans turned and slogged back the way they had come.

There were now about a hundred and fifty armed militia under her command, including three or four on horseback. Hers was the only chariot and she needed a driver. The headman promptly refused to have any part of the contraption but appointed a youth with wide shoulders and a narrow waist to take the reins. Time to take stock.

The Invasion had started after all. The Roman authorities had regained control of their soldiers and were transporting them across the Ocean and landing them in her territory, perhaps at other landing sites as well. There were definitately ships in the channel and in the Stura River which meant they were threatening the regional capital upstream. She could, in fact, see smoke rising from the direction of the river, black rolling smoke like burning thatch. She had seen only about one hundred enemy footsoldiers so far but there would be cavalry shortly. The Irish were able to load and land warhorses and the Romans were certainly able to do the same.

The armed militia were all watching her, shifting and hefting their weapons, occasionally glancing around for sight of the enemy. She could order them to fight or she could order them to disperse. It was her decision, they had elected her for this and they had gathered to defend their homes. She had not the heart to tell them that their homes were doomed anyway. They probably knew it, even though few of them had yet seen the number of ships she had seen at sea. Even so, they were not here to give up without trying, and there were only a few Romans ashore as yet.

With many protests, the horsemen were sent away to carry the word to neighbouring chiefs and to find out what was happening north of the Stura River. She stood on the shifting platform of the chariot and told the militia what they were going to do. There was growl of agreement from the middle aged and whoops from the younger generation. Many spat on their hands and took practice swings with sword and falcata. Then they spread out on either side of the chariot and began to walk back towards the sea.

The summer heat was building up, swallows flitted in the blue sky above. The horses in Ena's team did not appear to have completely recovered from their fright. Sweat had dried on their necks but foam still showed around the bits and dripped from their jaws. The wheels rumbled and swished over the dry, grass-covered ground. The warriors talked quietly as they walked along and there was even some laughter. She did not join in the simple jokes. Her neck was stiff and the muscles over her shoulders were taut. She found she was gently grinding her teeth and her mouth filled with saliva.

It was the javelins. Without even looking at her people, she knew that there was not a shield, or even a helmet, amongst them. Their method of fighting was to close as rapidly as possible in a wild charge and then to use their weight and swordsmanship to break up the enemy formation and kill the individuals. They had no throwing spears nor bows with them. The only javelins on the British side were the five short darts in the quiver strapped to the outside of her chariot.

She had seen about a hundred Romans, all with shields and armour. If they had only been armed with swords they would still have presented formidable opposition. Their javelins, though, would strike down her people before they could even reach the enemy. They could kill, probably, at thirty paces. Even if half of them missed…The cold arithmetic was frightening. Fifty of her people killed or wounded in the first volley. How many volleys could the Romans release before the Britons could close with them? How many javelins would each Roman carry? She felt cold. She was leading most of her people to death.

The flags were still fluttering, the red and gold shields in a block around the base of the flagpole. She saw the sharp stakes pointing outwards and the glint of javelin points. About one hundred paces from the Romans' front rank, she raised her hand calling on her warriors to halt. Some of her younger men surged forward and back, getting more excited. The older warriors got them under control, checking distances ahead of them. They were clearly outside the range of the javelins here, but well within the distance the British could cover in a swift charge which would bring them, still fresh, to within swords' length. The Romans did not stir nor respond to the British taunts. Ena still had a few moments before the insults were all expended and both sides would expect action.

Like a stone, the understanding settled in her mind that the British could not charge the Romans and survive. The Romans had no apparent intention of leaving their position. Perhaps she could draw some of them out. She wished she were a better driver. Or that she knew the capabilities of the youth with her. The headman strode up and down in front of the British foot soldiers, gathering their attention with his voice and movement. Then he turned and faced her. She told him what must be done.

With a smack on the shoulder, Ena galvanised her charioteer and the horses threw themselves forward. She felt a pang of jealousy at his expertise, took a dart from the quiver and balanced it in one hand while clinging on with the other. As the chariot turned and raced along the short front of the Roman position, she tossed the dart high into the air. It traced a graceful curve against the blue sky as there was a flurry of movement behind the wall of bright shields. The shields of the second rank became a roof. The dart, falling almost vertically, slammed into one of the shields and stuck, upright and harmless.

The resounding cheer from her supporters did not disguise from Ena that her provocative attack had not disrupted the Roman formation. It had not even wavered. What next? Try again, of course.

Her charioteer, snarling with excitement, lined up the team and urged them forward. She saw movement behind the shields. A crested helmet seemed to indicate the whereabouts of a leader. Aiming as carefully as the unstable platform permitted, Ena launched another missile into the sky. As it left her hand, however, shields opened like shutters and javelins shot out. Her charioteer's jaw dropped and his eyes squeezed shut, head sinking between his shoulders. Something flashed between her face and the charioteer's back. A javelin smashed through the wickerwork side of the chariot and scored agonisingly across her leg. A horse coughed and a snap and rattling sound came from one of the wheels as a stuck javelin was shattered by the whirling spokes.

The charioteer, unhurt, whooped in relief as he guided the chariot out of range, but all was not well. Ena, leaning against him, holding her calf, could feel that the rhythm of the chariot's movement was faltering and was slowing, despite the effort the charioteer was transmitting, through his back, to her. Biting her lip against the pain, she looked over his shoulder and droplets of blood dotted her face. Then, the wounded and labouring horse went down. The chariot slewed around and tipped them out onto the warm grass. Fortunately it was traveling quite slowly and did not roll over them.

Bruised and shaken, Ena struggled up with the help of the young charioteer. He had armed himself with one of the missiles from the wrecked vehicle and Ena still had her sword. Had it been in a battle with another British tribe, they would have been dead. The tribesmen, seeing a chariot overturned, would have rushed forward and annihilated the crew. The Romans did not move. Instead it was Ena's own followers who were rushing forwards, brandishing blades and roaring at the tops of their voices. She screamed at them to stop, and the nearest and the most cautious heard her and slowed uncertainly. The headman, not the fastest of the runners, heard her and joined his voice to hers.

The British charge stopped just outside javelin range, some of the participants actually being held back physically by others. Then, breathless, they began to withdraw step by step, backwards from the unmoving Roman shields. Ena limped on ahead of them, leaning still on the charioteer, until the warriors felt they could with honour turn their backs on the Roman soldiers and walk after their wounded chief.

CHAPTER 62

▼

BRITAIN

You would have thought that they had fought—and won—the battle of Zama. The initial suppressed yell of triumph when the chariot turned on its side was closely followed by another as the barbarian foot soldiers began to retire. Titus and Fangs went up and down the ranks, snarling and pushing until the glee subsided into so much nudging and grinning at one another. They were very young soldiers. I checked with Philip but his signaler was dead. The dart had some down nearly vertically over the shield wall and entered his chest just behind the collar bone. It had been very quick.

"Be quiet!" I had taken a very large breath and the roar was correspondingly quite impressive. It was time to settle them again.

"Watch your front. Rear rank, pass one of your javelins to the man in front. The farmers you have just frightened have retired but they have not gone home. Keep your eyes open and your mouths shut. We have lost one man killed and one of our heroes slightly wounded by a small boy with his slingshot. Where are you? Yes, you numbskull. Come here."

A very shame-faced young soldier with a small cut on his cheekbone presented himself.

"What is the penalty for deserting your post?"

His eyes popped open at the question and sudden fear flickered in their depths.

"Answer."

"It is...death, Centurion."

"Correct answer. I saw you leave your post without permission, throwing aside your weapons. You left your colleagues either side of you exposed to enemy attack."

"Centurian, there was no enemy nearby." A faint sheen of perspiration appeared on his forehead.

"No enemy nearby? So you were running away. Is that it?"

"No, sir."

I was pleased to see him fight down the sudden alarm. I turned to Fangs.

"What is the usual method of execution in these cases?"

"Centurion," Fangs was both formal and judicious. "If a legionary deserts his place of guard duty, he may be beaten to death by the comrades he betrayed."

Even the young legionary knew this was true and that such a sentence was carried out in certain cases.

"In this case, Centurion," said Fangs slowly after the awful truth had sunk in with all the soldiers, "as the individual concerned is hardly even a proper soldier yet, I recommend a lesser sentence."

"Very well. You hear that this experienced soldier, who had to go out with some of your colleagues to rescue you from a small boy and a woman in a chariot, you hear that he recommends a lesser sentence?"

The unfortunate gulped and nodded.

"Go out there and collect all the javelins. Do not come back until you have got them all and you have straightened the shafts. You made a very poor showing against a woman and a child. If the barbarians come back before you have finished, we'll all see if you can fight grown men. Go."

"Move!" supplemented Fangs.

The ranks were again steady, patrolled by Titus and the middle-aged legionary. No barbarians were in sight although several pillars of black smoke were visible to the north. The corpse had been moved out of the way and Philip and his surviving signaler were busy.

The scene in the channel and beyond was incredible. A continuous row of ships was beached on the outer edge of the bank across the channel and the channel itself was packed with vessels. Ranks of ships, crammed with men, supplies and animals, waited their turn at sea. Unloaded ships in the channel eased their way north to clear the way for loaded ones nosing their way in. Those on the bank backed away from the land, using oars and stern anchors, as soon as they had discharged. The bank was black with troops and animals all plodding northwards onto the island proper. The composite stream split on the island and gathered around unit standards planted or waved from the higher ground. Some cavalry units were already mounted and moving inland to clear the island.

"Any cavalry ashore on this side yet?" I asked Philip.

"On their way," said the Greek sailor, with a tired grin. "The First Cohort of Legion IX Hispana has been landed directly in the mouth of the river, the Stura. They'll be getting their cavalry ashore as soon as the legionaries have hacked a ramp up from the waterline. That should be soon now."

"Messenger coming," shouted Titus.

"What is that?" said Fangs.

"An auxiliary horseman…no, an auxiliary muleman," amended Titus.

The mule halted short of the sharpened stakes which marked our perimeter and no urging from its frustrated rider could make it approach closer. It stood, legs braced, ears twitching and intelligent eyes gauging the rank of grinning young soldiers it faced. The rider was obviously a cavalry trooper. The mule, it seemed, was more used to inert packs than to demanding human burdens. I went to the rider as the mule would not come to us.

"Longinus, Centurion," said the red-faced man in a slight Balkan accent.

"Longinus what?" demanded Titus who had joined me.

"Trooper Longinus Sdapezematygus, Centurion, Ala I Thracum,"

"Sorry I asked," muttered Titus, almost under his breath.

"What is your message, Trooper Longinus?" I asked.

"'From Aulus Plautius, Governor of Britain, to Titus Seleucus, Captain in the British Fleet.'"

The man began his recital in a monotone which suggested accuracy of memory. I stopped him until Philip could reach us and then told him to continue. It seemed that Plautius had come ashore at the mouth of the Stura River with the leading elements of Legion IX Hispana which was something he had no business doing. No Invasion Task Force commander should be on the beach when most of his force was still at sea. I could only assume that he wanted to set an example to the ordinary legionaries. Now, he had decided that all the legions were to disembark directly onto the mainland and he had to entrust this critical order to a foreign soldier on a mule. There was something wrong with our Governor's judgement.

"Why are you riding a mule?" Titus at last asked the question when Philip had bustled off to his flags. "Mix up in the ship-loading?"

The mule pointed its long ears at him and appeared to glare balefully.

"No, Optio. Horses refused the river-bank. Too steep, you see. Mules? No problem."

"Message passed, Centurion," said the surviving signaler. "Philip is waiting for a reply."

We looked north at the smoke as we waited. The mule decided that the soldiers were probably harmless and started to crop the grass. There was some slight shifting and shuffling in the ranks behind us but, considering the thousands upon thousands of soldiers within a few miles of us, it was remarkably quiet.

Philip pushed his way out into the open, the war wound to his buttock apparently forgotten.

"Legion II Augusta is in the channel."

There was a subdued cheer from the legionaries who were doing their best to evesdrop his report.

"They will follow the Governor ashore at the Stura River. Legion XX Valeria will follow."

At the mention of Legion XX Valeria, the handsome, contemptuous face of Hosideus Geta came to mind. Hero of Mauretania, second in command of the Invasion Task Force and overdue high honours for his military prowess. I hoped he had had a thoroughly bad crossing and that seasickness had wiped the sneer from his face. At least, he was in the right position to co-ordinate events and, if the Governor was unfortunate enough to encounter a barbarian with a meat-cleaver, he was in a position, heaven help us, to take over command.

Thinking of barbarians, I climbed onto the wreck of the chariot to survey the countryside. One of the horses was dead in the traces and the other was nowhere to be seen. The defaulter had gathered a sheaf of javelins and had been using a stone against the wheel hub to hammer out the kinks in those shafts not too badly twisted. He helped me balance on the upper wheel. The expanse of open country to the west appeared deserted except for one or two solitary horsemen some distance off but the grassland was dotted with low bushes and the occasional stand of small trees. Interestingly, there was no livestock. The alarm must have been given before the sheep were released from the pens. Formal scouts, or even more small boys with slingshots, would be watching us from cover. They would have seen the messenger ride in, and they would be ready for him when he rode out.

I jumped down and told the legionary with the recovered javelins what he was going to do to complete his rehabilitation. His face lost a little colour but he nodded abruptly and took his salvage back to the shield wall. I still could not see any sign of significant movement of troops other than the broadening span of smoke to the north. Philip was waiting for me with the messenger, Titus and Fangs. Even the mule raised its head expectantly.

"No formations of the enemy in sight," I told them. "Nor any friendly formations either. There are watchers out there."

"Legion IX Hispana is probably moving north from the river to cover the marines," guessed Fangs. Our Legion will turn south to link up with us when it lands."

"The Governor will not release Legion IX Hispana from the Stura until he knows that his orders for the others to land there have got through. That means," I said to the Balkan horseman, "that you go back and tell him."

CHAPTER 63

▼

BRITAIN

"Are you all right ma'am?" Segonax had halted his chariot, and the armed reinforcements from his tribe, outside the small stand of trees on the edge of the harvested fields.

Ena's leg wound had stiffened and she was having difficulty in flexing her ankle. It was a blessing in a way. She was no longer expected to lead her warriors in furious and useless charges on the enemy when she should be receiving reports, mobilising British resources and planning the campaign to throw the Romans back into the sea. Only by sitting in one place could she do this effectively, and now she had the excuse.

A trickle of reports was coming in with women and fast-running children. They were filled either with very good news or very bad news. They came on foot, on horseback and, in one case, on the back of the family cow. Some were injured, most were not. There were several 'sole survivors' who were rapidly turned around and sent back. Segonaox' father was too ill to move and she had no information about the whereabouts of the two other chiefs of the Cantii. She assumed they were engaged north of the Stura.

As far as she could discover, the British north of the Stura were being pressed back by the weight of Roman armoured infantry. The river valley was seething with the enemy, granaries, houses and the few standing crops in the fields were burning in front of them. More Romans were being landed in the river mouth and some cavalry had now been seen picking its way westwards. For the moment, the ground to the south of the Stura was relatively free of the enemy except for the signaling post overlooking the mouth of the channel. She described the situation in brief to the young leader, her former driving instructor.

"Ma'am, I have sent word by boat down the Medu River for Camulodunon, I hear that the High King is still in the capital."

"The Romans have masses of ships, Segonax. They might be in the Thames estuary already. What about the route through Lud Dun?"

"Riders are on the way. They have orders, of course, to report to Administrator Ceri there before pushing on to Camulodunon. Also, I have ordered all boats and ferries to the west bank of the Medu River where they will remain under guard."

"Right. Now. The snails will start pushing into this area from the Stura or by landings on the south coast. They will want to use the road to Lud Dun for any advance. We must disrupt their landings, slow them down, fight them in the open ground if we can, until the High King can get the main forces here. How many chariots with you?"

"Five here. Ten more soon."

"Keep the chariots for scouting the open country around the road and as a reserve here. Impress on the crews not to get themselves killed or their vehicles wrecked. They will be needed for the main battle."

"I'll tell them, ma'am. Then I'll take some of the footsoldiers forward and cut off the enemy signaling station, from the landward side anyway. Pity about the guard boat."

"I'm afraid the sea belongs to the Romans unless a really bad storm comes up. We must defeat them on land. We have missed any chance to defeat them on the beaches."

Segonax chose the fastest runners from among the many warriors anxious to go with him. Many of the older men and women were worried about families and relations in the Stura River valley but they were all grimly determined to strike at least one blow against the invader. They were not happy about being left behind and Ena had to limp out of the trees and speak to them as a group. While she was doing so, Segonax got his chariot and the younger warriors heading east.

Looking north, he could still see no sign of the enemy. The other chariots, scouting the uplands around the ancient road to Lud Dun, covered his right, even though he could not see them. He had chosen a chariot driver and now had time to survey the countryside and chat to those accompanying him on foot. The sun was high when he heard a piercing whistle from high in the trees. A small boy with a, now, dirty face and a slingshot, dropped from the branches. He had successfully eluded the authorities and, more importantly, his mother, all day. He had, he reported with some pride, kept the snails under observation. He pointed the direction. Segonax sternly ordered him home.

Creeping forward, Segonax saw the flags first. He did not have enough follow-ers to place a continuous ring around the signal post on the cliff's edge so he con-tented himself by posting two scouts on the southern side and the rest in small batches, in cover, on the other sides. He made sure that they all knew where he would be stationed, ready with his chariot and driver to intercept any messenger. Not all the warriors knew the countryside. He tried to pair townsmen with shep-herds or hunters and sent them off.

The last of the groups had not even gone out of sight when his driver gripped Segonax by the shoulder and pointed a rigid arm at the distant flags. A horseman was leaving the clump of figures at the cliff's edge and was turning north. None of the British was in position to intercept him yet. Segonax snatched the reins from the driver and started north, using every scrap of cover and fold in the ground to keep his vehicle out of sight as he hurried to cut off the messenger. His dispossessed driver watched the messenger and muttered reports of his progress as Segonax concentrated on his driving. His horses were the best and responded instantly to his practiced guidance. The erstwhile driver said that they were gain-ing, that the messenger was not moving fast, hardly more than a slow trot. There was something strange about the messenger's mount. Segonax did not worry about that. It was the despatch-rider himself he was determined to cut off.

The British chariot followed the shallow valley of a tributary of the Stura, the horses going well at a fast trot. The driver had temporarily lost sight of their quarry but they were still heading north-east and would be rapidly narrowing the distance from the messenger. Their way was suddenly impeded by a small, steep-sided stream-bed which joined the tributary. Without hesitation, Segonax turned sharp right up the shallow side of the tributary. He halted at a point just short of the crest and ran out along the drawbar. He saw the hindquarters of the animal just going behind a stand of small trees a hundred paces ahead. The des-patch-rider would not have seen the Briton's head appear above the fold in the ground. Perfect.

Segonax scrambled back into the vehicle and it surged onto the higher ground just as the messenger appeared on the other side of the trees. The driver, with the reins back in his hands, shouted with glee as the despatch-rider turned his head towards them. His animal stumbled or bucked and its rider, without hesitation, wheeled back towards the signal station.

"It's a mule. Would you believe it? It's a mule."

The driver hauled on the right hand reins to cut off the rider as he re-emerged from behind the trees. Segonax hung on with one hand and took a javelin from the quiver. He nudged the driver, told him to be careful with his horses' mouths and balanced the weapon.

Mules are strange animals, more intelligent than many people think. They can stubbornly refuse to move if they are not convinced that all is well, and will kick and bite ferociously if seriously annoyed. This mule took one look at the strange contraption rattling towards it, apparently chasing a pair of galloping ponies and being chased in turn by two very tall humans, and it decided that it wanted no part of this apparition. It displayed a turn of speed which would have done credit to the straights on the racetrack at the circus. The armoured rider bent low and clung on.

Even so, Segonax might have got close enough to bring down the rider had his driver been as expert as he was. Cutting as close as he could to a stand of low trees, the driver did not see a stump in the thick grass until the last moment and only just managed to avoid a collision. The horses lost their rhythm and the chariot its momentum. The legionaries scattered as the mule, yellow fangs bared, charged to safety in amongst them.

Segonax fought down his disappointment and annoyance and shouted that all his scouts should remain out of sight, watching the Romans who had again closed ranks behind their sharpened stakes. He gave his horses chance to recover their breath and drove them slowly backwards and forwards in front of the enemy just outside javelin range. The Romans showed no signs of stirring.

CHAPTER 64

▼

BRITAIN

The mouth of the Stura River, and the channel outside, was almost choked with shipping. In some places, determined centurions were getting their legionaries ashore by clambering from deck to deck until they reached dry land. There was no panic, the infantry were seasoned soldiers, but it was fortunate that the landing was virtually unopposed.

Legion IX Hispana was ashore and reorganised. The five and a half thousand men, fully armed but with only the rations they could carry, were deploying away from the beach to the north of the Stura. Legion II Augusta, under Vespasian, was now landing with Legion XX Valeria under Hosideus Geta pressing into the channel. Legion XIV Gemina waited off the coast.

Camp Commandant Anicius Maximus surveyed the scene with disgust. Someone had to take charge of this mess before it became a shambles. The Governor, it seemed, had gone off somewhere with Legion IX Hispana and his own Legate, Vespasian, had his hands more than full getting Legion II Augusta ashore. Anicius Maximus had no doubt as to who was best qualified to co-ordinate the landings on the Stura River. Ignoring the silent protests of his arthritic joints, he chose a prominent point and climbed towards it, gathering a trumpeter and two signalers on the way. His new batman hurried along behind him, carrying the Commandant's helmet, his day's rations and his folding chair. New arrivals in the mouth of the Stura river had their attention drawn by trumpet blast and were summoned by gesticulating signalers to report to the grim figure of the one Roman in Britain who knew exactly what everyone should be doing.

"Trooper Rufus Sita," said the Camp Commandant. "You are supposed to be with Legion XX Valeria. What are you doing ashore already?"

"Legate Hosideus Geta sent me on ahead, sir. My orders are to find out about enemy concentrations south of the, ah, the Stura River and report to him when he lands."

"Very wise," the Commandant actually thought that it was a deviation from proper planning and a typically undisciplined intrusion by an ambitious senior officer. "Have you got your horse ashore? Right. This is what you do. You see that smoke over there? The grey column in amongst the black? That's where you will find a turma of Ala I Thracum. My compliments to the decurion and he is to allow you to accompany him until Legion XX Valeria lands. Understood? Go."

The decurion was not at all pleased with the unwished for arrival of a supernumary who was also a former decurion of his own unit. His horses were fractious with the smell of smoke and the lack of fresh water. His men were already weary after the long voyage, the struggle to off-load their mounts and the tension of advancing into enemy territory. Their faces were streaked with soot and sweat and their shoulders spotted with ash. He closed his stinging eyes for a moment, then ordered Rufus Sita to remain close by him and waved the troopers to follow him around a burning cornfield.

"Where are the enemy?" Sita wanted to know. The other horse-soldiers, his former subordinates, took pity on his isolation.

"We haven't seen any," said one.

"They've all run for it," said another.

"Quiet," ordered the decurion. "Watch your front or the first Brit you see will be your last."

A farmstead, apparently intact, loomed in the shadow cast by the columns of smoke. The fact that it was not burning seemed somehow ominous amongst the general destruction. Several troopers adjusted their grips on their lances. Sita drew his sword. His hand was wet.

"There's a man in the doorway, decurion."

"I can see him."

It was a wonder that the thatch had not caught fire from the sparks in the air. Swallows flitted through the pall of smoke, hunting insects disturbed by the fires. An elderly man sat on a bench under the porch of the house. In his hands he held one of those broad, single-edged blades the Gauls called falcata. Silently the horsemen spread out into a semi-circle facing him across the bare ground of the farmyard. He did not move.

"Who speaks Celtic?"

"I do," said Sita.

"Tell him to lay down his weapon. We won't harm him."

There was a brief exchange.

"What did he say?"

"He told us to go to hell."

Half burned fragments of straw floated to the ground.

"All right," said the decurion. "Kill him."

No one moved.

"I said…"

One of the troopers rammed his heels into his horse's side and the horse jerked forward. The horseman poked out his lance and the old man easily parried it. He tried again and again his lance was knocked aside. The old man did not even get up off his bench. He did not have to. His house protected his back and the porch prevented an attack from the sides. The trooper tried again, unsuccessfully.

"This is becoming ridiculous," murmured Sita.

The decurion grabbed a lance from one of his men, turned his horse sideways and hurled the weapon with all his force at the seated man. The old man bent stiffly at the waist and the lance disappeared into the house.

"Enough!" shouted the decurion, throwing himself off his horse and drawing his sword. No one laughed.

"Wait," said Sita. "I'll go round the back."

"Set the house on fire," suggested one of the troopers, but the decurion was not listening. He stalked towards the porch. The old man, seated on his bench, watched him coming. He raised his weapon with both hands. He would soon have tired in this position but the decurion was now impatient to end this trifling incident. He stepped close and feinted at the old man with his sword, swaying backwards as the falcata swished downwards. The heavy blade thumped into the ground and the troopers were shocked by their decurion's scream. His sword, poised for the fatal stab, fell from his hand as the falcata sheared leather and flesh from his foot. Unarmed, he stumbled backwards and sat down in the farmyard.

"For god's sake," said Rufus Sita. "Medic, see to him."

He threw himself off his horse, took the medic's lance and walked up to the porch. Staying well out of range, he feinted a couple of times as the old man waved his heavy weapon, then he drove the lance into the farmer's chest. He dragged the corpse out of the porch and noted without surprise the frame which supported the farmer's withered leg.

The decurion sat on the ground steadily and monotonously cursing while the medic gravely bound his damaged foot. One of the troopers, trying to keep a straight face, returned his sword to him.

"You better go back to the beach," muttered Sita. "The Camp Commandant will be setting up a hospital there."

"I'm fine," lied the decurion between gritted teeth. "Get me onto my horse."

While they were doing that, one of the horseman called out that there was a runner coming. Breathless, Longinus trotted up to them, coughing in the smoke. He reported that he had escaped from the signaling station through the surrounding British warriors by a clever ruse. He had mounted a legionary on his mule and had run along beside the animal through the thick grass, staying on the unseen side nearest the cliff edge. When the mule and rider had been spotted by the enemy, he had dropped flat on the ground while the legionary led the pursuit back to the signaling station. No doubt, he said, that position was already overrun and he was the sole survivor.

He paused for praise. It was not forthcoming.

"British warriors," said the decurion with something like relief. "Mount up. You, Longinus, go on to the beachhead with your report. There is no enemy that way. The rest of you, follow me."

Fortune had totally deserted the decurion. Hurrying his unit through a smouldering village on the way to the Roman signaling station, his horse trod on an ember and he was thrown violently against a pommel of his saddle. He sustained massive internal injuries and had to be sent back to the beachhead with the medic.

His deputy took charge, although many would have wished that Rufus Sita could have done so, and they only paused when the Roman position on the cliff's edge was in sight. There was no doubt that there had not been a massacre. The orderly line of red and gold shields proclaimed that the legionaries were alive and under control. There was no sign of any British. So much for the report of the 'sole survivor'.

The deputy waved the turma forward and the cavalry broke into a straggling canter. Rufus Sita felt a deep qualm of uneasiness but the legionaries were waving at the oncoming cavalry. The deputy waved happily back.

Suddenly, the countryside erupted, spewing barbarian infantry with gleaming blades from behind every bush and out of every dip in the ground. Horses shied and bucked, unsettling riders encumbered with their long lances. Several cavalrymen were dragged from their saddles and many horses crippled by the heavy blades. The deputy hesitated a moment too long, his screaming horse went down and he died an instant later. Several troopers wasted time trying to get into line for a charge. Most followed Sita who did not even try to draw his sword but ducked his head and kicked his horse into an uncontrolled gallop towards the safety of the legionaries. They were the ones who got clear. The ones who stayed to fight, died as individuals or in small groups long before the first squad of shocked legionaries could reach them.

The British did not stay to fight the legionaries. They retired, jeering and waving captured weapons. A single chariot circled behind them like a sheepdog with its flock.

CHAPTER 65

▼

BRITAIN

"What is going on?" The High King of Britain was not a reassuring sight. He was grey-faced and red-eyed with weariness, his thin hair standing in spikes and his clothes travel-stained from days of ceaseless activity and the forced march from Camulodunon. His nephew Ceri, tired himself, had quickly hustled his uncle into his own house in Lud Dun. Togodumnos was a big man but he seemed to have shrunk since Ceri had last seen him.

"The Roman army is ashore," Ceri began.

"I know that much. And why didn't you know they were coming? I was relying on you."

Ceri smarted under the harsh tone but held his temper.

"The Romans managed both to resolve the mutiny and get their entire army into the territory of the Cantii in a matter of days. Our warriors had dispersed home and are still in the process of assembling again. The local militia are fighting hard, I hear."

Togodumnos' voice was hoarse with the days of cajoling, explaining, threatening and exhorting needed to get the British army in motion and he had a pain in his chest. He felt a flicker of respect for his nephew. He, at least, had not defended himself by pointing out that it had been the High King's own decision to allow the most experienced warriors to disperse at the news of the Roman mutiny. Togodumnos had been told, to his face, that he should have waited until the legions had marched back to Germany before dismissing the core of the British army. That was all very well for those who did not have any other considerations than the purely military. The Roman professional army could sit on the other side of the Ocean for ever, without either going back to Germany or invading Britain. In Britain, the High King's best men were urgently needed to administer the regions if they were not actively engaged in fighting. It was his decision to make and he had made it. He must now correct that mistake.

"You say that you hear that the militia are fighting hard, nephew. They are Cantii, of course. But it sounds as if you have not been there yourself? What's going on?"

"We need to talk about allies." Ceri handed him a cup. It was the first time Ceri had seen the High King's hand tremble. He put it down to tiredness. "But first, the enemy. Their fleets of ships are crossing the Ocean in both directions. Some of their ships have even been seen in the Thames estuary by our guard boat in the mouth of the Medu River. A lot of cavalry and some infantry are reported from the south side of the Stura. Chief Ena and young Segonax are co-ordinating resistance there. There is no word from the other two chiefs. A few families crossing the Medu report that the Cantii are destroying food north of the Stura, as instructed, but that Roman cavalry is hunting down the militia there."

The High King did not comment on his nephew's avoidance of his original question. He thought about Ceri's information of the enemy's movements.

"It sounds as if the Romans are clearing their right flank with their cavalry. If that is what they are doing, they'll probably advance up the road to Lud Dun when their build up is complete."

"Maybe."

"Yes, maybe. Ena and Segonax must hold the country south of the Stura and fall back as the legions advance. We must build up behind the line of the Medu."

The High King's eyes seemed a little clearer and colour appeared again in his cheeks. He smoothed his hair.

"You mentioned allies. I wonder if we have any. The Catuvellauni and the Trinovantes have mobilised, of course, about seventy thousand altogether. I am hopeful that a lot of stragglers will catch up later, but it may not happen. Your uncle Caratacos is on his way with about eight thousand Atrebates. He would have been here already but he had to make sure the northern Dobunni are committed. King Buduoc is bringing five thousand Dobunni, it seems. And that, plus whatever remains of the Cantii, is probably all that we can expect for the main battle for Britain."

"Say about ninety thousand altogether. We must still outnumber the Romans at more than two to one. That's not so bad. But what about our other neighbours?"

"Ah," said the High King, with a hint of humour. "You are referring to the aloof Durotriges hiding in their high fortresses? Or to the loudly patriotic Queen

Cartimandua who just somehow cannot get her Brigantes to move? Perhaps to the good King Prasutagos of the Iceni whose wife tells him when he may leave the house?"

Ceri had been restraining his natural restlessness until the High King had relaxed a little. Now, he sprang to his feet and strode about the room.

"The Irish, I suppose, are too far away."

"And disinclined to get involved. If we win, nothing changes for them. If we lose, the Romans will still be a long way from the Irish Sea. High King Conaire Mor still does not appreciate how fast these snails can move. That's why I am giving permission to Brigit Mong Ruadh to come as far as the Medu. She is an experienced soldier and her brother will believe her report."

The British High King drained his cup and held it out again.

"Why aren't you at the Medu?" he asked bluntly.

"King Buduoc and his five thousand Dobunni are going to get to Lud Dun before Uncle Caratacos," explained Ceri, his small, bright eyes fixed on those of his other uncle. "They had not yet dispersed to their homes when you ordered the mobilisation again. I am not going to leave Buduoc here alone."

"I see. You think that the loyal King Buduoc might defect, complete with one of our principal towns?"

"This town is the very point where the main road to your capital crosses the Thames and, into the bargain, is a big enough port for the entire Roman fleet. It would be a very big prize for him to be able to offer the Roman general. Big enough to extract a very pretty deal for the Dobunni and for the King himself."

"All right, Ceri. I get the point. I must admit to thinking that King Buduoc is something of a weasel myself. Anyway, I would not buy a second-hand chariot from him."

"Send him away," said Ceri. "Tell him to go back and guard our lines of communications or something."

"Ask yourself, Ceri," said his uncle, "if things go wrong, would you rather have Buduoc behind you or in front of you. Yes, you see. No, King Buduoc, with his brave Dobunni warriors, goes straight to the Medu River to reinforce Chief Ena if he can. To assist him to decide whether he can or not, I am going with him."

Togodumnos stilled his nephew's astonished protest.

"No, Ceri, you stay here and bring on the main army with your uncle Caratacos. I've done all the hard work to get things moving. Why should you have all the fun? I will be at the Medu."

CHAPTER 66

▼

BRITAIN

Ena felt she must look a sight. The minor wound to her leg was healing cleanly but that was the only part of her that felt clean. As a Celt, and more importantly as a Celtic woman, she did not wish to appear before the High King, even if he was a man and from the Cassi family at that, when she was not looking her best. There had just been no time.

Skirmishes with Roman cavalry patrols south of the Stura River were now a daily occurrence and the care of her horses, and even the most basic maintenance on the chariots, had suffered. Every day, the constant attrition had nibbled away at the numbers and the determination of her hungry and tattered followers. The smoke north of the Stura had finally faded and dispersed and the arrival of blackened and wounded fugitives had died away. From everything she had learned, the Cantii no longer existed north of that river.

The two missing chiefs had to be presumed dead and the tribal organization was too disrupted to elect replacements yet. According to his people, Segonax's father was on the point of death and, for the moment, she alone was the focus of loyalty and resistence in the land of the Cantii. She wondered if there had ever been such a dirty, bone-tired symbol of national resistence. She hoped that her mother and her children were safe.

When she drove waveringly up to the point where the High King sat slumped in the saddle, she found that the meeting was going to be even worse than she anticipated. A lovely redheaded woman sat her horse beside him. An air of authority surrounded her, and she was clean.

"Ena." The High King's red-veined cheeks were shiny with perspiration and his hair clung to his brow. "Have you left any Romans for us?"

"There are still more than enough to go around, unfortunately." Ena struggled to respond lightly and to keep her hands out of sight.

"Brigit, this is Ena, Chief of the valiant Cantii," the High King introduced her. "Brigit Mong Ruadh, military adviser to her brother, Conaire Mor, High King of Ireland."

"Ireland!" Ena exclaimed.

"Yes, Chief," said the Irishwoman in a high and accented voice. "We have heard great things of the courage and determination of the Cantii and now I can see why."

Ena felt her sunburned skin stretch as she smiled. She brushed some hair from her face.

"And this," said the High King, turning in his saddle, "is my colleague, Buduoc, King of the Dobunni."

"Yes," said Ena, looking at the thin man with the restless eyes. "I have met the King before. Welcome, sir."

"I hear the Cantii need help. Five thousand Dobunni are right behind me. You and I, we will chase the Romans into the sea together."

Brigit shifted uneasily in her saddle but said nothing.

"Very well," said the High King. "I will deploy the main army on the west bank of the Medu as it arrives. Brigit, will you accompany me? King Buduoc, I would be grateful if you would instruct your contingent to join the Cantii under Chief Ena in delaying and disrupting enemy activities as long as possible. Give me as much time as you can and then fall back on my right flank."

"Should we not hear Chief Ena's report on Roman activities?" Brigit was most deferential.

The High King wiped his brow and rubbed the hand on his left arm.

"Time is pressing," he said, "and I know I can leave the situation to the east of the Medu in the safe hands of the King and of Chief Ena. When the main army is safely deployed, we will discuss the matter again. Yes, Ena?"

Ena was disconcerted that the meeting was apparently over and stumbled over what she wanted to say.

"Segonax has done very well," she managed. "He's had a great deal of success in ambushing the Romans. Hides his people and springs the trap when they are not expecting it."

"Yes, yes. You have all done very well and you must continue to use those tactics until I can get the main army into position. Then we will fight a conventional battle and destroy the Romans. Very well done. Now, we must go. There's a lot for all of us to do."

Ena watched the High King ride away with his bodyguard and the Irish lady. She had not had time to even look at the other members of his party, and yet she knew that she had failed to convince the High King of something important. Buduoc was looking at her with a half-smile on his face.

"Impatient, isn't he?"

His saddle creaked as he turned.

"Here come my warriors. Now, let's go and kill some Romans. After you Chief."

The small army of Dobunni looked somehow alien to Ena. There were a number of chariots, but not many, and a small contingent of cavalry on big horses. Most of the well-armed warriors marched confidently on foot, looking at the signs of war damage, the empty homesteads, the deserted fields. Their ruddy, well-fed faces showed only interest, not strain. It was disturbing that very few of them looked at her directly.

Segonax came to meet them, driving expertly despite a bandaged hand. He still looked very young if you ignored the dark smudges under the eyes and the wispy stubble on his chin. The Dobunni chiefs gathered around King Buduoc and listened to Segonax's report of the day's deployment and action so far. It seemed unreal even to Ena, the verbal list of incidents and casualties, on the windy uplands where there was no smoke and no visible sign of either enemy or friendly forces.

"So," said King Buduoc, with a sly glance at his listening subordinates, "our strategy is a British build-up behind the Medu River for the main battle, and our tactics are to disrupt the Roman build-up by attacking any enemy found south of the Stura River. We want, as far as possible, to keep the Romans north of the Stura. Is that right?"

"That's right, your majesty." Segonax blinked tired eyes.

"Well," said the King straightening in the saddle and looking around. "That should be easy. There's no one here."

There was a shout of laughter from every Dobunni within earshot.

Segonax did not reply. He did not even smile. He put the fingers of his uninjured hand to his mouth and blew a piercing whistle. Tattered, dirty warriors seemed to stand up from behind every bush and rise out of every fold in the ground. They were few compared with the Dobunni but they appeared to suddenly people the landscape with unmoving menace. There was the faintest ripple of alarm in the Dobunni ranks.

"Very impressive," the King muttered, "bandits too can often hide efficiently from soldiers. How would they do against a proper army?"

"Do you see any Romans?" Ena was indignant. "No you don't, and the reason you don't is because Roman cavalry scouting into this area is routinely repulsed by my people. Don't call them bandits. They have been defeating what you would call a proper army almost daily, pushing them back north of the Stura River."

"We all look forward to seeing what the famous Dobunni can do," put in Segonax, calmly, "now that they are here."

"What I intend," said Buduoc, a slight flush appearing on his thin cheeks, "is to use my army conventionally, out in the open. I do not deny that you have done very well using slim local resources. You should continue as you are, as long as it is only cavalry probes you are dealing with. I doubt that the Romans yet know that the Dobunni are here and we must use that. I shall sweep round the south of your positions, Ena, and confirm that the Romans have not landed anywhere on the south coast."

Several of his chiefs nodded and made noises of approval.

"It will not be long before the Romans attach footsoldiers to their cavalry units to deal with your technique. The infantry will flush out the ambush parties and, once they are running, the cavalry will ride them down. When this first happens, send for me and I'll give the Romans a real surprise."

Ena looked at Segonax.

"It makes sense ma'am. The people are tired but we can keep going for a few more days yet."

She turned back to the small monarch.

"We think that the Roman break-out, when it comes, will be into this area and onto the main Lud Dun road. They will use it to go around the British line on the Medu."

"So much the better," said King Buduoc. "They will not be expecting me to attack them from their left flank."

"Very well," said Chief Ena. "I agree."

The Dobunni chiefs nodded and backed their horses away from the small group of leaders. The Dobunni army turned across the Lud Dun road and headed towards the south coast. Ena and Segonax gathered their followers and headed north, towards the Stura again.

CHAPTER 67

▼

BRITAIN

Caratacos arrived at the Medu River ahead of a huge pall of dust marking the advance of the main British army. Ceri, and Fox the Druid, were with him. The High King gave a ghost of a grin as the threesome rode up. Brigit, at his side, smiled approval which seemed particularly concentrated on the High King's brother.

"Thank god the Romans are such an idle race," said Togodumnos in unfeigned relief. "We thought that the defence of Britain and Ireland was going to be left up to Brigit and myself. Roman cavalry are already watering their horses in the Medu. I hope you have brought plenty of cavalry."

"All we could lay our hands on," said Caratacos cheerfully, "we emptied the farms."

"And the chariots!" Ceri's eyes were sparkling. "I'm sure the vibration of the wheels has done permanent damage to Lud Dun bridge."

"How are you, lady?" Fox enquired gravely, his ginger hair as bristly as a boy's. "My colleague, Niall, with your Irish troopers, is close behind us with the main army."

"How many in total?" The High King interrupted with unconscious rudeness. He was not referring to the little party of Irish observers.

"About seventy five thousand," said Caratacos, looking at his brother carefully for the first time, "not counting Buduoc's Dobunni and any of the Cantii who are still available."

"I have about ten thousand Cantii here, a mixed lot with no chiefs. King Buduoc, with his five thousand, is with the Cantii still in the field under Chief Ena."

"Has anyone notified Chief Ena that her mother and her children are safe?" Brigit intervened quietly. "If not, would it be all right if I send a couple of my troopers to do that when they arrive?"

The High King waved his permission. Fox could see he was very tired. Concern for the peace of mind of one of his subordinates was low on his priorities.

"Deployment," pronounced the High King. "Chariots upstream, to the right, all of them. Ceri, you will be in charge." He ignored his nephew's brilliant smile.

"Infantry." He spoke to Caratacos. "Deploy them along the Medu. Don't worry about the stretch where the river is tidal, the Romans won't risk that, but reinforce the guard boat station at the river mouth. I want to hear about any approach of Roman shipping." Caratacos simply nodded.

"Fox. Go back and tell the cavalry to halt on the higher ground behind the infantry. I will join them there shortly. Any questions? Well done everyone. Let's get on with it."

After they had all gone, Togodumnos slowly and inelegantly slid from his horse's back. His knees would perhaps have buckled had he not held on to a pommel of his saddle. With slightly trembling hands, he tied the reins to a bush and lowered himself to a sitting position. Then he flopped back onto the thick grass with a whoosh of expelled breath and looked up at the blue sky, a few wheeling swallows high up.

"Great Bel," he murmured. "Thank you."

He shifted slightly, feeling the kinks in his spine straighten. Then he took a few slow, deep breaths. He closed his eyes and listened to the thudding of his heart. After a while, it merged with the rumble and vibration of the wheels, feet and hooves of the British army, moving into the positions he had decreed. The sun shone red through his closed eyelids. His horse tore quietly at the grass. The wind dried his forehead and a great peace settled on him.

He thought of his father, the great Cunobelinos, unchallenged in his British domains, secure in his position and moving to the Otherworld full of successful years. May he only do half as well. Father, he thought, help me.

The impression of movement died away and a shadow fell over his face. It was Fox. It was time to speak to the army.

CHAPTER 68

▼

BRITAIN

If it had not been for all the visitors, life on the cliff's edge would have been just about as perfect as it gets in the military. I had had the entrenchment dug a little larger than normal military practice decreed. I could still man it effectively as the cliff itself provided very adequate defence on one side. Tents were not available, shipping space being far too valuable for any luxuries, but the weather was fine and sleeping in the open was no hardship at all. All the digging was done, routines for water and firewood collection had been established and, after the one disastrous skirmish with our cavalry, the enemy had disappeared.

We saw very little of our major infantry formations as they moved inland and, usually, only the routine cavalry patrols crossed our front. To our rear, however, there was a vista of continuous fascination in the daily arrival of loaded ships and the departure of empty ones. Philip and his signaler were busy with flags and dispatch-riders all day and often into the night. We legionaries had little constructive to do but a great deal to watch.

Unfortunately, this tended to attract considerable numbers of under-employed senior officers, mostly of the junior tribune variety, who tended to believe that the signal station functioned for their entertainment and that the junior centurion in charge made an adequate tour guide. They were not above justifying their presence by demanding that their remarkably trivial messages be passed by our signalers. Even junior centurions in the army learn how to deal with these intrusions. After the legionary legates got to know how their junior tribunes liked to spend their days, many of the most irritating visits abruptly ceased.

As someone said, all good things come to an end, and, about two weeks after the first landings, no less a person than Camp Commandant Anicius Maximus sent word that we were to prepare to move. Legionaries, it seemed, were not going to be wasted guarding facilities which were now some distance behind the advance and were under no apparent threat. The guarding of the signal station would be taken over by auxiliary infantry of Cohort V Gallorum. I was to report, with my century, to the forward headquarters of our Legion II Augusta at the tribal capital twenty three kilometers up the Stura.

Philip was not happy about the downgrading of his security but he managed to be civil to the young Roman centurion in charge of the incoming Gallic infantry. It was the first time I had encountered a centurion more junior than me. As a centurion of a unit of legionaries, I naturally took precedence over a centurion of auxiliaries. I was showing him around, and my young soldiers were being disgustingly condescending to the hard-bitten auxilliary infantry, when the hand-over time-table suddenly had to be revised.

It started with a shout from several sentries on the wall that a single horseman was approaching. Messengers from the landing site at the mouth of the Stura River were common. This rider, however, was coming from the south, not the north, and was carrying a branch of green leaves. A messenger allegedly coming in peace.

Leaving the optios to pair an auxiliary with each legionary on the walls, my fellow centurion and I stepped out of the gate. The horseman had halted about one hundred paces from the walls, well outside javelin range. He appeared to be alone but I well remembered how Celtic warriors could appear from under every blade of grass and I waved for him to come to us. His lack of armour or helmet and his brightly woven woolen clothing, confirmed he was a Celt. The torc at his throat declared he was of some importance.

He kneed his large cavalry horse into motion and walked it towards us. I did not turn my head at the clink and shuffle behind me as the soldiers prepared their javelins. He stopped within range but not too close to us. His long sword hung by its belt from a pommel of his saddle, out of easy reach for him.

I greeted him in Celtic, which surprised him. It surprised my fellow-centurion as well, although he had picked up a lot of the language from his auxiliaries. The Celt, rudely, did not provide his name or that of the person who had sent him.

"I am here," he said haughtily, "to speak with King Bericos."

No Briton in the field would refer to Bericos by his title. He was officially a traitor.

"He is not here," I told him, stating the obvious. "I can convey your message to him."

"Call him," ordered the self-important barbarian. "I will wait."

"Dismount," I told him.

"No," he said sitting upright and looking proudly over my head at the javelin points. "You cannot harm a messenger."

"Dismount," I repeated, "or my men will kill your horse."

His breath hissed between his teeth and he slid off the animal without a word. His quickness of decision reminded me very much of Cogidumnos. I called over my shoulder and a folding chair was brought out.

"Sit," I told him.

"Will you kill my horse if I don't?"

I did not reply and, after a moment, he sat on the chair. This proud man would not have accepted my orders if he was not determined to speak to Bericos. Judging by his torc, he was a senior man. I guessed that he would not accept any further insult to his personal dignity unless an even more senior man had sent him.

"Take the messenger's horse to water," I told the legionary who had brought the chair.

He took hold of the reins and gave them a little tug. For a moment the Celt did not release them. Perspiration showed along his hairline and his fist trembled. Then he slowly opened his hand and the messenger was left sitting horseless and weaponless.

It was time to repair a little damage to his self-esteem. As the animal was led away, I unhooked his sword from the saddle and handed it to him, hilt first. A very senior Briton had an important message for King Bericos who, as everyone knew, worked for the Romans.

The Camp Commandant would know where the King was, he certainly always knew where everyone else was, but I had no intention of sending an unknown British emissary into the militarily sensitive area of the landing beaches. If this was a trick, then it could only be either to gather information or to kill Bericos. The messenger was not going to be given the opportunity to gather information, and suitable arrangements would have to be made to protect the King.

I borrowed the Celtic messenger's own horse and sent Titus off to report to the Commandant. Then I instructed the Gallic auxiliaries to sweep the area around the signal station out to about a kilometer, and to post sentries at that distance from our walls. The legionaries continued to man the walls and the solitary Celt appeared to doze in his chair, the potential target of several javelins.

In the end, it was Cogidumnos, and not King Bericos, who arrived, escorted by some cavalry, our old friends Ala I Thracum. The messenger left his sword on the chair and he and Cogidumnos walked and talked alone for most of the afternoon. In the early evening, he reclaimed his weapon and his horse and rode away to the south. Cogidumnos settled into the folding chair. He did not, for once, look as cool as a fish.

"How many of them want to surrender?" I asked, coming up quietly behind him. He twisted around in the chair.

"What did he tell you?" His eyes were intent.

"Briton of rank, sent by someone more senior, wants to speak personally to the biggest traitor in Britain collaborating with the invaders? What's to tell?"

He subsided slightly.

"What are my options?" he asked, almost to himself.

"You don't have any. You tell Senator Sentius Saturninus. Even if you don't, I'll report to my superiors and they will tell the Senator. Depending on numbers, this could be the foundation of the force of British levies he wants to create. Better you are in the forefront rather than trailing behind."

"You're right," he said jumping to his feet and punching me lightly on the shoulder. My normal response to this sort of condescension would have been to punch him on the nose, but there was more to find out.

"How many?" I repeated.

"A lot. It's big." He nodded for emphasis. "If he's not exaggerating, that is. I'll be back at dawn."

Ala I Thracum, grinning and waving, thundered away after him. They hardly glanced at the stretch of ground where several of their comrades had been hacked to pieces so recently. There is nothing like a good massacre to raise the spirits of the survivors.

To work. I told the auxiliaries to set up standing patrols a mile out from the three faces of our entrenchment. I then took the grins off my legionaries' faces by telling them what they were going to do. They sorted out tools and went off to cut poles for the tribunal they were going to construct facing out from the inland side of our entrenchment. They had until dark to do it and then all they had to do was cook, wash, shave, clean weapons and prepare uniforms. If there was any time left, they could eat something and sleep. If they were not on guard duty, that is.

Cogidumnos did not arrive at dawn but it was not too long afterwards when a considerable column of men approached from the north. In the centre, the chubby and impressive figure of Senator Saturninus strode along. Next to him was the taller, rangy shape of old King Bericos.

The toga is a garment which imparts dignity, particularly when it is adorned with the purple stripe of a Senator, but it does not look well on a man on a horse. The Senator was wearing his, rather than military garb, and I suspected that everyone else had to walk out of deference to his choice of attire. His clothing made the point that a Senator clearly outranked a King.

The Senator greeted me warmly and nodded with approval at the new tribunal. I received the familiar hairy, bear hug from Bericos and I had an army breakfast of bread, bacon and hot wine served all round. It nearly emptied our ration stock but we were on the move anyway, the auxiliaries could find their own. The Senator quite enjoyed lying on the damp grass, chewing bacon and acting like the old campaigner he had, perhaps, once been. A runner from one of the standing patrols gave us only enough time to clear away breakfast and brush down the Senator's toga before a large British force came into view from the south.

The main body halted at one of the auxiliaries' posts and, after a pause, a small group of horsemen rode slowly forward. Gold and silver glinted at their throats. I sent Titus and a number of legionaries to meet them. There was an unheard argument but Titus is of stubborn peasant stock, not particularly impressed with rank even in our own Army and not at all overawed by that of our enemies. The British eventually dismounted and the legionaries neatly took away their horses. The Celts walked to the tribunal around which we waited.

They were dressed and adorned in their best, faces washed and shaved, except for the usual British moustaches, and their hair combed and stiffened with lime. Their long swords had ornamented hilts and they each wore an expensive torc. They were led by a thin man with slanted shoulders and flickering eyes.

"I want to speak to King Bericos of the Atrebates," said this individual in an unpleasing nasal voice.

"You may speak to me," said the Senator in his resonant tones. "I am Senator Sentius Saturninus. Who are you?"

"I am King Buduoc of the Dobunni." Bericos stirred beside me.

"You mean King Buduoc of the northern Dobunni don't you?" he rumbled.

"Ah." Buduoc sounded almost pleasant. "You must be ex-King Bericos. Do you let the Romans speak for you, now?"

I pinned Bericos' toe down with my heel, a trick I had learned in the City Cohorts, and he just managed to keep his temper.

"King Bericos," intervened the Senator, "is my valued colleague and assistant, as you are that of Togodumnos, the so-called British High King. Aren't you?"

"The Dobunni…" Buduoc began.

"The northern Dobunni," Bericos again amended.

"The Dobunni," King Buduoc repeated more loudly, "decide where their loyalty lies. Now it lies with me alone. I choose to offer that loyalty to the Romans."

"In return," said the Senator smoothly, "for Roman confirmation of your throne, I suppose?"

"And the total independence of the Dobunni tribe," responded the shifty King.

"No alliance preserves total independence. If Rome offers you its protection from the British High King, you will be required to make a concrete contribution to the aims of Rome. In this case, the warriors you have with you will suffice."

I am sure I heard King Bericos chuckle while King Buduoc, in front of his chiefs, tried not to squirm. Having come this far, he could not back out now. Word of this interview would quickly reach the ears of the High King, either of its own accord or because the Senator made sure he was told. King Buduoc would not be here now if he was trusted by the High King. He was probably a dead man walking before he came to my signal station. He would most certainly be one if he left now without Roman protection.

"I agree," he said, simply.

His chiefs looked shocked at his tame collapse but he really had no choice.

"Good," said the Senator, beaming on the uncomfortable monarch, "your men, ah, and women, will be of great service in guarding certain installations and individuals. I, myself, have need of a small bodyguard, for example. They will not need those horses and chariots, at least not initially. They will be left here under the care of the Army. You will need to accompany me at all times to receive my orders. King Bericos will answer any other questions you may have."

He surveyed us all with a bright smile.

"A good morning's work, I think. Now, King Buduoc, kindly have your people assemble in front of this tribunal so that I can explain to them how things are going to be. No, I'm afraid it is not possible for you to join me on the tribunal. Only the commander is allowed there. Army custom, you know."

CHAPTER 69

▼

BRITAIN

The tribal capital of the Cantii was almost a complete wasteland of urban destruction. No one likes to live amongst swirling clouds of ash and spikes of charred wood and even the labourers unloading the river traffic at the forward base of the army preferred to sleep outside the blackened stumps of the city walls. The fields and buildings all the way along the Stura had been comprehensively destroyed by the retreating tribesmen and they had not hesitated to torch their own capital.

Legion II Augusta was in an entrenchment constructed to the usual standard design but it looked incomplete as there were very few tents available as yet. The legate commanding our Legion, Vespasian, had one of the few large tents which doubled as his operations room as well as being his sleeping quarters. Normally he would not have had the time to welcome a junior centurion but, it seemed, he had a special job for me.

"The British, Victorinus," he said, "are a problem."

I sometimes state the obvious myself in a briefing, but this seemed to be carrying things to ridiculous lengths.

"I can," he continued, "leave these Bodunni or Dobunni people to Senator Saturninus, but I need to keep Cogidumnos and King Bericos close at hand for later. They are supposed to be recruiting people from the Atrebates for the British levies but very few have come in and I do not want to turn them loose on their own."

This was clear. However much the two were disliked by their own tribe, it was just possible that, unsupervised, they could gather recruits for themselves without handing them over to Vespasian. Things would be different when the territory of the Atrebates was liberated from the High King's control and we could closely supervise our allies. I had an inkling of the part he had in mind for me.

"The build up of munitions is taking too long and is absorbing too much river transport and pack animals. We suspected it might, if we could not requisition local animals. Well, you've seen the countryside. So, Fleet transports are no longer being unloaded on the beaches. They are going to accompany the army when it advances to contact by sailing up the Thames estuary. They will be unloaded when we cross the Medu River and when we take Lud Dun on the Thames. This means that the general advance is imminent."

"And my century is to guard the British allies?"

"You are getting ahead of yourself, Centurion." Vespasian's open farmer's face had clouded. I reined in my tongue.

"Your century is not going to guard the Brits. as you have in the past. An auxiliary unit has that job. I need every legionary I have, however inexperienced. You are going to get some first-hand battle experience. You are going to guard the artillery."

I knew that each century in a Legion has a catapult mounted on a cart and attached to a limber for ammunition. The catapults are the smaller variety, capable of mechanically driving an iron and wood bolt some three hundred meters. Naturally, these machines far outrange the ordinary soldier's javelin and even the arrows of the specialist archers of Cohort I Hamiorum. The Legion should, therefore, have about sixty catapults. It was impossible for one century to guard them properly. Vespasian was watching me doing the mental calculation. His cheerful smile was back on his face.

"Do not despair, Centurion. You have, what?—eighty men in your century. But there are two artillerymen and a driver with each of the catapults. Use them for security when they are not actually in action. I intend to use all the catapults as one unit and you had better make sure you don't lose any."

"When do we advance to contact, sir?"

"Shortly. Very shortly."

"Would you tell me the order of march?"

"Not for dissemination below your rank, yes. Warships of the British Fleet in the estuary guarding our right flank and looking after the Fleet transports in convoy. The puddle-jumpers, that is, the loyal Batavian allies, on the coastline. On their left Legion XIV Gemina with Legion IX Hispana behind it. On their left, ourselves with Legion XX Valeria behind us. Finally, guarding our left flank and, hopefully, fighting off the chariots, the gallant men of the Roman cavalry."

Again, I had to give this some thought. The whole army had worked out that the British main army had not yet been confronted and that the most likely place for them to give battle would be on the Medu River which stretched across our intended line of advance.

"It sounds, sir, as if the Batavians, Legion XIV Gemina and ourselves will close up to the east bank of the Medu ahead of the rest of the army. The puddle-jumpers have got their own equipment and techniques for river-crossings, but they are lightly armed. Which of the heavy Legions will cross first?"

He gave me a beatific smile.

"The one with the most boats and the shallowest water," he said.

We were going to be upstream of Legion XIV Gemina.

"If there are no more probing questions, Centurion? No? Then you may go."

Mail had caught up with Legion II Augusta and I was sent over to the aquilfer's office, a small tent next to the eagle's shrine. His clerks were still checking the tin labels and picking open the stitching on the mail bags, so I went in to pay my respects. He was immaculately dressed, as always, closely shaved and his hair oiled.

"That was a close run thing, over the water." He recognised me at once.

"It was the eagles appearing around the tribunal which turned the tide with the mutineers," I said, truthfully.

"The tide would not have run in so fast if certain insults, directed at the Emperor's messenger, had not created a following wind."

We both laughed and he offered me a chair. I told him about the signal station and the surrender of the first major British force. He told me that the registration of marriages was complete and that large numbers of families were on the move from the other frontiers. He had heard from Pytheas that contracts for the leasing of shipping had been signed.

We spoke of the forthcoming battle with the main British army. Despite Buduoc's defection, we had no doubt that there was going to be one. The Cassi family had not risen to secure the position of High King over several generations by worrying over the treachery of some petty monarch. The Cantii are also British and, surprised and unsupported, were fighting like furies. The High King had obviously missed his opportunity of fighting us on the beaches but his main army was intact and determined.

"What do you think of the influence of the Druids?" I asked the custodian of the spiritual life of the Legion. The acquilfer paused for thought.

"I have met several of them," he replied slowly, "educated and intelligent men. Because of their position as repositories of knowledge in a society where writing is discouraged, they bind together the Celtic nations. We Romans must divide to rule. The Order of Druids will have to be destroyed."

"To prevent them encouraging rebellions in our Celtic Provinces?"

"Not only that," said our Legion's aquilfer, "but they will never accept the divinity of certain of our Emperors, and that affects the hold the Roman Army has over its soldiers of Celtic descent. They must go."

I did not tell him that I had serious doubts about the divinity of our Commanders in Chief myself. It depends on how one views divinity I suppose. Traditionally, Roman gods make mistakes but are divine by birth and by success. The Emperor Claudius had been born into the right family and the Invasion of Britain might well provide him with significant success. Our disabled Uncle Claudius might, therefore, be on the verge of qualifying for divinity. No wonder the Druids had reservations.

A clerk brought a sack of mail for my century and I took my leave of the aquilfer.

"See you on the Medu River," he said as I left.

Most of my young soldiers got letters from their parents. Two were addressed to Fangs who received them with a gappy grin. They were addressed in the same hand, his wife, he told me, now arrived in Gesoriacum. There was nothing for Titus who pretended that it did not matter. I got a letter from my brother. Silence settled all over the Camp.

Marcus greeted me, hoped I was in good health. I was now an uncle for the second time. Unfortunately his lovely wife had passed away at childbirth despite the best efforts of the Greek doctors. Due to his distraction, the business had suffered. My personal bank account was safe but he did not now have money to pay me my share of the business, a matter we must discuss as soon as I could travel home. He was now actively tackling the business issues and, after proper mourning, he would marry again.

It took me a little while to absorb the news. Death during or shortly after childbirth is, of course, common. However good the doctors, and Marcus would have had the best, some such deaths are unavoidable. I could not picture my brother's wife as a drained corpse. She would always be a vibrant, laughing girl, one I had betrayed. She had, I think, found love and security with my brother for the rest of her short life. I hope so. The pain I felt then is still mixed with shame. Only Marcus has nothing to reproach himself for. Typically he was worried about not paying adequate attention to the business and endangering my interest in it. My only concern was that he was worried. I wrote back with condolences and reassurances, the trivia which somehow assists in the healing process. Late that day, I collected up the letters written by my men and delivered them to the aquilfer's clerk. We then got down to some frantic packing.

It is fifty kilometers from the remains of the tribal capital of the Cantii to the Medu River and I had to get sixty artillery carts down a single upgraded native road in two days. It had been straightened, resurfaced with wood and gravel and the undergrowth cleared back, but it was nowhere near normal military standard. The British had used it for local traffic and farm vehicles as there is a much drier main road running along the high ground to the left of our advance. Even with all the work put into it by the military, I was glad that the infantry had been banned from marching on the new surface and that the artillery took precedence over all other wheeled vehicles. The huge wagons loaded with bridging equipment had to follow our light carts as best they could.

For the artillery of Legion II Augusta, things went well. The last afternoon, in Camp five kilometers short of the Medu River, I congratulated myself hat I had only lost one piece. A cart's wheel had collapsed and I had had to leave its crew, under guard, fitting the spare. I thought then that they might catch up. We had seen no sign of the enemy during the day although the cavalry on our left had lost a few men in petty skirmishes. I left Titus in charge of the artillery park and I rode back down the road, the surface now torn up by wheels and broken by sharp hooves. We had been lucky it had not rained.

The sun was sinking behind my right shoulder when I found the cart. It was still on its wheels although the horses had gone, of course. There was no sign of the driver. The two artillerymen and my four soldiers had all died close to the road. Their bodies had been stripped naked and their weapons had been taken. They had not been mutilated much although one, a soldier who must have been particularly difficult to kill, was more or less hacked to pieces. Even then, there was sufficient left for me to recognise the old scars of a particularly savage mule bite on the corpse's shoulder.

The catapult was smashed and the ammunition had all been removed from the limber. I did try to move the cart but without any proper traces I could not get my horse to pull it. In the end, after a struggle, I simply set fire to it and rode back. Titus was on the point of leaving the Camp with a search party to look for me. I told him the bad news which the young legionaries seemed to have been almost expecting. Titus had had to get permission from the Camp Commandant to leave Camp. So I had to report to the Commandant and receive the tongue-lashing I was expecting for going out alone to do something the Legion's rear-guard should have done.

With those gleaming black eyes fixed on mine in the lamp light, Anicius Maximus then told me that the army would reach the Medu early the following morning. Scouts had reported vast numbers of enemy campfires on the other bank although not apparently grouped in any sort of order. The army would set off before dawn and the Legion would go straight into the attack without giving time for the British to redeploy. The artillery was to protect the bridging teams and I was to protect the artillery. I was to have the artillery ready to move well before dawn. If I let him down, he would take a personal interest in my future career, not to say my survival. The centurion of the rear-guard was waiting to see the Commandant as I left.

CHAPTER 70

▼

BRITAIN

Being High King of Britain involves a lot of entertaining and Togodumnos was doing his best. All the chiefs of the Catuvellauni and the Trinovantes were there, as well as most of the chiefs of the Atrebates. The chiefs of the Cantii were all dead except for one, and she was fighting out in front of the army's right flank. Every other leader in the army, however junior, wanted to be with the High King, to be encouraged by him, to eat and drink with him and to boast to him. Caratacos and Ceri did their utmost to shoulder some of the burden, making their rounds of the campfires, joking, slapping backs, sharing food, but it was the High King that everyone wanted to talk with. Togodumnos, grey-faced and shambling, tried to be everywhere, talking down the power of the Roman army, laughing scornfully over the cowardice of the Dobunni, praising the fierceness of the Cantii, pointing out the might and the valour of the British army.

Fox called a halt. The Cassi family, he declared, must have some private time for religion. He would go with them to a nearby sacred grove to commune with Bel. Togodumnos pretended reluctance but knew he must have rest. It was too late. In full view of the army, the ashen-faced High King pressed a great fist to his chest, stumbled and toppled like a stricken oak. Life still flickered as Caratacos and Ceri raised his shoulders. He could not speak but he smiled at them both before the light in his eyes went out. Stunned chiefs by the hundred assembled around the little group. Fox stood.

"The High King is dead," he pronounced. He looked east towards the enemy and back at them. "Who is the High King?"

They were experienced men and women who knew the dangers of delay. They were also the only people who had a say in the election of a new High King. There was no hesitation.

"Caratacos," they said.

He stood. Ceri stood beside him, eyes wet and the High King's sword in his hands. From memory, led by Fox, the ancient oath was recited in the gathering dusk by the assembled chiefs of the army of Britain.

"We will keep faith unless the sky fall and crush us, or the earth open and swallow us, or the sea rise and overwhelm us."

The oath concluded, Caratacos placed his hand on the sword's hilt. The horned helmet of wisdom was not with them, so he bent and placed his hand on the cool forehead of his brother instead. He straightened and faced the assembly. Britain had a new High King.

He looked at the pale, hard faces and the intent, light-coloured eyes and he thought he saw uncertainty behind them. There was no time for uncertainty.

"You may go home," he said, and the ripples spread outwards from him as if he were a stone dropped in a pond. "You have nothing to prove here. I know you all. You are brave and skilled in battle. I am the High King. I give you permission to go."

All movement in the crowd ceased. The intentness increased. The faintest of smiles lit the faces of the quickest and most intelligent. An evening breeze stirred the woven woolen clothing.

"I know that you are the mightiest warriors in Britain. Why should I not? I have fought against some of you myself. I have also fought beside you all, in my time."

He glanced at the darkening sky in the east and then back at the hundreds of leaders gathered around him.

"But this battle will be different. We will be facing the biggest slave-gathering machine the world has ever seen. No captives will be ransomed back to their families as is done in civilized warfare. Prisoners of war will be dragged to a market-place where pot-bellied, weaponless citizens will buy them with bits of silver. Free people, valiant warriors, will scrub the floors and nurse the children of those not prepared to die for their beliefs.

"Give up your freedom, say the Romans. Give us your land, cast aside your families and your religion. Come and work for us, in our fields, in our houses and deep in our mines and, when you have produced another set of children, do you know what we will do for them? We will make them into Roman soldiers to go out and rape more nations.

"A great Roman army has been forced to cast itself onto our shores like a stranded sea monster and, even now, is waddling towards us, eating up the land of the Cantii. Our brothers and sisters are attacking it, tearing off chunks of its blubber and slowing it down, but they are too few to stop it by themselves. Still, they have given us time. We can all go home now. Enjoy a few more months of freedom with our families before the slavers and the land-grabbers and the tax collectors come to steal our property and drag away our children.

"They are very efficient these Romans. Like little armoured snails they have crawled all over Europe, sucking the life out of the nations and making their children into more little armoured snails. They have done this from Asia to Gaul, to free Celts like us. They are so good at it they are frightening. Don't they frighten you?

"No? Well, you have my permission to go, if they do. We have the Romans penned behind the Medu River with our Ocean behind them. We are the barrier standing between these aliens and our homes. We could simply turn and walk away, other nations have done so. Still others have fought and been defeated in battle. It does not have to happen to us. We don't have to stay here with our friends and fight. We could fight as individuals in the doorways of our homes instead. We have time to walk away. Or, we could remember who we are and where we are. We could stay and smash the head of this reluctant monster and throw it back into the Ocean as our ancestors have done twice before.

"In any case, I am staying. I cannot leave the Cantii still struggling alone with the entire Roman Army. The Cantii and I will fight. Here. Anyone who stays with me will have to obey me, the elected High King. And I will redeploy the army of Britain as is necessary. No chief, however well-born or brave, will be allowed to argue or disobey. Anyone who thinks this is an infringement on a Celt's personal freedom may leave now. In the Roman Army they don't have that option. They mutiny and yet they are still forced to cross the Ocean. Those individuals who surrender to us will be treated properly, they do not want to be here in the first place. Those Romans who do not surrender to us will be smashed, here, on the Medu, by the High King and the free Celts standing with him."

There was no uncertainty now visible about the leaders of the army of Britain.

"Who is staying?" demanded the High King. He received his answer.

"So be it."

As they streamed away to their units, Caratacos put his arm round Ceri's wide, thin shoulders and hugged his nephew.

"Time for mourning later, Ceri. You've still got the chariots on the right. Find me Chief Ena of the Cantii or Segonax."

"I'm here, sir." The young soldier looked five years older since Caratacos had last seen him, and they had been a hard five years. "Chief Ena sent me with a message."

"I'm very sorry for your troubles and I regret interrupting," Brigit's high, accented Irish voice was like a blessing. "What can I do?"

"Brigit, please wait," Caratacos managed a smile. "Segonax, what is the message?"

"Columns of Roman cavalry, more than we've ever seen before, moving west along the high ground towards the Medu. They are not scouting, they are advancing. We cannot see what is to the north of them but we can hear the ground vibrating. Nothing to the south of the cavalry. We are sure it is a general advance by the enemy but not along the main Lud Dun road. They must have their right on the coast. I came as fast as I could but they should have been here by now."

"Well done. They will have stopped for the night. We'll see them at dawn."

"If they are moving between the high ground and the north coast," said Fox, "they may still try to cross the Medu lower down."

"And we haven't got anyone close to the river mouth where the river is tidal."

"That's right, Ceri," said Caratacos, "but we are going to have. I cannot move the infantry easily at night and the cavalry are in the correct place, behind the infantry. Ceri, get back to your chariots and move them around the rear of the army. Position them on my left. Destroy any attempt to cross the tidal stretch of the river."

"When Ceri moves, that will leave a gap on your right," Brigit said, as if to herself. "The Roman cavalry are heading for that point."

"Correct," said the High King. "Fortunately, we have Britain's experts at handling Roman cavalry right here. Segonax, the Cantii must be almost exhausted..."

"No sir, we are just warming up."

"...so," continued Caratacos, buoyed by the dirty young soldier's optimism, "the Cantii must fill the gap on my right. My compliments to Chief Ena and she is to fall back to this bank of the Medu and prevent the enemy cavalry from crossing. Tell all the Cantii already here to assemble on the right of the army and report to Ena. All right? Go."

He turned back to his nephew and smiled grimly.

"Are you still here, Ceri?"

"What about Uncle Togodumnos? Perhaps, Fox..." His voice tailed away. The Druid did not move.

"Fox cannot be spared. I intend to be wherever I am needed tomorrow so Fox commands the cavalry. The late High King's spirit is in the Otherworld. We do not have time for the proper disposal of his body now."

"Perhaps, here, at least, the Irish can help." Brigit's pale face was even whiter in the descending darkness. "We are not the British High King's subjects but we are fellow Celts, we have eaten and sung together and we have exchanged gifts. My troopers knew and liked Togodumnos and would be honoured to escort his body to Camulodunon. Niall will lead them. He is a Druid and will confer with Fox before they leave tonight."

"We thank you, Brigit. Will you wait at Camulodunon?"

"Oh no! You don't get rid of me that easily. I am here as an observer for High King Conaire Mor, and 'observe' is what I am going to do. Don't worry, I won't be in your way. Just make sure I can report to him that you won."

"What else?" the High King asked a smiling Fox.

"Perhaps a prayer?"

"Yes. Where is that sacred grove you mentioned?"

CHAPTER 71

▼

BRITAIN

Before dawn, getting the artillery on the move was a waking nightmare. Three of the drivers had managed to desert, despite the sentries, and several of the artillerymen developed vague but serious symptoms of illness. Two of the first carts on the move managed to collide with one another and got their wheels tangled. I was pleased to see that none of my legionaries became disconcerted by the uproar from their seniors and supposedly betters. Police training does have valuable spin offs. They took over the driving of the driverless carts, unsympathetically dismissed the whining of the supposedly sick, calmly ignored the clamour of the crews involved in the collision and lifted one of the carts to untangle them. I intervened only where necessary and not to reason with the unreasonable. My boot connected with more than one backside and Senator Asiaticus' vinestick saw good service.

By the time the heralds demanded for the third time "Are you ready?" we were, in fact, lined up in order of march, with my legionaries making sure that no one discovered urgent business elsewhere. We were tired, irritable, weighed down with armour and weapons, but we were ready.

Once we started to move west, it got better. Light began to touch the swaying tops of the huge wagons of bridging equipment rumbling along to our left. Soon, on both sides of the wheeled vehicles, forests of glinting javelins points seemed to bounce over marching dark blocks of infantry. Here and there, a helmet of a mounted officer reflected the backlight from the east. Long shadows began to appear in front of us. The ground shook. I could not see the cavalry to our left but I knew it was there, just as surely as I knew that, away to the right, Roman warships cruised beside the advancing army. The feeling of being embedded in an irresistible and single-minded force took hold. No one was now looking for an escape route. The nagging voices of the centurions and the optios died away.

I relaxed in the saddle, legs dangling, dust gritting between my teeth, and looked around. I could now see the nodding head of my horse and distinguish each of the artillery carts I was responsible for. I took personal stock. My chin-strap was tight and I would have to loosen it before the action. Shouting through clenched teeth is an artform I have never mastered. For now, it held my helmet with the transverse crest firmly in place. My mailshirt of silvered iron was already lightly coated in dust and I was wearing two tunics of red cloth, for cushioning, under it. I had considered wearing my light mail vest as well but had decided against the extra weight and the potential for permanent damage to the nipples. My baldric was over my right shoulder, on top of my red scarf still worn as a sash. My sword, still the short legionary pattern weapon I had first been issued with, now hung on my left side in accordance with my rank. I wore a wrist guard on both arms as I had no intention of being encumbered with a shield on the approach march. On the battlefield, I calculated, a spare shield would not be hard to find. Although saddles are hard on the thighs, I had decided not to wear breeches. I did not intend to fight on horseback, the animals are too unpredict-able, and soldiers, even on the battlefield, sometimes have to answer the calls of nature. No one was going to kill me because I had breeches tangling my ankles. I made do with a loincloth. My hobnailed shoes were comfortably laced, my money was safely buried where I could find it after the battle, my battered vine-stick was in my hand. I was ready for the Celts.

Ahead, there was a low persistent murmuring like beehives in the summer that grew in volume as the army advanced. I saw heads around me craning forward, towards the sound, and I jogged forward to the head of the artillery column. Sun-light gleamed behind the army as it crested a rise overlooking the grey snake of the Medu River and Roman trumpets blasted shatteringly right across the front. On the other side of the river a great black mass lay across miles of dark grey countryside. From it, a dull reverberating roar rose, spiked with the menacing snarls of the Celtic horns they call carnyx. We had found the main British army and they could see us outlined against the rising sun.

The voices of centurions and optios rose again, ordering, directing, chivvying units towards their intended positions. Guides, sent out overnight, rose from the summer grass and called forward their charges. Our guide, magnificent in full battle order, his black eyes glistening in the level rays of the sun, was none other than Anicius Maximus, Commandant of Legion II Augusta. He had a brief instruction for me.

"The tribune responsible for the Legion's artillery has had an accident. You know what it is supposed to do. You command the artillery. Any problems, see me."

Without pause, the army lapped over the crest and poured down towards the river bank, the artillery rocking easily along, the wagons of the bridging teams noisy with swearing drivers and screaming brakes. I loosened my chinstrap and snatched a glance at the enemy. The vast dark mass seemed to be convulsing, its edges advancing and retreating, the noise level grew to thunderous proportions. Its edges were far back from the other bank of the river but roughly aligned with it. The British general—High King, or whatever—had left plenty of space on the far bank to be out of our missile range and to give room to develop a mass charge.

Before the first of the huge wagons had ground to a halt, the artillery carts were turning into position, teams facing uphill, catapults pointing out over the tailgates. Artillerymen dropped to the ground, checked arcs of fire and ordered adjustments of position. Then the wheels were chocked into position, the limbers opened and weapons readied. While the artillerymen fiddled with the intricate mechanism of the catapults and laid their ammunition to hand, I wheeled my legionaries and spaced them in front of the artillery, facing the enemy. I then dismounted and tied off my horse to the wheel of a cart and walked along the line.

Titus and Fangs were walking up and down behind the legionaries, talking to them, joking, encouraging them. I walked in front of them and watched their faces, nice and white for the most part, with their eyes scanning the mass across the river. One of them, though, had a decidedly greenish pallor and, to his embarrassment, its owner suddenly vomited onto the grass in front of him. I was reminded of the gladiators' changing rooms at the arena. With my back to the river, I removed my helmet, the sun just catching it, and addressed my men.

"You are all young soldiers with long military careers ahead of you and you have all probably got the thickest of skulls under those legionary helmets. You will hardly feel the sword blows from those weaklings across the river. However, I am much older than you and have probably got fewer brains to scramble."

There were a few wan smiles.

"So, I am now going to do something pretty indelicate to protect those brains. You may turn away if it affects your sensibilities."

Naturally, they did not turn away but their eyes were all turned to me and not on the threatening mass across the water. I whipped off my loin cloth and tied it round my head before replacing my helmet on its new cushion and retying the chinstrap. I then turned and faced the enemy.

It was not a real laugh behind me, but it was definitely something that approximated one. Titus and Fangs kept the mood going and I could look to my left to see how the bridging teams were getting on. I looked straight into the black eyes of the Commandant. He held my gaze for a moment and then turned away without comment.

He had left a space between the artillery position and the parking place of the wagons. It was through this space that the assault cohort would lead the advance across the bridge. Presently, it swarmed with men of the bridging teams. I was almost shocked to see that already a finger of bridge-construction was stretching out into the current. It was being made by a series of small boats being put into the water side-by-side and anchored by sacks of stones thrown into the water upstream. The anchor ropes were being lengthened or shortened, to bring the boats into alignment with one another, and they were then tied off. Sections of planking were already being laid over the boats and tied to them, to bind the boats together and to form a walkway for the infantry.

Behind the wagons and the artillery park, a formation of white-faced legionaries was being marshaled into a column; the assault cohort, five hundred strong. Upstream, beyond the wagons, a flotilla of little boats was being placed on the water by hundreds of strangely equipped auxiliaries. I recognised Cohort I Hamiorum, the archers.

There was so much of interest going on that I needed the loud clearing of the throat from the Commandant, and his fierce glare, to remind me that I had things to do.

The artillerymen were all standing on the carts looking at me and I felt my cheeks redden. I walked down the line checking with each crew that they were satisfied with their position, they were all well within range of the intended bridgehead on the other bank and that their weapons and ammunition were ready. I reported all ready and Annicius Maximus, as usual economical on words, told me to carry on. I told my legionaries to sit down in front of the artillery in case of an accidental discharge or a broken bowstring and took my position on top of the centre cart.

The noise on the other bank had decreased to a continuous rumble, punctuated by the braying of an occasional carnyx. The bridge was halfway across the river and to the left, upstream; Cohort I Hamiorum was on the water.

"Make ready!" I shouted.

It sounded to me like the squeak of a mouse but the artillerymen bent to their windlasses. The ratchets clattered as the shuttles on sixty catapults dragged back the bowstrings. The legionaries on the ground involuntarily hunched their shoulders. I did not hear the one bowstring break but I did see the end flip forward and an artilleryman calmly unwrap a new one from round his waist. Ignoring his repair work, I inflated my lungs again.

"Load!"

Iron headed bolts rattled in the channels and their wooden shafts nocked to the straining bowstrings.

"From the right. One ranging shot each. Shoot!"

It occurred to me, too late, that I should be walking behind the artillery checking the fall of shot and making sure that range adjustment were being properly made. The range adjustments are made by raising or lowering the rear end of the channel in accordance with a graduated scale cut into a vertical bar at the back. It was too late for me to personally supervise each piece, but I could watch the strike of the bolts. Most landed well onto the far bank. A few splashed into the water. Several of the artillerymen had their hands raised. I had a second chance. Jumping down, I went to each of them in turn, pretended to understand their explanations of the range adjustments they had made, checked that the bridging parties were still out of harm's way and allowed one further shot each. I then went to report to the Commandant.

Glancing across the water at the enemy, I noticed that their leaders were still holding the tribesmen back from the water's edge and our archers on the river had tried a few ranging shots of their own. The sun illuminated the massed ranks of colourfully dressed Celts as they surged about and waved their swords. Suddenly, as if on a signal, the enemy's heads turned to their left, looking downstream towards the sea. A few individuals ran out of the crowd as if to see better. There was a partial surge in that direction but it stopped in a flurry of shouting and horn-blowing.

"What was all that about?" I wondered aloud next to the Commandant.

"I would think," he said, smiling grimly, "that the loyal Batavian allies have got something to do with it."

A young senior officer, a tribune, slid off his horse next to us.

"All right, Commandant," he said, airily, "I'm here. I'll take over the artillery now."

"Where have you been?" growled the Commandant ungraciously, "I heard you had had an accident."

"Yes. My knock-kneed horse fell over and trapped me under it. When they got around to dragging it off me, I had to go and change my uniform. Sorry I'm late."

Anicius Maximus raised his face to the sky with his eyes pressed shut. Silently, he extended an arm and pointed the Tribune at the artillery carts.

"They have been sited and ranged," I offered, suppressing a smile. The youth had no such inhibitions. With a grin and a wink, he strutted off.

The bridge had almost reached the other bank and still streams of men clambered cautiously along the wooden walkway carrying the small boats, coils of rope, net anchors and sections of planking. The working party at the forward end had started looking nervously at the mass of armed warriors surging slightly like the tide just out of our arrow range. There was now no virtually no noise.

"Make ready!" It was the fastidious young Tribune on the centre artillery cart. I hurried back to stand behind my men. The assault cohort got ready. Downstream, to our right, a succession of deep roars from the other bank reminded me of the chariot races at the circus. Our bridge-builders scampered back across their structure. The archers rocked in their little boats upstream.

"Load!" shouted the Tribune in a slightly strangled voice above me.

"Advance!" ordered the Senior Centurion of the assault cohort in a voice like iron and Roman trumpets shivered the air. It was answered by a mighty bellow from the Celts across the river. I could actually see their leaders pushing the enthusiastic throngs back into some sort of order. Led by the standard bearer and the Senior Centurion, the armoured legionaries stepped onto the bridge and picked their way delicately across the creaking structure. The new bridge heaved and strained as it took the weight.

Dozens of Celts ran forward and began whirling their arms. Small splashes appeared in the water around the bridge and the legionaries raised their shields. One of them fell into the water with a considerable splash and did not reappear.

"Slingers!" shouted the Tribune to his artillerymen. "Do not shoot."

He was quite right. No catapult crew could expect to hit single individuals at that range and, although we had plenty of ammunition, it was not unlimited. The slingers, on the other hand, had no ammunition limitations. Legion II Augusta erupted in a cheer as the shieldless standard bearer and the Senior Centurion reached the other bank. Another cohort formed up in column on our side of the river.

Moving fairly briskly now, the assault cohort shuffled across the creaking bridge bent behind their shields and carrying bundles of javelins and, no doubt, trying not to think of their chances of survival if they were knocked off the bridge into deep water. The tiny bridgehead on the far side started to expand. Little splashes marked the water next to the straining bridge and another legionary went in. One hand remained above the water for a while, gripping the side of a boat, but eventually it disappeared under the surface. Still the enemy did not charge. If it were not for their far-too-active slingers, I would now be wondering if they were afraid.

The Senior Centurion on the other side was frantically positioning his men as they streamed off the bridge, pushing and swiping at them with his stick. He did not think the Celts were afraid. He knew a charge was coming. He had almost his full five hundred men over. The standard bearer of the next cohort stepped onto the bridge.

The Celts charged. Like the shadow of a cloud rushing down a mountainside, the enemy surged towards the little bridgehead. The leading edge of the charge became a little ragged as the faster runners accelerated in front of the rest, but the mass swooped with frightening speed towards the armoured fist we had placed on the other side of the river. The legionaries, clusters of javelins driven into the turf next to their feet, raised their shields and braced themselves to launch their missiles. The archers stood in their boats and strained their bowstrings.

"Shoot!" shouted the youthful Tribune and, with the crack of bowstrings and the thump of shuttles, sixty iron-headed bolts soared over the water. I did not hear the order but flurries of arrows speckled the sky in front of the archers' boats. The assault legionaries launched their javelins.

The front ranks of the enemy shuddered and, in places, crumpled, but the momentum was huge.

"Reload and shoot!"

Bolts rattled in the channels, ratchets clattered. The archers, on their unsteady platforms, were shooting from the river as fast as they could draw string.

Some legionaries did get off a second volley of javelins. Most simply drew their swords and braced. The impact must have been violent and would have been overwhelming had not gaps opened up in the enemy mass due to the speed of the charge and the rain of missiles. The Roman lines staggered and sagged under the force of the collision, the legionaries fighting desperately for their lives and to stay on their feet.

"Advance!" I recognised the Commandant's voice. The follow-up cohort had paused on the bridge, not from fear, but from the stunning spectacle in front of them. The line of legionaries jerked into motion again, stepping quickly along the quaking footway.

The bridgehead was so compact, and the enemy masses so huge, that only a part of the British army could close with the Romans. Large bodies of warriors lapped around the bridgehead and spilled into the shallow water around the end of the bridge itself. The leading soldiers of the follow-up cohort engaged the enemy in the water with their javelins, exactly as if they were spearing fish. These fish, however, were lethal. Whirling blades cut the legs from under Roman soldiers and they died in the churning, muddy water along with the tribesmen. More and more legionaries got ashore and the Senior Centurion was everywhere, pushing them into gaps as his men fell. Those waiting for a gap to open launched javelins over the heads of those in front of them.

The crack and thump of the catapults was almost continuous and another cohort was forming up in column but some of the little boats upstream were being paddled back to our bank. The archers were out of arrows. A gap had opened in the Celtic mass around the bridgehead. The ring of warriors nearest to the legionaries were still closely engaged and resisting any attempt to replace them. Those further back, unable to come to grips with the Romans, but suffering from the hail of missiles, tended to slowly draw back from the fighting and only to rush in when tribesmen in the front ranks were killed. Each side appeared to be able to replace losses. It all depended on whether our missile supply held out and whether our bridge held together.

The Commandant appreciated this first. Before allowing the next cohort to advance, he sent the reluctant bridging teams out onto the bridge to tighten down the bindings on boats and footway. Legionary dispatch riders were sent back to Legion XX Valeria in our rear for more artillery ammunition and spare parts. There was nothing we could do for Cohort I Hamiorum, they would have to bring forward their own reserve of arrows. Fortunately, there was no shortage of javelins.

Quite suddenly, the British masses rolled back from the river. A few tribesmen did not disengage in time and were killed, but most moved swiftly out of javelin range unharmed.

"Stop shooting!"

I had almost forgotton the Tribune in the cart above me. Again, he was right. Bolts would simply be wasted at this stage. Cheering broke out and the surviving legionaries across the river slumped over their shields.

"Repair your weapons."

I was beginning to respect this Tribune. The artillerymen began to replace bowstrings and to screw down the torsion bars of wound gut. Then, without any further order, they started an ammunition count.

The column of legionaries waiting to go across had still not started to move when word spread that the First Cohort would be the next to go. This formation is traditionally the most prestigious in a Legion and is led by the Chief Centurion. In this case, it became obvious that the Legate himself, and the aquilfer, were going too. The Commandant had a brief word with Vespasion before the First Cohort advanced. I strained to eavesdrop.

"Whoever is in charge over there," said the Commandant, "has got some idea of generalship."

"Because he held them back out of missile range until we got that cohort over?"

"And because he has pulled them back again. He can't use the full weight of his army against that little bridgehead. He wants us to expand it, then he'll charge again."

"Well Commandant, you know what they say. 'In the first charge, the Celts are more than men. In the second charge, they are less than women.' I should have an easy time of it."

"I think that was a quotation from a dead man, sir. Good luck."

I jumped up and grabbed the Tribune's sleeve.

"The bridgehead is going to expand. You might want to reposition."

I looked around while he thought about that.

Astonishingly, it was already early afternoon. Most of the bridging teams' wagons had been pulled back from the river bank, leaving piles of spare equipment which was being neatly stacked. Beyond, the archers were still on the river although without any present targets for their reduced supplies of arrows. The First Cohort was bustling importantly across the bridge following the aquilfer to resounding cheers from behind me. Vespasion in his shining cuirass was close behind the eagle, stepping cautiously over the frayed ropes and splintered planking. A fourth cohort of legionaries, overtaken by the First Cohort, was still formed in column waiting their turn to cross.

On the other side of the river, like a crowd at the sports, the vast masses of the enemy sat on the grass and cheered their slingers who darted about among the many bodies littering the ground in front of the Roman position and launched their primitive missiles. Was it my imagination, or had the numbers of British decreased? I could not tell for sure. The roars we had heard coming from the other bank downstream of our position had died away. I could even hear a few birds singing.

"Right!" shouted the artillery Tribune. "Water and feed your horses."

Again, the order made perfect sense. We did not know the extent of the expanded bridgehead yet and we were going to be busy enough shortly. I found I was ravenously hungry. Cold bacon, bread baked as hard as a biscuit and muddy water, a meal fit for an Emperor. My soldiers all laughed and joked as they ate, sitting on the flattened grass and watching the strangely domestic scene of the artillery horses sucking river water.

There was a murmur from the waiting cohort behind us and the hollow sound of horses trotting on the grass. The Commandant rose and saluted the army's second in command, and Legate of Legion XX Valeria, Hosideus Geta. He had a small escort of swarthy, frizzy-haired cavalry, dressed in bleached wool and armed with long lances, Mauretanians I supposed. Geta stared across the river, barely acknowledging the Commandant's salute, then he dismounted.

"I take it that that is Legate Vespasian commanding over there," he made it more a statement than a question and the Commandant simply made no reply. Geta's eyes swiveled round and looked properly at him for the first time.

"Right. My artillery and bridging train are right behind me. I need to confer with your commanding officer."

"Have you sent ammunition for our artillery?" the Commandant's question was blunt and a faint flush appeared on the brown cheeks of the Hero of Mauretania.

"I have none to spare, Commandant, and your artillery seems to be under-employed anyway. They will have to make do with what you've got for the time being."

"There are many Celts who would not agree that my artillery has been under-employed," Anicius Maximus did not appear to be impressed with Hosideus Geta. "What was that noise we have been hearing downstream?"

"Oh, the puddle-jumpers got across on their rafts and air-bags when the tide was turning. They were attacked by the barbarian chariots, hundreds of them apparently. Absolute carnage, I'm glad to say."

"I take it that the Batavians did well?"

"Didn't kill many crews but slaughtered the horses. They've made a barricade of the wrecked chariots and are waiting for the next turn of the tide for their reinforcements. Now, I've got to see Vespasian and I'm sure he has no time to come here."

"Yes," said the Commandant, fingering his chin which looked freshly-shaved. "Barricade, you say?"

He looked sharply around and caught me with my mouth full.

"Centurion Victorinus."

I scrambled to my feet trying to simultaneously dispose of the food, empty my drinking water out of my helmet, hide the loin-cloth wrapped around my scalp and brush off the grass from my tunic. My antics seemed to cause some innocent merriment among the onlookers. I vaguely heard the Commandant issuing a string of orders, fortunately not to me.

"Legate Geta," said he, fixing me with a stern gaze, "needs to go across to confer with the commander. Your century is under-employed" he emphasised the word without any sign of amusement. "Escort the Legate across and space out your men on the bridge as you do. They will be passing equipment across hand-to-hand until the Legate is ready to come back. Clear?"

The bridge swayed underfoot and the current swirled and sucked around the boats. We trod with care over the creaking structure, my men with their shields slung over their backs. Closer to the shore, the body of an archer was pressed against the bridge by the current and there were pathetic heaps of sodden clothing and wet metal in the muddy shallows under the bank.

The bridgehead was very crowded with some eighteen hundred men, dead and alive, packed into a small section of riverbank. The centurions, directed by the harsh, carrying voice of the Chief Centurion, struggled to sort the legionaries into sections of responsibility and to have the wounded attended to behind the raised shields of their comrades. The whiz and crack of the slingers' stones was continuous. Geta and I pushed our way to where the three cohort standards were planted around the Legion's eagle. A stone pinged off the metal bird as we approached.

"Hosideus Geta!" Vespasian greeted the army's second-in-command with a cheery smile and gave me a brief nod. "Welcome to wild Britain."

A stone rang on his helmet. He barely blinked.

"I don't think much of your legionary engineers," Geta's smile was a little strained. "That bridge is shaky and you haven't even got half your Legion across yet."

"Ah," said Vespasian. "Well that is where you can help me Legate. If your people can bridge the river just downstream of here, Legion XX Valeria can cross and link up with the right of my bridgehead. That will give us two bridges in case one fails and double the size of our bridgehead for the break out. It will also give us double the amount of artillery support because these barbarians are going to try a massed charge again before dark. I'll bring the rest of my Legion over tonight."

"Can you hold them with what you've got?"

"Have to," Vespasian remarked cheerfully. He looked at me. "How goes it, Centurion?"

"The Commandant's compliments, sir. He's sending over a whole lot of palisade stakes to keep off the chariots. And there is one other thing."

"Thank old Maximus for me, will you. Not that we've seen any chariots or cavalry, yet. What was the other thing?"

"If you can mark the limits of the bridgehead at last light. We will fire a few ranging shots and set the artillery to shoot safely even at night."

"That's ridiculous," Geta exclaimed. "These barbarians won't attack at night."

"Normally, Legate, I would agree with you." I thought then that Vespasian would make a great politician. "But these Brits seem very determined and, even an occasional shot will discourage any sneak attacks on the bridgehead."

A stone, its force almost spent, smacked into Geta's upper arm, making him flinch. Vespasian turned to me.

"At dusk, I will plant a cohort standard at the right and left limits of the bridgehead. You can try your ranging shots then. What about the second bridge, Geta?"

"Tonight. Legion XX Valeria will bridge the river downstream of you and I will lead it across at first light."

"Fair enough," said Vespasian. "See you in the morning."

Substantial piles of sharp palisades stakes had grown on the bank above the bridge. Several entrenching tools had been tossed on top of them. My men were already withdrawing back across the river, one of them being more or less carried. We followed smartly behind, stones splashing and rattling around us.

The Senior Centurion of the next cohort was waiting impatiently and we had barely stepped off the bridge when he ordered his men forward. A Mauretanian led forward Hosideus Geta's fine horse and the second-in-command made a short speech of thanks to the Commandant and departed.

"All right," said Anicius Maximus. "What's really happening?"

So I told him.

The bridge parted when the cohort was half across. Two legionaries lost their balance and fell in. A section of walkway also fell into the river when the bindings securing it to the boats separated. The current pushed the two halves apart but the anchors for most of the boats did not drag far. The soldiers on either side of the gap managed to shuffle their way to safety.

There was a deep roar from the barbarian army and nothing their leaders could do could hold them. The sun was setting behind the British army as it flooded down the gradient again towards the bridgehead, now packed with armoured men and fringed with sharpened stakes. Vespasian had opted to keep the bridgehead as compact as possible. The British had no really effective missiles and he had no wish to provide a wider target for the masses of Celtic swordsmen to attack.

The Tribune had not redeployed the artillery, waiting for me to get back with up to date information on the Legates' intentions. They were now shooting into the sun and perhaps it was just as well he had not moved the carts, they still had fairly accurate points of aim on the other bank. I do not know what happened to Cohort I Hamiorum but I saw very few boats upstream of the bridge. The Commandant, I saw, had the bridging teams scrambling out along the partially disintegrated bridge.

"Shoot!" ordered the Tribune and the familiar multiple crack and thump announced the departure of a volley of iron-headed missiles over the water.

"Reload and shoot!"

The collision of the Celtic army against the legionary bridgehead was at least as heavy as the first mass charge, possibly heavier on the left where there were fewer archers and they could not release their arrows fast enough to break the impetus of the charge. The javelins did much execution at close quarters and the palisade, no doubt, checked some of the impact on the shield wall. It was not as easy to see what was happening this time as the light was now behind the attackers but the legionaries had two big advantages. The second and third lines of soldiers in the bridgehead could now keep up a continuous hail of javelins over the heads of the first line and the legionaries were trained to rotate with the front line so that fresh soldiers were continuously replacing tired ones. The barbarians could not properly bring their numbers to bear on the smallish bridgehead and resisted being replaced in the front line even when they were almost exhausted.

It was dusk, and the bridge repaired, when the attack rolled back, leaving many more bodies on the field this time. Vespasian had the limits of the bridgehead pegged out with cohort standards. We loosed our ranging shots and secured the artillery pieces before dark.

Fed, and the guard list settled, I lay down on the grass under an artillery cart with Titus and Fangs. The quiet talk of the legionaries, and the snort and stamp of the horses nearby, was soothing, but nothing is more soothing than survival of a day's battle. To our right the distant grind of wheels and extravagant shouting announced the arrival of the bridging train of Legion XX Valeria. To our left, through the night, the creaking and sucking sounds of the repaired bridge told of the silent crossing of hundreds of burdened legionaries from Legion II Augusta into the battered bridgehead.

CHAPTER 72

▼

BRITAIN

They had built a big fire at the foot of an oak tree and a large cauldron provided hot beef stew to all the visitors that night. Fox, as the man of religion, presided over the cauldron. Brigit, in her observer status, sat on the edge of the firelight but did more than justice to her food. Caratacos sat with his back against the tree trunk, his face ruddy in the firelight, but rose to greet each of his subjects with a bowl of beer as they came to report to him.

Ceri was distraught, his wide shoulders hunched, his little eyes dull.

"Those German savages," he snarled bitterly, "shot our horses down like deer. Wrecked more than half of the chariots. When we dismounted and attacked on foot, they retreated behind the wreckage and even into the water." He added sadly "I lost a lot of crews. We killed a lot of them but there were always more, floating over the river like scum on a tide."

"Can you hold them?" Caratacos asked, mildly.

"Yes!" Ceri's voice was sharper, eyes brighter. "Most of our javelins went into the river but I have people out, gathering up theirs. Later, I'll set fire to the wreckage under cover of a feint attack. See what they can do, when they've got nowhere to hide."

"Good," said the High King. "Do it."

Ena had washed her face and hands in the river before coming. Her woolen tunic and trousers were still muddy and splashed with blood. It was not her blood.

"There are a lot of enemy cavalry," she reported. "Several nations. I have even heard some speak Celtic. I had a crash in my chariot and have to get about on foot but my people are fighting as if they are possessed. We have had to hurt the enemy's horses. Horrible. Sharpened stakes in the riverbed and hidden in small bushes. Ropes in the long grass stretched between trees. When the horses are down and crying, we kill the riders. We have killed a lot. Riders, I mean. And horses."

"How is Segonax?"

"Wounded again. Still fighting."

"And your people?"

"Still fighting," she repeated, her eyes lighting up. "Alive or dead, the Cantii are staying right here."

"Thank you Ena. Have some food."

So they came to the oak tree. Chiefs of the Catuvellauni, the Trinovantes and the Atrebates. They came with news of Celtic bravery, of enemy atrocities and of casualties. Swimmers could not get close enough to cut the anchor ropes, as the bridge was full of armed men. The current was not powerful enough to drive tree trunks launched upstream through the bridge structure. They also reported a second bridge was stretching out across the river. They made suggestions. They stayed to eat and to drink a little and to talk. Then they left.

Fox carefully lifted the cauldron off the fire. It was nearly empty.

"What do you think, Fox?" asked the High King. Brigit watched silently.

"The Cantii will fight, perhaps to the death," replied Fox slowly. "Ceri's charioteers will try once more but, if they don't succeed, they will break. It is disastrous for a unit armed with what is supposed to be a war-winning weapon to see it casually demolished. I think that they will break."

Caratacos took a careful swallow of beer.

"What about our infantry?"

"Just the reverse of what I would have thought." Fox's tone was that of a scholar, dissecting a problem. "The Catuvellauni, the power-base of the Cassi family, they are on the verge of breaking. Of course, most of their best warriors were with the charioteers. Still, it is surprising. The Trinovantes are afraid that the Catuvellauni are going to desert them. Remember, they overthrew the puppet king Caesar installed all those years ago. At the instigation of your family. They are watching which way the Catuvellauni are going to go."

"And the Atrebates?"

"Most surprising of all. They are determined to fight. You must have made a big impression while you were their administrator."

"Or," said Caratacos, "they like the idea of one of their own being High King."

"It amounts to the same thing," said Fox and Brigit, unseen, nodded.

She started when a figure silently appeared next to her. Caratacos saw him.

"Bivan! Come and join us. There is still some food and drink left. How are the tides on the Thames mud flats?"

"Low tide when the sun is highest." The Silurian pilot rarely used many words.

"Very well," said the High King and appeared, at last, to relax.

Fox, ginger hair bristling, rubbed his hands and held them out to the fire.

"What about my cavalry?"

"Cavalry, Fox? Cavalry is for scouting and hunting down a beaten foe. Ask Ena. It's not for attacking unshaken armoured infantry with unlimited supplies of missiles. We'll see what the dawn brings."

Other figures appeared at the edge of the light of the dying fire. Central was that of an elderly woman, perhaps fifty years old, with a small boy protectively beside her and a sleeping toddler in her arms.

"Is my daughter here?" Her voice had a local accent. The pitch and tone was that of an educated woman.

"Who is your daughter, lady?" Caratacos scrambled to his feet.

"Ena, Chief of the Cantii," she said, looking the High King in the eye. "I am her mother and these are her children. Is she here?"

She was not tall. Her shoulders were narrow and slightly bowed with the years, her hands large and shapely, her hips broad. She held her head up, graying hair drawn back from the narrow face, her eyes, which should have been dulled with age, sparked with interest.

"My daughter?" She repeated.

"She was here, mother," Caratacos replied. "She was here but she went back to her warriors. They are some distance upstream. Not easy to find in the dark."

"Did she get anything to eat? I've brought her clean clothes."

"She had supper with us. Why not sit down and rest. I'll see she gets the clothes tomorrow. Fox?"

Fox was already stirring the fire and replacing the cauldron. In the increasing light, Brigit could see that the boy's eyes were moist. He was about seven years old and had been looking forward to seeing his mother.

"Your mother is fine, darling," she said to him, " and so brave. She is an example to us all."

"Yes," he said, fiercely, "the bravest. She is not even frightened of wolves."

"There you are, you see."

"Have some food with us, mother," invited Caratacos.

"I have eaten enough, with the families back there," she inclined her head to the rear of the army, "but, perhaps, the youngster."

"Of course," said Fox, looking for an unused bowl.

"I have eaten enough, too," said the boy stoutly, although his eyes kept straying to the cauldron.

"Ah," said Caratacos, "but this is special food. Warrior food. Here, try some."

"Don't leave any bits," admonished his grandmother gently.

"How are the families?" asked the High King.

"Doing their duty. Supporting the warriors."

"Are they frightened?" Brigit asked in the small pause which followed.

"Frightened, dear?" said the old lady. "Frightened of death, no. It comes to all of us. Frightened of slavery, frightened of separation, yes. Very much." She turned to face the High King. "Don't let it happen, dear."

After they had gone, Brigit dug in her bag and produced a small harp.

"My intuition tells me," she said lightly, "that business is done for the moment. Does anyone remember 'The Repulse of the Swan'?"

Even Bivan smiled.

By first light, the army was on its feet, coughing, yawning and shuddering with the pre-dawn chill. Hedges of hands were held out to the revived camp fires and, wherever dry mouths could produce sufficient saliva, food was chewed. Caratacos could offer no further help to Chief Ena, fighting the enemy cavalry on his right, or Ceri, with the remains of the British chariot force on the left. The battle would be won or lost, this day, by infantry, by what happened in the centre. The chiefs' nagging voices rose above the rumble of the crowds of warriors. The Catuvellauni assembled slowly on the left, the Trinovantes on the right. Between the two tribal masses, the smaller contingent of the Atrebates was pushed into a dense, narrow-fronted column. The warriors grumbled and joked and hefted their swords. There were no shields and almost no armour. They preferred to have space around them in which to swing the heavy blades.

At the river's edge, a large block of enemy infantry was across, hiding behind their shields and a fence. About two hundred paces down stream, the new bridge stretched from bank to bank. On the far bank, a dark mass had gathered at that end of the new bridge.

As the first rays of the sun lit up the clouds above the high ground behind the enemy army, a tremendous fanfare of Roman trumpets broke out. The army of Britain responded with a shattering roar and the jarring braying of the carnyx. The dark mass on the far side of the river began to uncoil across the new bridge and to pool on the near bank. The warriors began to surge and elbow one another, the chiefs' voices rose and became shriller. The only thing which prevented an immediate charge was the appearance of the High King alone in front of the army. Nothing he said could have been heard but he raised his weapon above his head. Not his magnificent sword of office but a common falcata, the heavy, single-edged blade of the poorest infantryman. The heaving and shoving in the ranks subsided a little. The front ranks still had to dig in their heels to hold their position. The enemy continued to stream off the new bridge and to add to the expanding new bridgehead. It had nearly touched the edge of the first bridgehead, hopefully masking the artillery across the river. Caratacos released the infantry of the army of Britain.

He had barely swung the blade forward when the running front ranks of the Atrebates reached him and lifted him off his feet. Carried along with the country apparently streaming past him, Caratacos felt a huge release in tension. The mighty forces he had assembled, guided and restrained were now unleashed out of his control, for better or for worse. There was nothing he could now do except the one thing he had been trained to do since boyhood, and that was to fight. For this moment, he was no more than an infantryman with an infantryman's heavy weapon in his hands.

Caratacos saw no missiles but the Romans must have launched them, and some must have found their targets, as the press of running, panting bodies around him slackened and he got his feet on the ground. The impact, when it came, was not as great as he had expected. The dense, fast-moving column of frantic tribesmen crashed into the thin lines of braced legionaries and smashed right through them. Caratacos stumbled over stabbing, kicking armoured bodies before finding himself suddenly, frighteningly, knee-deep in water. The ranks in front of him had disappeared, the press behind him lessened and he looked straight across the river at the massed artillery of the Roman army.

Automatically, he crouched in the river while shouting an unheard warning. Splashes appeared in the shallows. A missile flitted past his ear and thudded into something behind him. Icy water groped at his groin. Left or right? The bridgehead to the right was larger and fortified. It was enveloped by the Trinovantes and it was unlikely that he could reach the front rank to influence matters. More splashes and thuds. The new bridgehead was to his left. The Romans had only just got their lead elements ashore. They were neither fortified behind a palisade nor were they yet properly deployed. To the left, then.

He shouted to the breathless Atrebates crowding the riverbank close to him and waved downstream. Many heard him and started to push their way along the riverbank and in the shallows. One of the tribesmen, wading along rapidly ahead of him, was suddenly flung sideways against the bank. Caratacos had not even seen the bolt. A splash to his right was immediately followed by a savage tug on his underwater trouser leg. Missed. He had gathered a number of Atrebates who were forging their way along the riverbank and next to it. They could hear that the tribesmen they were now passing were Catuvellauni, striving to disintegrate the new bridgehead. The new bridge was ahead, laden with armoured soldiers unable to move forward or back. He sank below the surface.

Groping forward, the air bubbling in his ears and his feet slithering on the muddy bottom, Caratacos vainly tried to see what was ahead. He heard the heaving, sucking noise of the bridge as he bumped into a straining anchor rope. There was no time for his knife. He rose with the water streaming from him and wildly swung his falcata in a horizontal arc at the legs of the soldiers on the bridge. Had he had his feet firmly planted, the legionary would have lost at least one leg. As it was, in fright, the Roman lost his balance and went over the side with a shout and a splash. It gave Caratacos just a moment to slam down his blade on the anchor rope where it strained over the side of one of the boats. Other legionaries, struggling to maintain their balance on the heaving, crowded bridge, tried to poise their javelins. More warriors in the water were hacking at anchor ropes and swinging at Roman legs. The end of the bridge started to drift away from the bank.

Unfortunately, this took the legionaries out of range of the flashing British swords and allowed them space to launch their javelins without worrying about the danger of losing their legs. What it did do, was to separate the legionaries in the bridgehead from support from across the river. Ignoring the danger of a javelin or a bolt in the back, the sopping tribesmen climbed the bank, wet wool clinging to their limbs, and attacked the legionaries facing the Catuvellauni from the rear. There must have been a very senior officer in the bridgehead—and, in fact, Caratacos did see gold and silver armour amongst the dull iron of the legionaries—because the Romans did not panic. They closed ranks and the rear rank faced the water. The Atrebates in the river and on its bank had no impetus to push the Roman line back from the water's edge. The Romans on the bridge, relying on their colleagues' armour and shields—and their own expertise—to avoid killing their friends, launched javelin after javelin into the backs of the Atrebates. More javelins were passed hand-to-hand along the bridge.

The best warriors of the Catuvellauni had pushed their way to the forefront of the British masses and were hacking and chopping at the shield wall in front of them. Sword and falcata, swinging in flashing arcs in the early morning sun, sheared off sections of red and gold shields and, sometimes, sparked on legionary helmets. The flickering and darting short stabbing swords of the legionaries found homes in abdomens and rib-cages. The bodies piled up. The bridgehead shrank.

The Trinovantes had not been able to break into the other bridgehead. Flights of missiles, and a hedge of sharpened stakes, broke the impetus of their charge and kept them out from among the five thousand organised legionaries on shore. The longer sides of this bridgehead allowed more tribesmen to come to grips with the legionaries, but the British refused to give way to their fresher colleagues anxious to come into the front line. Only a few of the clearer-headed devoted time to uprooting or flattening the palisade stakes behind which the enemy fought. The Roman legionaries routinely rotated their front-line soldiers and it was not long before the exhausted Trinovantan front-line drew back a few paces. The pressure from behind them had eased due to the continuous rain of javelins thrown from the Roman rear ranks. Those few paces brought them into the javelin killing-ground. They tried throwing back the twisted Roman javelins which lay everywhere, without much effect. Then, they withdrew another few paces.

With a shudder, the bridgehead of Legion II Augusta seemed to change shape and to swell. Undamaged shields were passed forward to the front ranks. They advanced several paces and another volley of javelins took flight. The Trinovantes started to give ground, rolling back up the slope they had charged down. On the downstream side of the bridgehead, the palisade fence was dismantled by the legionaries themselves. Then, the bridgehead disgorged a huge armoured column across the littered ground towards the embattled remnants of the bridgehead of Legion XX Valeria. The Catuvellauni, seeing the threat to their rear, broke and ran.

Most of the Atrebates, trapped on the riverbank or in the water, were killed. Caratacos was not killed. Sinking below the muddied surface of the river, he dived under the bridge between the rolling corpses and the plunging javelin points, which he heard rather than saw. He came up for breath, eyes streaming with water, and found a footing on the slippery bottom. Roman trumpets and Roman shouts filled the air. Roars of battle had given way to cries of the wounded. Something splashed in the water in front of him. The artillery would hardly be shooting at a single individual but the river's edge was clearly no place to be. He scrambled up the wet bank and found a long British sword in the battlefield litter. His falcata was at the bottom of the Medu.

He was downstream of what was left of the second bridgehead. In the centre of a low wall of wool-clad bodies was a clump of armoured figures around some tilted standards. They seemed to be content for the moment to cheer and wave their weapons.

Ahead of him and to his right, the infantry of the army of Britain was streaming back up the slope. Most of them were walking and looking back, but many, he felt, were not going to stop. Most of the chiefs would have been in the forefront of the assault and most would not have survived. His new sword felt very heavy and he rested the blade in the crook of his left arm. There was no sign of Roman cavalry yet, thank god. Just as that thought came to mind, horsemen appeared on the slope ahead. The small body of priceless British cavalry had come to cover the retreat of the infantry. Fox must not charge.

Switching the blade of his sword to rest on his shoulder, and with his shoes squelching like those of a wild fowler, the High King of Britain put his head down and wearily slogged his way alone up the slope. Fox recognised him when he got close and rode forward to meet him.

"Shall I charge?" Fox, his face pale and his ginger hair catching the sunlight, asked without unclenching his teeth.

"No!" Caratacos was out of breath but gave the word explosive vehemence. 'They'll murder the horses. As long as the cavalry is intact, they'll be more cautious pursuing the infantry."

"Very well," said Fox, slipping out of the saddle. "Your horse, sire."

It was no time for elaborate courtesies and Caratacos accepted Fox's leg-up into the saddle.

"Thanks, Fox." He was recovering his breath.

Still thinking of Roman cavalry, Caratacos stared up stream and then glanced at the united bridgehead on the riverbank. The new bridge had already been anchored again and armoured soldiers were steadily flowing across. There was, as yet, no general move forward but there must have been at least six thousand legionaries across and on their feet. No doubt many Romans had been killed and wounded but the sights which drew the eye were the lines and heaps of British casualties, thickening to piles and a wall of bodies around the Roman bridgehead.

"The infantry? How many stayed with you, Fox?"

"A thousand, perhaps. More in the trees. Of the rest, some of them are making for Lud Dun, but most of them are going to chance a crossing of the Thames over the mudflats. I don't see any of them making a stand. I've sent Bivan on."

"Good. Thanks." The High King looked at the sun. Almost at its height : low tide soon.

"Who is this," said Fox, peering upstream. A small band of scarecrows around a slow-moving chariot approached. "Is it Ena?"

"No," said Caratacos from his high saddle. "Another woman driving. Chariot's weighed down."

She did not have to haul the horses to a stop. As soon as the driver stopped encouraging the sweat-stained beasts with words and with the reins, they stopped by themselves. She leaned her hands on the sides of the chariots and bowed her head for a moment. When she raised it, they could see she was more tired than the horses. Over the pallor of her face lay a film of sweat and dust. Specks of ash coated her teeth and a column of red down her neck marked where she had lost an ear lobe. She recognised the High King.

"Cavalry." Her voice cracked. "Celtic cavalry and some other heathens. They are across the river. Ena was captured, alive I think. The Cantii are being destroyed. I have been sent with this one. Ena said you must keep him."

She sat on the side of the chariot and Caratacos saw the crumpled, unconscious figure of Segonax.

"I will keep him. Now, we must go."

"Yes, High King, you must go. Rally the army of Britain. Come back and avenge the Cantii." She raised her head. "We stay."

She stepped down from the chariot on unsteady legs and Fox went to her. He did not touch her. Her little band gathered around her. They looked down at the stirring Roman formations.

There was movement behind Caratacos. Horses stamped and shuffled, saddlery creaked. The horses were edging forward. Individual tribesmen on foot filtered through the cavalry and began gathering around the Cantii. The High King felt a rising pressure in his throat and behind his eyes. Fox looked up at him.

"We stay, also" he said, "but the cavalry must go or there will be British bodies littered behind every bush from here to Lud Dun. Keep the cavalry between the Romans and our people. When you have made a new army, come back and destroy them. Until we meet again, then."

Caratacos was within a hair's breadth of ordering the cavalry to charge. A feminine Irish voice spoke.

"No. You are the High King of Britain. You are not an ordinary soldier. You may not indulge yourself."

"Goodbye for now," said Fox to the High King. "Goodbye, Brigit, dear."

The Cantii and a few other tribesmen, began to walk down the slope with Fox. They did not wave. They knew that a single gesture might launch the cavalry whether the High King wished it or not.

"Time to go," said Brigit, tying her horse to the chariot. "I'll bring Segonax."

"Cavalry!" shouted the High King in a strangled voice. "About turn. Forward."

Bivan was not a horseman. He was a river pilot since boyhood on the Severn estuary. He had, in manhood, become an expert on the Thames estuary and was fascinated by the weather, currents and tides. He could ride a horse but found them silly, unpredictable and illogical. Worse, they had to spend half the day eating and not working. The most you could say for them in his mind was that they could move fast, when they felt like it. Even he, though, was appalled by the shambles he saw on the left of the British army.

At first, he had been almost carried along by the crowds of retreating warriors making their way rapidly north across the rear of the British positions towards the estuary and the precarious escape route across its tidal mud flats. The mood was strange. It was, initially, sour and irritable with a strong element of shame. Fairly rapidly, relief lightened the mood and the first signs of self-justification. After all, not one of the Romans could stand up to them, warrior to warrior, at swords' length. They had hidden behind their shields and thrown things, and even that had not been enough to fend off the British. They had had to come to the battlefield with machines to shoot arrows even further. They had no idea of civilized warfare.

Bivan was sure that, in their hearts, the Catuvellauni and the Trinovantes and the few surviving Atrebates all knew that the sordidness of warfare waged by missile from behind machines and armour was beside the point. They knew that they had fought with the bravery of their ancestors. It had not been enough.

The recovering mood of the throngs of retiring Celts did not survive the sight of the demolition of their magnificent chariot force. Shouts of anger and dismay did not halt the crowds. A great blanket of gloom settled over them but they carried on shuffling towards the north and the Thames crossing.

Ceri was standing alone in his chariot with his spent team facing uphill as if they did not want to look at the carnage along the river's edge. There were a few other chariots parked carelessly nearby, their crews, like Ceri, gazing downhill. Bivan pretended not to notice the tear tracks through the grime on his cheeks when he spoke to the commander of the British chariot force.

All along the riverbank, hordes of yellow haired warriors seethed about several pillars of smoke. Some of them picked at the shattered wreckage of chariots and bodies, presumably looking for any booty that had been overlooked. Apart from some jeering, they took no notice of the British infantry retiring across their front.

"I count about six thousand here," said Bivan, "and I saw masses of snails waiting to cross. Why don't they attack?"

"They want us to attack them. Again."

"These don't look like Romans."

"No," said Ceri, turning his ravaged face towards the older man. "They are Germans, I think. Do you know what they are doing, Bivan. They are making fires of the chariots and," his voice cracked, "they are eating my horses."

"Enough," said Bivan, sharply. "Time to go. Leave them to the horse-goddess. Those savages do not know that they are in her land."

Ceri, with a visible effort, turned away from the foreigners and their fires. The crowds of British infantry leaving the battlefield had thinned out and did not yet seem in any danger of a Roman pursuit. He wiped his hand down his face.

"I must get to Lud Dun," he said.

The Silurian waterman shook his head.

"The roads will be crammed with refugees and, in any case the High King is on his way there with the cavalry. Leave your chariot and come with me across the Thames. You will be there quicker in the long run. Send your other chariots after the High King."

"Have we got time before the next tide?" Ceri was looking at the high sun.

"Who am I?" demanded Bivan, indignantly.

For the first time, the shadow of a smile appeared on the dirty features.

"The best estuary guide I know. I hope."

In the end, they took the chariot as far as the southern edge of the marsh, turned the weary ponies loose and tipped the battered vehicle into a ditch. Then they joined the tail end of of the refugees' column, following the wide trail of footprints and flattened vegetation into the muck. Bivan had thought to act as guide for the infantry but many locals must have joined the retreat. The British infantry were well on their way across the Thames and the low tide had yet to turn.

CHAPTER 73

▼

BRITAIN

The artillery of Legion II Augusta was in a bad way. The shock of discharging so many bolts without maintenance had reduced many of the catapults to combat inefficiency. On top of that, they had shot off vast amounts of ammunition and very little remained in the limbers. The young Tribune, after cheering and jumping up and down like a schoolboy, had driven his artillerymen to weapons' inspection and maintenance duties. I decided, based on my quickly expanding military experience, that he was a young officer of promise. He was bent over a catapult, which looked to me more like a half-built dog-kennel than a weapon of war, when I pointed out that our colleagues in Legion XX Valeria had no apparent intention of parting with any of their ammunition to assist us. Their Legion was still in the process of getting across the river on their new bridge. I suggested that my century cross the rickety old bridge to salvage what artillery bolts we could find on the battlefield.

The bridge, deserted now except for a few tired members of the bridging teams, swayed and sagged in the current. The lashings were all loose and the planking broken in parts but we crossed without incident into our Legion's bridgehead. I was surprised that we had not yet deployed. The Celts seemed to have left the field, heading west and north towards the Thames. To the south I thought I heard a Roman cavalry trumpet. I pushed my way through the unemployed legionaries, ignoring their protests and the protective snarls of their centurions. Our Legate, Vespasian, stood, legs apart, under the eagle. Some very angry officers stood around him. I reported my presence and my mission.

"Very well, Centurion," he said, with a rasp in his voice. "Go collect your bolts. You will be the only Roman on this side of the river doing anything useful."

"Here he comes now, Legate," muttered a red-faced tribune.

Ploughing through the painstakingly aligned ranks came a vision in silver and gold metal, unmarked by mud or blood. Legate Hosideus Geta of Legion XX Valeria, having had his bacon saved by Vespasian's professionalism, had come to call. Watching without being noticed is part of a patrolman's training and I managed to remain close to the eagle.

"Legate Vespasian!" warbled the Hero of Mauretania. "I received your request to pursue the fleeing British and it does you great credit. Your Legion has behaved heroically and done its duty admirably but now it must be exhausted."

A sort of silent convulsion swept outwards through the legionary ranks. No one looked round but the tension hummed like a bowstring. It did not halt Geta's flow.

"As soon as I can get the rest of Legion XX Valeria across, I shall lead the pursuit to the north. Legion II Augusta, once its administration has been resolved, should swing wide to protect my left flank."

There was a certain amount of wordless growling among the senior officers of Legion II Augusta. Vespasian's calm, firm voice spread oil on the water as he took the army's second in command in a friendly grip by the elbow.

"Absolutely, Legate," he said. "Now, there is something I want to show you out there between the two bridgeheads."

I summoned Fangs and Titus with a jerk of my head and we forced our way out of the right hand side of the bridgehead, Fangs giving vent to some colourful language when his tunic caught on a splintered palisade stake. I saw some British cavalry at a distance but too far to be a danger. The century lined up at the water's edge and started to sweep up the slope to recover expended bolts. Particularly close to the river's edge, this involved the gruesome task of extracting them from what had once been living soldiers.

The two Legates, in their expensive and distinctive armour, were having an intense private conversation in the open.

Warning shouts from the legionaries in the bridgehead drew my attention to the slope ahead. The cavalry had gone, but a small party of armed Brits was walking down towards us. There could not have been more than a hundred of them and they were walking almost casually, in a loose group rather than in any formation. It seemed excessive to take precautions against such a trifling threat, but they were armed, showed no sign of intending to surrender and were still coming on.

I told Titus to gather our legionaries and hurried over to the two Legates. They barely acknowledged my presence or the message. They still had things to say, apparently. The Celts were getting disturbingly close.

I sent Titus with half the century forward to get between the Legates and the enemy and told the rest of the men to stack the recovered bolts and to form a second line. It was at that moment that an artilleryman across the river lost his head. Titus was in the act of waving forward his half-century when an unseen force flattened him to the ground like a little girl's doll. I got to the wavering front line of my century just as the British were cut down by a volley of javelins from the bridgehead. They had not got to within twenty paces of the palisade fence.

Titus' eyes were open. The machine-driven bolt had gone in under his arm, just above the upper horizontal plate of the loricated armour he was wearing. The grooved end of the wooden shaft protruded obscenely, its iron head was deep in his chest cavity. He looked at me and gasped.

"When are you going to return that tunic you borrowed?" then he closed his eyes and whispered something like "Domitilla", or perhaps it was just a sigh, and he was gone.

To anyone watching, it would have appeared as if Fangs had his hand on my shoulder in an act of consolation. In fact, he had secured a good hold on the neck of my mail shirt. Small, pot-bellied and elderly he might have been, but sword-drill for eight hours a day for twenty years had given him a grip which could have throttled a horse. I could not break free. I could not desert my century, run back along a splintering bridge and hack a criminally careless artilleryman into small bloody pieces.

The Legates, affecting not to notice, walked off to their respective Legions. After a while, we went on collecting artillery bolts.

Before we were finished, both Legions moved off leaving us, the dead and small groups of keening Celtic women looking for loved ones, on the cluttered field. By late afternoon, a body of cavalry arrived at the artillery park across the river and the drivers started to hurriedly hitch up their teams. Several troopers crossed the river to us. They were, they said, from Ala Indiana Gallorum, had successfully forced a crossing of the river higher up and had now returned to escort the artillery across. I was to turn over the salvaged ammunition to them and to report to the Legion's headquarters. I sent six men back to bring forward the century's eight pack mules and the two men I had left guarding them before the battle. I got Fangs to sort out weapons and rations for us from the carts. I did not trust myself in the artillery park.

We caught up with the main body of Legion II Augusta only a few kilometers to the west. My century gave a small cheer when we saw that the entrenching of the overnight Camp had already been done. I led them to the space for the special service section and they thankfully sat on their bedrolls. It had been a long day. For me it was not yet over. I reported to the Commandant who was sitting on a folding chair in the open next to his bedroll.

"You will hear the bad news yourself, shortly," he said, by way of greeting. "Legion XX Valeria has apparently been overly-enthusiastic in its pursuit. I hear that considerable numbers of legionaries as well as several units of auxiliaries have got themselves into serious trouble in the marshes of the Thames estuary. Take a horse, go and see what's happening."

Of course, he could have sent any one of a number of centurions but I had to admit that my contribution to the war effort that day had been modest to say the least. He could also have sent any one of the hundred and twenty dispatch riders of the Legion but they were possibly not of sufficient seniority. I was the obvious choice and I willingly went.

It was still light in that long northern evening when I was back again. I was under the escort of a very surly turma of cavalry attached to the Governor in person. Their decurion handed me over like a misbehaved schoolboy to the Commandant who now sat, clean and freshly shaved, in his newly erected tent.

"What happened?" was his very reasonable question after dismissing my escort.

"Cavalry under command of Legion IX Hispana rounded me up and took me to the Governor," I had to admit. "He has given orders to prevent scouting of the fringes of the marshes. He interviewed me himself. I think there has been a major disaster, the tide swallowed up a lot of soldiers."

"And?" he demanded, black eyes fixed on my face.

"And Hosideus Geta was with the Governor when I arrived. He was very—excited."

"And?" the Commandant's voice was just tinged with impatience.

"Well. He was saying that he had only been able to reach the marshes when the tide was coming in because he had been held up by Legion II Augusta. He said we had not been ready to advance. He said that, in the end, he had had to go on without us."

The Commandant stood up sharply and a flicker of pain crossed his face. He pointed to the fallen folding chair.

"Wait here," he ordered and walked stiffly away in the direction of our Legate's tent.

It was almost dark when he returned. He had special orders for me.

"Tomorrow, you will go back and look for those renegade Brits, King Bericos and that Cogi—whatsis. You will not find them."

"I will not...?"

"You will not find them. You will ride all the way back to the landing beaches looking for them. They are needed to facilitate the Roman advance and to recruit British levies. Clear?"

"But I will not find them."

"That's right. Instead, you will get some personal mail of the Legate's onto the fastest ship you can find. You have a friend in the Fleet. That little Greek fellow."

"Philip. He's in the Fleet's Communications Division."

"Right. Use him. When the mail is safely on its way, then, and only then, you will locate the British allies and bring them back here."

It was hard not to smile but his stare did not waver.

"And where are they likely to be found?"

"With the bridging-equipment wagons just across the river."

"Right, sir. The mail?"

"Being prepared. Bad luck about your Optio today. Tell that toothless old man he is promoted. The extra pay should come in handy."

When I told Fangs, his grin was a fearsome thing to see and he asked me to take a letter with me for his wife. It was not easy for me to see Fangs as a family man although I knew he had a wife and children in Germany. He laughed with delight when I mentioned this, his middle-aged wife, Julia, he said, had packed up what she could and had made her own way to Gesoriacum where she was waiting with thousands of other soldiers' families. There was one other sensitive matter I needed to touch on.

"See, here, Optio," I adopted a haughty command attitude which seemed to amuse him even more. "I can still call you Fangs, but I won't have these young legionaries doing so, bad for discipline don't you know."

"All right, Centurion," he conceded. "It's Macer. I'm the newly-promoted Optio Fangs Macer, at your service."

It was about eighty kilometers miles back to the beaches. Fortunately, our mules and baggage arrived overnight and I was able to recover my breeches and a battered document case I had picked up somewhere. I was therefore able to present a fairly professional appearance the following morning, with my bedroll, rations for myself and a small sack of barley for the horse all tied to the back of my saddle. I received Legate Vespasian's package from the Commandant and raised my eyebrows at the name of the addressee. The Emperor's mail takes priority over any other communication, of course, but I had one detour to make on the way to the beach.

I thought I knew exactly where Titus had fallen, but the battlefield looked very different that morning, all white bodies and black birds. The legionary burial parties had arrived on the field but scavengers had already been busy overnight and most of the remaining dead had already been stripped and robbed. Many of the Celtic corpses had disappeared altogether, presumably located and removed by relatives. The burial party had started to gather the Roman dead and I found what I was looking for amongst them.

Ignoring the protests of the optio in charge of the Legion II Augusta burial party, I made my own pyre out of broken palisade stakes and a damaged section of bridge planking. Titus had been stripped. I managed to remove the missile that killed him and I washed him in river water. It was a real struggle to get him decently dressed but, at last, he was back in the tunic I had borrowed from him. I placed the coin I had been saving for my own funeral in his mouth, said a prayer and set the pyre alight. A little of my food ration went on the pyre with him. When it had burned down I gathered some ash and sealed it in a little pot I begged from the burial party. So I said goodbye to Titus forever.

The Emperor's mail was now seriously delayed, but I judged he might forgive me if I collected my buried money on the way. A very nervous Celt took me across the river in a ferry that had been resurrected from somewhere. My horse behaved itself and we got across without incident. I recovered my money and set off east for the coast.

I had intended to travel along the high ground where the damage of conquest was probably less intrusive, but time was now pressing. The upgraded native roadway had been broken up and churned into porridge by the passage of the army and the wind carried the taste of old ash and death. I did not see one unburned homestead nor one living animal that was not under Army control.

At a ford over a small stream, a group of British labourers, old men and boys mainly, were relaying the wooden rail and plank approaches. Their guards were obviously Celts and, from their moustaches, woolen clothing and lack of armour, British Celts at that. Their leader, sitting his horse with his legs dangling, challenged me quite sharply. I immediately backhanded him with my vinestick as a lesson in our differing status in the Army of the Empire. His eyes reddened in pain and hate but he adopted a more civil tone. The prisoners enjoyed the scene, jeering and laughing loudly. I had no doubt what was going to happen as soon as I rode on but, in these things, nature has got to take its course. Conquered Britons also had to learn at what level they fitted into the Imperial hierarchy.

Philip, when I found him, was annoyingly uninterested in the perfectly co-ordinated advance of the army and its brilliant defeat of the main British forces on the Medu River. All he wanted to talk about were winds and tides, fleets and flotillas and the amazingly boring problems of supply and storage. He was, he told me, being transferred back to Gesoriacum. He agreed to get a message to his father confirming the resounding Roman success, but weighed Legate Vespasian's letter to the Emperor in his hands, making it obvious that he was privy to information not normally accessible to front-line centurions.

"You know," he said finally. "You could just as easily leave it here."

I was about to tell him it was from the commander of a legion addressed to the Emperor and he had better get on with it, but, of course, he was well aware of that. The inference I was supposed to make was that the Emperor was coming to Britain.

"When does he get here?"

Philip looked peeved that I had not had to prise the information out of him.

"Did I say he is coming? What I can tell you, though, is that my father has been visited by a Praetorian Guard officer and told that if he transports one soldier's family from the Continent to Britain before he gives him personal clearance then any contract he has will be cancelled."

"That does not mean that the Emperor is coming here," I had decided to needle my know-it-all nautical friend. "There's no need anyway. The British are defeated."

"You know that, and you have told me that, but the population of Rome does not know that. Not yet. The population of Rome might be under the impression that the Emperor is required in person to finish off a difficult enemy. How would it look if the Emperor, hurrying to save his army from an undefeated foe, had to cross the Ocean at the tail-end of a convoy of women and children?"

Put that way, the warning issued to Pytheas by an officer in the Emperor's own Guard made a lot of sense. Philip had to grin at the imaginary scene he had conjured up. Even Uncle Claudius at his most benign might suffer a loss of his sense of humour if his glittering rescue expedition were to be led onto the beaches by shiploads of argumentative women and wailing children.

"If he is on his way," Philip went on, "and successfully concludes the war, his reputation will be secure."

"And so will his position," I agreed, and told him about the Praetorian on the Rhone who knew all about elephants. "Those pens the Fleet is constructing near the beaches, they will never do for elephants. They are too large and the walls too low."

"They are not for elephants," said Philip. "They are for British slaves."

I told Philip to forward the Emperor's letter from Vespasian anway. If Emperor Claudius had already set out from Rome he might get it on the way and, if he had not, leaving it in Britain would serve no purpose. I also gave him Optio Fangs Macer's letter for his wife in Gesoriacum and a letter of my own to Pytheas, Philip's father and my own business associate. The Fleet apparently had a full military post office in the town now and the cross-Ocean flow of mail was established. I declined an offer of a place on a transport going down to the Medu River, it was packed and I had heard stories about the waters of the Thames estuary. Devastated countryside, haunted by armed Celtic bandits and patrolled by renegade British soldiers, seemed preferable.

King Bericos and Cogidumnos were exactly where the Commandant had said they would be, fretting under the dubious protection of a few wounded Batavians. I got the usual extravagant welcome from the Brits which immediately aroused deep suspicion, it appeared, in the minds of their guards. Communication was not possible, I could speak no German and they understood neither Celtic nor Latin. They would not release the British, and I would not go without them. In the end, nothing would satisfy the Batavians but that they accompany the Celts they had been told to guard. It was only a few kilometers to the Camp of Legion II Augusta but some of the more seriously wounded of the Batavians were soon in difficulties. My little party arrived at the Main Gate Right with several German protectors being helped along by the British they had been told to guard. Most professional officers and men of the Legion could speak some German in those days and the Batavians were soon released from their duty to their satisfaction.

The Commandant nodded sagely when I reported to him. I had been away nearly a week and Legion II Augusta had not moved. The Batavians had crossed the tidal marshes onto the north bank of the Thames and Legion IX Hispana and Legion XIV Gemina, under the direct command of Governor Aulus Plautius, now held both banks of the Thames at Lud Dun. Legion XX Valeria, still counting the cost of its rash pursuit, had been placed in reserve.

"I was wondering about that," growled the old soldier. "The Governor has pushed a lot of cavalry through onto the north bank. They report no contact with the retreating enemy, but no one is stirring. Come with me."

Vespasian was leaning back in a wicker chair with his feet on the table, occupying his time by tapping his shoes with a stick. An overturned pot of ink lay in the corner of the tent and several documents lay scattered on the floor.

"Welcome, Victorinus," he said. His face brightened and he took his feet off the table. "Have you got my Brits?"

I reported the safe dispatch of his letter, the state of the country east of the Medu and that I had indeed brought up his loyal British allies. After a prompt from the Commandant, I also reported the rumour of the Emperor's imminent arrival.

"Yes, yes. Anything is possible," he said, airily. "Meantime, we must make use of this period of—ah—reorganisation."

He swept a few crumbs of British earth off his table and spread a map.

"My area of responsibility is all the country south of the Thames. As soon as the army resumes its advance, other formations will continue north and occupy the enemy capital. Legion II Augusta, and its auxiliaries, marches west. The first tribal area we will enter will be that of the Atrebates, here. King Bericos' land. I have some recent intelligence from a wandering Gallic medicine man but it is low-level and most of it I could have guessed for myself."

Local response, at least on the coast, to the potential return of King Bericos had seemed lukewarm at best. It also seemed unlikely that his support would be greater closer to the tribal capital, Kaleoua, where a member of the Cassi family had been the effective ruler for many years. Perhaps, though, now that the main British army had sustained a major defeat, more of Bericos' supporters might declare themselves.

"I want," said Vespasian, "to locate and organise Roman sympathisers among the Atrebates."

"King Bericos?" I asked. "He's not young…"

"No. The King of the Atrebates is needed for a particular function and he has no male heir if he should be killed. He stays here. Take that Cogidumnos. I will give you a cavalry escort, or would you prefer the British levies?"

"Not the levies, I think. They are seen as being one of the causes of the British defeat and we have been using them to guard British prisoners. Celtic troops, yes, but I think that they should be troops from a population which has already lived and prospered under Roman rule. Is Ala Indiana Gallorum available?"

The Commandant left.

"Assessing the mood among the Atrebates is important," repeated Vespasian, "and recruiting levies equally so, but this Legion's long-term goals are further to the west. Any information you can glean on the Durotriges tribe will be helpful. Also, I hear there is a large island off the south coast which is within my area of responsibility."

"The Fleet might be able to provide some information," I suggested, "or the merchant skippers operating across the Ocean." I took note of the narrowing of the clear eyes in the farmer's face. "But, of course," I continued hastily, "I will gather as much information as possible."

"Good. Have a cup of wine with me and then go and brief Cogidumnos. I am sure that the Commandant will find you some Gallic cavalry."

CHAPTER 74

▼

BRITAIN

We circled around Legion XIV Gemina, who were in Camp south of the Thames at Lud Dun, and picked up the Kaleoua road to the west. Travelling through undevastated countryside in Britain was an uncommon pleasure. We had to keep alert for bandits or armed fragments of the British army, but the sight of unburned fields and intact homesteads tended to be relaxing. A few locals were seen at a distance but quickly ran away when they saw Roman cavalry. This did not auger well for our intelligence-gathering mission.

The thirty horsemen of Ala Indiana Gallorum were commanded by a stocky, fresh-faced Celt from Lughdunum on the Rhone in southern Gaul, where the Fleet has its inland base. The Celts in that region had been subjects of Rome for more than a hundred years and he was endlessly fascinated by the way the wild Celts of Britain lived. He pointed out to me, several times, that Lugh and Lud are different names for the same Celtic god and that the name of his home town, Lughdunum, means exactly the same thing as the British Lud Dun, the Fortress of Lud. In the end I had to point out to this earnest young officer that, if the Celts had ever learned to write, the spelling of the towns' names might have been as close as the meaning. The ensuing silence was short. The Decurion was a hard man to put down.

The Gallic cavalrymen were all looking about them with the same interest. They were imagining themselves, perhaps, in the huge Celtic armies of history, rolling across Europe with their cities on wheels amongst the horsemen, charioteers and footsoldiers. This turma of Ala Indiana Gallorum, with their shaven faces and uniform helmets and shields, looked nothing like the warriors of Brennos or Vercingetorix. They looked what they were, Roman auxiliary cavalry, under the command of a Roman Centurion. My own Celtic descent I kept to myself.

They were interested in everything about Cogidumnos. His moustache and length of hair were now appropriate to a British chief. He wore comfortable woolens and a gold torc gleamed impressively around his neck. I was amused to see how his aloof manner and cold glance quelled any jokes being made at his expense. Even the Decurion was wary of him. He gazed about like a landowner in his own fields and tried to suppress the unmistakable glimmer of excitement in the back of his eyes. He had come home.

On the second day, the cavalry had great fun trying to catch a tribesman to question. Most of the men disappeared into the nearest thicket like bolts from a catapult. The shouting and laughter from the unsuccessful pursuers was eventually beginning to get on Cogidumnos' nerves, and on mine, and I spoke sharply to the Decurion. Before he needed to take any positive action, a young trooper whooped in triumph. He had managed to catch an old lady in her vegetable patch. He rode proudly back with her tucked under his arm like a bundle of sticks. She was not a bit dismayed, screaming at him from close quarters and striking out at him with little, knotted fists.

"Put her down!" Cogidumnos' voice came out as a snarl. I was astonished to see that he was really angry and had his hand on the hilt of his long sword. "Put her down. Now!"

Neither the Decurion nor I had time to intervene. The trooper dropped her as if she had suddenly developed horns. She stumbled as her ancient knees absorbed the minor impact, but she retained her balance by gripping her captor's foot. The young cavalryman was still looking open-mouthed at Cogidumnos' red face when the old lady put her shoulder under that foot and heaved upwards. He missed his clutch at one of the front pommels of the military saddle but managed to hook his knee around one of the rear ones, so he did not fall clear. His horse skittered, and his colleagues jeered, as he carefully hauled himself upright again. Eventually, he gave a shame-faced grin. Cogidumnos relaxed and dismounted.

I gave the Decurion a moment to get his men settled down and then instructed him to put out sentries while we waited. Cogidumnos talked quietly with the defiant old lady and, after a while, she began responding. This was going to take a while. We dismounted and had something to eat.

When I took some food over to the two Brits, the old woman was looking hard at him with a puzzled expression. He was staring off at nothing much, his expression grim and calculating.

"What's happening?"

It was she who answered in a broad local dialect I could barely understand.

"Foreigners. Black Irish, they say. Men and women, going to Kaleoua to take away Caratacos' family."

"Who is Caratacos?" the Decurion had come up behind me. His Celtic had a strong Gallic accent but she undertood him.

"He's the High King."

"No," said the Decurion confidently. "The High King of Britain is Togodumnos."

"Wrong," said Cogidumnos. "Togodumnos is dead. Caratacos is his brother, they have made him High King. He's sent an escort to move his family and they are ahead of us, at Kaleoua." He looked at me. "It's a big opportunity."

To say that I saw an image of honours and promotions in front of my eyes would be to exaggerate. Slightly.

"Are you sure they were Irish, grandmother?"

"No. Maybe Irish. I don't know. Just foreigners," she nodded at the Gallic Decurion, "like him."

"How many of these foreigners?"

"Maybe a dozen."

Could I afford to send one messenger, or two, back to the Legion? If I did, what could the Legion do to assist, other than to tell me to wait where I was until a more senior person arrived? If I waited, either the High King's family would be gone or the more senior person would claim all the credit for its capture. Either way, no honours or promotion for Centurion Aurelius Victorinus. I obviously could not spare even one messenger.

"All right. Eat, grandmother, no one is going to harm you."

"They had better not try."

A few paces away, I gathered Cogidumnos and the Decurion into a small orders group.

"Irish?" I asked Cogidumnos.

"If so, they have got to be escorting the family westwards. The British will attempt some sort of defence of Camulodunon, if ever the Roman army decides to move itself, and there would therefore be no point in the High King's moving his family into danger."

That made sense to me.

"Decurion," I demanded. "How skilled are your men in street fighting?"

He looked shocked.

"They are cavalry, Centurion. Cavalry in enemy towns means hamstrung horses and troopers killed by women throwing roofing tiles."

I had not seen a tiled roof in Britain, but I could see what he meant. We could not attempt to capture the High King's family in Kaleoua itself, not with cavalry. We must circle round the town and ambush the family and escort as they made their way to the west. Luckily Cogidumnos knew the area well.

"I suggest we ride slowly north until dusk. The locals might think that we are heading for Camulodunon. Then we turn west and go around Kaleoua."

"We can't get lost," asserted the Decurion. "If we go too far to the north, we'll strike the river Thames."

"The only way you will get lost", said Cogidumnos, fixing him with his customary cold stare, "will be if you do not listen to my directions."

The night was clear and cold enough to see the horses' breath as they plodded through the leaf-litter at the edge of the woods leading down to the Thames. The Gallic Celts are a superstitious lot and the troopers were nervous about enemy woodland at night. I said a prayer myself, but not as a protection against the spirits of the enemy's ancestors. My wish was for good fortune after a particularly long night march. We crossed several small tributaries of the Thames during the night and the men ate cold food in the saddle so, although tired, we were not particularly hungry or thirsty when the first gleams of light appeared behind us. The horses, on the other hand, had not had the opportunity to graze and, for the sake of their efficiency, I was glad when Cogidumnos called a halt.

He and I walked forward to the road and checked its surface. Fresh droppings, together with wheel tracks and hoofprints told us a story.

"Can this be them?" I asked. "The manure is still warm in the centre and we are not far to the west of Kaleoua. The party would surely not have set out so late in the afternoon. Would it?"

"Have you ever tried to get a party of women and children ready to go on a journey?"

"I see what you mean. Well, if they stopped for the night, they have to be close ahead. We'll give the horses a quick feed of grain and press on. That's not a problem."

"No. Your problem is how to separate the Irish from the family. Kill the Irish and capture the women and children. Tricky."

"Let's go talk to the Decurion."

The calculations for the plan turned on the number of warriors in the escort and, for that, we had to rely on the estimate of one old lady. She had, indeed, been a very sharp old lady and I was inclined to take that chance. The Decurion led the advance party of eight cavalrymen and I the remainder. The horses had perked up considerably after a good helping of energy food and we all set off at a smart trot down the road, my party several hundred paces behind the Decurion's.

It was getting quite light when the Decurion raised his hand to halt his advance party and as a signal to me. I also caught a faint whiff of woodsmoke. When I was sure that the Decurion was looking at me, I pointed at a thick stand of trees to the right of the road and he nodded emphatically. Cogidumnos and I bustled our score of excited cavalrymen into the wood and had them tie up their horses on the far side. It was no place for a fight on horseback even before we modified it. Horse-hobbles, knotted together, made good trip ropes and cavalry lances were planted, butt-end first, amongst the trees. By the time I concealed the soldiers, sword in hand, that stand of trees was a cavalryman's nightmare.

I heard several distant shouts from further down the road and then the section of Gallic cavalrymen galloped back into sight, giving every appearance of a panic flight. This might not have been altogether a pretence, as a riderless horse cantered at the back of the group and I counted two troopers short in the Decurion's party. Behind them, frighteningly silent, galloped a much larger group of horsemen, well mounted and armed with swords but without spears or shields. The old lady had not been far out in her estimate of a dozen, and they certainly gave every appearance of being Celts. Torcs shone in the early morning light, indicating chiefs or at least senior and successful warriors. I felt far less confidence that they would be taken in by my plan. I had barely time to modify it.

I told Cogidumnos to stay put. He simply nodded. I gathered up as many troopers in the wood as I could and led them scurrying and cursing quietly through the grasping undergrowth back to the horses. We were mounting up when the noise of conflict rang through the wood. Cogidumnos and the Decurion were engaged with the Irish, if that is what they were. The temptation was to simply kick the horses into a wild gallop around the wood but I held them to a quieter trot while events unfolded in the unseen skirmish. I had six excited troopers with me, without their lances but with their long cavalry swords drawn and their shields on their arms.

As we rounded the wood, reining aside to avoid another riderless horse, I could immediately see that the Irish had not been drawn into a headlong mounted rush into the trees. Only a small group of Celtic warriors sat their horses, holding the reins of several more. Most of the Irish were among the trees and on foot. The horseholders were straining to see the progress of the close-quarter fighting which sounded fairly desperate. I released my little command at them.

The only reason why all the horseholders were not killed in that first charge was that the released, riderless horses got in the way. The Gallic troopers were not to be denied, though, and they started to carve their way through the turning mass of frightened horseflesh and to cut down the unarmoured Celts. I marked down a bulky, well-dressed warrior who was holding no horses. He took a glance in our direction, shouted something towards the wood and fled. My horse, already at full stretch, closed the distance rapidly as he tried to get his mount settled into its stride.

For a Celt, he was not an outstanding horseman. He looked back once, wide-eyed, gauging the distance between my blade and his body. While he was doing so, his horse had decided to go one way around a tree. When the Celt looked forward again and saw the rapidly approaching obstacle, he decided to go the other. The horse shaved past the tree but its rider, totally unbalanced, collided with the tree trunk with a force which made even me wince, and he fell senseless onto the ground. My legionary sword was too short to finish him off without dismounting and I had other things to do. He was not going to be going anywhere soon.

The only horsemen still in the saddle were two armoured Gallic cavalrymen. A number of riderless horses were circling or grazing. The ground at the edge of the trees was littered with prone bodies. Soon, other troopers appeared from the wood and waved their weapons and cheered. Cogidumnos, I discovered, was unhurt and so, surprisingly, was the aggressive cavalry Decurion. He did a quick head-count and announced that we had lost six troopers killed and four badly wounded. Cogidumnos had been examining the enemy dead. They were definitely Irish, he said, holding up a handful of torcs he had stripped from the bodies. There were eight dead Irishmen and one wounded warrior he had prevented the troopers from finishing off. Plus, of course, the Irishman who had tried to ride through a tree. I sent someone to pick him up. A heavy casualty list.

The elated Decurion issued orders to his medics and walked around slapping backs and congratulating his men. While they tidied up the scene, stacking weapons and catching horses, I went to inspect the captives. My man was still unconscious, breathing noisily through a broken nose. I had a cavalry medic set it as soon as he had the chance. The other foreigner was bigger and younger. He had run onto a cavalry lance which had been planted like a pike amongst the undergrowth. The small iron head had driven through the muscle and flesh between the bottom of his ribcage and the top of his pelvis. He was in a lot of pain but stood a good chance of survival if blood poisoning did not set in.

"All right," I said. "Let's go and get the family."

We had to leave two medics with our wounded and the spare horses, but we took the two living Irishmen, slung over their horses' backs. I still had seventeen troopers, some with minor wounds, and their Decurion and Cogidumnos, in my little cavalcade. Hopefully, there would be no more than two or three of the family's escort left.

The Decurion reported that he had had only time to note several large wagons around a cooking fire before the escort had driven him off. He could not estimate the sort of opposition we might still have to face.

Even in the most isolated places in Britain, there are frequently watchers, and this was not an isolated place, it was the main road from the nearby tribal capital. Where the spectacle to see is that of a small-scale battle, small boys are soon to be found behind every tree. The slingshot stone missed me, but it must have stung my horse like a giant hornet and I had to spend some time getting it under control. One or two of the troopers were also hit with hurtling stones before they could get their shields up. The small boys fled unscathed.

Somewhat embarrassed, we rode quickly on. The only comfort I could offer myself was that I had not been unhorsed in front of Ala Indiana Gallorum. Cogidumnos drew level with me.

"Those dirty-faced urchins did not come from the campsite. They ran back towards Kaleoua. We will have more company later."

"Then let's get on with it."

Armoured horsemen are not ideal for hunting down fleet-footed children who know the ground, so I did not further deplete my small force by sending soldiers after the slingshot specialists.

The wagons were still there with a haze of woodsmoke still hanging over them. A teenage girl came out, shaded her eyes against the sun and then suddenly bolted back within the campsite. There was some half-glimpsed movement behind the wagons and then everything was still. I was sure that the British would have been preparing to fight ever since the Irish rode out to drive off the Decurion and his party. Their wagon teams were in the centre. There was no sound except for our horses. We halted at long arrow range, about one hundred paces. I nodded to Cogidumnos.

"Go tell them they are under arrest," I said, using police terminology without thinking.

He kneed his horse forward a few paces and did just that, at the top of his voice. There was a short pause, and then a feminine voice piercingly screamed a name. His name.

"Cogidumnos!"

He turned a pale face to me, lower jaw dropping.

"Scota," he whispered. "It's Scota."

Then he did a very shocking thing. He drew his long sword and, with a Celtic scream, kicked his startled horse into a full gallop, directly at the silent wagons.

I had seconds to make up my mind. I had never liked Cogidumnos, the man was normally too full of his own importance, and now he was behaving like a love-lorn youth. I was very tempted to leave the fool to his fate. On the other hand, he was widely believed, by people who matter, to be vital to the successful conquest of Britain. The capture or death of the High King's family, on the other hand, would be prestigious but would not affect the outcome of the war.

"Charge!" I said. The troopers, in a loose line, kicked their horses into motion. The big horses quickly got into their stride and it was too late to stop the cavalry when Cogidumnos' horse went down just short of the wagons. He hit the ground heavily, sword flashing as it bounced from his grasp. He was trying to get to his knees as we thundered past. I resisted the temptation to kick him in the head.

Arrows and stones rose in flight from between and under the wagons. As we got in close and tried to find a way through, cauldrons of boiling water rained down on us from the wagon tops. Hunting spears and sharp stakes jabbed at our horses' bellies from under the wagon beds. The drawbars of each wagon or cart had been tied to the wheel of the next one and the spaces in between filled with luggage and cut thornbushes.

We made attempts to get the horses to leap the barricades but the noise of beaten metal and the waving of firebrands from within, and the minor injuries the horses were receiving from the thorns and sharp weapons, convinced the creatures that we were all safer outside. After much waving of our swords and ineffectively poking about with our lances, we withdrew with as much dignity as we had left. Cogidumnos was dazed but on his feet when I gripped him by the wool around his neck and dragged him back to safety at a smart trot.

After I had berated the crazy Celt for a while, I realised that he was just not concentrating and I left him, weaponless, to recover his wits. Another of my troopers lay prone on the turf and yet another had stayed in the saddle but was crying with the pain of severe scalds to his neck and forearm.

It was time to deal with the problem with a bit of system.

"Did anyone hear any male voices or see any men there?"

There was much shamed shaking of heads.

"Barbarian bitches," muttered one of the Gallic troopers.

"All right. Get those Irish prisoners over here. In the open."

They willingly dragged the prisoners off their horses and propped them up in front of the wagons. The one with the hole in his side promptly fainted. The other one, snuffling through his remodeled nose, told me his name was Niall. If it is possible to look dignified with his facial injuries then he somehow managed to do so.

I shouted towards the campsite, in my best Celtic, that their escort had been killed, except for the two sorry captives they could see, and that the womenfolk should surrender and I would spare their lives, something like that. A feminine voice in a foreign accent shouted back that if I wanted them, I had better come and get them. Niall's battered face twisted into a grim smile. The defenders could not recover their arrows but they did not appear to be short of anything else, including cheek.

"Charge them again," urged the Decurion. I did not tell him to do it himself, he probably would have done so. He was one of those military numbskulls whose helmets have taken a considerable battering over the years.

"They are only women," he asserted, angrily. "Obviously, their husbands have not kept them under proper supervision."

There was a stange wheezing sound and I was surprised to see that Niall was actually trying to laugh.

"Keep them under supervision?" he managed. "You speak Celtic but you think like a Roman. I suggest you go and try and teach them a lesson."

The Decurion was not quick-witted enough to think of a clever response. He contented himself with cuffing the prisoner about the head instead.

Ignoring the uneven confrontation, I again addressed the unseen Irishwoman.

"Surrender," I ordered, "or I will kill these captives."

"You do that," was the reply, "and I will kill Scota."

Cogidumnos lurched to his feet but the Decurion was ready for him and quickly wrestled him back to the ground. I whispered harshly in Cogidumnos ear.

"Be still you fool. Have you forgotten? She is a Celt too. You people are forbidden to execute a female prisoner."

His eyes cleared.

"But she will know," he muttered slowly, "that Romans kill prisoners without a second thought if it means winning. You've got to convince her that you will do it."

"Oh, I'll do it all right," I said confidently. On my instructions, the captives were gagged and their wrists tightly bound behind them. Niall was suspended by one ankle from the branch of a tree. He turned helplessly below the creaking branch. Firewood was gathered and set on the ground directly beneath his head. The big youngster was propped on his knees in the open, braced against the legs of a trooper whose sword blade lightly rested on his shoulder. Female faces had appeared above and between the still wagons.

I walked up to stand alongside the half conscious Irishman and shouted towards the wagons.

"Come out and talk."

There was no response and, at my signal, the trooper placed the point of the blade in the hollow of the captive's collarbone. I shouted again.

"Come out and talk. Or I'll kill this one and still have a hostage available for bargaining."

A woman dropped lightly down from one of the wagons and, making sure I was watching, stuck a large Celtic sword in the ground. She then walked athletically forward to the edge of effective bowshot from the wagons. I was not looking forward to negotiating with a woman but I planted my own sword and walked up to her.

"Have all you Romans got those tiny little swords?" she said sweetly. I felt my ears reddening. She was attractive in a mature sort of way. Pale skin, pale eyes and thick red hair with a few strands of silver. She was not muscular but had a physical poise that I had seen on the most successful gladiators, the ones who were almost never taken by surprise. Her eyes did not waver.

"I am Centurion Aurelius Victorinus, Legion II Augusta," I said a bit pompously. "Roman Army."

"And I am Brigit Mong Ruadh of Ireland," she said. "What do you want, soldier?"

I swallowed my annoyance at her tone, delivered in a light, accented voice, and reminded myself that Celtic women often hold positions of command.

"You have a woman, Scota, kidnapped from the Continent by British marauders. She was under the protection of Rome and she is to be released to me, now."

"And, if she is not, you will cold-bloodedly slaughter two wounded and defenceless prisoners, is that right?"

"The preparations for torture and execution were only to get you out here to talk. I do not intend to destroy this proof that Irish Celts are assisting British Celts in their quarrel with Rome. The British main army has been destroyed and the Roman Army is taking possession of the conquered territories. The Irish should know, we are in Britain to stay. Ireland is not that far away."

She did not react at all to the threat. She must already have considered the consequences of the fight between the Irish escort and Roman cavalry. Misunderstandings do occur in wartime, and an encounter-skirmish between two groups of armed men can be explained away as a mistake. If, however, she refused to hand over a prisoner abducted by the British from the Romans, she would be clearly siding with the British. I had no idea who this woman was but, the more senior her position, the more she would commit the Irish people to any defiance of Rome.

"I hear what you say," she said non-commitally. Then she gave a dazzling smile. "By great good luck, resolution does not rest in our hands alone."

The one thing an officer in enemy territory must not do, is to concentrate on the obvious threat and forget the possibility of others. That military error was exactly the one I had now committed. Of course the cavalry Decurion, his men, and even Cogidumnos bear some responsibility, but none so much as myself.

While we were all involved in the small drama being played out in the open space in front of the campsite, a vast crowd of people was drifting silently, like cloud-shadow over the countryside, to envelop us. They were women and old men, mostly, with the usual coveys of small boys, but there were also men of military age, many of them bandaged. Each adult seemed to be equipped with a weapon of some sort and the crowd numbered in the thousands. It seemed that most of the population of Kaleoua had come out on foot to take part in the debate, and they were still coming.

A two-wheeled cart, drawn by two small horses drew up at one side of the open space where Brigit and I still stood, weaponless. The driver tied off his reins and sat facing us on the tailgate. The crowd pressed slowly forward, forming a dense collar right around the campsite and my much-reduced turma of Roman cavalry. The lack of noise among that multitude was unnerving. The cart-driver raised his hand almost informally and, with a great rustling, the tribespeople settled down in the grass. The warriors had clustered close to the cart and the only Atrebatan still standing was an evil-visaged man with a recent facial wound, probably from an arrow. The cart-driver looked about him with interest. Faces in the crowd turned from us to him.

"First," he said, as if continuing a conversation. He had a high, clear voice which easily carried to all parts of the crowd. "First, some introductions. I am the Chief Magistrate of the Atrebates. In the absence of our High King, I am the senior representative of the people here." He nodded slightly towards the wagons. "We know, of course, the ladies of the High King's family. We have also got to know Brigit and her party. We do not know you, sir."

I told him who I am and he smiled most pleasantly.

"Be so good, Centurion, to tell your men to put away their weapons. They are quite insignificant, in the circumstances."

I did so.

"Thank you. Now, if you would kindly have Niall lowered to the ground? The counsel of a Druid is always helpful in these matters."

"Druid!" the exclamation was jolted out of the Decurion and his troopers assisted Niall to the ground far more gently than they had hauled him up. Niall, his hands freed, held out a grimy palm under the Decurion's nose. After a moment, the cavalry officer returned a small golden sickle to the Druid. The Decurion was embarrassed at being caught out in a little private looting and his men looked at him thoughtfully.

"Good," said the Magistrate. "I see you are injured Niall."

"Nothing serious. I collided with an oak tree."

"Most appropriate for a member of the Order. I presume you were about to harvest some sacred mistletoe at the time of the accident?"

They laughed a little at the in-joke. The rest of us just stared. It did give me an idea, and I offered to have my medics see to Niall's injuries and those of the Irish warrior who was still sitting on the turf. It was respectfully declined but a tribal doctor went to the wounded youngster.

"Very well," the Magistrate turned to business. "We understand from our military people," he gracefully indicated Scarface who stood glowering beside the cart, "that our High King fought the invading Roman army on the Medu River. We are informed that, having destroyed a large part of the Roman army, the British army withdrew to prepared positions on the Thames. Is that also your view of the battle, Centurion?"

"British casualties were very heavy and the Roman army's relatively light. Your army fought from behind the Medu River and yet had to retreat. It was a British defeat."

"Despite the fact that thousands of your men perished in the swamps and marshes of the Thames River estuary," Brigit interjected.

I tried to restrain my tongue.

"They died due to lack of local knowledge. It will not be the same again. They died in the pursuit of a beaten army, that will often be the same again."

"And yet," said the Magistrate, reasonably," if the Roman army was victorious and intact, where is the general advance? Yours is the first Roman military formation we have seen."

There was a concerted grunt of agreement from the audience.

"We do things methodically. Armies have been brought from all over the world, carried across the Ocean in fleets of ships we built on the way and have forced a disputed river-crossing and defeated a more numerous enemy. Certain additional preparations are being made. Then you will see a general advance which will certainly bring major Roman formations to the land of the Atrebates."

There was silence. The Magistrate did not move his head but his eyes scanned the crowd.

I pressed on.

"For that reason, the family of the High King wishes to leave you and, for that reason, they wish to take with them the unlawfully abducted daughter of your King, Bericos."

He waited until the rumble of quiet discussions in the crowd died away.

"All that is as may be. In one aspect, though, you are undoubtedly wrong. Scota may or may not have been unlawfully abducted but her father, former King Bericos, is certainly not the ruler of the Atrebates."

In the sections of the crowd I could see without turning around, there was much nodding of heads. Bericos would not be willingly received back as monarch, if at all. If I wanted to keep Scota, I had to demonstrate her status. Thankfully, a British woman's evidence is given equal weight with that of a man.

"Scota can confirm that she was abducted against her will and that she is, in effect, a prisoner."

"Just so. You would wish to take her into your custody?"

"I would wish to take her back under the protection of Rome. A protection, incidentally, that she sought of her own free will and from which she was removed illegally and by force."

Scarface took a step forward.

"She ran away to Rome with her father and that Cogidumnos there. Now, they return bringing an alien enemy to our land. They are traitors, all three."

Cogidumnos appeared next to me and I must confess I was not unhappy. He looked coldly about and then addressed the Magistrate.

"We are not traitors, nor did we run away to Rome."

That interested the crowd greatly and it surprised me.

"The Cassi family penetrated this region by force and guile and overthrew Bericos and those of us who supported him. We were forced out of our homes, away from our families and out of our land in Britain. We fled for our lives from the Catuvellauni tribe, aliens from north of the Thames. We did not flee, as you say, to the foreign Romans. We fled to the other part of King Bericos' domains, the ancestral lands of the Atrebates on the other side of the Ocean. Those lands from which your ancestors emigrated to come here. Bericos is King there, just as he was King here."

The Magistrate was listening carefully but his eyes were intently scanning the crowd and assessing his people's reactions to Cogidumnos' continuing argument.

"It is true that the Atrebates on the Continent are subject to Rome. Everyone over there is. It is true that the Romans gave us shelter and supported us. Now the Romans have a quarrel with the High King and have already defeated him in battle. They will come here, with or without us. With or without Bericos, King of both branches of the Atrebates, they will come. You may support the foreigner, the so-called High King, Caratacos, or you may support your own King, Bericos. Either way, the Romans will come. King Bericos will come with them."

"Thank you, Chief Cogidumnos," said the Magistrate. "We need to discuss further what you say."

Everyone was aware of Cogidumnos' change in status, imparted silently by the crowd and confirmed by the Magistrate's use of his title. No one protested outright. Therefore, it became a fact. After a moment, the Magistrate, still seated on the tailgate of his cart, turned to Brigit.

"Brigit Mong Ruadh," he said. "What is your position, here?"

"An observer only," she said lightly, "and a friend of the High King's family."

"And the deaths of your gallant companions?"

She glanced at Niall. Without a word being spoken, agreement was reached.

"A tragic case of mistaken identity," she said. "I thought the High King's family was at risk and ordered my people to defend them. The Romans probably thought they were being attacked by a band of warriors from the High King's army."

I nodded at the Magistrate and glared at the Decurion who had opened his mouth to speak. Scarface turned his flushed face towards the Magistrate who put his hand on the warrior's shoulder until he relaxed.

"Just so," said the Magistrate again. He gazed calmly about as some muttering and shuffling in the crowd died away.

"Now," he said. "The Princess Scota and Chief Cogidumnos, being Atrebatans, must stay here with us."

I tensed and saw the Irishwoman do the same. Neither of us liked the idea of being deprived of our hostages. Cogidumnos whispered harshly so that both of us could hear.

"It's all right. It's all right!"

"They will, of course, be perfectly safe," soothed the Magistrate, although their safety was not what was in the forefront of my mind. "If any charges were to be brought against them, they would be heard in a proper court of law in my jurisdiction. They will also be given the opportunity to address a general assembly of the nation on the subject of the status of Bericos, former King of the British Atrebates."

Cogidumnos caught my eye. Bericos had just been granted official standing in so far as the overseas branch of the Atrebates was concerned. More importantly, no one had objected. Unless the High King could inflict a serious defeat on the Roman army soon, Cogidumnos would be able to convince the general assembly to acknowledge Bericos, King of their overseas branch and friend of the Romans.

The Magistrate had not quite finished.

"Until the general assembly makes its decision known, military operations by the armed forces of the Atrebates are suspended."

In other words, the Atrebates were out of the war.

A long exhalation swept the crowd. Its individual members seemed to relax. Many placed their weapons beside them on the grass. The remaining details did not take long to finalise.

Scota, thin and bright eyed, walked alone from the wagons and stood smiling up at Cogidumnos. With clumsy fingers, he undid the brooch at his shoulder and swirled his fine woolen cloak around her. Then they went and stood together among their people.

The Magistrate asked Brigit to convey the good wishes of the Atrebates to the High King of Ireland, confirming my suspicion that she was a person of consequence there. She made a short speech of thanks and assisted the Druid to get the wounded Irish warrior over to the wagons. She jerked her long sword out of the turf and ran her fingers along the blade to remove the dirt. Then, with a wide smile, she raised the point and made a vaguely obscene gesture with it in my direction. Roman dignity is all very well but I actually wanted to laugh and, somehow, the crowd perceived this. The round of laughter was polite and there was no jeering. Her high, reedy voice could be heard within the campsite as the wagons were unchained by the women and the teams hooked on.

He then looked at me.

"The family of the High King are not combatants. It is the decision of this assembly that they may continue on their journey unhindered."

He had not appeared to consult anyone in the assembly but I could see by simply looking around that he spoke the truth. That was the sense of the assembly. High King Caratacos was obviously still held in high regard by many. How the Magistrate was going to prevent me chasing after the wagons, and arresting the family again, I was about to hear.

"I am sure that you have excellent medical people in the Roman army," said this barbarian Magistrate, "but we have doctors and surgeons here of high repute. They have examined your four wounded soldiers in the wood and will soon attend to the unfortunate man with the scalded arm. They have decided that your wounded need several days of rest in our hospital for military casualties. They will receive the best of treatment there alongside our wounded from the battle on the Medu River. You and your men will be our guests until your wounded are discharged from hospital."

CHAPTER 75

▼

BRITAIN

The following day, I was standing at the same spot looking at the wagon tracks heading west, when the small cart rolled up behind me and the Magistrate sat on the tailgate and swung his legs.

"A fine woman," he said conversationally. "Sister of the High King of Ireland, you know. A widow, now. Some children, I believe."

I looked at him with a pretence of amused indifference.

"Ah, well," he sighed. "We all waste so much of our lives. I understand one of your wounded died last night. My condolences. I see your men are building eight pyres for the funerals so I have brought you these. I hope they are suitable."

He handed me a leather bag. Inside were eight small funerary urns of glazed grey pottery. I still had the ashes of my friend, Titus, in a similar pot, wrapped in my bedroll.

"The families of my men will be very grateful. I am very grateful."

"Just so," he said.

"I cannot let you go, you know," he said without looking at me directly, "at least, not yet. You could easily overtake the High King's family and they would not be able to fight off your professional soldiers. They would try, and you would have to kill them."

"And anyway," I added for him, "your people would not allow it."

"It would be a breach of the law of hospitality. Charges would be brought and I would lose office. That would not be in your best interest."

I did not press him to define the word 'your'. After a moment, he went on.

"The Atrebates want guidance from the High King and messengers have already left. I suppose you also want guidance from your general. I cannot let you or your unit go, as things stand now. The warriors will be very alert to see that you don't go without my permission. However, it might be possible for, say, two of your men to slip away unnoticed. Such things do happen, no matter how strict the watch. Tonight will be almost moonless."

"Just so," I said.

That night, two of my Gallic cavalrymen slid out of their bedrolls, slipped the tethering knots on their horses and walked them quietly past the loudly snoring warrior on guard. They got about two kilometers from the camp when they found themselves surrounded by the dark shapes of armed Celtic warriors and were quickly disarmed, separated from their horses and hustled into a dense thicket where they were going to be held under guard for the rest of the war.

The ambush party was so busy settling their prisoners into their new home, and congratulating themselves, that they did not see the second pair of cavalrymen I had sent out, stealing past on horses with muffled hooves and without the harness decorations Gauls love so much. It was not until late afternoon that the British were sure that four cavalrymen had escaped and not the two they were ready for. After the initial anger, the British gradually recovered their sense of humour and rueful grins appeared among the warriors. Perhaps because of the pain of his recent face wound, Scarface did not smile. My men had been told publicly that they were guests of the Atrebates, so I did not believe that they would be killed out of hand. Nevertheless, I was relieved when the first two cavalrymen were delivered safely back to me. Then it was only a matter of waiting for instructions from Legion II Augusta.

They were a long time coming, and when they came they were not to my liking. The cavalrymen delivered a sealed letter and confirmed that they had not been questioned by the Atrebates nor had anyone interfered with the letter while on their way back. The seal was still intact.

Before reading my instructions, I talked with the two men privately. Nothing had changed as far as they could see. The Roman army still occupied entrenchments on either side of the Thames River. The victorious legionaries were again complaining about bridge-building and road repair work. Provisions, they had heard, were being delivered to the army by the Fleet operating up the Thames as far as Lud Dun. Their colleagues in other cavalry units had told them that they were probing well to the north of the river and had made no contact, so far, with any significant body of the enemy. What was Governor Aulus Plautius waiting for? They did not know. I had a good idea. Uncle Claudius was on his way.

The written instructions I had waited for with such anticipation were an anti-climax. I was to stay where I was, support Cogidumnos and protect him if possible, forestall any rebellion on the part of the Atrebatan allies and to promote the interests of Rome. King Bericos would not travel to Kaleoua yet. He was required for a planned function in the enemy capital, Camulodunum, when it fell. I should report as often as I deemed fit and await further instructions. Great. I wondered which clerk had written this hazy wish-list while Vespasian was doing something more important. Only one thing was as clear as springwater. I was to stay where I was.

Cogidumnos was anxious to get his chance before the general assembly of the Atrebates, and Scota as well. The Magistrate showed no sign of any urgency but was always unfailingly polite in putting off setting a date. The conquest of south-east Britain was still not completely settled although the balance lay heavily in favour of the Romans. The Cantii tribe was destroyed, the little army of the Dobunni had defected under its ungrateful King, and the Atrebates were beaten. Cogidumnos told me that the word from the Durotriges to our west was that they had declared their neutrality as had the southern Dobunni. Only the large tribes of the Catuvellauni and the Trinovantes were still in the field and the Catuvellauni, the Cassi family's own power base, were wavering. The serious strategic error of the previous High King, and his sudden death, had shaken the foundations of Cassi power.

The newly elected High King of Britain had had an almost impossible task. He had had to take over the consequences of his brother's mistake and his brother's choice of ground and, even so, he had nearly held the professional army of Rome on the Medu River. Battles with barbarian armies do not usually last beyond one day. To fight a two-day battle in those circumstances he must have a considerable personal following. Everything I had seen among the Atrebates tended to confirm that. No doubt he was now working frantically to reorganize and revive the British army.

Aulus Plautius had halted his victorious army while in pursuit of a retreating enemy. That might prove to be his own strategic blunder even if dictated by the highest political needs.

Cogidumnos had not traveled far from Kaleoua to garner support for King Bericos. He said this was because the situation was so volatile still and he did not want to away from the centre of things if a general assembly were to be summoned at short notice. Also, I suspected, he did not want to be too far away from Scota. Things did not seem to have progressed far on that front, and she spent a good deal of time with the younger warriors and the charioteers. Young British women are very open in these matters and, when I asked her about her admirers, she did not blush or look coy.

"Victorinus," she said, "I have lived in Rome far longer than you have been in Britain. Here, if a woman wants to consort with a man, she does so openly and, therefore, can do so with the best man who is willing. Is that worse than the Roman women who have to do so in secret and with the lowest form of male life?"

I decided to be as open.

"Are you going to marry Cogidumnos?"

"There are times when he remembers that I am a woman and forgets that I am the King's heir. At those times, I think it is possible."

He had gathered about himself a substantial body of the older warriors who had not been at the Medu battle and who believed that they were being prepared to guard the Atrebates in the place of the numerous casualties sustained there. I assisted with a basic training plan and lectured on simple tactics. My cavalrymen put on several demonstrations of infantry drill. Legionaries they were not, but they provided interest sessions and attracted more recruits for Cogidumnos. He was assembling a very credible body of British levies. Better than that, they were not led by a neurotic and dangerous turncoat like King Buduoc, but by a man known to both the Romans and the tribespeople and whose career depended totally on the favour of the Roman Empire.

The Magistrate did not intervene in these activities and, from his demeanour, it would almost seem as if he were totally unaware of them. Then, one day, long after my surviving wounded had been discharged from hospital, many of the tribal veterans of the Medu suddenly disappeared. The wailing of the women first alerted us and I was not surprised when the Magistrate sent word that a general assembly had been summoned.

Cogidumnos immediately went into a huddle with Scota and I walked over to the large, thatched courthouse building. The Magistrate sat amongst a large and agitated group of tribal elders but immediately excused himself and came out to where I was waiting politely on the porch.

"The news," he said lightly, "is mixed. It seems that your Aulus Plautius has been superseded by a more senior general, Claudios or some name like that."

"Claudius, yes."

"He has brought massive reinforcements including elephants. I would like to see an elephant. He forced the Roman army to advance and was repulsed with great slaughter by the High King north of the Thames. Claudius and his army are in Camulodunon licking their wounds. So it is said."

He looked at me sidelong as he recounted this report. No defending army voluntarily gives up its own base, and no defeated army occupies its enemy's capital.

"It's another British defeat," I said, bluntly. "Do you want my advice?"

"I shall certainly listen to it."

"Get the general assembly to recognise King Bericos. If they will not have him, then get them to elect Cogidumnos. Do it now. Then send a message of submission to Emperor Claudius by the fastest riders you have."

"Is it so urgent?"

"Yes. In these circumstances, the Romans have only two policies and they are official. They are clemency and atrocity. You would not wish to see atrocity in action. Scarface and his party have gone to join the High King, haven't they? Well their actions were without your permission, weren't they? You are responsible for the entire community, not just a few disaffected warriors. Atrocity will set back a community by decades. Do it now."

So, he did. When Legion II Augusta came marching in, Vespasian was greeted by King Cogidumnos before a parade of a depleted turma of Ala Indiana Gallorum and rank upon rank of the British levies of the loyal Atrebates tribe. The parade commander was myself.

When the feasting and the entrenching was done, I found myself, not for the first time, standing before Legate Vespasian in his newly-erected tent. Behind him, Camp Commandant Anicius Maximus surveyed me with a bleak but not unfriendly stare.

"I thought I sent you on a scouting mission," said Vespasian, easily. "I did send you on a routine scouting task didn't I? Yes, I believe I did. Did I tell you to slaughter the escort of the representative of a foreign power? Did you tell him to do that, Commandant? No, of course not. Our relationships with Ireland may never be the same. Did we tell you to chase the British High King's family into exile. Did we?"

I got as far as saying 'no sir', but he was not to be stopped.

"Is it part of a routine scouting mission, with no less than thirty auxiliary cavalry, to take possession of a sovereign state and to install a new king on the throne? Is it? Because, if it is…" he waved broadly at the ten thousand or so soldiers of Rome who surrounded his tent, "…if it is, then what the hell am I doing with all these people?"

Even the Commandant appeared to be amused.

"The Emperor said he wanted to interview the Centurion personally, sir."

"And that's another thing," continued Vespasian in a tone of mild exasperation. "There I was, all washed and shaved and making myself pleasant, presenting

King Bericos, and the ten other so-called British kings, to the Emperor to make their formal submissions in the captured British capital itself, and what does the Emperor say? Does he say 'Legion II Augusta, hey? Fine body of men. Well done, Legate Vespasian,'—did he say that, Commandant? No, he didn't. He said 'Vespasian, I want to see Centurion Aurelius Victorinus before I leave Britain. See to it.' That's what he said."

He nodded solemnly, several times. I was taken by surprise when he added.
"So do it."
"Do what, sir?"
"Go and see the Emperor, you idiot. Haven't you been listening? Why did we promote this man, Commandant?"
"Very difficult to imagine, now, sir."
"Exactly. Are you still here, Centurion?"
"No, sir." I hurriedly left.

I passed Legion II Augusta's former Camp south of the Thames in a heavy autumn rainstorm. The walls had been flattened, of course, and the grass would eventually grow again but, like all former Camps, it had a desolate air.

I had been provided with what the Decurion had assured me was his best horse. For a man of his aggressive temperament, his best horse turned out to be an excessively muscular and exuberant brown animal, forever hungry and with a minute brain containing the one belief that food lay just over the horizon. He was hard on the arms and the thighs but he certainly covered the ground. He needed to. The Emperor was well ahead of me and making good time towards the landing beaches. He had no intention of being marooned in Britain by the winter gales.

I followed the wide track left by the Praetorian Guard, some six thousand of them I had heard, and the copious droppings of their animals. I kept a lookout for the manure of the sixteen elephants in the party but small Celtic boys had, no doubt, quartered the ground before me. The absence of elephant dung suggested that many a British household had been presented with a trophy turd by one of its younger members.

By the time I reached the Medu River, I still had not sighted the Emperor's escort although my horse was still going as if it had six legs. Guards on the bridges and ferries were my old friends the loyal British levies of the Dobunni tribe, occupying themselves mainly by lounging about and spitting in the water. Interestingly, many of them had shaved off their moustaches since I had last seen them.

Over the Medu, the countryside was beginning to recover. There was some rebuilding work going on the homesteads. Bundles of reeds and thatching grass lay beside the road awaiting collection and some old men and boys were carrying recently cut poles into the farms. There were very few women about, but if I were a farmer with the Praetorian Guard marching past my door I would also make sure that the women made themselves scarce. There was no livestock, nor any wheeled vehicles, to be seen, they had all been requisitioned by the army. Ash no longer blew about on the wind, the recent rains had settled it and the ground was absorbing it. Farmers are always ingenious at hiding seed grain from even the most thorough military search and, with a few handtools and a lot of labour, they would be able to prepare and plant some fields for next harvest. In the meantime, life would be hard but there were fish in the rivers and hares to be trapped. The most enterprising would have already scavenged and concealed weapon points from the battlefield to make hunting spears, so the deer and wild pigs could expect relentless hunting in the cold weather.

I spent one night with a group of convalescent wounded and sick on their way back to their units. They were from the hospital originally set up by our Camp Commandant above the beaches. The mixed party consisted of both legionaries and auxiliaries and, I suspect, were none too happy at the sudden end of their quiet life. Apparently, a ferocious giant of a Praetorian Guards' officer had physically hurled a reluctant sailor out of the hospital door while clearing the wards. That sounded familiar. They had not seen the Emperor in person, but they had been driven off the road by Guardsmen earlier that day. He should reach the coast tomorrow.

Dawn saw me clinging to the saddle pommels as my horse evidently thought the rising sun was something to eat. It would have been remarkably easy for a few Celtic farmers to pick me off during the first mad canter. I had to stay on the road surface, or my horse would have done their job for them, and they could easily have stretched a trip rope across the road at hock height for the horse or head height for me. Perhaps the Praetorian Guard, sweeping across the country-side, had subdued the locals completely, or, more likely, the army had confiscated even the farmers' ropes.

By noon, grimy, saddle-sore and weary, I came into the presence of my Commander in Chief. Uncle Claudius' fine head of white hair stood out amongst a disorderly mob of elderly men disguised as soldiers. The amount of gold and silver on the armour weighing down those old shoulders would probably have paid the salaries of Legion II Augusta for the year. Towering above them, was the long forehead and slanting eyes of none other than Valerius Asiaticus, contender for the throne, Senator of Rome, murderer by proxy and municipal lead thief. Our Emperor had taken the excellent precaution of bringing along all those who might want to overthrow him while he was busy conquering Britain. I wondered if any battlefield accidents had reduced the number while he had been in the country. It was only a pity that Asiaticus had not inadvertently stepped in front of a catapult. That only happened to the good.

A military flunkey tried to bar my way, perhaps he had not seen a real centurion before, but what really brought me to a halt was the spectacle being viewed by the Emperor and the other military sightseers. A huge stockade was full, completely full, of British prisoners, men and women, dirty and tear-stained and bitterly silent, and a few wailing children. A contractor and some sort of a medical man were examining them and registering them. They were destined for the slave-market, the profit of the Imperial enterprise to Britain.

Surrounded by his potential rivals, the Emperor was, not unnaturally, quite alert to his environment and he immediately spotted the small disturbance caused by the intrusion of a real live soldier. He crooked a finger at me and, with a sneer at the flunkey, I marched over and saluted my Commander in Chief. He took a lurching step forward on his thin legs and gave me a charming smile.

"Aurelius Victorinus. There you are. It's a long way from the Water Commissioner's office in Rome. What are you now, a centurion? Well done. Why haven't you got any decorations?"

He turned to a shining pillar of steel and horsehair behind him.

"Pollio, this centurion has not got any decorations. See to it."

Rufrius Pollio, now the Prefect of the Praetorian Guard, smiled grimly at me. Even through his clenched teeth, I got a whiff of garlic.

"It looks to me, sire, that the man is more in need of a bath than a medal."

The ancients around the Emperor tittered dutifully.

"I prefer the smell of sweat and horses, Pollio, to the scent of intrigue."

The tittering stopped. Claudius turned back to me. He waved his hand at the crowded stockade.

"See what you have done," he beamed innocently while I tried to swallow something in my throat.

His eyes immediately narrowed in concern and he turned away towards the contractor.

"You!" he roared at the contractor. "Come here. What's your name? Ambon? Right. Make sure you treat the slaves properly. I don't want any damaged goods arriving on the Continent. Is that doctor properly qualified?"

Asiaticus eased up alongside him, his eyes glimmering under his brows.

"I understand from Governor Galba that the doctor has done good work for him, sire. Phylus is, apparently, well qualified in the field of eye ailments and also speaks the language. He's a Gallic Celt himself. He knows the people well."

"And they seem to know him well. That slave just spat in his face. Bring her here."

The woman seemed small even amongst the old men in armour. Dirty and emaciated, in little more than tatters, her defiance surrounded her like an almost visible aura.

"Your name?" The Emperor's tone was mild. "Translate, somebody."

The tall Gallic medicine man did so, and she replied with a brief addition.

"She says her name is Ena, sire," Phylus cheeks showed some colour.

"She said more than that," said the astute Uncle Claudius. "What else?"

While Phylus was trying to make up an answer, I replied for him.

"She said, sire, that her name is Ena and she is not going to answer any more questions from a treacherous Celt who oozes along in snail slime. It loses something in the translation."

We all had a good laugh at Phylus, only he and Asiaticus did not find it amusing. Claudius, widely regarded as a fool, picked it up straight away.

"Senator Asiaticus," he said, wiping his eyes, which were, nevertheless, dangerously alert. "Do you have a keepsake, something to remind you of Britain? No? Well, why not take this British slave? I doubt you will forget the place with her in your household. Yes, I am prepared to sell her to you. Just see my procurator."

Asiaticus could hardly turn down such a suggestion coming from the Emperor. Putting a good face on it, he loomed over the young woman, and, grasping her jaw, glared down into her unwavering pale eyes. Seeing no sign of any intimidation, he pushed her face roughly away, his iron signet ring raising a spot of blood on her white cheek. She still did not look down.

"Yes," said the Emperor, cheerfully. "Yes, Senator. You are going to have trouble with that one."

Tiring of games, Claudius lurched into motion, summoning me with a jerk of his head, and I followed his broad shoulders as he barged his way out of the circle of spectators, several of them nearly being trampled underfoot as everyone tried to get out of his way. A glistening sentry held open the tent flap of an enormous red leather edifice that was the Emperor's office on the coast of Britain. Inside the tent, he sat behind a large desk, rested his elbows on it and clasped his big hands.

"Sit," he ordered.

There were several folding chairs with ivory frames, normally reserved for Senators. As there was nowhere else, other than the floor, I sat in one of them.

"I want to hear what you have been doing," he said in a businesslike manner, "but not now. I have a long journey ahead and time is pressing. We have been very successful in Britain, you and I. For me, that means that everyone now accepts that I am, indeed, the Emperor of Rome. It does not mean that there is now no danger threatening me personally, it simply means that it is now illegal. For you, it means that I can give you any job you want. If you want the army contract to provide woollen winter trousers to the legions, you can have it."

He paused, watching me with those clever eyes. He was not joking, but there was something else.

"The dangers that threaten you personally, sire, they would not be found at the frontiers. You have proved the Army correct in backing you. They must be centred on Rome. Narcissus, as always, will be watching the Court. You are thinking of the population of the City, the mob."

"You look like a soldier but you were trained as a policeman." He gave a rueful grin, not a bit like his politician's smile. "Policemen rub shoulders with the population all day, eat and drink with them, deal with their tragedies, watch over their triumphs. They know what the population thinks, better than the Emperor. I need a policeman in Rome, right now."

"I'm ready to leave now. I just have a few funerary urns to deliver on the way."

"Good. The commander of Urban Cohort XII is retiring just as soon as he gets my letter. That's your job."

He lurched to his feet, knocking over the chair he had been sitting on.

"I cannot promise you a long career," he said as he shuffled quickly round the desk, "but I can promise you we'll have some fun."

He backhanded me across the upper arm as he went past, then his bulk darkened the tent doorway and he was gone.

I watched the Emperor's ship depart for the rest of his Empire, silver trumpets blaring, seamen shouting, gulls crying and the banks of gleaming yellow oars driving the resplendent hull to the shrilling of a flute. There was no room on board for a buck centurion. I just had to wait for the next ship, to squeeze in amongst iron-clad, overweight and sea sick Guardsmen. 'Justitia' was still being loaded. At least it was not mules.

No sooner had the Imperial ship cleared the channel than the first of Pytheas' ships sidled in to the wharf, heeling with the weight of humanity above and below decks. Several more such ships, I knew, waited their turn out on the Ocean filled with the families of the legionaries of the Province of Britain, come to join their men. Women and children, bundles and boxes, were already pouring over the sides and over the bow of the beached ship. The younger generation of passengers on the beach ran and shouted and stretched their limbs while their elders eased their weary backs, squabbled and laughed. They looked up beyond me, and rapidly began to assemble their goods and children and to clear the beach.

A vast, almost soundless movement behind me developed into the shuffling of thousands of bare feet and a few deep shouts of command. An immense, dirty column of woollen-clad prisoners wound its way down to the beaches, silent and smelly and nosing towards the ship so recently emptied of incoming soldiers' families. The head of the column rose up over the ship's side and, with a faint, continuous wail, poured into its hull.

"Excuse me, sir." A short, plump, middle-aged woman with a pretty face touched with colour at her daring in addressing a legionary officer. "I'm looking for Legion II Augusta. Can you help me?"

She had several large bundles and was wearing a new woollen cloak for traveling.

"Going to join your husband?" A fairly silly question, but her obvious excitement and anticipation was an antidote to the slaves' fear and anguish as they waited to board.

"Yes, he's now an optio in the Legion, due for retirement shortly." She was proud of her husband and looking forward to the hard, but secure, life of a citizen-colonist in a newly acquired Province.

"You are Julia Macer, Fangs' wife, aren't you?"

"Oh, no." She laughed. "But I know her, she's on one of the other ships."

"All right," I said, all business. "Do you need any food, money?"

"No," she said, the smile disappearing. "My husband has arranged all that."

"Of course. Silly of me." The smile reappeared. "Legion II Augusta is marching west. After a few days you will come to the land of the Atrebates. They are British but you do not need to fear them. See King Cogidumnos, he is a friend of Rome and his people will help you. Or see Scota, she is his—lady. Just keep going west and you'll catch up with them. If you fall into the sea, you've gone too far."

She laughed and shouldered her bundles, thanked me and set off.

After a while she turned once and smiled again. I watched her little figure merge with the many others walking away to the west, towards their husbands, to become families again. Far ahead of her, Legion II Augusta was ploughing its way steadily westwards through and over the British enemies of Rome and towards the distant Ocean. Beyond that Ocean, so I had heard, was Ireland.

THE END